Umail

First published in paperback in Great Britain
www.rhonawhitefordauthor.com
Text © Rhona Whiteford 2021
Rhona Whiteford asserts the moral right to be identified
as the author of this work
Editor: Liz Harris
Cover design: Lucy McSpirit - Freelance Graphic Designer
Cover painting: Rhona Whiteford
ISBN 978-0-995-7483-2-3

.

.

This novel is entirely a work of fiction. The names,
characters and incidents portrayed in the work are the
product of the author's imagination.

.

Printed and bound by
Flexipress Printing Ltd
Unit 1, Windmill Avenue, Ormskirk,
Lancashire L39 4QB

Rhona Whiteford lives in Lancashire, England
with her family and their animals.
She has been writing professionally for 35 years.

For my daughter, Laura.
I taught her to read and now she inspires me to write.

A
BOUQUET
OF
NIGHTSHADE

Rhona Whiteford

Chapter 1
England 1895

'Poor child, poor child'
Christina Rossetti

A HEATWAVE ravaged Manchester: the heart of the city was a furnace where people and animals lay sprawled in the throbbing temperatures. Sophia worked on; the windows, high in the walls, were open, the ceiling fan turned briskly, and the stone floors and thick walls kept the workroom at a very tolerable temperature. The table itself was ice-cooled because the temperature was vital if the bodies of the deceased were to be preserved at all.

She leaned backwards a little, pressing her knuckles into the small of her back and felt a pleasurable relief. That done she reached up to wipe her brow with the back of her gloved hand, trying to move a long curl of hair that dangled limp in front of her eyes, but as this glove was rubber it merely slid the hair across her skin uncomfortably. Finally, tired out, she dragged off both gloves and washed her hands. More of her hair had escaped its clips and she pushed it back into place and re-fixed the plaited coronel more firmly on top of her head, secured loose curls away from her neck; such long hair was heavy – heavy and hot, despite fans and ice. She smoothed her skirts and that action reminded her of something she had omitted to do; she had not pulled the sheet back over the body of the woman on the table. She did so quickly. Decency - especially in death.

How could I forget to cover her? Poor thing. Ashamed.

A long tress of the woman's blonde hair had fallen over the edge of the table and exposed like that it was somehow unseemly, unseemly and indescribably sad. Sophia reached for the hair, intending to tuck it neatly under the sheet, but as her fingertips made contact, she experienced a huge jolt of energy that surged through her body, stunned her.

She could not move her limbs. Her eyelids fluttered. Her breathing became low and deep as though she were drawing air infinitely slowly through layers of wool, from the soles of her feet upwards. Screams filled her ears. She felt her head yanked roughly back by the hair and a huge, hard hand caressed her exposed neck before it clamped tightly over her mouth and nose. She clawed at the hand and arm, felt it covered in hair…a man.

Then a great coursing silence engulfed her, wrapped her in its folds, imprisoned her. Sophia could not have said how long the sensation lasted but it disappeared abruptly, leaving her shocked and frightened, yet this was soon followed by a sense of solemn awe that wrapped around her like strong arms bringing comfort and security, bringing her back into herself. Nevertheless, she had to grope behind her for the tall stool to sit on; tried to steady her breathing. Tried to think.

This is what she felt before she died – was murdered. Her family said it was murder. They were right, weren't they? Oh, oh, how terrified she was.

She did not question the knowledge or the way it came to her; she did not need an explanation from anyone else because she had had similar experiences all her life, even in her infancy. Because of this she felt no fear of the occurrence, but what she had seen, experienced, sent a tremor through her soul.

8

My gift – Mother said. A 'sensitive', aware of spirits, forces and currents of existence beyond this life. A gift that can be used for good. Always good. But what does this vision mean?

Spiritualist churches had thrived in the city for several years now; mediums, real or bogus held séances in their parlours, even in theatres especially commissioned for such events and people were comforted or exploited, entertained or disgusted. It was the current vogue and one she often heard of in her own business; the bereaved were desperate to contact their dead, and it was common for whole families to visit a medium to try and do just that. Sophia had never been to any sort of séance and her own gift was never spoken of to anyone now her mother was gone, certainly not to her father; it frightened him.

But now she too was afraid because never before had she felt the death of someone else, the violent death, the murder of a person and, more particularly, one whose body she was preparing for burial.

For the deceased on the table, she had worked with even more care than usual because she was young, not more than twenty-one or two, she thought. It was not an unusual age to meet death, even in the middle classes and in these modern times, but they had been told by her family that she had been murdered and that was uncommon in the middle classes.

There was more: she was the second person, and of similar age, to be found dead in identical and very strange circumstances. Both victims had been brought to *Arnold Kelley and Daughter* for preparation and Sophia and her father had been disturbed to notice similar odd marks on both bodies even though their deaths had no obvious single cause; this knowledge pulsed in her mind, her heart, insisting she noticed it, did something.

Her muse was interrupted by a burst of laughter that came from the kitchen, deep and hearty, but still she stood, turning the thoughts over.

A door opened down the corridor. A voice called, a mellow voice, a kindly voice.

'Sophia, my dear, where are you?'

'Busy,' she answered. 'In the workroom, Father.'

'We have a visitor. Can you come?'

'I will. A moment.' Succinct.

She made no move though.

The police doctor had examined both victims, but he had found nothing of note. No post-mortems had been carried out because he had said there was sufficient evidence to show both had died of asphyxiation, a fact he said was proven by their blue-tinged lips. He suggested it might be due to tight corsetry and possibly over exertion in the tremendous heat, causing lack of breath. In both cases the Coroner had listened to his evidence at the Inquest and had ruled that both deaths had been caused by misadventure.

But how desperate the families were, she remembered, *Each family, at two separate inquests, a short space of time apart, had been convinced it was murder because their daughters had been well and happy, and would never, as some people suggested, take their own lives. That was written in the Manchester Evening News too - how we are ruled by the screeching of gossiping harpies.*

It was a relief to all when suicide was ruled out; the police had readily agreed with the families because there were two similar cases. Everyone had accepted that, and although it was possible for a family to be unaware that one of them was so desperate, so desperate in fact that they would take their own life, two such cases in identical and very strange circumstances made it likelier to be foul play; hardly a nonsensical misadventure caused by tight corsetry in a heatwave.

Sophia's mind raced around possibilities, chased by horror.

She stared down at her hands clasped tightly in front of her, her knuckles white.

She had been told that each victim had been found positioned very carefully and respectfully on the ground. They were in separate locations in the city centre, but ten days apart, and were found at the time they should have started work. There were no signs of violence on the bodies or in the surroundings. The small amount of evidence was unusual, and all things considered led to the police calling it murder. Sophia felt that had to be so.

She gazed at the body, deep in thought and shuddered.

Such fair hair, a little longer than mine, but just as curling. I'll dress it beautifully, in the style she did herself. Mind - it was only a little disarranged when she came to us. Now I know that could have been from the attack or simply from her being handled since her death, taken here and there as we decide what to do. But if she was attacked, as I saw – shouldn't it have been in greater disarray?

She was acutely aware that all her senses were heightened; every detail of the vision was etched on her mind; the poor woman's final dreadful moments, for surely, they were just that. It was deeply moving. She forced herself to be practical, resolving to think more about this later when she was at leisure. That would be when today's funeral was over. But they had no date yet for the funeral of the woman who filled her thoughts.

I'll put some colour on her eyelids and lips, cheeks too; Goodness knows she needs it... Her family will want to see her looking beautiful and they're trusting me to prepare her, another woman to make her respectable again. Death is bad enough for someone as young as she, but to be murdered too... How must her family feel? And that look on her face...I felt her horror. Who'd do this – and twice? It must be the same

11

person - killer. Everything looks identical.

She stood up, suddenly resolute. *I've had enough for now,* she told herself, *Oh, and how long before we get some normal summer weather? Bring on the gales and drenching sheets of rain.*

She longed for the cold, the intense icy cold of a winter's day outside, she knew she couldn't bear the heat in the city for much longer. Fortunately, the body she was preparing for burial would wait, and she had just finished the final injections of the embalming fluids. She quickly collected all her instruments in an enamel tray, ready for cleaning. The syringes rolled annoyingly across the other items and she thrust the tray away from her onto the draining board and washed her hands again.

Her eyes fell on a tiny posy of flowers. She had found it tucked down inside the bodice of the dead woman. The first victim had had one too, but of different flowers. She quickly took the tiny thing and opening a cupboard, took out a small flower press.

I'll keep it preserved here, with the other one. Strange there should be two. It may be important.

That done she looked at the body once more.

Poor, poor girl.

She turned away, pulled off her overall, wrenched off the long sleeves that caught her wrists and the whole long length of it dragging everywhere, trapping her calico skirt in its folds. Even her muslin blouse refused to co-operate and clung like a damp second skin. Her own body felt like a furnace.

I've been working since dawn. I need a rest, that's what it is.

The door burst open and a girl bobbed her head into the room, her bright auburn hair a flash of colour. She wore it in a huge, heavy bun at the back of her neck, a parting in the middle of her head, which suited her completely, despite the workaday severity of the style.

'Master wants you, Miss. You've to come and see summat special!' the girl told her, as she came fully into the room. She lifted the lid of a laundry basket to look in. 'I'll take this over, now it's full, Miss.' She heaved the basket up onto her hip. The laundry fella's here already. Things're drying quick in this heat and he's out to make his fortune! The master said...'

Sophia saw her huge brown eyes gleaming with mischief, skin glowing in the heat. Even in her drab cotton work dress, with a long hessian apron, the girl looked sparklingly alive and vibrant.

'I know, I know.' She forestalled the end of what her father had said. 'He called for me. But what's so exciting? Anyway – you're supposed to knock, Alice. Try and remember.'

'Yes, Miss. I know, and you'll never guess what 'tis, but you'll fair swoon like them society ladies when you see, Miss...' She was halfway out of the door before she'd finished speaking. She was petite but very strong, each step she took was filled with bright energy.

'Yes, yes. I'm coming as soon as I can, tell him.'

Alice dashed away, laughing.

Sophia shook her head wondering how it was that the girl was always even tempered, a very spirit of joy. Perhaps the young woman whose body was on the table was once the very spirit of joy. Perhaps she lightened people's lives, loved, had wild and beautiful dreams of her own future, was beloved by her family, had given her heart to a young man – perhaps she'd dressed herself nicely to meet someone...

Quick footsteps in the corridor. Alice was back and a little more urgent.

'Miss, *please* come. You're wanted.'

'Yes.'

Sophia stood looking down at the covered body.

Alice reached out and gently lifted the cloth away from the face.

'She was lovely.'

'Yes.'

'You're worried about this one aren't you, Miss?' she asked, gently.

'Everything's strange, I have to admit.'

Alice continued, her voice low and practical, all her bubbling liveliness pushed aside.

'She is slim and tall too, tall as many men,' she said, thoughtfully. 'Clothes of proper good quality; that walking dress was fine lawn and the little lilac cape was silk; dainty but it was stained so, on the back. Wasn't she left on the pavement round the back of the Royal? Anyway, I washed them carefully for her, just as you said, for when the family come and see her. Like as not they'll want to bring other clothes for the burial. There has to be summat lovely instead of all this horror. I mean, I know this is an undertaker's an' all, but some things don't feel right, do they? And no hat; you noticed that when she came in and that's unusual on such a day and for a ladylike person. Don't you think so, Miss Sophia?'

'Yes, yes I do, Alice. Practical as ever. You notice a lot of things yourself.'

'Me mam said that were me being just plain nosy.'

'Maybe. Useful though. Look at the hands.' Sophia drew back the cloth a little more and lifted one. 'This woman's hands worked hard, but at what? She looks ladylike but did she have a family, children to wash for? She was no seamstress either, no pricked fingers, no callouses, no broken nails, but they are muscled, a little reddened too, perhaps they were in water a great deal. Very clean. If only mine were as unmarked.'

'Well, I'm doing a lot o'washing, Miss. Just your delicate linens and all, but even that gets my hands in't soapy water. Yet

I've still got the blue seams from the coal dust. Now that were from hard manual labour, since I were ten. Ehh, six long years, sorting coal at the flippin pit-brow day long. At least when I were housemaid that last year there, me 'ands were dry mostly. I suppose every task leaves a mark.'

*Everything leaves a mark...*Sophia suddenly remembered what she had found when she picked up one of the woman's hands to clean and trim the nails again. *That was very odd; the other body had something grey under the nails too, something foul, the texture and the smell. Both of them had scratched or scraped at something.*

Shocked, she instantly recalled the feel of those hands on her face and her neck. It came to her that the victim, in her final desperate moments, had clawed at the back of the attacker's hands or arms, and that the foul substance was scraped off his skin, or worse, was his skin. She would not forget that smell and the texture of the stuff. It was an effort to continue the train of thought. She shuddered.

Alice saw it. 'Perhaps you could do with a cuppa, Miss – for the heat?'

'I could really, you're right.' Then Sophia brightened. She'd remembered. 'A nurse, of course; I think her mother told us, didn't she? She worked at the Manchester Royal Infirmary; found round the back near a warehouse of some kind; you were right. Nurse Worthington, Adeline Worthington. A fine profession for a bright young woman: She wanted to become matron one day.'

She bent to cover the body again but paused to gaze again at the woman's face, her eyes now closed, and her features composed, youthful. It had taken all Sophia's art to change the expression fixed on her features when she'd died.

'You know, Alice, she was lovely in life. Such thick, dark eyelashes. What a difference the shape of a few features makes.

Father remarked so. It's a dreadful thought that she is the second we have dealt with in as many weeks. Awful. Why, these two young woman with their whole lives ahead of them? Who did this?

'Wants the 'angman's noose, whoever it is.' The girl's voice thrilled with indignation.

'Yes.'

'You'll be coming to the kitchen then, for the tea? Please, Miss! The Master keeps catching sight of me. And you'll really want to see what's there...'

'Thank you, yes. Now off you go!' Sophia answered and waved at the girl, shooing her away. She drew the cover up again.

The police will surely investigate such deaths quickly. I wonder if Nathaniel knows anything.

His face came floating unbidden to her mind, dark features scowling, brooding almost, certainly intense.

My very own Heathcliff. Miss Emily Brontë must have known someone like him to paint such a man with words. Or is he more of Mrs Gaskell's John Thornton? Yes. She smiled at the very idea of Nathaniel but a worry took root and blossomed. *Will he tell me if he knows anything? How goes the investigation? Perhaps he doesn't yet know, and when he does, he must tell me. I'm involved. I've tended both the victims and he knows I wouldn't gossip. He may be an officer of the police, but he knows little of women, or me – daft lad, as Alice would say. Maybe he'll learn.* Her mouth narrowed, yet her eyes sparkled.

Alice wants taking in hand, perhaps, she thought without any real intention to accomplish the task. *And I suppose I should hurry up and see whatever it is in the kitchen everyone's so keen for me to view.*

The vision was still upon her though. Sure enough, the

heatwave had drained her energy and led her to a mild discontent that was unusual for her, but the feeling that was building inside her was fear.

She fetched the trolley and quickly, with the ease of practise, she moved the body onto it and back into the refrigerated room for the present. She looked down thoughtfully.

I will do my best with her. Adeline Worthington shall look as beautiful as I can make her. God grant there are no more poor girls like these two. What occupation did the first girl have? She explored her memory, finally remembering that the mother had been so proud of her daughter being a pharmacist's assistant, an assistant to her own father, in fact. They had the big new shop on Market Street.

Ah yes, Hepplestone's, she was Sally Hepplestone. She worked with her father, as do I. Now I remember, I had no visions when I touched her, although she bore similar marks on her body to Adeline Worthington.

But time moved on and it was time she answered the summons.

It must be a person we know and not a customer, nor anyone official if they are in the yard kitchen.

The tiles on the floor of the corridor rang with the quick tap of her heels, but it was the sound of more laughter from the kitchen that made her slow down and listen. She was curious.

A man? Young too, and hearty by the sound. Father laughing; now there's something strange – and welcome. He rarely feels like laughing in this heat.

The workroom was at the back of their premises and opened out into the extensive yard for easy access when loading and unloading bodies. Also facing into the yard were the stables, barns and vehicle storage, workrooms and the outside entrance to the yard kitchen. Behind the kitchen door the men's voices made the deep continuous murmuring of a beehive in full summer.

That's a comfortable sound, and pleasant. It has been a trying day so far, she reminded herself. *Frightening, if I am wholly honest, disturbing at the very least, and my mind feels heavy with it all.*

She took a hot breath, felt a pulse of foreboding deep inside as her mind flashed through the scene she had witnessed; she trembled, clasped her arms round her shoulders, felt nausea rise up, her head spun, she groaned aloud.

What an effort it took to push the thing away, compose her mind to normal thoughts, not visions of tormented death. A delightful and renegade breeze slipped under the back door, so she leant back against the wall to rest a minute, lift her skirts a little and feel the coolness on her legs.

She must go in! She grasped the awkward door handle with both hands, and wrenched it sideways, which was the usual method employed by the household to open it, then stopped in her tracks in the open doorway. Sitting at their table was a young man, an exquisitely handsome young man, an enquiring expression lighting his face as he stood politely.

'Sophia, ah my dear, you are here at last. This is the new curate of St Ann's, Reverend Knightly. Reverend Knightly, my daughter, and senior partner in the business, Miss Kelley, Miss Sophia Kelley.'

Chapter 2

'No man is an island'
John Donne

'MISS KELLEY.' He offered his hand, palm upwards, an old-fashioned courtly gesture, she knew, but nevertheless she put her hand in his, and to complete the ceremony he bowed quickly over it.

'Mr Knightly.' She bobbed her head in acknowledgment. *I'm Miss Emma Woodhouse now!* Eyes twinkling at the thought.

The young man smiled.

What a ray of sunshine! She decided and returned the smile. 'Pardon me, *Reverend* Knightly.'

Both men had risen to their feet when she entered, and the younger man stepped round to pull out a chair for her at the table; there was something about the way he moved that caught the eye and held it.

'Shall I make tea, my dear?' her father said. 'We hold very easy ways in here, Reverend Knightly, as you see; no ceremony in the yard kitchen; we're too busy by far. Old customs like tea in the kitchen, are most comfortable for me.'

Her father seldom waited for an answer where tea was involved. He moved to the range and swung the iron hook holding the kettle round so that it was over the hob then lifted the large blue teapot and red tea caddy from the shelf.

'Black Indian tea. Can you do with that, Reverend Knightly?

For if not, we've none of your Lapsang Souchong or Earl Grey's blend here,' Sophia's father announced.

'I am fond of black Indian, thank you, and I do not require a slice of lemon.' She saw a twinkle light his eye. His voice was attractive, very pleasant to listen to.

His host smiled. 'Good, good, my own preference.'

The greetings over, Sophia sat back in her chair and sighed; this was exactly what she needed, a pleasant chat with interesting people. The vision stayed at the back of her mind; haunting, teasing, frightening her, even as she set out to be sociable, to feel the balm of ordinary life.

There were times when she was overwhelmed with the goodness and beauty she experienced in her visions, as she called them. Some brought comfort, but there were some that were deeply affecting because they were awful, inexplicable and intangible. Of course, she couldn't prove she had seen Adeline Worthington being assaulted, nor did she know if the same hand killed her, but what she could do was close a door in her mind and push the vision resolutely behind it to the deepest, darkest recesses to be released and examined later. At the moment, fate had brought a pleasant diversion in the form of a handsome stranger and she was ready to benefit from it.

'This is a good, homely scene,' said the visitor. 'And the coolness is welcoming, considering what we are faced with outdoors.' He pulled gently at his high collar and flapped the edges of his coat. It was then that she noticed he had a scar on one side of his face. It was long, thin and jagged, going from his brow to his chin; an old scar, healed and white.

But it doesn't spoil his looks, she thought, and felt in insistent urge to run a finger down the length of the scar. Sometimes Sophia could sense a pulsing history from a single touch and gazing at his scar she felt her hands grow warm and the fingers tingle. A single touch might tell her if a person or an object carried heavy, troublesome memories, or was imbued with all things good and pure. It was another familiar experience.

Her mother had cherished her gift and Sophia was used to its place in her life, glad of it often. But she did not explain these mystical experiences and knowledge to anyone else, not even Nathaniel, she simply helped people if they had a need, in any way she could. Her parents had argued about it and it was the only jarring note in the enduring love of their marriage; Mother saying it was bestowed by God for the help of souls in need. Her father viewed such visions as trickeries and the mediums who pretended to have them as agents of the devil, exploiting the bereaved with fairground tricks. He did not want his daughter to be associated with those clairvoyants and mediums, the charlatans whose theatrical séances terrorised, not comforted; the only positive outcome being the growing wealth of the mediums.

So, faced with the interesting visitor, of course Sophia suppressed the urge to touch the scar. Sometimes the impulse could not be denied because of the wrench exerted by a past catastrophe, but today, it was merely laced with curiosity and, if she were honest, the interest of a new acquaintance too.

The kitchen door opened suddenly, and Alice flounced in with a pail to put beneath the sink where there was a drip from one of the pipes. She bobbed a curtsey to her master but catching Sophia's eye in passing she raised her eyebrows suggestively and flicked a sparkling glance at the curate. Sophia scowled and used her own expressive eyebrows to tell Alice to go, and quickly. For once she did as she was bidden, and the sound of trilling laughter danced in her wake across the yard.

It was so infectious that Sophia was forced to bend and pretend the hem of her skirts needed some adjustment and the

21

young curate's obvious discomfort helped her subdue a snort of laughter. He looked increasingly warm in his plush coat. Her father had noticed and invited him to take it off if he liked, to feel at home, especially when there was weather that'd cook an egg on the pavement. But Reverend Knightly demurred like a gentleman born.

'No, no, no. I am quite easy now.'

Sophia relished the sound of his speech. It bespoke the higher classes and from down south near London. It was deep, beautifully modulated, respectfully low with soft vowels and hardly a movement of the perfectly formed lips. Such an accent was developed in infancy under the influence of governesses and tutors who gently guided their charge, then a life of public school, probably Eton, almost certainly Cambridge, beautiful drawing rooms and balls of the highest quality, possibly even aristocratic society. This flitted through her mind in an instant and when she raised her eyes, she was surprised to find him gazing at her.

'Oh yes, everyone feels at ease here, Reverend Knightly,' she said, determined to push the dreadful vision to the very back of her mind for now, and to enjoy some light, harmless chatter with an attractive man. Then, instead of lengthening the moment, it was easier to rise and help her father with the refreshments. She collected cups and saucers, a jug of milk from the small pantry at the back of the room, and the bowl of sugar.

'And it's a cool place here in the summer,' she added. 'As is the whole of this side of the house, and the workroom at certain times of the day.'

She saw a thought sweep across her father's face even before he asked, 'Is the new cool table working as we hoped?'

'Oh, yes, it is indeed,' she said, then to Reverend Knightly, 'We have a new device that keeps the deceased cool to prevent deterioration, especially in weather such as this. It is a folding board and has a place for ice blocks underneath – quite the novelty in our business.' Her mind's eye swept round the workroom with its marble examination table and the refrigerated body storage room lined with stone. In the past they'd had stone shelves set deeply within the walls. Everything was secure and cool. She was reassured.

Her father took the teapot and filled it. 'All of this is worth the investment to keep the deceased preserved until we can do our more creative work, shall we say. This summer!' He shook his head, pursed his lips.

Glancing at the visitor Sophia saw his own mouth twitch a little. 'Oh, Father, Reverend Knightly may not be used to stark, practical talk such as ours - about bodies.' She watched his reaction. 'It can be tactless for some people, even the clergy.'

He answered with careful solemnity, 'Anything to do with death is my concern, but it's true, I am more concerned with the preservation of the soul than the more flamboyant and decorative trappings of modern mourning.'

'Ah, you mean the tinted creams that disguise death's ravages to the face, the favourite hair styles, the best clothes and other embellishments,' Sophia suggested, mischievously.

'Indeed, you read my mind.' He paused a moment to gather his ideas, eyes lowered. 'I have discovered that the bereaved today are greatly troubled by appearances, as if by the observances and ceremonies society has contrived, they keep the beloved lost one with them in this vain world a little longer.'

'To that end, there is a fashion for photographs taken of the departed loved one; they are in life-like poses, sitting or standing (with props!), babies sometimes in cribs or in the arms of siblings,' she said, watching closely for his reaction. She suspected him of subtle sarcasm.

He added, 'And surrounded by a floral exuberance worthy of Her Majesty.' He clasped his hands on the table, as though in prayer and then cast his eyes heavenward.

There was a heartbeat's pause before she laughed, a delighted burst of merriment.

'You are teasing! Our dear Reverend Williams, ever the scholar, doesn't indulges in such frivolity.' She found herself delighted at this irreverence.

'Yes, I believe I am teasing, but so were you!' he pointed out and grinned. Sophia thought it boyish and disarming. 'We will be friends, I think, Miss Kelley.'

'I'm sure we will.'

They exchanged a smile. His showed beautifully even teeth and a curling mouth. He wore his hair short, without the long sideburns many men preferred, and he was clean shaven, newly shaved she thought. He had glossy auburn hair and deep green eyes. She noticed they were fringed with thick dark lashes that a woman would envy.

What does he think of us, I wonder? What do we look like to him? Perhaps he doesn't notice things; many men don't. She patted her hair and felt the bouncy familiarity of her massed curls.

He smiled at her gesture and she had a spark of inspiration.

I think he has sisters and lots of female relations. He is very easy with a woman – and many men lack that skill too. It will stand him in good stead with the parish!

'The tea is brewed,' her father announced, and still having the previous subject of their talk in his mind added, 'And can I knock down your mockery of these post-mortem photographs, that some of these pictures are the only images people have of their lost relative. Don't hold with them myself, but people do find a comfort, I believe.' He poured the tea. 'But here is news, my dear; Reverend Knightly will be officiating at the funeral this afternoon. I understand our old friend is not himself.'

'He is in his cups, you mean, Father?' She flicked a glance at the curate.

'Aye, almost as gone from the world as the bodies we tend. The poor old man. I am fond of him.' He shook his head and passed a cup to Sophia. 'Taken to his bed I hear, but with a little sherry in a flask.'

Sophia laughed again. 'Oh Father, if he takes any more into his body, we will not need anything else to preserve it when he passes away.'

Both men laughed with her.

She felt a stab of regret. 'But you know, he often takes to his bed in the afternoon, but then he's very elderly and may simply be tired. And the 'solace' may dull any aches he has. I don't really wish to malign him. He is a good man and our friend.'

'Aye, that's true enough,' her father added.

David Knightly smiled.

'You seem sure that I will not pass this observation on to Reverend Williams, Miss Kelley.' It was a statement, spoken with kind confidence and both she and her father exchanged a glance. It wouldn't be right to upset the old man, whatever state he was in.

'No, I do not think that,' she reassured him.

'But we have only just met.'

Have we? I suppose that may be true, she thought as her father reached for the sugar bowl and grinned at her. *He's one of those souls you feel you have met before somehow. Perhaps it's just that he is a very likeable man with a smile that makes you warm to him instantly.*

'My daughter is a fine judge of character, Reverend Knightly. You will find that she is always to be relied upon.' He spooned four teaspoons of sugar into his cup and stirred vigorously, beaming at them both.

David Knightly turned to face her.

'A worthy testimonial, I should say. Thank you for your early trust, Miss Kelley.' He looked into her eyes. 'On the strength of that may I presume to enquire about something that puzzles me?' He caught her father's eye and added, 'And I ask in front of Mr. Kelley so that he may be assured I mean no impertinence.'

She smiled permission, her father nodded, put down his cup.

'I must confess myself curious about your role in the business of undertaking funerals. Is this a role that ladies of your station, your higher class, are accustomed to hold, dealing with the deceased each day? I come from London and life and traditions seem quite different from those here in Manchester particularly. This city is nothing short of a rocketing powerhouse!'

He smiled charmingly, and she knew well that some people may have thought the question impolite, but for the openness of his smile that made it completely devoid of censure.

Her father sat back in his chair, a smile playing on his own lips. 'My dear?'

Here Sophia was confident.

'My role has always been one left to the women in our society, at least for many centuries of our Christian society, as you must know. And you'll find that up here, the working classes and the poor, always have a woman in the local community, even of one street or courtyard, that undertakes the laying-out of the dead.'

'I suppose that must be the case in the south – though I wouldn't know.'

Sophia's father added, 'It is a caring role, that final ministration to the body and it can be the greatest comfort to the bereaved. And there is always a local woman who is the midwife for the lying-ins. Some do both jobs! Is that not so, Sophia?'

'It is. I do think though, that since our lives have become more affluent, beginning with the wealthy industrialists, our middle classes, as we seem to call them, have taken some of the caring roles from their womenfolk as being undignified in their station. But it is not undignified to me, to us.' She exchanged a glance with her father. 'Quite the opposite in fact. And there is something else; we have a new band of people now, women, those who have a caring role as a real profession, such as nurses, midwives, teachers and as I do, as an undertaker. I've heard of many women who are doctors too, one here, at the university – but that seems a step too far for some of their male colleagues.'

She could see agreement and interest brightening his eyes but felt no undue personal pleasure in the response; she was more concerned to explain how seriously she took her profession.

Am I talking too much? Why do I feel the need to justify what I do? Do I sound as though lack confidence?

Her father sat forward now; hands clasped on the table in front of him, a quick smile thrown in his daughter's direction.

'Reverend Knightly, I see you are curious as to both our roles in your own new life here,' he said and grinned at the younger man, who Sophia noticed, still appeared very interested. 'My wife and I were of these poorer classes, but forty years ago - which doesn't seem long to me. I was employed in the cotton mills on Ordsall Lane, a carpenter by trade, employed to refit the looms and fix up all structures of the kind. My wife kept a small provisions shop in our home, from the front room, and it was well frequented. We lived in one of the terraced streets, Stone Street, close by the mills and what is now the docks for the new canal. She was the very woman, being full of compassion and skilled with her hands, who people called to lay out their dead in our own neighbourhood. So, when I found myself laid off work, I turned my hand to coffin making, and at that time it was an unheard-of refinement for the poor. We began to make a small charge for her service and I had to charge for the wood and labour, of course...'

'And your business began, I see,' Reverend Knightly finished for him, nodding.

Sophia poured their visitor more tea. 'And I, having been brought up in much wealthier circumstances, being educated too and used to helping my parents in all parts, have succeeded my mother in the business and with great willingness.'

'And talent,' her father added. 'My daughter is very well regarded, and her services are often sought, particularly for females; people find it a reassuring dignity. And now, Reverend Knightly, she takes more of the management over each day – not that I'm ailing at all! But I find myself enjoying it, I can tell you. My daughter is the senior partner here. It is a fine thing to be so proud of an offspring who so ably takes the reins of a prosperous family business.'

'I am delighted to have joined a parish where such goodness and skill accompany a necessity of life – and death. I beg your pardon if I seemed too intrusive in my wish to know about you.'

'No, no, lad.'

'I also wish to do well here. I'm from a privileged background and all the necessities of life were simply managed by someone else. It is I who am the poorer. I don't even make my own tea, in fact, I cannot. Am I not a weak creature? And I thank you for being so open. I'm honoured by your trust.'

Sophia's father was pleased with the new curate. He sat back on his chair, relaxed and proceeded to probe the visitor about his reasons for coming up north when so many found life in the privileged home counties far more congenial that the heart of a big city.

'Ah,' Reverend Knightly laughed. 'Why leave all that comfort and ease, why not marry a rich heiress, perhaps a debutante, and continue in the way of all landed gentry?'

'Yes!' Sophia said. Her father smiled smugly.

'The answer is that I wasn't serving God well enough – the Church is my vocation, not the second-class gift to a second son. I was given a good living in the church on my family estate, a wealthy estate, but the people didn't need me greatly. My abilities were not stretched. In short, I was bored. Another clergyman of less energy or wealth would be able to grow in that situation and better himself and the parish. My bishop down there, felt I would find my métier here in a city parish, so he wrote to his friend Bishop Moorhouse at the cathedral.'

Oh, how very pleased with ourselves we all are!

Her father was thoughtful. 'Forgive me, Reverend, but you look quite the gentleman and your clothes and manner bespeak it so. Do you think the poorer folk will accept help from one of such a higher class? Will they talk to you, as they do to Reverend Williams?'

Down to brass tacks, Father! Sophia enlarged on his theme.

'Who looks a little more worn and one of them. They appreciate his great learning and value his choice of a simple way of living. They often give him small presents of an egg, a loaf, none of which are easily spared, because they like to help one in need themselves.'

'More approachable, you think.'

'Well...'

He laughed. 'I like people, Miss Kelley, I genuinely like them, the servants who do the menial tasks, the wealthy lords of the land, the lawyer, the baker, the ordinary everyday mixture of people on the streets. They fascinate me. And I've always had the same response back. Already I find a great humanity here among the poor.'

Yes, I believe you.

'As far as my wealth goes – it has never gone to my head, don't worry.'

Her father said, 'I believe the vicarage now has a washer woman who comes in, and a maid to help the housekeeper, Mrs Biggs, plus a manservant to do odd jobs. Would that be your doing?'

'It would, although do not assign me moral approval without knowing I am merely seeing to my own comfort; I am but a babe in arms as far as looking after myself goes. I truly cannot begin to wash my own shirts! And Reverend Williams's household arrangements needed some help, in the material sense only. We are but two bachelors and need looking after. For myself, I discover that I am very adaptable. In my family home we would no more think of having tea in the staff kitchen than you would think of sitting down in the middle of a railway track to do the same. But I am enjoying this Northern custom greatly.'

'And you have trusted us with this view of yourself, Reverend Knightly,' her father added, his tone contemplative.

Sophia smiled a little, hesitated before she said, 'Speaking of trust again, there is something that has worried me, well, worried Father and me.' She glanced at her father, saw him nod permission.

She was about to speak further when there came shouts of greeting from the stable yard outside, loud male voices, some hearty and good natured, another annoyed. A door banged loudly then swift, heavy footsteps crashed along the passage and the kitchen door was flung open.

Chapter 3

'How do I love thee?'
Elizabeth Barrett Browning

A YOUNG MAN swept into the room, in haste, and familiarly. He glared at everyone in turn, his eyes lingering suspiciously on the comfortable demeanour of the visitor and on the clerical collar he wore under his smart, sober coat. He wore the uniform of a police officer himself. He was tall, strongly built.

'Has something happened to Reverend Williams?' He blurted, then shook his head abruptly, as if to chastise himself. 'My apologies, sir, I am accustomed to see another clergyman taking tea at this table.' His voice was deep yet quiet, shot with authority; his dark uniform added to the air of power, as he stood before them.

Sophia swung round in her chair.

'Good morning, Nathaniel; I see you've returned.' She raised an eyebrow, at his hasty entrance, yet her face was lit up from within.

'You're all right then? You're well, Sophia?' he demanded, but softly. His eyes swept hungrily across her face, troubled, and at the same time he took up the hand that rested on the table and pressed it to his lips. Her hand was hidden entirely in his huge one.

She stroked his cheek gently when he released it.

'As you see. Fit as a fiddle – but quite wrung out with the dreadful heat.'

Ah, Nat. At last! You've been gone so long. Everything in Sophia's world took on a different light now he had returned.

He did not look relieved by her assurance. His mouth narrowed.

'There was a report of a young woman having been attacked near the Shambles. I thought... but thank God.' He seemed to recollect his manners and turned at last to the curate who had risen to his feet. 'I'm Sergeant Roberts of the Manchester City Police.' He put his thumbs in his belt and looked steadily into the eyes of the other man. Sophia was both surprised and, if she were honest with herself, a little thrilled to see a challenge.

Her father made the introductions. 'This is my daughter's fiancé, Sergeant Roberts. Nathaniel, this is Reverend Knightly.'

The atmosphere had an unexpected frisson of excitement. Bizarrely she found herself thinking about the comic opera they had been to see after Christmas, *The Pirates of Penzance,* with the song, *A policeman's lot is not an 'appy one!* She glanced at him and saw at once that he was completely, serious; what was she thinking? She was fully sobered in a second. Another young woman attacked.

Nathaniel continued, 'Your business here, sir?' A quiet enquiry. A straightforward, appraising look.

'Steady on there, Nat, lad; there is nought to worry the law here,' Sophia's father said, smiling. He tapped the top of a chair, nodded the policeman to it, and filled another cup with tea. 'Reverend Knightly is the new curate of St Ann's.'

Her father was a big man, vigorous, a good peppering of grey in his otherwise dark hair and looked hale and well at sixty. He was clean shaven, disliking the variable fashions of whiskers as fripperies. All the men on the yard were expected to be clean shaven too – our professional style, he said.

'David Knightly,' said the curate, standing and offering his hand to the policeman. Nathaniel ignored it, nodded curtly instead and sat down at the table. He removed the truncheon and lamp from his belt and put these items and his helmet on the floor at the side of his chair, to make sitting for a time more comfortable. He was opposite the visitor.

Angry and worried, and … jealous? Sophia wondered, surprised at, yet a little pleased by the notion until she saw his expression grow colder. *He can look quite sinister at times, especially with that hooked nose and shadowed chin. Perhaps this is a suspicious expression that policemen cultivate.*

She looked from one to the other and found herself comparing their appearance and attitude. She was interested to see that Reverend Knightly returned to his seat calmly and was not disturbed at all by Nathaniel's confrontational manner, nor his lack of social manners.

They are almost mirror images, are they not? Both tall and well set up, one crowned with that strong auburn hair and blessed with sea green eyes. Mr Knightly – Reverend Knightly. And the other, such a glowering other, dark eyes and a black cap of thick curly hair almost covering them. Nathaniel, love.

The new curate looked urbane and relaxed, unusual in a curate, she had to admit, but a pleasant change from a frail old man sometimes confused and sometimes appearing to be in his cups.

And this new man has a sense of fun. I think that charming, but Nat, Nat is enraged for all he shows only his policeman's calm. What makes him so terse today, surely not appearance of a clean and handsome new curate in an immaculate black frock coat. Surely something of far greater importance – this attack on a woman? Still, he has taken a direct dislike to our new friend here, and that's intriguing.

She turned to him. 'Nat, a young woman, you say, near here? Is she alright?'

Nat pushed a finger inside the high collar of his uniform and eased it away from his neck; the silver numbers on the collar winked as they caught the light. Sweat trickled from his brow and down the collar of his tunic. His hair was damp too.

'She is. She was out on an errand and was attacked in an alley near the Shambles, early this morning before the start of business, about eight o'clock, I believe. She fought off the man – she thinks it was a man, a foul smelling one. She saw nothing because he came up behind her and threw an arm round her neck and the other round her body.'

Sophia heard this with an inward shudder of remembrance.

A third young woman?

Nat had not paused in his speech. 'Apparently, she was very distressed when she spoke to my constable. It was he who passed the information to me, remembering that you might be abroad at this time of day, and in the area. He knew I'd want to be informed so that you might be warned.' Tension laced his voice. 'Have you been out? Did you see anything,' Nathaniel swept his gaze round the table, 'any of you?'

There's that anger again. There's something more than he is telling now. Aloud she said, 'I've been in the workroom all morning and Father's been making final arrangements for the funeral later. Neither of us has been out. You can ask the men on the yard what they have seen too; they come in and out as you know.'

The curate leant almost imperceptibly towards her as he turned to answer for himself: 'I've been with the worthy Reverend Williams, but I think he may have had his mind elsewhere.'

Sophia saw the ghost of a smile round his lips. 'I'm certain he will vouch for you,' she said, 'We've known him a long time and he can be trusted in matters like this, at least.' There was a warning in her tone; Reverend Williams had been mocked by her enough for one day and she was uncomfortable that the new curate now wanted to continue the entertainment. Something more serious was afoot. David Knightly inclined his head in apology and flushed deep red.

He has the manners to look contrite at least, she thought. *But, oh it's my fault; I encouraged his theme. I'm not being true to myself at the moment. How could I imply, before a stranger, that poor old Reverend Williams was a drunkard?*

Then her mind instantly pivoted to what Nat had said.

'Nathaniel, what does this young woman look like? I may know her, but I've another reason for asking, which I'll tell you in a minute.'

Nat reached for his teacup, but paused to consider, and when his eyes flew to hers and she saw fear in them, she knew he'd understood the way her thoughts were tending. His expression darkened, he swallowed.

'She looks…' he began slowly, as if unwilling to voice the notion, 'I suppose something similar, erm, a little like you,' adding with more conviction, 'but perhaps only the height and colour of your hair, now I recollect.'

'Oh Goodness, that may be Jenny Hargraves. She is secretary to one of the partners at the Phoenix Assurance. We've passed the time of day often. How is she?'

'I believe she's badly shaken.'

Her father spoke. 'Tell him what else we noticed, lovie.'

'We've had two young women brought to us for preparation and we're curious, no,' she paused and exchanged a look with her father as she found the words she needed, 'not curious, more worried about them too. Both the families and the police agree they were murdered, Nat. Did you know about them?'

'I have heard but haven't been given the details yet. I was

away, as you know,' Nat, took out his police notebook and pencil, 'visiting London and the Metropolitan Police there,' he added with an almost reverent tone that could have sounded self-important, to a stranger, but that Sophia knew was far from studied nonchalance. He was wholly serious about the role of the police and he was anxious to secure promotion to Inspector when a vacancy came up.

The curate listened attentively; he wore a calm poise that Sophia guessed would make any sort of confidences or confessions easy to utter in his presence. He, like Nat, was a young man waiting to rise in his chosen calling; she and her father had heard that Reverend Williams would be retired by the Bishop soon enough. Perhaps this Reverend Knightly could be his successor in a busy city parish. She could see that he had a quality of stillness about him that was in no way menacing or watchful; it was more akin to the timelessness of a clear night sky, appearing endless, yet one felt it pulse with energy and distances. And possibilities.

'But Miss Kelley, what is this thing that makes you a little uneasy?' David Knightly asked, sitting forward. His voice quiet, focused, and disturbingly hypnotic. 'I may be able to help, or possibly hinder, and not be invited to tea again!'

Nat coughed, interrupting. 'Go on, Sophia; what have you noticed?' He held his pencil over the book.

'Yes, explain, my dear,' her father said.

'It might be a coincidence, but both have...they both have a look – just a look of me also, as I said about Adeline Worthington, Father. We all four have roughly the same colouring and size, that is all, yet two of the four are dead. Sally Hepplestone and Adeline Worthington are the two who are dead. The one who was attacked today might be Jenny Hargraves and then there is me.'

Nathaniel's eyes sought Sophia's and held them for a

heartbeat, full of disquiet.

Reverend Knightly nodded. 'It's very strange. Can I ask how the two women died, Mr. Kelley? Or perhaps Sergeant Roberts might know.'

'I do not.'

'Well, Mr. Kelley, would you know if it was by some strange means they were killed? Perhaps, an uncommon illness? These things do happen, even to the young and healthy.'

Her father exchanged a look with Sophia before speaking.

He said, 'We're not experts in medical matters such as a doctor might be, I mean those doctors or sometimes even pharmacists who do examine a body post-mortem, to discover if there is anything of note. No, we are not experts, yet we're very familiar with death and how some people may have come to meet theirs.' He took a long drink of his tea, appearing to consider what to say next. 'Who could do such a thing to such young and lovely women? Why would they do it? But I'm wandering, aren't I?' He put down his cup and laid both palms on the table. 'I'll make my point. Both of the women had a blue tinge to the lips and some discolouration, tiny burst blood vessels around the whites of the eyes which we have seen in those who die of pneumonia...'

Sophia added, 'And lack of air generally. Remember the tiny baby last year that had been found dead, under the pillows of the parents' bed, smothered, by the look of things. And then there is consumption. It is common, as you know. And the smog does stick to the back of your throat and cause a wheezing at times.'

Her father nodded, unbothered by her interjection. 'Or it could be a deceased person had been in the cotton trade and had spent a lifetime breathing that fine, dusty, cotton-laden air in the mills, but not necessarily as a weaver or anyone on the mill floor. There is a lot of that round here, in the North, and we've that many cotton mills here, we're called Cottonopolis by the rest of the world. You're from London way, you say, Reverend Knightly? Well, this breathing trouble is not confined to one class, though it is prevalent among the poorer classes. We had a mill owner last year, a very grand and wealthy gentleman, but he spent each day walking around the weaving sheds, watching, talking, breathing the dust. His family told us he always was short of air and his lips were blue at the end as he fought for his last breaths.'

Nat had made notes as he spoke, his whole body attentive.

Sophia's father held up a hand. 'Wait, Nathaniel, lad. There's a more important point I must make to sum up. Your Dr Johnson, who examined both bodies when they were taken to the mortuary at Newton Street Station, found nothing to indicate a cause of death, other than their blue lips. Y'know, it could be that they were suffocated, because we have been told of no other illnesses. But the inquest found that both deaths were due to misadventure.'

'I see, Arnold, thank you. I'll make a report to my Inspector. I have the names of these women. I take it they have been buried?'

'One was buried last week, and one still awaits burial.'

'Ahh.' Nat wrote a comment in his book; another detail to be added to the rest, pocketed his notebook, picked up his equipment.

'Father, what about …' Sophia began but he appeared not to hear and stood up as Nat did. He had to reach up to rest a hand on the policeman's shoulder.

'You'll let us know what happens about the enquiries? I'd appreciate knowing. Mind how y'go, lad,' he said as he opened the kitchen door for Nat and patted him out.

'Nat, wait for me, please. I'll walk with you to the yard gate. Excuse me, father, Reverend Knightly,' Sophia said and David

Knightly got up too.

'I must also take my leave to prepare for the funeral later. I'll see you then.' He rose to follow the others, but her father called him back.

'The deceased, for today's funeral that is, that is Henry Arkwright. He knew Reverend Williams well and I reckon the family might be pulled up short to see a new man, but needs must, as they say, eh?'

'Short notice, indeed – but the day has come, and we can't wait in this heat...'

'Am I to take it the Arkwrights have asked you to speak the funeral service?'

'They don't know yet, but, as you say, what alternative? Don't worry, I'll do my very best.'

'By the way, David...' Sophia heard her father begin.

The door closed on the conversation and Sophia caught Nat's arm as they walked down the corridor.

'What ails you then?'

'Nothing but care of you.' He snatched her to him, almost crushing her in his embrace, planted a hard kiss on her lips.

She pushed him back. 'You missed me then?'

'Always...' and kissed her again, only to push her quickly away just as the yard door flew open. A middle-aged man took a step in, pulled up short. He was a man with an outdoor complexion; he wore a horseman's tidy work clothes, a hessian apron over breeches, gaiters, open neck shirt, waistcoat. His face was one of those that, although very plain in feature when in repose, as soon as it was animated with an emotion became truly interesting. He was dark haired, clean shaven and had been gifted with a hooked nose that gave him an air of being immense dignity. He was a horseman in every inch of his being; the Yard Manager and Head Groom.

'Eh, sorry, Miss!' said the man. 'Wanted a word wi' Arnold about summat. 'Ope I'm not disturbing ought?' He grinned. He was a tall, slim man with military bearing.

Nat glanced at the man dismissively and to Sophia said, 'I will see you later.'

'Albert. What is it?' She found herself grinning too as Nat stalked past Albert and slammed the door after himself.

'Ehhh, He's a tender, shy young lad that one.'

'Well?' Sophia said, shortly, arms folded, eyebrows raised.

'Right. Just the final arrangements for later, Miss Sophia. Are we to put the new velvet pall on the coffin? Eddie wants to know so that he can finish up and close the hearse.' He smiled at her and pointed meaningfully at her shoulder where a long coil of hair had fallen, unravelled messily from her tidy working hairstyle when Nat caught her.

'It's hot, Albert, nothing more!' she retorted.

'Aye.'

'The new black velvet, as you say. Thanks,' she said. 'Right, go on. Off with you.'

'One other thing, Miss Sophia, I've had to take Samson off work for this afternoon and replace him with Captain. He's lame on the nearside foreleg – abscess below the knee. I were wondering if you had a syringe I could have to use for the draining.'

'Really, draining with a syringe? Poor Samson. A fly bite gone bad or what?'

'God knows there's enough flies about. No swelling there last night but Davy did say he'd a small scratch, but from where I've no idea. And about the syringe, I were talking to Davies from Smith's yard, last week and he saw one used for this job by the head groom at Lord Montague's. I usually nicks the swelling with a sharp knife, but I believe this'll be better and drain more cleanly. No pus running down the leg. I'll poultice it as well, like.'

'I thought you already had a few syringes, bought specially for injecting oils – your clock-mendings, remember?'

'Well, yes, Miss, 'course I remember, 'he snapped. 'I just need a bigger one – for the pus.'

Sophia tilted her head a little, a questioning gesture. 'No need to let the heat get to you, Albert. Send Davy across when I'm in the workroom.'

'Miss.' Raised eyebrows, were his final word.

David Knightly left a second after Albert. They would see each other later, he told Sophia again.

She re-joined her father, a mix of emotions roiling around inside her, disquiet about her vision and the so-called coincidences, pleasure in the contact with Nat, the new curate and yes, even Albert.

Cheeky old thing. 'Father,' she said as soon as she entered the kitchen, 'Why did you stop me speaking?'

He knew what she referred to. 'Best to keep those details between us for the time being, and obviously Nat. Tell him later, if you walk out this evening. Both of 'em with that puncture wound under the ear, tucked away and no earring on that ear, not found nearby neither. And the expression on their faces; don't forget that. I haven't seen the like of that before. The little posy too. Each of 'em had one, didn't they?'

'Yes. I preserved them both.'

'Good, good. Why would two young women have one? Is it the current fashion? Are these details important? We shall see. But for now – we're busy, and Alice says our dinner is on the table, ready. Come on, lovie. I only hope it's the *cold* roast from yesterday; perhaps with some of Benjamin's tomatoes, a pickled walnut…'

'You and your pickled walnuts, Father! You'll end up looking like one.'

'I'll look like one for real, soon enough, as most of our clients do, once they are boxed!'

'Father!'

She took his arm now as they strolled to the main house kitchen for dinner, leaving the men to the yard kitchen where Alice was now ready to dish up their meal.

Chapter 4

'Hope may vanish, but can die not'
Percy Bysshe Shelley

SOPHIA LOATHED FUNERALS in a heat wave. Lunch was eaten and it was but one short hour before the next funeral. What bothered her more than anything was the thought of changing her cooler clothes for the formal mourning dress that was required. She shuddered. Apart from the black costume with its long skirts wrapping her legs, the second skin of black cotton gloves that encased her sweating hands, the boots and black stockings that made her feet swell, the prim black veil of her tall hat pressing a skeletal hand on her face; apart from all that, it was the stench of a summer funeral that she could not abide. In weather such as this year, it was unbearable. She stopped what she was doing and closed her eyes, frowning as remembered scents swam, eel-like, along the stream of her thoughts. Perfumes were the worst.

She put her hands to the small of her back and stretched luxuriously before she remembered that very shortly, she would have to lace herself up in her stays to make her costume fit properly and not only that, but there were also tiny buttons, hooks and eyes by the score and boot hooks, ribbons and no end of laces to reckon with.

Perched on a high stool at the workbench and staring at the wall tiles, chin on hand, she looked forward to everything with deepening dread.

My stays will be like those straitjackets they use at the Lunatic Asylum, and I shall be shut up there in truth if my life continues like this. This heat will be the death of me then I'll have to join the long line of clients we are receiving so regularly. Ten years working with Father. Arnold Kelley and Daughter, Undertakers of Distinction. *But, oh, ten years of summer corsetry and mourning dress. How can I go on in this heat?*

But Death knew no festival times, nor seasons and Sophia's world was filled with the business of the deceased and the bereaved. When her parents had started the business, it was unheard of for women of the middle classes to attend funerals and show their grief in embarrassing tears, whereas the poor knew no such restraints and women wailed and wept their loss to the graveside. But now middle-class women were expected to attend funerals and to be dressed appropriately in mourning black and weep at will.

But why must they smell so? The women are worst of all. They drench themselves with perfume to hide the smell of mothballed funeral garments and sweat. Sour perfumes too. Men don't bother with anything other than tobacco and strong spirits. All packed together in the funeral carriage, smelling like a thick soup made with perfumes and farmyard dung. The poor don't attempt to hide their smell. At least their funerals are more honest.

What with all the talking, shouting, wailing and laughing, do not forget the laughing...strange that they would laugh, yet they do, they sound, and stink; a chicken coop stuffed with fussy, mangy old birds that have been soaked in 'Essence de Violette.'

So, instead of walking sedately alongside the mourners' carriages, Sophia usually paced ahead of the horses or positioned herself next to the horses' heads; their dignified pace as they pulled the hearse, easy to match. She would inhale the heady scent of their hot bodies and hay-perfumed breaths, the sharp-sweet oil on harness and hooves as they climbed the hill to the church, headbands crowned with dancing black ostrich feathers, all nodding in time. And the chime of their bits as they mouthed them, the creak of the harness and the ringing clash of hooves on cobbles was music to her. The horses, whom she loved, gave her some relief from the foul miasma and endless screeching that surrounded a summer funeral.

But it was with weary resignation that she anticipated that afternoon's walk in the heat along the road to the church, a long enough walk in high-heeled boots. She would drag her feet past the running sewers and alleys of the terraced houses, close packed and noisome, the dark courts and soaring warehouses, past the old disused graveyard and the sludgy River Irwell idling by. This would be a middle-class funeral, an expensive and exclusive observance. It was what people wanted and her father said he was prepared to provide it. But remembering his roots came easily to him and often they would provide the funeral arrangements for many of the poor known to him, who lived in the area once home to her parents. They would be quiet, simple and dignified events, so as not to excite envy, that ravening beast that preyed on the poor. There would be no charge.

Her mind returned unwillingly to the coming afternoon. She knew that on a day like this, with blistering blue-white skies, the glass of the hearse would cook the air until the rear door was opened to release it like a foul wild animal to leap at her. This would bring the smell of the body itself, embalmed or not, leaving the odour of death lurking at the back of the throat and nose for some hours.

And furthermore – I detest lilies; they reek of decay. People would be shocked to hear that an undertaker loathes them Still, they are styled as emblems of purity and innocence, but to me they are a stark reminder of loss and pain.

Her mind followed the route of the funeral procession across the square and through the arch of St Ann's Church door, blessedly cool though it would be, the air would be awash with a new cauldron of smells.

That cloying incense! I thought only the Catholic churches used it and St Ann's is not Catholic. How can people stand it every day? And poor Reverend Williams. Forever forgetful and untidy; stale grease all over his chin, creased vestments, as usual. He smells no better than the body on some days, she thought. *Old he may be, but he doesn't have to be dirty. Am I uncharitable once more? Maybe he's not cared for well enough. Still, the new curate has made some good changes in the household arrangements. I think I'll enquire of Reverend Williams's health... But thank Goodness for Reverend Knightly today!*

At heart though, she felt her good fortune with all the fervour of one who has worked hard to live up to the success of her parents and to do them proud. Their business flourished as they dealt with people of the middle classes, respectable, wealthy people who had the leisure and the money to mourn their dead in style, having no need to beg an hour off work at the mill. Yet people with money felt the same pain of death as the starving poor.

And there she was, Sophia Kelley, a young woman engaged in an enterprise as one of its prime movers; one of a thriving group of professional, articulate women with skill and society's approval. Her Majesty had gone a long way to show the country that women could fill many roles; but there was a longer way to go as many men did not agree with their monarch.

Why do I love what I do? It's the people, I think. They are so vulnerable faced with death - most of them, that is. It's strangely fulfilling to be of such great help. It's not the organisation and preparation, it's the comfort, and they welcome it. Usually. She opened the neck of her blouse to waft cooler air to her skin. *But why do I feel so unsettled today? All I see is Death. What about the world out there, the city? It's full of life and joy, troubles and love and is decidedly not the daily route of the workroom, the parade to church, the long trail to the cemetery.*

She felt that if she could see a little more of the world from time to time then she could be deeply content with her role in the business. *Times are changing; it's almost a new century! I shall be thirty years old on that New Year's Eve, and it'll be a landmark in everyone's lives. The century itself will turn in five short years and nothing will stop either event. 'Variety is the very spice of life that gives all its flavour'. So says Mr Mark Twain!' How often does father use that quote himself? It may be what I need.*

She thought about her father, what it was that made him the man she loved and a man to be proud of. They earned a great deal of money in their business and yet lived plainly enough as they had always done. When her mother, Annie, had been alive, he had bought her extravagant gifts from time to time: a ruby ring, a pearl brooch, once a beautiful silk dress he had had made. All were given as surprises; nothing delighted him more than to be romantic, for what else mattered in life? And theirs was a marriage of romance. 'Aye, and hard work too!' he would say.

She had died suddenly ten years ago; she sat down in her chair, after a busy morning, smiling at some remark her husband made, turned her head and, sighing a little, quietly

47

slipped away before his eyes.

There wasn't a day that Sophia failed to think of her, and her father said the same, but for all her psychic gifts she had never heard her mother's voice or had any vision of her, nor any dreams in the ordinary way people dream of loved ones departed. What she did have, however, was a profound sense of peace whenever she thought of her mother, a sense of nearness, of strength and warmth. And that was something to cherish each day.

Chapter 5

'Darkling in the eternal space'
Lord Byron

TEN O'CLOCK THAT NIGHT and still the heat pressed a smothering hand over the city. Sophia gazed up at the sky; the moon had probably risen but was not to be seen. Sometimes she could be glimpsed if the wind was strong enough to clear away the cloud and mist, but tonight and for many nights past there was not even a soft sigh of wind to lift the shroud of smog that draped the chimneys. They thrust themselves up through the haze, making their escape, breasting the horizon like sentinels to puff out their own clouds of smoke; hundreds of them venting fumes and gases from cotton mills, flour mills, dye works, chemical works, brick works, glass works, foundries and coal mines. The fires could not be doused - if only they could. Even in a heatwave, steam power was life. Coal was life. Add to these giant chimneys thousands of small household fires sending their smoke upwards from thousands of small chimneys and Phoebe would shed no silvered light over the city that night.

Sophia walked with Nat, her arm sandwiched between his bare forearm and the warm, damp cotton of his shirt. He was deep in thought and she was still hot. They strolled past the city warehouses and the network of canals and the wharfs, and out to the short stretch of pathways along the River Irwell that remembered once being countryside. Ragged tenements boiled across the land beyond the scrubby trees and parched grasses; warehouses leaned drunkenly against each other shoulder to shoulder on each bank of the river to form, in places, a dark tunnel across it.

It was good to linger like this with the day's work done and with someone as familiar as herself.

The man I will spend my life with... What would my life be like without him?'

She had found herself questioning their relationship sometimes. Did people do that before marriage? Were thoughts like this better left until the time was right. But when would that be?

She was uneasy, sometimes quite bereft when he was away, frequently annoyed by him when he was with her, proud of his strength of mind, his cleverness, his integrity, his reputation, his handsomeness too; she thought him handsome, yet other people thought him grim looking. She loved his rare impulsiveness, his frequent passion, his constant care. Kindness. What stopped her marrying him now, next week? She did not know and pushed that thought aside too. What she did know was that he was always at the back of her mind, in the corner of her eye and there in her heart. Yes, her lodestone.

'Oh Nat, church this afternoon! It was unbearable.' She groaned at the remembrance. 'Lord above, we have a funeral each day this week, two tomorrow! Why must people die in a summer like this?' She sighed. 'But on a brighter note altogether, Reverend Knightly looked very collected and cool, even in his vestments. And church is cool, if smelly. He was eloquent too; the family were properly comforted.' She squeezed his arm affectionately.

'Ahh, the smart new curate. Hmmm.' He sneered.

'Very smart and very fashionable.'

'As am I!'

She laughed. Her fingers lingered on the hair on the back of his hand and forearm and she felt the memory of her vision that morning, felt her head heavy.

Not now...don't let me have a vision now... She squeezed her eyes shut for a second to dispel the feeling, shook her head, breathed deeply.

'Still no air out here,' she murmured.

Nat laughed gently. 'No, no there's not one breath of air.' He stopped and gently pulled her round to face him. 'You are quite beautiful, you know. This soft stuff...' he said, fingering the muslin of her sleeve, 'the fall of the fabric, the colour – it's so very much part of you. Blue is your colour; exactly the same shade as your eyes.' He sighed, his face serious. 'I don't like the life you lead, love. I often wonder if you do.'

She was shocked. 'But I do like it; you must know I do, perhaps not in this heat,' she interrupted but he didn't seem to hear. 'I do complain, I know it. Yet I do love my work.'

'I'll do my utmost to change that for you.'

'Please don't trouble yourself...'

He did not hear. 'It's not the life of a lady,' he murmured. He cupped his hands gently round her face and bending, he kissed her, softly at first to seal a promise and then with a desperate passion as though he knew he would have to fight her to keep the promise.

Sophia gasped for breath. He released her.

'Nat?' She pressed him away firmly with both her hands on his forearms. Something was heavy on his mind. 'But I do lead the life of a lady.'

For answer he simply shook his head, and she knew he was too full of his thoughts to speak just then. He drew her arm through his, pulling her closer to his side, which she did not resist, hot and damp though he was.

He feels like a boiled ham. Thank Goodness for the muslin petticoat too and this scooped neckline. A lot more comfortable than my black.

They walked onward. A man on the opposite bank of the river hurried along with a pair of rabbits dangling from his hand and a lurcher trotting behind. The man waved, and Nat returned the greeting. There was constant noise on the evening air, shouting, screaming, laughing and bangs from the rows of terraces in the dip. Music, singing from the public houses. They didn't notice it, being the normal evening sound of the city. Dogs barked; children yelled. An owl screeched nearby.

'You know, I'm not one to sit in idleness. I'd be bored. I need to do things, things that matter to people. I'm a woman with a profession.'

'There's a determined light in your eyes, my love…but what a profession, handling bodies day in and day out like a butcher.'

Now she gasped, indignant. 'I hope I don't make such a mess of my clients, and it's a worthy job.'

'But not for you. It lacks grace and sensitivity. It's unclean at its basest level.'

'Hoity toity! A nurse handles bodies also, and the living are properly unclean and alive enough to continue producing what is *unclean* from many orifices!'

'Sophia!' he exclaimed.

'Nathaniel, you're a little delicate for a policeman tonight! What's more, the living talk and complain and scream, swear, shout and sometimes do violence to their rescuers. My work is silent, until the funerals that is. And for those occasions I need to be grace and sensitivity personified! In fact, very ladylike.

Our services are for the middle classes who think very highly of manners – and themselves.'

He groaned. 'I want a more fitting occupation for you.'

'*You* want that for me? Is it in your gift? Or do you have another gift in mind, my love? Ten children? Is that what *you* want? They are especially foul as far as I can discover. And I'm too old for more than five!' She made a moue of disgust. 'I am twenty-five and that is very old for a first marriage. I am called a spinster by the terms of polite society. Of course, it doesn't matter how old a man is as he is expected to have relationships before he finally settles on a wife and then, if he is discreet, he can have a mistress or two also. And many children that give *him* little trouble.'

'Stop, stop, stop! You're misinterpreting me.'

'I have a profession like many women of my class, and I have opinions that matter to me.'

'This I know!' His tone wry.

'You're taunting me now?'

'There is no need to be confrontational and contrary, wilfully misunderstanding me. You know I value everything that makes you the person you are.'

'My work is part of who I am! Oh, go on with your thoughts as they're so pressing,' she snapped, exasperated because he was right in some ways. She could sense he was upset about more than her professional status and her role as a wife.

He put his hand over hers that lay on his arm, raised his eyes into the far distance of his mind.

'You read that book, *A Tale of Two Cities*? Mr Dickens? and talked to me often enough about it,' he began, excitement sparkling in his voice now. 'I'm going to take you to Paris and to see all the sights there, the places made famous by the story – oh, and the Eiffel Tower, but that wasn't there then, in the story. It's just like Blackpool Tower, but taller – nearly double.'

He warmed to his theme. 'Both cities, but London first, I think. The underground railway – with electric powered trains! Just think. And, very new indeed, there's that new bridge over the Thames, Tower Bridge they call it – opens up in the middle to let ships pass. You'll be amazed - looks like a castle, it does. We'll go there first, If I can get leave to consult with Inspector Reid once more – he of the Ripper case, remember?'

'Yes, yes!' *I have heard all about it, endlessly!*

'Then you can come with me and we'll explore the new museums and the National Gallery.' He was gabbling feverishly, walking faster and faster, so that she had to skip to keep up. 'And there's Her Majesty's museum, The South Kensington; they are building a new home for it on Cromwell Road. I'm told it'll be a grand place like a palace itself. So many galleries and museums, love. There's the British Museum with the Elgin Marbles, and all those curiosities from Egypt – Egyptian mummies! And I do think you'll be interested in the way they preserved their dead! And we've already seen those Pre-Raphaelite paintings, which you admire, here at the art gallery in Manchester. There're more galleries in London, so many more.'

'Nat! Calm yourself.'

'You deserve to see the world, and all its fine things, not stay cooped up with the leavings of death each day. I want more for my wife, much more.'

'I help to make those leavings dignified, to help people bear the loss. I am not the attendant at a public mortuary that deals with old bodies fished from the River Irk or left in a builder's ditch. I do not fill the mass pauper graves with my own hand. The leavings of death, indeed! Nor do I push the plague cart round the cobbled streets.'

'Take breath yourself. I merely want to look after you!'

'You have no need to shout.'

He thrust her hand from his arm and strode onward a few steps.

'Now you are a toddling baby.'

He swung round. 'You are too proud sometimes,' he told her, his face now furious. 'These deaths of the poor in their noisome garrets – the grubby bodies mean as much to their families as the perfumed ones of the rich.'

She was silent, stood very still, her head down.

He continued on this theme now. 'I see the poor every day, wallowing in their muck. The majority cannot help their dirty state. They have no food, huddling in their foul cellars with no fires, no clothes and riddled with illness. You must be aware of this.'

'I am. I give wherever I find a need. It sounds to me that you wish to keep me in an ivory tower, secure from the outside world. I'm content with my profession but, yes, I want more from life for myself, not just to be a wife, by the way. But I know what you want,' anger sparking in her tone, 'You want me to reside in your house and in your heart you want me to be a lady without occupation other than the home – probably in a villa in Moss Side, near Inspector Caminada's own house. Women can do more in these times, Nat. The Pankhursts were born in Moss Side, by the way; it's a well-to-do leafy suburb for the militant classes.'

He walked on with great long strides. Sophia ran to catch up with him and tripped on the tussocks of dead grass. 'Nat, Will you stop?' she cried.

'That was unfair!' he muttered and slowed only a little. 'I'm the one who wants you to see more of the world, spread your wings!'

'Right now I do not want to have an itinerary planned. And by the way, would we be going on this odyssey of yours before we're married? Plenty do, these days – always have if truth be told. I don't think my father would want that – nor would I. I want to be properly married, in church. I want to make a proper commitment before God.'

He sounded shocked. 'Of course we would be married.'

She had not paused. 'It's important to me. And Nat, you know something so against convention would prevent your promotion. But what I really want before all of that is to find out what ails you right this minute? All this extravagant planning. You're unlike yourself.'

'And you are *exactly* like yourself; you can do no wrong.'

He stopped abruptly, stared at her with wide eyes for a full minute until she cried, 'Nat!' again.

He exhaled sharply, exclaiming, 'Love, I'm sorry. I feel strange tonight. The heat, events...'

'Why? What's happened to make you so agitated? You're my rock. You can't crumble.'

'I'm your rock...' he whispered. He threw a glance down the length of the sluggish river, his expression troubled.

She followed his gaze. The water was slightly clearer away from the centre of the city. There, dead animals, old boats, crates and broken goods snagged on the wrecked branches of last winter's storms, all stirred up each day by the traffic on the river. Here the surface looked like water at least, although what lay submerged was unknown and the only blemish was a scum of coloured foam held in the curve of the river and a woman's bonnet floating past on a piece of wood.

'This case, for that's what it is; the Inspector was talking of it today, saying each murder was separate, but the fact is we've two murders that are almost identical. It has the potential to grow, to be something so much worse.'

'Worse? You mean you think there'll be more?'

'I do. In fact, I know it! What I heard in London convinces me of that. And I want to help put a stop to this train of events here before it escalates into something more horrifying – like Whitechapel. So, I can say that a small part of my agitation is ambition; I need to be promoted to Inspector. I'm capable, more than many others. I'm only involved at my level, as a sergeant in the uniform division, at the moment. It's frustrating. I want to be a detective, as Inspector Reid is, a man with the same tenacity, the same integrity, the same record of apprehending the criminals, all so that I can have more power to prevent more death by catching the killer.'

'But what's to stop you, love?'

'Fear.'

Chapter 6

'I fear you more than any spectre'
Charles Dickens

'FEAR?' she echoed.

'Fear that anything could happen to you,' he told her.

He stopped walking and he turned her to face him again.

'Nat, I'll be fine,' she said.

'You are too complaisant – and naive.'

He shook his head, a brief smile, more of a stretching of the lips, a sadness. She took a breath to protest but he looked so serious that her comment died before it reached her lips.

'There are two young women who have been murdered and one attacked. They all resemble you, even if it's only slightly - you said so yourself. Inspector Reid would say *that is already a pattern*; he is ever searching for patterns of behaviour in criminal events of this kind. His theory is that criminals create their own patterns of working, patterns that satisfy them, identify them to themselves, to the world in the same way a carpenter or a farrier would do. When the detective can make out the pattern, he is a giant step nearer to getting his man.'

He's shaking. Unlike him.

'Inspector Reid is astoundingly thorough in his investigations. In this case here, there're too many similarities in their appearance, the fact that they all pursued a profession, were ambitious and they were unmarried. And there is the location of all three women – all were in the centre of the city. You live and work in the centre of Manchester. There are too many matches involved for it to be mere co-incidence. Yet the means by which the two victims met their deaths is a puzzle, apart from the colour of their lips and the small bleeding in the eyes, both, Arnold said, the result of lack of breath, suffocation, not strangulation. You didn't see marks on the neck, did you?'

Sophia bit her lip, remembering the instruction from her father. 'No, we found none to indicate that.'

'I must speak to the woman who escaped, Jenny Hargraves, ask in what manner she was attacked.'

'Shall we walk on? Come.'

They moved on slowly, heads together. Minutes passed in silence. He seemed to her to be his calm self again, focused on the conversation.

She said, 'But there're more details about the two deaths that Father wants you to know, and only you at this time or he would've enlightened you this afternoon. Reverend Knightly seems a good man; I find him very pleasant indeed, and he spoke with compassion at the funeral. However, he's not long been here and Father, I can tell, won't yet give him close confidences.'

'Your father's a man of extreme good sense.'

'You don't like him, the curate?'

'I do not.' He stopped walking again, but she pulled him on gently. His eyes were alight with interest and anticipation. 'What would Arnold have me know, love?'

She told him about the other four features of the deaths that were identical in both victims: the pin prick behind the ear, that same ear being sore looking and missing its earring in each victim, the small posy of flowers pushed inside their bodices, hidden from view and first seen by her when she examined their clothes, and, even more disturbing to Sophia, the expression of frozen terror.

'It'd be useful if I could see the remaining victim, if Arnold would permit it.'

'Yes, I think you should, and I think Father would allow it because of the murder. He usually adheres to the wishes of the family if they request me to tend a female relative, but this is an unusual death.'

'One other thing, Sophia, love, the other earrings, the ones left on the ears of the victims – where're they? Did the family take them in each case?'

She thought for a moment then replied, 'They did, but I think both families would lend them to me for you to examine, if I ask. They don't know of anything other than that one earring is missing, and I think they presume it lost in a struggle. Why?'

'Inspector Reid said that a murderer sometimes keeps items from the victim as a trophy of his deed.'

'Oh, Nat. I can hardly bear to think of that!' she cried. 'A trophy, something to value? To take something so personal, the poor girls' treasures, pretty things that they liked. I feel worse for knowing that somehow,' she told him.

Nat stopped. It was now fully dark. 'We'll turn around and walk back the way we came. There're no ears to listen in on this path. If we go through the streets as we sometimes do, voices can carry and there's always someone abroad.'

'And look, the moon has managed to peep out through a tear in the smog. I love the glitter of it on the river. It makes you forget it's just foul water.'

'It's a sewer, not a river. They've built those new sewers under the city, haven't they? The old Romans built some, I think. There's that stream under Hanging Bridge, the River Irk. A suitable name! Maybe all the filth will flood down the new sewers one day, and the river will be a crystal stream giving only pleasure. The factory poor'll perhaps be sweeter smelling by then too.'

'I'm amazed that you can be so fastidious, working as you do in the Deansgate slums and in the swills around Piccadilly. How sweet smelling are your criminals and prostitutes?' she wondered, her tone dripping sarcasm.

'Me fastidious? I have a nose sensitive to assault. That's all!'

She caught a glint in his eye. 'Nat! Don't tease. This is serious.'

'It is.' He was silent for a while, deep in thought.

They strolled, his arm round her, their heads as close together as his greater height would allow. She watched their feet striking out, watched them scuff the grit on the path and marvelled how Nature always strove to take back ownership of the land. On the edges of the path were new strands of grass, lime green in the evening light. What took her breath away was a flower: a white Water Lily, a scattering of disc like leaves, deep green and washed bright with the water they rested on and a single ivory flower bud, just opening to reveal the tips of its feathered golden centre. There it was, nudging the wreck of a small boat embedded in the silt of the river's edge and, to complete the wonder, hovering over it on glittering bronze wings was a dragonfly clothed in emerald and sapphire silks.

'Oh, look, Nat. How breathtakingly lovely. Nature can't be stopped, can she?' Sophia didn't hear his answering grunt but raised her eyes to scan the banks of the river. 'There, look, by that wall, Meadowsweet, lovely.'

He patted her hand.

They were passing the remains of a collapsed shed. 'See that, almost buried by flowers. Look, a tiny ash tree, elderberry too. And there's bindweed, all those lily-like trumpets, and rose bay willow herb.' She disengaged herself and went closer to bend down and examine something scrambling between the other plants. 'Look, Nat, the purple vetch too.'

He was forced to smile, she knew.

He said, 'I'm surprised they've lasted long enough to grow at all. Kids'll eat anything round here. When we go to London then I'll take you to Kew Gardens. I'm told they have wonderful glass houses, all heated throughout the year. There're plants from all over the world.'

He was used to her interest in plants and flowers of all kinds and she was delighted that he'd thought of this.

'In any case I'm amazed things grow here,' he said, 'It's a midden - those tenements are the foulest in Manchester. So many people trying to live in there. And they stink. See, the tenants are making a whole mountain of their rubbish. Mind, work's scarce and I suppose they must needs do something with their time.'

She sighed, exasperated suddenly. 'Well, thank you for the social commentary.'

'I can see past the flowers.'

'So can I, but there are people who live there who will be cheered by them.'

'More cheered by money for the rent, food for today and a job for tomorrow,' he said.

'Very practically put. Thanks for the idea of Kew, but do you have to bring things down to the lowest level? These flowers aren't spoiled for me. There might only be the odd one, but I just like to find a little brightness in even the worst of days. Goodness knows this has not been the best.' She was cross with him.

'I know, I know. It's my fault. I've had my mind filled with death - no, evil, that's what it is. Come on, we'll walk in silence and listen to the birds,' he said, but a piercing screech, a range of foul language followed by answering wails and shouts from one of the back yards made them both laugh.

'But back to the business of the day. May I?' he wondered; his tone playfully polite.

'Go on, go on.'

He was all seriousness once more. 'If I can look at the body, then I'll have my own observations noted and maybe some good evidence too to support the alleged murder, as well as observations from you and Arnold. The only halt to my enquiries might come from our Inspector Bateman. He's possessive, that's his problem. He avoids letting his uniformed men give any help at all to the Detective Division.'

'He wants the glory for his own men?'

'Always. I think it's a fault. We should aid each other – all the Divisions across the city, without petty rivalries. There're places and situations that a man in disguise might go that are never open to one in uniform. And another thing, if the officer has to halt when following a suspect because he has strayed into another division, then the criminal gets away. If I could present everything we know about these two murders along with some concrete evidence to Inspector Caminada, I think he'd be very interested indeed. Y'know he's truly dedicated and as famous here in Manchester as Inspector Reid is in London.'

'But the Ripper was never caught.'

'True, but although Reid didn't bring the Ripper to justice, the killing stopped; there're many who say it's because of his zealous detection methods that Jack knew he would be caught – and soon. He needed to go to ground – and speedily.'

'Inspector Bateman wants to keep you for himself as a valuable officer. Isn't that so, Nat? Come on, admit it,' she said as he shook his head. 'You should be proud of that. I know I'm proud of you.'

He squeezed her hand. 'I could do Inspector Bateman's job without any extra effort at all when he retires. That's one thing I want, and if that came about then I'd have my uniformed men assist the Detective Division when they could. We've a common goal and can reach it more effectively and quicker if we cooperate.' His tone was vehement, passionate. 'But if I show myself adept at uncovering information, perhaps I can work directly for Inspector Caminada, you know, maybe transfer to his division, if it's allowed. I could learn the craft from him and be promoted that way. I think that'd be what I'd prefer.'

'But right now, to test our suspicions and fears, would Inspector Bateman allow you to pass on the information to Inspector Caminada?'

'I don't know until I try, but I suspect not. He's always been a bit on the strange side. The investigation's taken a slow start. Now another young woman has been attacked today, the Inspectors should get organised.'

'Inspector Bateman will be interested to know you met the famous Inspector Reid?' she enquired.

'Possibly, but it was by accident. I was sent down there on a mission to discover how the Metropolitan Police control unruly crowds, as their reputation, described by the newspapers, is truly astounding. Shall we say - I found they have effective methods, and none too gentle. Inspector Bateman'll be impressed by that alright.' He laughed. 'A lot of work for the hospitals…'

She persisted with her own train of thought instead of asking him to describe his enjoyment. 'Then you will take your information to him?'

He stopped walking and pressed her hand where it lay on his arm, saying earnestly, 'I'll do that. I was shown a great deal of the evidence Inspector Reid collected and I'll never forget the photographs of the victims. Such horror. I don't want a fiend such as that to stalk the streets of our city, love. This coincidence of appearance is too close to you to be comfortable; I'll stop at nothing to protect you.'

'I know that, Nat,' she answered softly. She could feel him shaking again, leaned her head against his arm. 'You know, these two women weren't mutilated as the Ripper's victims were, but I think they died stricken by some nameless horror. I saw it on their faces. But, a different killer, surely, someone whose mind is warped in another direction? Am I wrong about killers' thoughts; their minds being distorted in different ways – each one unique? But maybe you think the Ripper has come North?'

'No, I think you're right. It is a different person entirely, one who does this for a completely different reason, as you said. The problem is I can't tell what that is yet.'

She could not suppress a shudder at the idea and Nat put an arm round her shoulders.

'Ah!' she exclaimed,' There's something else; another detail that may be important.'

'Yes?'

'I kept the flower posies in each case, as I said. Each flower has its meaning and you know I'm always careful how I use flowers myself. No, don't tease me!' she added when he looked round sharply, a smile playing on his lips. 'And I've kept them safely for you and have written down each message.'

'I can't tease you about this, love. Good evidence, that's what it'll be. But who's the intended recipient of the flower message? That's the thing.'

'That's the thing...' she repeated, thoughtfully. 'What I can't understand is why your Dr Johnson didn't find the posies, or perhaps he did and put them back in place, tucked in the fabric so that they wouldn't be dislodged. If he didn't find them, it's possible he didn't examine their clothes, or more importantly, didn't examine their bodies properly to find a cause for their death. He may have missed something else. The only evidence he gave to the inquest was that they had died of suffocation. And I must say that I didn't find any other signs of injury on their bodies, no stab wounds or blood, nor were their necks broken.

They strolled on.

'You know, in defence of Dr Johnson, the bodies brought into the mortuary at Newton St. have usually met their end by some very obvious means, such as a cut throat, obvious strangulation – and sometimes with a garotte still lodged in their skin, or they have other catastrophic injury; they have been under the wheels of a dray or a train. I don't think Dr Johnson is aware that people can be killed by less dramatic means.'

'It doesn't excuse him,' she said.

'No.'

Both lapsed into thoughtful silence.

They were now approaching one of the many bridges that spanned the river and beyond that the tower of the Cathedral could be seen in the far distance. The riverbank was gloomy where it plunged beneath the stone arch. There, all was black.

'Hurry under the bridge, Nat, you know I don't like the smell of the place. I've had enough assaults on that particular sense for one day,' Sophia told him, and she tightened her grip on his arm and increased her own pace. 'Hurry. I'll hold my nose! The path is narrow.'

He laughed and they hurried onward.

Once under the arch they were assaulted by the musty air, a little cooler than that in the open, and of a different quality altogether. To Sophia it seemed thickened and she felt as though currents this air curled about her. Nathaniel shuddered.

'Ugh, I don't like this, Nat!' she cried and walked faster.

'Strangely, me neither! There might be bogey-men...' He laughed. 'I'll arrest them!'

'Shhh!'

It was a deep bridge, maybe twenty paces from one side to the other and they had almost reached the centre point when there came a noise, a groan behind them, in the gloom.

Nat stopped abruptly and spun round, pulling Sophia behind him.

'Who's there?' he demanded.

The groan again.

'Is someone hurt?' Sophia called.

A voice came from one of the murky recesses in the side wall. 'I am here,' it said.

It was a man's voice, deep and strange.

Nat pressed Sophia back and retraced their steps alone, searching the gloom, which, always deep in daylight, was now myriad shades of black that surged and slithered in the faint glow on the water from a bridge lamp above.

Suddenly he stumbled over something lying in the path but managed to keep his feet. There was a muffled cry and Sophia jumped aside, shocked. The movement allowed a little light to penetrate; it showed a leg stretched out on the ground across the very path they had just trodden. Nat went forward.

'You there, I'm a police officer. Get to your feet.'

'I cannot.'

'I've heard that before, man. Get up I say.'

There was silence.

Sophia called, 'Why does he not move?'

'I am hurt, lady.' She thought the voice faint with pain.

'Who are you?' Sophia asked.

'I am Michel,' he said, and he pushed an arm into the softness of the lamplight. 'I need help...'

The arm was covered in a ragged coat sleeve, torn and crumpled. The hand shook and there was blood shining on it, easy to see even though the man's skin was in the shadows. Sophia could smell it too.

Nat made up his mind. 'Give me your hand if you want help standing. I can't quite see you there,' he said and waited while the man made a Herculean effort and pushed his body forward to extend the hand.

Nat grasped it and the man cried out again.

'Steady then,' Nat said, bracing his legs and holding out his other arm to grasp the man's and help him balance as he rose.

The hand clasped in Nat's was dark, with dirt Sophia imagined, given the state of his coat sleeve, but when his body rose shakily and he turned his face to them under the glow from the lamp, they saw that his skin was black by nature, and that he had only one arm. The empty sleeve was tucked back inside itself at the elbow. The man could barely stand; he looked as though he had been beaten and was covered in blood and dirt and he grimaced in pain as they moved him.

Nat drew him forward, holding him upright as he stumbled. Sophia put her hand to his good shoulder to help, but as she touched him, she felt such a shock of empathy that she gasped aloud and tripped on the rough ground herself. That was the second time that day she had felt such a powerful connection to another newly-met person.

Chapter 7

'What a piece of work is a man'
Shakespeare - Hamlet

BUT SHE DIDN'T FALL, instead she bumped against the man's side and he groaned, a loud agonising sound. He threw his single hand across his body to protect the empty end of his arm, but the unexpected movement made Nat stagger; it was an effort to keep his balance.

'We make a rum sight, lad!' Nat said. 'People will think we've been drinking all night. Sophia, lead the way up onto the bridge. I've got his weight and I think his injury is too painful on that side for any closeness.'

The man was covered in foul mess and blood, so she was glad to do as she was asked, but Nat had not asked her to be silent. She couldn't have managed that in any case.

'Michel? Can you hear me, Michel?' she asked; he nodded, his face set in a rictus of pain, lips clamped shut as though to keep a scream inside. 'You've been beaten badly. I know you can't talk for the pain, but we'll help you, don't worry.' His eyes widened, showing starkly white against his dark skin. 'Just nod...' she told him, 'if you understand.' He nodded slowly then suddenly a scream burst from him, high pitched, tormented.

'Sophia, don't press him now.'

'Press him? I'm just reassuring…'

'We'll take him to the Infirmary. It's not far to Piccadilly,' Nat interrupted, edgily.

Michel continued to moan and give short cries. He bit his lips, and they ran with blood. Sophia rounded on Nat.

'*Not now? Not far?* She was incredulous. 'Look at him, Nat. Too far for him, in this state. It's a mile at least. What are you thinking?' she snapped. Before he could answer, an alternative presented itself. 'We can go home, to the yard. We can put a cot in the harness room for now; it's dry and draughtproof. There're plenty of blankets; I know it's a warm night, but he's had a shock and will need some heat. I can get the stove lit there and boil water enough to tend his injuries.' She was trying not to breathe the smell coming from him in heavy, pungent waves. 'We may need to send for Dr Smith, but we'll see.' She took it for granted that Nat would help this man who looked to be genuinely and desperately in need of help.

Nat staggered under Michel's weight. 'You're right, yes. We'll get to the yard; it's near. Look, he has fainted – or worse. He'll be in the best place then!'

Sophia snorted. 'I shouldn't laugh! But it's more of a shock to hear you making a joke. Can you manage him? I need my overall. I've had enough bodily fluids for one day.'

'He's a solid weight, muscled. He's been well beaten though. But the arm; how he came by that injury staggers me.'

'He's so black – his skin, I mean. I've only seen one of his kind before. We almost missed him under the bridge, with him being dark as the night itself. He sounded like us though, didn't he?'

'From the little I heard,' he answered. 'But I suppose he should sound like us; he's a man after all. There are lands full of black skinned people.'

'But that's not here, in Manchester! That's all I mean to say.'

'No, not here.'

'And I guess these people from different lands may speak a language of their own and not English,' she said; a heavy layer of sarcasm. 'He did speak English though, didn't he?'

Nat was intent on his task and grunted as they moved onward slowly. He was tall and powerfully built, but the injured man seemed a similar size and a dead weight.

Ten minutes later Nat staggered through the yard gate. Sophia hushed the dogs when they rushed over, growling, to sniff at the intruder, but they were soon satisfied that the strange person was no threat and settled back down to their job of night-time guarding. All three of the big watch dogs returned to their beds and lay back down with comfortable grunts.

Nat swayed unsteadily by the harness room door, waited until Sophia put the lights on. They had electric lights in the yard – every modern convenience. As soon as they could, Sophia and her father had decided that oil lamps and gas flames were too much of a risk in such a big stable block and had had one of the new electrical systems installed, at huge expense.

She put a horse rug on the top of the long table before she motioned for Nat to lay the man down, which needed both of them to achieve. The stove was soon lit; it was always put out overnight but laid ready; she put the kettle to boil on the stove top. Harness gleamed in long rows in the soft light against the wood panelled walls. The air was redolent with the scent of the clean leather and bright metals.

Along the passage, the horses in their stalls snorted at the disturbance; Sophia walked down the line, quietly, swiftly, calling each one until they settled. The air was heavy and fragrant with their bodies and hay-laden breath. It was cool for them inside the building; the brick and cobbles resisted the heat.

Michel mumbled incoherently, his head tossing from side to side, sometimes moaning softly on a single note, other times drawing his teeth back and grunting with pain. He was covered in filth and now they were in a confined space, the smell was worse than anything Sophia had ever encountered. They took off his outer clothes carefully and were about to take his shirt and ragged underdrawers, when he snatched them with his good hand – his only hand. His eyes flew open and Sophia saw he was embarrassed; it lasted but seconds before he fell back with a sob, resigned, and his eyes now stretched wide with pain. Her heart went out to him and trying to give some small reassurance she told him she would find him some replacement clothes later; his own were only fit to burn. He breathed noisily through his mouth, his lips were drawn back, baring his teeth. How white and even they looked, underneath the coating of blood.

Strange, but he seems familiar. This is the second time today I have felt a connection with a stranger, had that feeling of déjà vu. It may be that it is just the attraction of a soul similar to your own. Sometimes you simply like someone on first sight, you have a natural sympathy. Then there was that vision I had when I touched the poor body, poor Adeline. I ought to be used to such experiences by now – but I never am. And three such feelings in a single day! The more it happens, the more wonder I feel, but the more puzzling it becomes too. But how could this man be familiar when I know have never met him before? I would remember if I had met a man with his skin colour.

Michel screwed his eyes tightly shut. Now and then a low whimper escaped but when they helped him remove his undershirt and disturbed the amputation site, he roared and fainted.

'Oh, Lord! Look, Nat! What a mess, a filthy mess. What is

72

that black stuff?'

'Tar. To cauterize the wound.'

'Tar? *Hot*, you mean? *Boiling* tar?'

'A sailor's trick.'

'So, he is a sailor?' she wondered. 'Hot tar!' She shuddered at the idea.

'The new Ship Canal, remember? Vessels, ocean going ones arrive from all over the world now – and depart with our goods.'

Sophia looked up from the old cloth she was tearing to use as wash cloths. 'How encyclopaedic, Nathaniel,' she remarked.

He stretched his lips slightly, 'I try to be. It pays to know things. I'll find out about our friend here before long.'

'Will you? Hot tar though? But, yes, that would cause this blistering and, ugh, almost crispness. I've seen some sights, Nat – but this...' She looked up at him. 'I'll go for my overall. Better get my gloves and a bowl while we wait for the water. You'll stay here?'

'Where else, now we've brought him here?' he said and took a small, cotton horse blanket, one used for the ponies that drew the children's hearse and draped it over Michel's lower body. 'For your modesty...' he said.

Sophia turned and gave him a questioning look, so he added, 'The men you usually deal with here are dead. This one is very much alive.'

'He's only just alive!' she retorted. *What is he thinking? The man is beaten half to death. Perhaps Nat thinks I can't help but fall into another man's arm, or perhaps thinks the novelty of his skin colour will excite me. There are times when he is very, very stupid.*

She glanced back as she reached for the door handle; for a moment she imagined a strange expression on Nat's face. Was he sulking? But why? Was it suspicion? – which was natural, given they had found the man, a stranger, and a vagrant by the looks of it, amidst the usual garbage of the city. But this was an unusual vagrant. Was it fear in his eyes? Maybe he sensed the man could be dangerous. She saw that he was watching her.

'Sophia, love, this man will have his own need for dignity and more importantly to me, I'm thinking of yours. Don't be made insensible to these things by reference to the dead. Your only experience is with the dead, mine is with the living – trust me. You see only dead bodies.'

What? What does he mean?

She stared at him, puzzled, betrayed, struggling with all her emotions and trying to control a building indignation. He in turn held her eyes with his and as the seconds passed, she found resolution and respect in them, and deep love.

She let out a ragged breath. 'Yes, you're right,' she said. 'I know you are.' She managed a small smile, then went quickly on her errand.

Returning five minutes later, she found the room quite crowded. Albert, with the other grooms and yard lads, were down from their quarters in the loft, having been woken by the disturbance.

She stared at them all. 'Well, what's going on here? This is not a travelling show at the end of Blackpool Pier,' she told them tartly as she swept the whole circle of them away from Michel.

Nat stood near Michel's head, looking on, his arms folded. It was Albert who spoke up.

'Who's this then? We heard the commotion.' He nodded down at Michel. 'What's he doing here, Miss Sophia? In the harness room too?'

Albert's inner sanctum...

She ignored him, watched Michel's breathing. He remained unconscious and moaning, but his body was not still; there was spasmodic twitching, and he arched his back and tried to turn. Nat gently pushed him down.

Sophia turned to Albert and felt herself growing angry.

'There was no commotion, as you well know, Albert. We found him half-dead under Victoria Bridge. And look at him; would you leave such a one on the ground and walk by?' she demanded.

She knew that Albert would influence the other men and she wanted him to follow her lead, not his own ideas. No need for the men to revolt because she wanted to help someone.

'I might at that!' he replied, and the other men shuffled their feet uncertainly and glanced at each other. Albert smiled kindly. 'There again, Miss, I've known you a long while and I know you couldn't do that. I'm surprised at 'im though.' He nodded towards Nat. 'I didn't think police were here to help.'

Nat kept his expression blank. 'I think I know when someone requires help and is not just skiving. There is more to being a police sergeant than cracking heads in public houses. But I can crack heads with the best of 'em – needs be.'

Albert and the lads exchanged glances at Nat's remark, but when Albert stepped forward to take a better look at the injured man, and murmured, 'Eh, that's bad, poor sod!'

The rest of them nodded to each other, shuffled in a more positive way, unfolding arms, stepping up to take a look for themselves.

'He's black i'n't 'e? We don't see many of 'is kind round here, eh?' Eddie remarked and the other lads agreed.

'Well, he's round here now. Sergeant Roberts thinks he's off a ship,' Sophia said.

One of the younger lads was bending to get a closer look at Michel's amputation site, couldn't help himself but blurted out his feelings.

'That's bloody 'orrible, that is – begging pardon, Miss.'

75

'Pardon granted, Davy. Now step back, would you? In fact, all of you get out! You should be abed. There is work to do in the morning,' she snapped. 'This wound needs to be cleaned up and I'm sure the wounded man needs some quietness.'

None of the men had moved when suddenly Michel regained consciousness. He opened his eyes and cried aloud, 'Que dieu me vienne en aide!' and groaned long and painfully.

'Aye, God help him alright!' Albert said.

'You understand him? French?' Nat looked at the wounded man with some interest.

'Aye, I know a bit.'

Michel's many cuts and grazes were bleeding freely in the growing warmth of the room and when he began to thrash about and try to rise from his prone position, he inadvertently banged the amputation site and roared anew, grasping the wound with his hand.

Nat and Albert managed to restrain him; Sophia told him gently that they were sending for the doctor.

She looked round at the men and resting her search on Davy, the youngest.

'Davy – go for Dr Smith, at once. Run all the way and tell him I need him immediately. Someone as skinny as you will be a good runner. No need to tell a great story either, get back here as soon as you can,'

'Miss!' he answered and bolted from the room.

'It's as well,' Nat said. 'Quiet there, man, we're trying to help you,' he told the injured man as he began, with effort, to try and move again.

Michel was not to be so easily restrained. He managed to rise halfway to a sitting position but then he rolled right off the table onto the wounded arm.

A great shout went up from everyone and many hands raised him up again.

'Thank the Lord, he's fainted!' Sophia said. 'Oh, the cap of tar has burst open – dear me! There's a little pus round the edges too - thankfully not much. I expect the tar cauterized the wound.'

'Eh, God, is that a bit of skin?' cried Ernie bending down to peer into the pool of mess and blood now on the floor. He was a tall wiry young man of eighteen. He favoured a long fringe of hair; it shielded his expression as he bent but when he looked up and pushed it away, Sophia realised that he was truly horrified.

She rounded on him, 'You have seen worse when you bring in our customers. You idiot boy. Go to the kitchen and get me a bucket of hot water and a pan. The doctor will want a great deal of boiled water. While you're at it, refill my bowl here – look, the kettle on the stove.'

Ernie was quick to move, Sophia's expression and tone of voice lent him wings. He emptied her bowl into a spare bucket and refilled it from the small kettle then flew to the yard kitchen and returned in a short time with what she wanted.

'I'll try to clean him a little so that the doctor can see the cuts from the muck. Oh, the smell!' she exclaimed as she began to wipe long smears of dirt and dried blood from the man's shoulders and neck. 'It's difficult to see a bruise, but there, there is a huge one; purplish now, hard to see on his dark skin. Turn him to the light. Can you stand back, lads? You're blocking my view - yes, all move.'

They shuffled back a step, too intent on the work to miss anything.

Nat said, 'Let's lift him, while we have many hands and turn him on the good arm so that you can clean his back.'

They did and all gasped to see a deep cut the length of a forearm on his back. Michel began to groan, and Sophia worked quickly before he became fully conscious; sweeping strokes with her cloth made the wound bleed afresh but she got rid of much dirt and they could all see that he was deeply bruised and swollen.

'Looks like 'e's been kicked, by God!' Albert said. 'You'd have big boots to do that damage, I'd say.'

Davy said, 'It's red, i'n't it?'

'Course it's bloody red, bloody idiot…' Albert told him and clipped him round the back of the head.

Sophia covered the cut with a clean and much-folded piece of cloth, and they laid him down on his back again.

'If he lies on this padding the blood will be stopped from flowing too much until the doctor gets here. More water, Ernie. This is full to the brim with filth and gore,' she added and dropped her soggy wash-cloth into the fluid. 'Throw that cloth away too. And empty the bucket down the grid – carefully, don't slop it, rinse it away with plenty of water or the dogs'll get wind of it.'

Ernie, who was a friend of Davy said, 'How does someone lose an arm like that? It's all ragged round the edges, i'n't it? Looks like it's been ripped off and had paint slapped on it.'

'Tar, hot tar. To stop the bleeding,' Nat told him and watched his reaction with interest, his arms folded.

'Ughhh. Brutal – done a purpose like?'

Albert nodded. 'Definitely – sailor's trick. Does the job, stops the blood, sometimes kills 'em though.'

Ernie winced. 'Mind you, me brother got splashed with iron ore down at the foundry and he screamed fit to bring the whole place down. Metal stuck on his hand. Me dad shoved it in a bucket of water for it to go 'ard, then knocked it off in the end with a chisel.'

All the men grimaced. Sophia bent over Michel's face, watching his eyelids flicker.

'Pass me another rag someone.'

Albert obliged. 'Does Arnold know, Miss?'

They all turned as a voice from the doorway answered, 'He does now.'

As he came into the room there were a variety of greetings, some muttered, some merely a nod or a raised eyebrow, all respectful.

He said to Sophia. 'What have we here, my dear? Who is this?'

She explained how they had come to trip over the man, under the last bridge and as he could see, the man was so injured that he couldn't be left, could he? And she'd sent for the doctor.

'Yes, of course, my dear. We may not take in every vagrant the city breeds, but I wouldn't have walked past this man myself. You did right, as always. He looks badly injured.'

Davy burst into the room, calling, 'Doctor's following. I've got one of 'is bags 'ere, Miss!'

'Leave it there, Davy,' his master told him. 'Eh, this man's in sore need of Dr Smith tonight.'

Davy was the youngest of the yard lads, at fifteen, and giving his master a puzzled look, as though he were doubtful of his sanity and reason, he blurted out, 'But he's a darkie, Master Arnold.'

His master shook his head slowly but softened the coming rebuke with a smile. 'So are you when you get sunburned – as you are now, on the face and hands. This is a fellow human, whatever his colour. We are all the same in God's eyes, made as He wills it, but in another colour. We've plenty of Chinese people living here. Now, they're very different, lad.'

Davy looked a little subdued and Ernie pushed him playfully, remarking, 'Any road, you're a right collection of colours y'self; yer arse is lily white...'

'Watch your manners, Ernie, lady present...' Nat told told

him.

'Sorry, Miss Sophia. I forgot meself,' Ernie muttered, but turned to Davy and mouthed, 'Lily white!' at him, which pantomime Sophia intercepted and told him to get her more cloths from her workroom.

'And quick as you like, Ernie, or I'll have Albert take you to the top of the Blackpool Tower and drop you over the edge when we go to see the Illuminations this year. Maybe they'll put lights on it, being new.' Her smile lessened the tension and they all laughed.

Sophia was intrigued. It was strange to notice that the men were disturbed in very different ways by the newcomer amongst them, even one so helpless, and she realised that they couldn't decide how to react; their pity battled against suspicion and distrust of anything new and also the fascination of finding a new person in such condition and in their familiar surroundings. But Nat's expression and demeanour told her he was taking his time to process his reactions and was weighing up the likelihood of this fellow being a villain or a victim. Only her father was quiet and seemed willing to receive a stranger in need.

Michel groaned and began to move again, his eyelids flickered, and his limbs twitched spasmodically. Blood ran from the edges of his mouth.

It wasn't long before Davy voiced his own concerns again. 'But 'e won't speak proper, will 'e? Ah mean, they cannot, can they?'

This time it was Albert, the senior, who shot him down.

'Hold y'tongue, lad. You do talk some nonsense. Different peoples in the world have different speech, as you would know if you staggered farther than the public house on Jackson Street on yer afternoon off. He probably speaks better than you. Go and see to the horses, gentle them, this disturbance is waking them up too much and they've work to do tomorrow – as 'ave you.' He paused because the boy hadn't moved. 'Go on, gerra move on.'

Davy was staring at the man on the table. The man's eyes were open.

'I speak English and French. I am Michel Bonaventure, from Orléans in France.' His voice was soft and deep and his words perfectly enunciated, though slowly delivered and with difficulty.

They were all stunned into silence for a moment and it was Sophia who spoke first.

'Michel, don't worry. We will help you. I am Miss Kelley, and this is my father, Arnold Kelley. We have sent for the doctor to look at your injuries.'

He lay unable to move but spoke clearly again. 'I thank you and I will repay your kindness.'

She had brought a jug of water and a glass and, holding his head up gently, offered him a sip, which he took. Then suddenly his eyes looked heavy, everything was an insurmountable effort. His eyes rolled back in his head and he fell into unconsciousness again.

Sophia breathed a deep sigh of relief. 'Let's hope he doesn't wake again for a while,' she said.

Her father said, 'I'll make tea, my dear. Nat, you'll be staying?' he asked as he turned to go. Nat said he would.

He stood with arms folded across his chest. He looked troubled; it was something he did often; this man bothered him more than he should. Michel was a stranger, deeply unconscious and was in no fit state to stand, let alone cause anyone any trouble.

But Nat's not that shallow. He must suspect something else. Policeman's gossip perhaps

The doctor arrived within five minutes. Dr Smith was on friendly terms with them; they had met often in a professional capacity for the past three years or so. He was a very pleasant man in his mid-forties, a steady sort, she always thought; worked hard to keep his wife and four children in comfort; chatted fondly of them at times.

After nodded greetings the doctor said, 'What do we have here?'

Sophia smiled inwardly; this seemed to be the usual opening gambit from doctors. She admired Dr Smith for being fascinated by the new medical developments at a time when many of his profession were suspicious. He was thoroughly immersed in his work and seemed to slide into a room without causing any disturbance in the air; just a quiet presence bringing help. His appearance was unremarkable, even though he was tall and broad shouldered. He had very dark brown hair, a small, neat goatee beard, wore spectacles and a neutral expression. In fact, he looked like a doctor. He also looked as if he were absorbed in the interests of the patient, which is what would impress if you were that person. They met quite regularly, usually alongside death beds and at funerals, as was common in their allied professions.

He pronounced the amputation a recent one.

'Very badly done by an amateur wood whittler with a squint, possibly the palsy, and definitely wielding a rusty meat cleaver.'

Sophia watched him unpack his bag of instruments; he followed modern antiseptic methods to limit the spread of infections and she was pleased to have anticipated his need to boil the instruments. He gave the man an injection of morphine for the pain. While they waited for the instruments to be ready, he helped her finish washing Michel himself and dressed the minor cuts, noted a couple that would need stitching, especially the one on his back. He did the back first as it was quicker to do than the arm, and he bandaged what he could.

'Now for the main act in this feast of entertainment.' He paused, looked about the room. 'Miss Kelley, have your men nothing to do? Sleep, perhaps?' he asked, pleasantly, smiling as he glanced at the group of men.

Albert replied that they'd willingly lose sleep to watch the best free entertainment this side of a bare-knuckle fight.

'Putting a bloke back together instead of taking 'im apart. You're a master at it, I can see that, Doctor,' he said. 'Chop away, we're all impatience, like a young lass walking out with our Davy here.'

'Oy!' Davy responded, but half-heartedly Sophia thought. He looked a little green about the gills to her.

Sophia's father had returned with the tea in the ten-pint teapot they used for the yard and when even more instruments were boiled sufficiently, Dr Smith set to with a will to put the man back together. Davy was sent to get the men's mugs and serve them all.

The doctor had no sooner stitched one of the longer cuts to his torso than the patient woke with a start and began screaming again and this time thrashing both his arms and his legs.

'*Je meurs! Je meurs,*' he cried.

'No y'not, lad, you're not dying yet,' Albert assured him.

Sophia could see that the man was shocked, and she suddenly wondered if he might not be dying after all, when a second later blood sprayed along the wall and splashed on the floor. Dr Smith pushed a cotton pad on the source and with the other hand rummaged in his bag and produced a face mask lined with cotton gauze and a small bottle of liquid.

'Sergeant Roberts, hold this over his nose and mouth. Miss Kelley open the bottle. It's chloroform. You have heard me speak of this; it will put our friend to sleep while I work on him,' the doctor snapped urgently, above the shouts of the patient and the men's loud comments.

'Hold 'im there!'

'Wait. I've got 'is leg.'

No sooner had the doctor poured a little of the chloroform onto the mask, than the patient began to relax and after seconds, was fully unconscious again.

The doctor cut away the slab of tar, removed the remainder of the pus and the ragged edges of the skin, then filed the edges of the bone, which were sharp as though broken off. Davy ran out at this point and they heard him being sick in the yard. Working slowly and carefully Dr Smith was able to draw the edges of the skin over the end of the amputation and stitch them neatly. Michel remained unconscious, occasionally twitching and shaking.

'This should heal well, if he doesn't get more infection in it. It must be kept free of dirt and not moved for a few days. Do not remove the bandage until I'm here to see how the wound fares. Now I'll wait until he comes to, check his breathing and his pulse, then I'll give him some of my wonder medicine for the pain and to aid sleep – indeed to bring sleep flying home to nest firmly in the mind for some time.' He took off his spectacles and wiped the lenses which had splatters of blood and other matter on them.

'What is this drug?' Nat wanted to know.

The doctor motioned him aside and murmured, 'I would not have the lads here know that I carry morphine, or indeed, a syringe or two, in case they mention it in the hearing of those who deal in misuse, perhaps at one of the public houses. You understand me?' he asked, and Nat nodded. Sophia listened. 'There is a market for such goods, Roberts. It's morphine I give him, to bring him a restful sleep for six hours at least.' Louder he said, 'He must needs be watched to see that he continues to breathe.'

Then he took out a bottle from his bag and turned away from the sight of the stable lads to fill a hypodermic syringe. He held it up to the light and depressed the plunger until a small drop appeared on the tip.

Sophia and her father used syringes in their own work to inject preservatives into the bodies of the deceased. She watched Dr Smith press the point gently into a vein that stood out on Michel's inner elbow. His skin was a lighter shade there and she could see the vein empurpled. He pressed the site firmly with a finger as he withdrew the needle and left it there for a few seconds. When he removed it, she saw a tiny hole, slightly discoloured round the edge. She had seen similar tiny wounds under the ears of the two dead women. When she used a syringe in her preparations, there was not even a tiny residue of blood, because it had ceased to flow on death. She suddenly knew what had happened next to the woman in her vision. She had been injected while the blood still flowed, but with what, she didn't know, something to quieten her. She had died of asphyxiation.

It didn't occur to her to question whether her imagination had invented everything, she had had many other experiences that had showed her places and events at a distance and for her sight alone. In each case she had been able to verify the truth of her visions when she heard from witnesses about what happened to someone.

But in this case, she understood that she was the only witness to the attack on the girl. Usually her clairvoyant experiences occurred between herself and another living person; she would meet them or touch them and by some special alchemy of the mind, or spirit - by clairvoyance, she would know of a significant experience they had had and sometimes feel their emotion as her own, even if they had not spoken of it or indeed, they often told her, they were not even thinking of the event. When she caught people's thoughts, knew what they were thinking just then, that was telepathy. She had read of it in the library. This time the person was dead and that brought her psychic skills to a whole new level.

I've had this vision but was it simply clairvoyance as I've come to know it, or a different form of sensitivity? Such a powerful image.

She didn't hear the doctor leave and barely noticed Nat's departure; she was so deep in thought.

Chapter 8

'Truth is always strange'
Lord Byron

SOPHIA LOOKED UP at the light in the loft windows. It was one o'clock now and the men had had just closed the door. Michel had been carried up there and put in a spare cot, all the while sleeping very soundly in the arms of morphine. She had wanted someone to be within earshot if he cried out and the men had readily agreed.

They lived up there, above the stables. None of them were married, and it was to the spare cot in the general room that Michel had been taken. Albert had his own bed chamber and a sitting room above the harness room, reached by its own passageway, which privilege was his as Yard Manager. Sophia was always intrigued, on the rare occasions she had been invited in as a child, to see how well kept and tidy it was, especially as he was on his own because at her age then she thought all men had to have wives. Now she knew that some didn't want one and some couldn't get one. It was true of women too. The world was changing.

As they were moving the sick man she'd said to Albert, 'You'll keep a close eye on the patient, won't you?'

'Course I will, Miss. Never worry,' he told her then to Ernie, 'Oy, keep an eye on the patient in there with you lot. I'm relying on you, lad.'

'I'll keep me ears open too. Eh, Albert, just call me nurse!' Ernie said.

'I don't need tempting!'

She knew how warm it would be up there; although the whole building was brick and floored with cobbles at ground level, making it cool for the horses, their body heat rose through the wood of the ceilings. This was welcome in winter but on nights such as they'd had this summer, it made sleep difficult. All the windows were flung open and down in the yard where she stood, she could hear the men's restlessness, the mutterings and snores as they settled down. But no noise from the injured man, no cries and groans.

Her father brought her some more tea before they went to bed themselves and they stood by the back door in the cool of the night. Nat had gone home when the men had left.

'The lads'll keep an eye on him, don't worry, lovie,' her father said.

'Yes, they always want a finger in any pie, and they're full of their ideas, are they not?'

He laughed. 'We Mancunians, and I suppose Northerners in the whole, are generally used to forming opinions and sharing them, whenever or wherever that is.'

'I wonder what brought Michel to this, Father; not just the injury and beating, but being poor and being here – in England instead of France?'

'Misfortune stalks some people. They start off with all the advantages and the devil steps right across their path and they cannot get him out of the way. That may not be what happened to Michel here. He may be at fault himself – who knows? We must wait to hear his story when he can talk without strain.'

She put her arm through his. 'It is very late, one o'clock; we must go to bed, Father.'

He chuckled a little. 'Now I am the child? Have I reached that venerable age?'

'No, no. You're well and vigorous – in your prime. I just feel tired myself.' They turned to the house door. 'Father, did you think Nat a little suspicious of Michel?'

First he rescues the man and then is suddenly wary of everything. Michel cannot even rise from the bed.

'Yes, of course, and rightly so, my dear. See his point of view; we know nothing of this man yet. It is the proper suspicion of a police officer, and also a man to whom you are promised in marriage. Think about it carefully, my dear – that's all. You are tending a young man, who when he is fit will be strong, aye, and intelligent by the sound of him. But we'll see.'

'Yes, we'll see.'

'Goodnight, Father, goodnight.'

'Goodnight, my girl.' He kissed her fondly.

There was only time for a few hours' sleep before the needs of the day were upon everyone. Dawn was at four o'clock and Sophia woke quickly and padded to her bedroom window. She had slept in her shift on top of the bed covers and felt quite rested considering the short time she had enjoyed. She gazed out over the tops of the city buildings; the tower of the Cathedral seemed close from her vantage point, its gothic spires and beautiful decorations pointing upwards, forever upwards. On the far distant horizon behind the ancient structure, she could just glimpse the ghostly hills of the Pennines sweeping ever northward. Dawn broke and the sky blazed through myriad shades of grey, each back-lit by gold as it rushed towards peerless cerulean blue, and all accomplished before another hour had flown. The smoke from the forest of chimneys was dragged upwards and northwards, away from the city, she guessed by a strong wind high up. The men were down in the yard at five o'clock and the work of feeding and mucking out the horses began. She could hear them calling and laughing as she dressed before going down to make herself tea.

It was soothing to stand at the door of the yard kitchen and sip the strong brew. She loved the beginning of the day which for her was always filled with possibilities. All the doors were open in the yard and she watched Albert as he walked down the line of stalls, greeting each of the animals. He was proud of his charges; there were none better behaved in Manchester, and Goodness knows, horses pulling a hearse should not misbehave.

She couldn't hear him from the back door, but she could recite his speech unaided; it was the same each day.

'There, there, my black beauties.' He spoke softly to them as he passed, greeting each horse with a rub of their soft muzzles and a small piece of apple or the like. 'All ready for your work, eh? Just what's needed; calmness itself and not a hint of flightiness in any of you.' He moved down the line of stalls. 'All as beautiful as each other.'

The black horses were Thoroughbred and Shire cross; Albert loved the type, as did she and her father. The ponies were next; small, rock steady, pure white ones from the Welsh mountains, only turning from grey to white when they reached maturity. They were used for the children's hearse and needed all too often. Albert and her father agreed on that too.

Both of them kindly and compassionate. Firm friends – which is to be expected after forty years together, master and man.

The horses were nodding their heads, anxious for their first feed; Ernie and Davy were taking round the feed buckets now. Each day they needed at least three pairs of the huge black horses and usually the ponies too, to be fit for work. The fashion was tending to a hearse drawn by four horses, and then there could be two carriages for the funeral party. They kept a pair of horses ready in case of sudden lameness, so that meant there could be times when they needed eight, or ten of the black horses each day. It was a big stable. There were always horses taking their rest days too.

She smiled as she remembered Albert always told new yard lads that horses are delicate creatures, prone to either small injuries, or to devastating ones, 'One or t'other!' Only the day before he'd told her of a cab horse killed when a horse-drawn tram collided with it on Market Street. There were commonly pulled muscles, strained tendons, shoes dislodged or thrown, many things that could disrupt the smooth running of the funeral business and her father planned for avoidance whenever possible. And he was as fond of the horses as she was. 'Rest is best,' was a one of his guiding principles for their health, so they were allowed two days off each week and if an animal needed to recuperate from anything, 'doctor grass' would sort it out. They rented several acres of pasture from a farmer a short way down river.

The horses will love their rest in this heat.

Her father joined her at the door with his own mug of tea. It was half past six.

She said, 'It's Crimson, Captain, Duke and Duchess for the meadows today, and another blazing hot one by the look of it. It is the Elphinstone funeral at eleven and the Makinson one at two o'clock – the baby, remember?'

'Ah, yes. Will it be Ernie and Davy taking them today?'

She saw him watching the young man in question as he strode across the yard with two galvanised buckets full of water. 'Those buckets were worth it, expensive but at least they don't get trampled so easily as the old ones. Captain's a one for trampling on things. Eh!' He laughed gently. 'We need water laid on in the stables now. Can't think whey we haven't done so already. We've the electric lights – that's a life saver. Now, water - continuous flow, small stone troughs. I'll see into that today, find out how to go about it. Less time fetching buckets too.'

'You're right, Father. That's a good idea, though Goodness knows why this flies into your mind after the night we've had, and yes, Ernie can ride Captain and lead Crimson Girl and Davy the other pair. He'll bring back Lady Midnight, Jason, Samson and Merry Maid. It's only two miles and most of it along the riverbank, and you know there's little other traffic about in the city this early. Ernie has done it many times before, I know he's not been alone, but it's about time he learned to take the responsibility, Father. He'll be the responsible one looking after the horses and Davy.'

'It's up to you, and I would do the same. D'you know, my dear, how proud I am of the way you manage the men? Well, I am.'

They were interrupted by Alice, calling from the kitchen door.

'Miss Sophia, Mrs Kittering says the yard breakfast is ready. She says it's early.'

'Why is that?' Sophia asked when she joined her indoors.

'She was wakened in the night by all the fuss, she says, and she says she was just up and about early. That's all as she told me, Miss,' the girl said, 'An' she wants t'know does the bloke in the loft want summat?'

'How do you know about him, Alice?'

Alice winked. 'Oooh, Miss, we was looking out of the window, after hearing all the row. Is it true 'e's black, Miss? I couldn't see owt much of him but his shape.'

'Very true that he's black, Alice. Now go and get some tea

and bread and butter for the *injured man* and leave your gossiping.'

Alice bobbed a curtsey. 'Sorry Miss Sophia, it is just that cook says...well, it's just a bit strange, that's all.'

'Well *you say* no more, Alice. Off you go!' She shook her head at the girl's comments. 'I expect a great many people will say the same, do you not think so, Father?'

Her father reached up to take the rope of the outside bell and gave it a couple of rings to summon the men for their breakfast.

'Yes, they surely will. This city's full of folk from all over. I don't know why it's news. It's not as though there are no other people of varied colours and different tongues round here; there're the Chinese, the Polish and the Jews too, though many of them have been here since Napoleon was a lad. And those Red Indians at the Wild West Show, remember? People just like to be shocked by something different, my dear.' He finished his tea.' I reckon as how we'll be seeing folk from the farthest corners of the world, now we've this new canal – ocean going vessels. Manchester'll be a melting pot of colours soon enough.'

'You're probably right, Father. Have you been up to see the patient?' she asked.

'You're going now? If so, then I'll come along.'

'Yes, I'm going. Dr Smith'll call again this morning, I expect.'

Before he could say anything more, the men came in from the yard but stepped back from the door to give way to Sophia and her father.

Albert nodded a greeting.

'Morning Arnold, Miss Sophia. Visitor's awake and better looking, now most o'the muck's gone. Not spoken though, apart from *Good Morning*, polite like!' He grinned. 'Not used to them sort of manners up there, are we lads?' he threw over his shoulder at the other men and they all made various noises of agreement from grunts to sniggers until Sophia glared at them and they trooped indoors to their breakfast. She and her father continued to the loft.

The light was always dim up there before the sun moved round the building later in the day. It took seconds for their eyes to adjust from the brightness outside and then to see the shape of a body beneath the grey blanket. When the injured man managed to turn slightly and show his face, it was his eyes and his smile that Sophia saw first and found herself drawn to, but there was also an oddly good feeling around this man. They exchanged greetings and enquiries about his health and how he had slept as though he were a guest in the main house.

Her father sat down on a chair near the cot.

'Now then, you don't know who we are, my lad, nor we you. I would rectify that if you are up to it. We have a business here and we need to keep things running smoothly. Each day is very busy, but you're welcome to our help notwithstanding.'

Michel groaned as he tried to turn further and pull himself upright on the cot and seeing his difficulty Sophia stooped to help.

'No, this I can do myself; I thank you.' He held up his good hand, palm out.

A clattering sound on the wooden steps caused them all to turn and see Alice burst into the room carrying before her a large wooden tray laden with pots.

'I've brought the bloke's food, Miss Sophia,' she called and then at the sight of Michel, now upright and looking straight at her, she jolted to a stop and after staring open mouthed for a second or two, she ventured a whisper to Sophia.

'So, that's 'im then? I've never seen nothing like that – apart from when blokes came up from the pit and before their bath, like. They were proper black then too.' She giggled.

'But mine, *mademoiselle*, it will not wash off,' Michel told her.

Alice started. 'I didn't know 'e could talk like us, Miss,' she mouthed to Sophia, sceptical, and repeated to herself in an awed whisper, 'Won't wash off...'

Sophia's father stepped forward, making Alice start as she appeared not to have noticed him in the shadows. He shook his head at her.

'Thank you, Alice. Now you can tell all your friends that you have met someone who is from a different country. And you will need to address Michel here directly as I believe he speaks English well. Michel, this is our maid, Alice,' he said.

'*Mademoiselle* Alice, I am pleased to meet you,' he said.

For a moment Alice was unable to answer, just stared, astounded, then, after bobbing a curtsey she put the tray on the table and muttered, 'Thank you, I'm sure.' Then she ran off downstairs.

Sophia smiled at Alice's retreating figure as her father turned to speak to the injured man.

'Now then, lad. Last night we heard that you are Michel Bonaventure from Orléans in France. I am Arnold Kelley, and this is my daughter Miss Kelley, and we are Undertakers, we deal with the preparation of the dead for their funeral. Do you understand this notion, I wonder? Do they have such things where you come from?'

'I come from France,' he said.

'Ah, were you born there, not in some other land?' Her father asked tentatively.

'As I said, born in France of my parents. There are people of all nations there – and all colours. France is a civilized country, Monsieur Kelley, and of course we have *les entrepreneurs des pompes funèbres*, which is how we term your 'undertakers' in French. Yes, I understand how it is that you are wondering about me,' he said, 'And I thank you for taking me in. I must now explain how I came to be needing help, perhaps?'

Sophia handed Michel the cup of tea that Alice had brought.

'You'll need to try and drink this first. You're badly injured, and the explanation can wait,' she said, glancing at her father, 'Hmmm?'

'Maybe not, my dear.' He watched the man. 'I think I'd like to hear this story, as you are able to speak so readily this morning, erm, Michel. And pardon me for any assumptions I make at present. We know nothing of you. Tell me, you were savagely beaten; were you in any way to blame by starting a fight? You have a recent amputation; was there evil work afoot to leave you like this? I cannot keep you here long unless you tell us all.'

'Ah,' Michel gasped as he tried to sip the tea and then looked around for somewhere to put the cup. Sophia pulled a chair to the bedside for that purpose, but the movement of placing the cup caused him pain and he winced, cupped the end of his injured arm with his hand.

'I understand you, *Monsieur.* I see someone has treated my injury. It is well bandaged. I hope it is clean?'

'Our own doctor, Dr Smith, came in the night to tend it and re-stitch it. He said it should heal well now,' he reassured him.

'Ah, bien. I should like to thank him a million times, this doctor. And when I have money again, I will pay him. I do not take charity. My wound, it was a mess. This I know because I am a surgeon myself. I am – I *was* surgeon on the *Roi de Marseilles*, a cargo vessel, a steam ship that travels between the Gold Coast and the English ports. I was attacked on board ship by some of the lower crew; they think I am of the same metal as the captain who is a violent and unpredictable man.'

'Attacked? Why would that happen to you, as the ship's surgeon?' Sophia was shocked.

Michel closed his eyes a moment.

'It was an event waiting for a vital spark, a powder keg to be sure. Someone had to pay for what happened on board. The men, they were cooped up. They were… opprimés…the word… ah, oppressed. They were punished for every tiny mistake. Flogging, flogging. One night the captain, he went ashore, and they were as little children; they broke into the cargo hold and were soon drunk on rum, sherry, wine – anything. *Mon Dieu!* Me they want to drown in a vat of wine. Bien sûr, I resist. I was on the steps to go down to them and I see the way they are – I try to climb up. They catch at my legs. In the struggle, my arm is out of the hatch. *Alors*, the ship lurched, the door slammed onto my arm – it is sliced off! It was that simple. They tried to help me then and used the tar to cauterize my wound, which was beyond any pain I have known before. I feared the worst. I expected to die of gangrene before three days were gone – that is if I survived the night without further injury. The crew, they were close to real mutiny, hating the conditions under which they toiled.'

He stopped speaking abruptly.

'Take your time, lad. We're listening. Take your time.'

Michel nodded, drew breath. 'The captain, he is a hard man and when we docked finally, here in Manchester, he put me off with my bag and half wages. Me, I staggered away from the place. Now it is that I am useless as a surgeon, I am tossed aside. Just like that.'

'A terrible tale – if all's true,' Sophia's father remarked.

'Father!' Sophia was shocked, but he was ever one to speak plainly.

For her own part, she was one who had to force herself to think clearly, to be brutally honest with herself. She felt strangely drawn to Michel, not because he was a handsome man; his features were fine and strong, and although his skin colour was unusual in this part of the world, she found it beautiful, but he also had a compelling personality, one she felt was truthful and kind.

'It is true, this my story. The filth you saw on me – and I thank whoever cleaned me up, that was the welcome I got at the docks. Three days pass, I think. My bag and money, they were soon stolen, and I was too injured to prevent it. I have tried to find help, but each time I approach someone who looks to be of my own class, I am pushed away – I smell, I look different, as you see. *Alors,* I find that you Englishmen are suspicious, and I look worse each day, especially as I have to steal scraps from the market to eat. I am destitute.'

He lay back, rubbed his hand around his face and head, saying, 'I am in need of a shave and a hair cut too. I am ashamed of my appearance.' His hair was close curled to his head and his beard of similar appearance. Sophia wanted to touch it. She wanted to help this man.

She sat on the next cot, leaned forward. 'Where did you learn English if not here?' Now he had found the strength to speak more than simple thanks, she found his voice was musical.

'I learned at the Sorbonne, the university in Paris, from many of my fellow students and I took lessons also, thinking one day to come to England. English is the *lingua franca* now because of your Queen Victoria and her grand Empire.'

Sophia saw that her father was going to persist in his interrogation as he said, 'You were found under the bridge, left for dead. But who did this? Why would they, if you had nothing to steal and were already injured like this? Who'd do that?'

'I was attacked by thugs who do not like the look of me - for amusement. That is all I know. It is right, I have nothing left to steal.'

'You don't seem bitter at the attack or the loss of your arm,' Sophia said.

He shook his head. 'What is the use? It is gone! What use bitterness? I am here now, I am alive, I seem in good hands and I am thankful. I will repay you when I can stand unaided. And of course, I regret my arm, I feel its loss most intensely; I am surgeon; how can I continue to follow my profession, my calling? But what recourse have I? None!'

His voice was quiet; to her his story was one of horror and yet he showed courage, endurance, and hope in the future. Sophia admired him, this vagrant who many hours ago had been close to death under a bridge in Manchester.

She was pleased when, after listening quietly, her father finally smiled and nodded in agreement.

'Well, well, it's a fair tale, I'll say that. And I'll say warmly that I believe you. Forgive me for my plain speaking, but I've a daughter and a business to protect. You are welcome to stay as long as you've need, and you can hardly move as it is. Dr Smith, who redressed your arm, will call this morning so you'll be able to have a chinwag with someone who's of your own profession. But now, work's to be done and my stomach shouts out that it's time for breakfast. If you've need of anything, call out and someone will come.'

He patted Michel on his uninjured side as he passed and turned to Sophia.

'Come, my dear.'

As Sophia glanced back, she saw only a smile and a brief wave of the man's hand.

She and her father had finished their meal and were about to go on with preparations for the funeral later that morning when Nathaniel arrived. He put his head round the door and announced abruptly that he would have a quick word with Michel.

'I'll come with you, lad...'

Sophia was surprised when Nat replied, 'I would talk with him alone.'

She exchanged glances with her father and feeling a little hurt on his behalf and cross with Nat for his abrupt statement she said, 'A police matter, I expect; something to do with the attack maybe?'

He merely smiled, shaking his head briefly and left the room. Her father had returned to his newspaper, The Evening News from the previous day, so she muttered her excuses and slipped out of the kitchen to follow Nat. He was at the top of the steps by the time she saw him and thankfully he left the door to the loft ajar, so she ran lightly up and stood as casually as she could near the door to listen.

She heard Michel groan and the cot creak and guessed he had moved to see who entered.

There was no greeting between the men.

'Now, what have you to say for yourself, man?' Nat demanded.

Chapter 9

'Thoughts are tyrants'
Emily Brontë

SOPHIA CREPT CLOSER and looked through the crack at the hinge end of the door. She saw the sick man rub his eyes and face his visitor calmly.

'I was brought here, and I think it is you that I need to thank for that service. A thousand thanks. You are Sergeant Roberts, non? I am Michel Bonaventure and I was told by the men that it was you and Miss Kelley who found me under the bridge. My mind, it will become clear in a few days. This I have seen on board ship after a man suffers an injury such as mine; deep trauma affects the mind. To remember, it is hard.'

'On ship?' Nat was terse. He stood next to Michel's cot and stared down at him, arms crossed, expression neutral. Michel managed to pull himself up and lay propped on his good elbow.

She watched as Nat moved round the other side of the cot and the light from the window showed his face clearly. He had always been able to control his expression so that whether it was blank or smiling, to most people his thoughts were hidden; Sophia was well aware that her own face told a rich tale whatever happened. As she peered through the gap, she saw the tension in his body, he quivered like a bow string, waves of suspicion and anger swirling around him.

Michel, she realised was once again prepared to justify himself patiently. He explained, as he had done for Sophia and her father, how he came to be destitute and attacked and Nat listened without interrupting at all.

'I will leave as soon as I am able. Do not worry that I will outstay the welcome I have been given.'

'I don't ever worry about helping a person in need, but I have to say that you seem a familiar sort of man, very easy in your manner and as I'm a police officer, I like to study such things and place them in the big scheme of events. We do not see many men of your colour in the city, but now that the Ship Canal is open, perhaps that will change. Nevertheless, we've troubling times in Manchester.'

Sophia noticed that Nat was at his sententious best.

He continued, 'However, you say you are a ship's surgeon - well! And from France. This city is open to all the world, I know that sure enough, and we have people from every walk of life here. But you, Dr Bonaventure, as I should call you...'

'Michel, please.'

'You find yourself in hard times. I hope we can... no, I'll rephrase, I hope I can trust you.'

He stared down at him, but the expression on his face was hidden from Sophia now by fold of someone's coat on a hook.

Michel tried to push himself up further into a sitting position but fell back exhausted and after a slight hesitation, Nat bent forward and lifted him up easily.

'I have trusted you with my life, my friend, and again I thank you.'

Nat merely grunted. To Sophia, the voyeur, it sounded as though he wasn't satisfied, and this troubled her, but not for long because hearing the yard gate latch, she turned to see the doctor arriving and waved him up.

'Good morning, Dr Smith, this is convenient. I was just going in,' she called, very relieved to have an excuse to be outside the door when she heard Nat's heavy steps approaching down the long room.

'How does our patient do this morning, Miss Kelley?' the doctor called, running up the steps lightly.

'Quite remarkably well, considering the ordeal. You'll want to talk to him particularly, I think, when I introduce you. In fact, you'll be very surprised indeed.'

'Oh? I'm agog with curiosity. And you, are you well? You look remarkably well, despite a broken night.' He smiled, adjusted his spectacles on his nose – a habit of his when greeting people. His eyes, warm and confiding, gazed into hers.

Dear me, dear me. Always a little too long doctor. 'I'm well, as you see.'

'Good, good. Lead on Miss Kelley, charming as always.'

Nat had arrived at the door, stepped back to allow him. Sophia made the introductions and saw how astonished the doctor was when she added that his patient was a fellow physician and surgeon.

She and Nat left them to talk and they walked down to the yard. He leapt the final two steps and caught her in his arms to lift her down.

'You feel a little better, then?' she asked, smiling.

'You always surprise me with this ability to know my moods; and you're right, I am full of anger today – boiling anger – as well as this heat. And no, I don't feel better, as you put it. My uniform is stifling me. I want to hit someone, something.' His expression was forbidding, his muscles, where she held his arm, tensed.

'Apart from me?'

'Apart from you,' he said and kissed her lightly, relaxed a little.

They sat on the bench outside the yard kitchen, usually the hottest spot, but the sun had moved, and it was dim and cooler under the overhanging roof. She told him to undo his jacket, cool off while she got him a drink, said not to be silly, no one will think the worse of you in this weather – Goodness knows she'd want to walk alongside the hearse later with bare feet and a sun bonnet. Once he had a glass of lemonade in his hand and at least looked less angry with the world, they talked about Michel, and his story.

'He didn't say he had a family, or a wife perhaps in Orléans? It would be sad for him to think of her not knowing of his plight. Don't you think so, Nat?'

'Possibly. But has he such a pining wife? You can ask him in your tactful way. People seem to open up to you, love. No! Do not pinch me, little minx. I meant it kindly.' He rubbed his forearm dramatically. 'I'm sorry for the man, I'll allow, and I know he can have nothing to do with the murders, being helpless as we found him – and probably had been for a few days. I want to blame someone, and he's a stranger, and he looks different, so he'll do. Yes, you'll tell me it's a base impulse – a prejudice against strangers. I'll tell you I'm not behaving like a good police officer, I know it, but these deaths are evil, whoever is the victim, the working girls of Whitechapel or professional young women like you, love. My own love...' He pulled her towards him, but she pushed him gently away, smiling.

'You are too angry and hot! Much too hot to want to hold.' She glanced round to see if anyone was looking and saw several of the men in the yard look away quickly. 'Ah, well...' They were engaged to be married – sometime. She did not yet know how she really felt about being married. She loved him, yes. Passionately? Usually. How would she feel if they parted? Bereft. But to become a woman such as he seemed to want, centred on the home, his work, his wellbeing, made her long to be alone on an island.

But yes, I love him truly and sometimes very, very dearly.

She would think about this later, but less pleasurable things weighed heavily on her mind.

These murders...

'Nat, will you be talking with your inspector today? Last night you said you might give him all the information we found about the two women.'

'I will try, of course, but there are four young women, remember?' he said, and she nodded; the reminder was a chill wind across her heart.

But she spoke briskly. 'Yes, I do remember; how can I forget? And I remember that we have two funerals today. My Goodness, it is as hot as an oven already and I must wear my full black costume, trussed up like a goose for the roasting.'

And now I am pushing the murders to the back of my mind. It's difficult to face. So difficult...

'Sophia...stop talking,' he said softly, and this time drew her to himself very gently and slowly, so that they could part with a kiss.

She watched him do up his uniform jacket, deft, strong fingers, the fabric across his arms and shoulders straining, settling, enclosing. He grimaced as he tried to button the top button against the column of his neck. The veins stood out on his forehead and by the time he'd finished he was sweating once more.

'I'll be off now. Until later, love.'

He adjusted his belt, clipped on his equipment, put on his heavy helmet and strode away across the yard, nodding at one or two people, official again.

She threw herself into the morning jobs as efficiently as ever and even had time to tend the pots of flowers that she kept in the yard near the kitchen door; geraniums and busy lizzie, fine abundant, brilliantly coloured flowers that thrived in the dry heat and were very far from the solemnity of the lilies. This was the hottest summer for many years – and after the winter they had had; called an Ice Age by scientific men and   something less scientific by ordinary men, the men who worked on her yard. Ice to be thawed to water the horses, rugs for them day and night, everything splashed with filth from the roads.

No funerals for more than a month, the ground being too hard to dig. At least the storage of bodies wasn't difficult as they were frozen solid. The horses not here to be stabled at Johnson's as usual. Extra feed. Thank Goodness for our big outhouses. But now – all is heat and colour. What a difference. Drought too at the moment.

But her thoughts were jumbled up and her feelings were mixed. She was strangely buoyed by being able to help someone so desperately in need as this French surgeon, although the city had many people in need, children especially. This Frenchman, Michel, who was more intriguing by the hour, had crossed their path dramatically and that was why it was so unusual and quite special in an indefinable way. On the other hand, she was angry and fearful, angry with Nat for being so suspicious, so much like himself really, and she was fearful because of the two dead women. It was unheard of for an undertaker to be upset by the deaths of people with whom they had no close relationship, but this time there were special circumstances.

She felt the connection, especially as she had had the vision.

The first funeral of the day was performed without a hitch and having changed from her hot costume into a cooler outfit for the dinner time break, she went to the workroom to finish preparing Adeline Worthington for her funeral. Prior to that she was to lie in the Chapel of Rest for her family to visit privately.

Nat called again before dinner time and found Sophia in the workroom arranging the dead woman's hair. He explained he'd been instructed by his inspector to go and visit the Worthington family and get permission to view the body and make what observations he could. He had gone and had been granted permission by the victim's brother, who was a solicitor. His parents were indisposed, he said.

Sophia was dressing the poor girl's hair.

'She'll look her best,' Nat ventured, as he watched Sophia work.

'Under the circumstances, she will. What d'you want to see then - as a police officer?' she asked.

He wanted to see the pinprick mark under the ear particularly. The body was covered with a cloth, leaving her head free. She had drawn the cloth up to the woman's chin when Nat arrived; it felt right to do so; the deceased was a young woman and although she found she was a little embarrassed in front of the man she was going to marry, more urgent was the need to protect this young woman in death. It wouldn't change the way she died but she deserved the greatest dignity now. Sophia felt a wave of intense shame, remembering her reaction when Michel was brought in.

Using a finger gently, Nat lifted the curl of hair behind Adeline Worthington's ear and bent to examine the area. He said, 'How did you come to notice it?'

Sophia was uneasy; she was not used to dealing with murder victims, nor, if she were honest, watching Nat do so. She paused to collect her facts and impressions.

'I suppose it was actually the absence of one earring that made me look around her ear and neckline, under her hair too, thinking it had caught there or had fallen into her clothing. Her ear was reddened too, as though she had been rubbing it, or had hurt it somehow. It was then I saw a tiny amount of blood around the edge of the pin head mark. I think something pierced the big blood vessel near there while she was alive, perhaps injecting a drug that paralysed because we all think death was caused by suffocation; the blue of her lips, the little haemorrhaging marks in her eyes. Last night, Doctor Smith put his finger on the edge of the needle as he withdrew it to staunch the flow of blood from the tiny wound from the patient who was alive and left such a tiny ring round the wound. When I saw that whole procedure with the hypodermic syringe, it made me think, perhaps this is what was used on the poor woman.'

He shook his head. 'How do you do it? That's certainly an idea, but we don't have any means of ascertaining what drug, if any, was put in her blood. A pity. You're such a clever one, love. You'd make a good detective; you are so observant in everything, not an item passes you by. I sometimes think your mind must be like a camera that takes the sharpest of photographs.'

He stood back and looked at the dead woman's face carefully.

'The eyes, of course, are hidden from view now, but that little detail of the pinprick behind the ear is so important yet cannot be seen upon a quick examination. It appears that our police surgeon, Dr Johnson, didn't perform his examination too well. He always seems a plain man to me, a nonentity if I'm honest. Perhaps I am speculating too much; I've no knowledge of the man other than the fact he always does the examinations very quickly and appears uninterested – yes, uninterested.'

He stood back, arms folded, thoughtfully gazing on the victim's face.

'But you, love, you always do your utmost. You've disguised the colour of her lips very well; they were quite blue I believe. To have blue lips and bloodshot eyes, means that that was possibly the final means of her death. You and Arnold thought so too. But to inject her with something that paralyses first, it's as if the murderer were toying with her, though, drawing out the end, making it more horrific for her.'

Sophia nodded.

They were quiet for a space then he said quietly, a note of profound sadness in his voice, 'He must have revelled in this slow death...'

She could only nod in agreement, the vision she had had flashing across her memory. This death made her acutely sad and uncomfortable.

How could someone do this, kill such a young woman - anyone and in such a ... such a theatrical way?

'You know, you've arranged her features so kindly. It might be some comfort to her family.'

'Oh, Nat, there will be no comfort to be had at all.'

There was a pause, his expression changed to one of realisation. 'No, no, of course not.'

A bell sounded in the yard.

Chapter 10

'I hold it true, whatever befall'
Alfred Lord Tennyson

'THERE'S THE DINNER BELL. I should hurry, we're busy again this afternoon. But I almost forgot, here're the posies,' she said and brought a small flower press from the shelf. She undid them carefully and placed the two pressed posies on the bench and they bent over to examine them closely, heads together.

She lifted one, a tiny, flattened bunch of blue and white and greens and placed it onto the bench. She felt as though it would burn her hand, such was its significance; the person who had made this and placed it in the dress of the dead girl was the murderer.

She pointed. 'This one was left with Sally Hepplestone, the first victim. It has the clearest message, Nat; the daisy's for innocence, the nettle for pain and the forget-me-not represents hope and optimism, apart from its more widely known message of remembrance. Now, if I read them together as a complete message, which is what such posies are used for, and obviously you've to know the language of flowers to read it - then I think they say *remember the pain of this innocent.* And we will – Oh, Nat, I know I shall, for ever.' They held each other's eyes. 'But the posy could have another message entirely; it could also mean *hope must bring pain for the innocent*. That is much more chilling, don't you think so?'

He stood up, hands on hips, exhaled noisily. 'It is – I do. And the other posy?'

'Mmmm.' Just as carefully as she had done for the first posy, she placed the second one onto the bench. 'This one's even more disturbing to my mind. It was the one with the poor woman here.' She moved over to the body, put her hand on the shoulder and once more felt the slow bloom of fear, shuddered.

Nat saw this. 'Sophia, you are feeling alright?' He lifted her chin with his hand; looked into her face.

'We've been so busy, but I'm fine, I'm fine. The flowers though, they bode nothing but ill.' She pointed to the second posy.

'This was left with Adeline Worthington here. The posy has honeysuckle, which represents affectionate devotion, and there is carnation, purple carnation. It is dyed specially – a simple process. And this particular colour symbolises many negatives: fear, antipathy, capriciousness, changeability, unreliability and a whimsical nature. I think they can all be contained under the term *coquetry.* And there is deep blue periwinkle which for centuries has symbolised death. In Medieval times they wove it into garlands for condemned criminals.' She sighed, a ragged sound.

'The condemned. Hmmm,' he mused. 'The meaning? You find these things out better than me, love.'

'The meaning. Ahhh, yes.' She took a breath, her eyes fixed on the fateful posy. 'I think it's intended to say that devotion can be distorted by coquetry. Purple is a colour of mourning so that makes the final message one of death. The periwinkle confirms it; *this coquetry has led to your death*. These are both dire messages to give such young women.'

'They are,' he agreed heavily. 'But does that mean that the

111

murderer knew the women and wanted them to have the message before they died? They are not the sort of posies a lover would give to his mistress, are they? The language of flowers has been subverted; these posies show only evil intent. And I wonder, did the victims see the posies themselves or are they intended for some other person or persons to interpret – their families for instance?'

She shook her head, eyes downcast.

He continued slowly, 'Y'know, if there had been just the one posy, the first one, then we might have thought that a lover had given it to her, if we didn't know the language of flowers. But as we do – you do, then to have two, one for each victim is not a coincidence, is it? And for the second message to be so much more sinister – then that bespeaks murder and both killings are connected by this evil narrative.'

She passed her hand over her brow. She felt hot, almost faint.

'Nat, you are the detective, or will soon be. I'll leave this to you. I can't fathom the mind of a murderer. I'm an undertaker; I deal with the bodies and the funeral. I know I'm observant, but that's all I am. *Apart from the fact that I have visons that show me things that have happened elsewhere and to other people...*In any case I must go to dinner now. Have you seen what you wanted to see here?' She indicated the body.

He said he had, and they parted, he assuring her that he would call again tomorrow, as he was on duty for the rest of the day and would try to call on Inspectors Caminada and Bateman that evening.

'One day they will see what a great detective you will be, Nat, you see,' she told him.

He rushed away again, intent on business.

She heard the door to the workroom close and walked back to the body to gather up the things she had used to dress the hair, but her own limbs were feeling heavy and her eyes refused to focus. She groped her way to a chair by the bench and sat down carefully as different sensations wrapped themselves around her; scents, sounds textures. The room swam, her vision blurred. She smelt coal dust and city heat: a mixture of dust, horse dung, sewage and unwashed bodies. Suddenly there was light behind her, but she was in a dark alley. It was deserted. A pit opened in front of her, no - a cellar hatch, the coal hatch to an enormous cellar. Morning light behind her.

It was then she felt strong arms around her body, a man's arms, a tall man; the rough scrape of fabric on his arms scoring her skin through the light cambric of her dress, her walking out dress.

The attacker held his hand close over her mouth and nose, the other arm was now clamped tightly across her body, pinioning her upper arms. She fought for breath, for life. She writhed fiercely and managed just once to scrabble at the hand on her neck and rake her nails across the skin, then reach up and backwards to try and snatch at his face, but it was turned away and she felt instead a man's neck and her nails scratched desperately. The smell of his hand, the taste of it against her lips sickened her. Her breathing became difficult, as though she drew each breath through a thick carpet. She was crushed close to his body and could not now reach behind to grab him, nor did her heels make any contact as she tried to kick back at his shins, but her kicks became feebler by the second.

He released her nose and she dragged in the air fiercely. But he kept his hand on her mouth and dragged her head sideways then pushed his face against the side of her head until his own mouth was pressed close as a lover's to her ear. She felt his tongue slowly lick it. She retched and then, beyond horror, his teeth nibbled at her earlobe. Her whole being filled with mounting cold panic as the nibbles became bites, harder and

113

harder bites until her whole ear seemed to be in his mouth.

She tried to buck her body away from him but could not do more than squirm weakly. All the while she could hear her own muffled screams in the background; but the noise foremost, the one that made her shudder with revulsion, was a slobbering, growling moan and a clanking noise such as that made by crockery in a sink. She was puzzled until she realised that it was his teeth playing with her enamelled earring. She struggled to breathe at all, felt herself growing weak, sinking into an abyss. A sharp pain on her earlobe brought her fully aware once more and she heard so clearly the awful sucking noise right inside her ear and then felt his mouth leave it wet and throbbing.

She realised her own mouth was free and she dragged in breath desperately, once, twice, three times as she built enough air and courage for a desperate scream, but before she could give vent, he held up before her eyes a hypodermic syringe.

'Be silent!' he hissed in her ear and she was.

He moved quickly to snatch both her hands in one of his and held them effortlessly behind her back. She concentrated on the hypodermic syringe filling her vision and saw that a dot of liquid was suspended easily just below the tip of the needle. She swallowed the howl she was desperate to release then, mesmerised, her eyes followed the path of the needle as he moved it from her vision round the side of her head. She froze, then felt him lay the cool glass of the syringe against her neck. If she kept still, maybe he wouldn't hurt her. She would not move, would not move. She would escape if she stayed still, did what he wanted…escape. There was a tiny pinprick of pain and she knew he had pressed the point into her neck below the ear. She imagined with horror that he was injecting her with a sleeping drug; she had heard about this obscene practice that led to a rape. This was happening to her…. The pain deepened; her limbs were weak as water. She couldn't move…

'Miss, Miss, wake up!'

Sophia felt her shoulder shaken and opened her eyes a little, ready to scream aloud, but caught herself in time as she focused on Alice's face close to hers.

'There you are, Miss. Nodded off? It'll be the heat. Meself, I'd 'ave liked to stay in bed the whole long day, I would, just lie there with a cool, cool breeze and nothing t'do.'

'Asleep? Have I been asleep? What time is it, Alice?'

'Dinner is on the table, in the house kitchen – only just served and it's cold pork pie, thank the Lord! If Cook makes me fry anything, I'll drop dead, I will,' Alice rattled on noisily. 'Listen to me   dropping dead in an undertaker's! I call that proper funny. Shall I tell Master you're coming then?'

Sophia stood up and wiped her brow. 'I was tired after last night. How's our visitor?'

'I don't know, I'm sure. No one's told me nothing. Am I to take him food, Miss?'

Sophia gave the girl a gentle shove towards the door. 'I'm here now. Come on, we will see what we can do.'

As she closed the door behind her, she remembered the smell of the attacker's hands – remembered? No, she only remembered what she had experienced in her vision. She was not attacked. But it had been so real.

The smell on his hands had been the same as that substance under the fingernails of the victims. She had not told Nat about that yet. She should.

Chapter 11

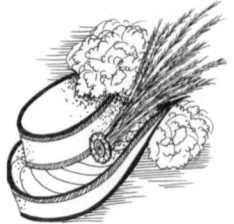

'The wonder of a mother's love'
Christina Rossetti

THE AFTERNOON PASSED, as Sophia knew it would, in sweltering discomfort. The funeral was dignified and long with weeping relatives clutching each other, plying fans feverishly; droves of black and grey figures staggering in the heat. She was exhausted and when Alice popped her head round the door of the workroom with a message, she snapped at her.

'Now what's the matter? Has Michel been polite to you and you think it strange?'

The sarcasm was not lost on Alice. 'No, Miss – and I was brought up to value good manners, especially in a mining town.'

The girl stood with hands on hips, which was her usual pose and not defiant; Sophia knew it. She tempered her answer with a smile, albeit a tired one:

'I'm sorry, Alice. It's unlike me.' She put a hand to her head briefly, asked quietly, 'What is it then?'

'There is a lady to see you. Mrs. Worthington, her mother.' She nodded at the body on the cool table. 'She says it's very urgent she sees you now. I've put her in't little parlour next to the   Receiving Room. Tea's on the way, Miss.'

'Tea? Yes, that would be good.' Sophia smiled again, disappointed with herself for her sharpness; Alice did her best,

116

and it was good. She noticed the girl watching her. 'Mrs. Worthington will appreciate that.'

'I'm doing it for you too, Miss,' she said. 'You need it.'

Sophia nodded her thanks, moved the body onto a trolley and wheeled it into the body storage room.

Arnold Kelley and Daughter, Undertakers of Distinction, required an extensive property in which to run their business. Sophia needed to find a core of calm within herself before she went to what she knew would be an emotional interview. In her mind's eye she ran around the whole enterprise, taking stock of the responsibility she had, delaying the moment when she must go and speak to the grieving mother.

She cast her eyes round the workroom; next door was her father's office, her own office, then the yard kitchen for their own men and sometimes other professionals and craftsmen who called on funeral business. Photographers and mediums frequently tried their luck, but her father would not tolerate either of them. But there was the cabinet maker who undertook to make coffins and who rented a workshop there in the yard and there were daily callers: the candle makers, the shroud makers, the florists and funeral furnishers and the feather man with armfuls of black feathers to decorate the horse headdresses, making them regal in their funereal livery.

There was the blacksmith who had his forge there to deal with their horses and did whatever metal work was needed for the business. Then there was the muck heap that was taken away regularly by the farmer who cared for the horses at grass, the huge barn for the bedding, forage and feed for them; weekly deliveries there. The Undertaker's yard was a busy enterprise. The main house kitchen was across the corridor and was where their housekeeper, Mrs Kittering, prepared food and organised the house and the other two servants: the whole business moving effortlessly on its daily rations of food.

At the front of the building were the public rooms and these had been made as solemn, yet as welcoming as was needful. Sophia was proud of them. There was the Receiving Room for mourners, where they were met with condolence and sensitivity. There was a small lady's desk in rosewood that reminded one that this was a business. Sophia's father had removed his cumbersome old mahogany desk, wanting to put his daughter forward as the face of the enterprise and he insisted she meet all mourners herself now.

She had chosen to decorate the walls with dove grey silk wallpaper and hung huge swathes of grey drapes at the windows, all edged with black; that same upholstery covering the chairs. In the corner of the room, to be seen as people entered, was a black marble plinth that held a white urn filled with Arum lilies, or whatever was seasonal, but in white, brought each week from a hothouse in the suburbs. She detested the lilies, but the clients expected them. A tall stained-glass window was set in the wall next to it. Sophia's mother had commissioned it from the Pre-Raphaelite artists, William Morris and Edward Burne Jones and it was the most beautiful depiction of an angel in prayer that Sophia had ever seen, all in blues and golds. The artists had done a similar one for Winchester Cathedral.

Behind the window was the corridor that led to the two viewing rooms, or Chapels of Rest, as they were now fashionably known. She had designed this décor also. Both rooms were serenely respectful under their swathes of black muslin and crepe, the air redolent with the scent of flowers and all bathed by the soft glow of huge beeswax candles in sconces. A single sculpture, a mourning angel with hands clasped in prayer and wings held aloft, commanded one room, bestowing an air of eternal calm and comfort. The other room had a stone cross and at its base, a sculpted child that knelt in graceful grief, with knees drawn up and enclosed by cold arms. Its head rested on its knees; eyes closed.

In each chapel, there was a black draped bier to receive the coffin and a number of chairs or a settee for the mourners. Outside on the square, the front of the business was presented with discretion, a lace curtained gothic window and grey and gold signage proclaimed to the city that this was an establishment of the highest quality.

Sophia and her father had their living accommodation on the two storeys above the business rooms and the servants were in the garrets at the back of the house. On hearing of Mrs. Worthington's visit she ran quickly up to her own rooms to wash herself, tidy her hair and change into her navy serge skirt and a plain white blouse. She walked quickly to the little parlour. She felt it was owed to all grieving relatives to show respect, to be in control of herself, so that she could offer what help was needed.

And this woman's daughter had been murdered.

Alice was in the room when Sophia arrived; she'd brought the tea and was pouring a cup for Mrs. Worthington. The girl had even put on her clean apron and cap.

'Good afternoon, Mrs. Worthington,' she said, sitting down next to the woman on the settee. 'Thank you, Alice,' she said. The girl left quietly.

The room was tastefully appointed. Sophia hoped the shades of grey and lilac might be soothing to a grieving heart. They were restful colours. There was no brightness to tempt joy into the life that, for most people bereaved, must continue blighted and with little comfort. It was a calm and ordered space.

When the door closed, Sophia spoke gently:

'You wanted to see me, Mrs. Worthington. How can I help – in any way at all, how can I help you?'

A slow tear moved down the woman's cheek.

Sophia offered a lace edged handkerchief of her own from her pocket.

'Will you have the tea, Mrs Worthington?'

The woman wiped her eyes and nodded mutely, took the cup and saucer. There was a taut silence for several minutes as she stared at the cup and saucer in her hand.

Sophia tried a gentle prompt. 'Perhaps you want to discuss the service? I could send for Reverend Knightly? He's the new curate and is very kind indeed.'

The bereaved mother shook her head, murmured, 'No, it is you I wish to speak to, Miss Kelley.'

Then she began to shake, so much so that the tea splashed into the saucer and Sophia had to quickly relieve her of it, then bent and put her arm round the older woman's shoulder.

'I'm so very sorry about what happened to Adeline.' Sophia's voice rang with sincerity.

The woman began to sob, great breathy gulps of anguish. 'It's my child I want to speak to really. My child, my girl, my only daughter, my beauty, my beauty.'

'Yes, yes,' Sophia murmured.

There were pauses in the waves of grief when the mother spoke quickly, muttering, almost to herself. 'Why did this happen? Why would someone hurt her?' Now and then she directed a look of such pleading sorrow at Sophia that she felt the same emotion swelling in her own breast.

'My dear daughter! Harmed, destroyed, taken by a monster surely. Oh, I can't bear to talk about it, but I must! How will I survive with this loss? Ah, the very idea is hard to think of. What had she done that deserved such a thing? She was so young; she'd only just begun her life. How will I live all those lonely years without her?' She paused and covered her face with her hands. Tears ran between her fingers. She took a huge deep breath and wiping her eyes with the back of her hand, she flung herself back in the seat, threw an arm over her forehead in distraction.

'Her poor father is already lost to me. He can't understand.' She looked intently at Sophia, her desperate eyes begging for understanding. 'He can't.'

Sophia shook her head. 'I hear that he's ill.'

'Ill, yes, very ill. But my dear girl; she was well, so beautiful, so sparkling with life. She was all dressed up to spend a day with friends, she said, some other nurses from the hospital – but they said they knew *nothing* of such an outing planned.' She shook her head, spread her arms out, a mime of incredulity. 'She wouldn't tell me an untruth, her mother; some malign influence was on those other girls – or on her, Miss Kelley.' Her face flushed red, her mouth open in horror as she gasped, 'Will the police catch him? Will he be brought to justice? No! No, he won't!' She began to shake all over, moaning and crying in turn.

Sophia held her until the fit of despair quietened and Mrs Worthington sat up.

'Miss Kelley, there is something I wish to tell you; I have found someone,' she whispered, and dragged the handkerchief down her face in great rough and ragged sweeps. 'Someone who can talk to people…people who have passed over…' She opened the handkerchief and laid it over her face and covered that with both hands. Her shoulders shook then with dry, silent sobs.

Sophia waited again, patiently. She was used to the role of comforter to the bereaved.

But she wasn't used to the feeling of deceitfulness that stole over her this time.

She had examined the woman's dead daughter, she knew what her injuries were and how, more than likely, she had met her death. She knew Adeline had been almost suffocated, drugged then suffocated until she had died. The suffocation was provable, but the only real evidence of the drugging had come from the appearance of a small puncture wound and, from this point on things became unprovable: the vision that Sophia had had of the hypodermic injection, the sensation she had felt of becoming paralysed. This was what no one else would believe. And Sophia couldn't tell why the drug was used other than to immobilize the woman.

Adeline's mother cleared her throat, held the handkerchief tightly in her hands as though it were a life raft, and she tossed on the awful ocean of grief.

'I've been contacted by a woman who can talk to people who have passed over, talk to them in the spirit world, I mean.' She spoke quickly as though to utter the word, 'dead' in connection with her daughter made the fact finally indisputable. 'She wrote a letter to me – this woman. My husband can't help me, at the moment. He is...' She paused. Sophia saw her struggle for breath and courage. 'He's just ill, as you say – ill.'

Apparently, Mr. Worthington had not spoken a single word since they were told of Adeline's death. A police constable and the doctor had called at their home, and they had been taken to identify the body in the Police Mortuary at Newton Street. They had not recognised her at first, thought it was a mistake – someone else's daughter. The constable had told Nat that it was the expression on their child's face that floored them. She had been of a sunny disposition by all accounts.

Sophia poured fresh tea and handed it to Mrs. Worthington, who this time was able to sip it before putting it on the table.

'Who is this woman who can communicate with the other side, Mrs. Worthington? How did she come to know of your loss, I wonder?'

'Everyone knows now. It's two days, I think...two days...' She broke off again to take up the tea and hold it on her lap.

'Gossip is very quick to travel. But what did the woman say

she could do?' Sophia pressed.

'She's holding a séance, this evening, for a handful of select-ed people who are recently bereaved. She is Irena Petrovna, a Russian apparently. She says she's held these séances in the homes of all the more prosperous people, and even gentry, hereabouts. How am I to believe this? And how am I to believe she can speak to my own Adeline? I don't know what to think, what to do.'

Sophia bent and gently removed the cup again and then took hold of her hands. 'Have you ever been to a séance before, Mrs Worthington? I mean, do you know what happens at such events?'

'I have, I do. I attended one some years ago, when Adeline was a child, but I didn't take her, naturally. I went with my friend; both of us for curiosity's sake only.' She paused to gath-er the memory. 'As it happened there was some sort of emana-tion, I think they called it, a green mist that went everywhere, quite off-putting, and much screaming and fainting. It was very strange; a stream of air, coloured air seemed to flow from the mouth of the medium – just coiled upwards. I remember thinking it was like the variety performance at the Palace The-atre. If only Adeline were here now, it's she I'd ask – how ab-surd am I? I wouldn't need to go if she were here, would I?' Her voice had risen to a shrill note, a tiny hysterical giggle escaped her, and she snatched her hands from Sophia's and began to wring them in distraction.

Sophia said, 'I'll go with you, if you like. Would that help, do you think? There, there.' She spoke with deliberately low tones and very slowly. 'That is, if you want me to. What do you think? We would go together. I can't take Adeline's place, but I can be there if needed – another woman to be beside you. Just another woman.'

All the agitated movements stopped abruptly as Mrs.

Worthington stared deeply into Sophia's eyes, taking her time to consider.

'I think that's what I hoped you might say, Miss Kelley. You're kind – like Adeline.' She sat back and looked at Sophia steadily for a minute or so, taking in her hair, height, her face and her dress. 'I think you are a little like my Adeline in appearance. It's…it's… odd, really. Very odd. How will I feel walking along with you? The last time I walked out with anyone, just a few days ago, it was Adeline. Oh, Miss Kelley, this is the worst time of my life.' She reached for her tea and drank it in one mouthful then looked at the pot. 'May I?' she asked.

Sophia poured her more, which she gulped down this time, desperately and had a third, added sugar herself.

'I must be strong at this time. My husband, Henry, he can't be. He has been broken by events,' she gabbled now.

'So Mr. Worthington won't be well enough to go to the séance this evening?' Sophia ventured.

'He's taken to his bed. Once we were told she was…' She bit her lip for long seconds. 'That she was murdered, and then we had to go and see her, well, he collapsed, gripped by such desperate anguish that I thought he wouldn't survive. He's always been a very strong man, but this has taken the heart from him. She is a nur…she *was* a nurse, but you know that. She would help her father, but I'm at a loss and that's why I wondered if this Irena Petrovna, this Russian woman, can help in some way.' Her voice now was flat, bereft.

Sophia would not tell this mother of the vision she had had of her daughter's dreadful bewilderment, her tumbling confusion, her paralysing terror. That would be breathtakingly cruel. Nor would she share any of her own past and often more positive clairvoyant experiences. Nothing was going to make her feel better at the moment – or ever. Instead she decided that going with her to the séance would simply offer support.

But she admitted to herself that she was very curious too, curious about the skill of this medium, her authenticity, and she was also curious because she had never been to a séance herself, she who was so familiar with clairvoyant experiences of her own.

At least I might prevent the poor woman being exploited in her grief. But I know exactly what Father will say about this.

Her father was wary of her gift, not understanding it fully, and if she was honest, she felt he simply didn't want to understand. He was a devout church-going man, and she knew very well, just plain distrustful of things he hadn't seen with his own eyes. A practical, well grounded man. Furthermore, he detested the use of such gifts for unfair profit, as he called it.

She and her father never recommended that clients consult a medium; the idea of talking to the dead was anathema to him and the persistent popularity of charlatan mediums was his constant bête noire. A memory was instantly recalled; he once threw a man out onto the street, lifted him clear off his feet, when he called to offer his services as a medium, 'So that your clients could speak, one last time, with their loved one in the Chapel of Rest. Satisfaction *guaranteed*,' he'd said.

But there was Mrs Worthington, seeking comfort from a séance. She stared straight ahead, her cheeks once more tear-drenched and Sophia thought that in all her years as an undertaker, she had never seen an expression of such profound sadness. Sophia put her arms round her again and the bereaved mother cried silently for her daughter.

How strange is grief? From mild dismay bordering on indifference to that bitter anger and raw desperation and the paralysing shock for Adeline's father. Perhaps it all depends on the depth of love for the departed? Maybe. And the circumstances of their death. How many old people have we seen that have died peacefully in the fullness of time, and after a good and meaningful life, well loved by their families?

Her own mother's death was due to a seizure, the doctor said. She had died smiling at her husband, the very thought of him in her mind as she passed away. Even though she'd been in the room herself and had witnessed everything, she'd been so profoundly shocked that even now she remembered almost nothing of the moment or the aftermath, even as a medium herself, one gifted with the sight, she recalled nothing of the most awful moment of her life. It was surely like this for Adeline's father especially as it was a very different death from that suffered by his daughter and showing her final moment etched on her expression to be one of horror.

But these two young victims – their deaths are terrifying – they terrify me. It is inexplicable. I feel helpless. These murders: the deaths are felt by so many more people, felt powerfully too, even by people with no knowledge of the victim or the family. All this emotion rippling outward across many lives.

It was only a minute or so before the mother disengaged herself gently and spoke, yet it felt longer to Sophia.

'Thank you, Miss Kelley.' Her voice was full of tears, her thoughts tumbling out in gabbled speech. 'I'd be very grateful if you would come with me tonight. The séance is to be held at the medium's own home, in Chorlton, at seven thirty. I think I'll need someone to remember what's said by everyone. Will Adeline speak? Will she sound different? What am I to expect?' she said. 'Could her spirit appear? People say they do appear. I'd be horrified – I know. How will I bear it? But I must. And I want to do this before you prepare Adeline for the Chapel of Rest, so that I have heard her voice before I see her again. Rest, yes, I want that for her now, *rest*.'

'Of course.' She gave her another handkerchief. 'Mrs Worthington, do you believe in the spirits?'

'I think I do. Everyone seems to speak of messages from, from... people who have passed away. I want to believe too.'

'I see.'

It was decided that Sophia would arrange for a cab to take them there and then wait for them until it was needed for the return journey. She knew of a reliable driver who owned his own horses and vehicles, a man who would stay outside the property to help if necessary; the horse would be glad of the rest instead of racing around the city all evening. She would tell her father, despite his opinion on the subject and because she disliked deceiving him knowingly. He would worry all evening as it was and would insist that she did indeed use Tommy Patterson's cab, a man he knew well and trusted.

It was half past four by the time the grieving mother had gone, and it was time for the men's tea. Although she didn't look forward to wearing her more formal 'visiting' clothes in the heat, she felt a quiver of fascination; did this Russian woman have any true supernatural gifts like her own? But there was also, lurking devil-like in a dark cave of dire possibilities, the chance that the woman was genuine and would have, and worse, would give voice to an experience such as Sophia had had.

What will I do if that happens? One thing is sure; I'll have to try and shield Mrs. Worthington somehow.

The proposed visit filled her with foreboding.

Chapter 12

'Lost in darkness and distance'
Mary Shelley

THEY SET OFF at half past six in order to make their way across the city at a steady pace; it was still hot, still dusty and the cabby was careful of his horse. Crowds thronged the streets, and the noise was as great as in the middle of the day; the shouts of newspapermen, pie-men and other vendors, the clash of hooves, grinding of wheels, the thunder and screams of the steam engines pulling away from Victoria Station, song, shrieks and oaths from public houses; everywhere laughter, talk, calls, music.

It wasn't too long before they reached the building site on Oxford Road, where a huge building was nearing completion. Inside the cab they had been silent so far. Sophia tried a light comment.

'The new building looks quite grand. The Refuge Assurance Company, Father tells me.'

Mrs Worthington glanced at it for a second and nodded slightly.

They passed the University, and a way down the road, Whitworth Park where the open space and fresher air was being enjoyed by many people that evening. They sat on the grass; strolled arm in arm with friends; children and adults played together; they walked dogs on their leashes, and everyone seemed to be enjoying the slightly cooler temperature away from the press of the streets and buildings. Sophia noticed that her companion looked away from the park where families and couples were happy together; instead, she stared pointedly at the opposite side of the street, crowded with terraced houses and small shops. She noticed a tear slide down the other woman's cheek.

The cabby called down from the seat up front, 'Not far now, Miss Kelley.'

The passenger windows were open, but the women were forced to fan themselves busily.

'Thank you, Tommy,' she called, and to her companion she said, 'Medlock Avenue, Chorlton – do you know the area?' she asked. She heard him answering, 'Aye.'

Adeline's mother stirred herself from her reverie. 'I do. It's a well-to-do neighbourhood, certainly. My husband has many clients who live there, I believe.' She looked at her fan as though wondering what it was for, let it fall into her lap.

'Of course; he's well regarded as a solicitor.'

'I don't know what will happen to him now. My son, Gerald, works with him, a junior partner. I know he'll look after everything, but Arthur's at a loss, as am I.' Her voice tailed off.

They arrived at the medium's house in a few minutes and after helping the ladies out, Tommy Patterson prepared himself for a wait, unhitched his horse from the cab and walked her to a municipal horse trough at the corner of the road. When the mare had refreshed herself, he took her back and hitched-up in case Miss Kelley needed him in a hurry, but in the meantime, he gave the mare her nosebag, took out his pipe and settled back inside the cab for a rest.

The house where the séance was to be held was a grand villa, one of many in the secluded road. Here Sophia saw much to admire; the ornate brick decorations, the wide bay windows on either side of an imposing portico supported, tastefully by Corinthian pillars. All was set in a good-sized walled garden with mature trees of every exotic species that modern specialist gardeners collected. There were maples, magnolias, azalea, oak, birch and several different firs, a verdant collage, myriad greens with swathes of russet, ochre and peach as islands in a fertile ocean. And the early evening light was at such an angle that it stretched their shadows across the lawns and paths as if they were giant hands pulling the visitors inward. Indeed, people were being admitted to the house when Sophia and Mrs Worthington came through the gate and they joined them.

The door, highly lacquered in black with bright brass furniture, stood wide to receive them. Waiting at one side with arm extended in welcome, there was a middle-aged man. He wore a white linen suit with a startling blue cravat at the throat and he was deeply tanned; Sophia guessed it was the kind of tan gained by many years abroad in hot climes. He sported impressive black moustaches and held himself very upright, a military bearing; that and his height cloaked him with subtle power. He murmured discreet greetings to each individual as he guided everyone indoors where they gathered in the hall. A strange yet fearful excitement rippled round them in a fast tide.

The hall itself was an imposing space floored with marble tiles that were welcomingly cool on such an evening, and though they were creamy white when in shadow, in the evening sun they were bejewelled by the light from two tall stained -glass windows. Here there was more to delight the eye as the window depicted exotic scenes of golden deserts, pyramids, palms, and outlandish figures forever fixed in dramatic action.

Sophia noted with some pleasure the three large pots of Japanese ceramic that caught the eye, each holding an abundant and vigorous plant. There was a palm, an aspidistra and a large basil, which delicate plant released its sweet scent generously as people stirred the air nearby. A maid was waiting for the visitors and quietly gathered their outer garments. Everyone avoided eye contact with each other, remaining silent as they gazed around or studied the windows. There were eight visitors.

The man in the suit gave a curt, military nod and addressing them all said:

'I, Ivan Ivanovitch, greet you and welcome you to this house. If you will wait here for one moment...' His voice was deep and quiet.

A murmur of surprise rose from the waiting group as he suddenly turned and ran lightly up the staircase, disappearing into the shade of the landing. All was silence. A long minute passed then suddenly, from the balustrade above, came the slightest sound, a susurration of the tiniest, sweetest bells. Everyone's eyes flew up to discover the source but instead they were rewarded with a tantalizing sight that was surely connected; a cornflower blue veil moving along the landing, as though travelling unaided, a gossamer flying carpet on the warm air. Sophia felt a tension wrap around the group in the hall like a shroud.

Suddenly but soundlessly, there now appeared at the top of the stairs a figure, and they saw that this was the source of the veil; it was wrapped around the head and shoulders of a small woman and sailed out behind her as she moved. Beneath this mist of fabric, she wore a long white linen shift dress, cut straight and belted with a rope of gold that was studded with bright blue stones. Her arms were bare, and her skin was sunburned as brown as that of the man who had greeted them.

131

She wore a plain gold band about her forehead and beneath it streamed her hair, long and luxuriantly black. Sophia caught her breath at this vision. She leaned a little to the side, keen to catch a glimpse of the face, expecting her features to be as beautiful as the rest and complete the whole astounding image, but as the woman stepped into a beam of light from a higher window, Sophia was shocked to see that her features were so pale, so small, so utterly negligible and inexpressive that they faded almost to invisibility. It was as though a spectre was before them.

She has no face... she thought. *This must be the Russian, the medium, but how unlike the person I imagined. How could this frail person survive a Russian winter?* It was an incongruous idea, but it seemed to suit the circumstances. *And she is dressed as an Egyptian ancient of some sort.*

The phantom, as Sophia then described the vision to herself, floated down the staircase and had gone almost halfway when Ivan Ivanovitch reappeared and followed a discreet few paces behind. As the woman reached the floor of the hall, she paused; he stepped to her side with balletic grace and with a subtle yet dramatic arm gesture, he urged her forward into the painted light. Drawing himself to his full height, his voice throbbing with emotion, he spoke to the visitors.

'Ladies, gentlemen, I present to you all, the Countess Irena Petrovna. She welcomes you and begs you will be silent for the present. Sounds from the living cast a shadow on her aura; they may disturb the spirits that even now clamour for her attention, entwining her mind, her being, her soul.'

He bowed to the Countess and she, staring unfocused and straight ahead, drifted slowly across the hall. As the strange figure passed Sophia, a wave of disquiet shivered through her body. She supressed the feeling, but not without some difficulty, convincing herself it was nothing more than the anticipation of an unusual event. She was here to support Mrs. Worthington; yes, she was curious, but she was resolved to protect the bereaved woman from anything that would cause her more distress.

The Countess Irena paused in front of a long curtain of claret silk which dressed an alcove, and in a single movement she draped it gracefully over an ornate hook fitted to the edge of the wall. Now that the extent of the alcove was opened to the light, they all saw that the back wall was painted with a beautiful scene. It was one of the current fashionable landscapes of a classical countryside, somewhere warm and bright and painted in the style of the Renaissance masters. The Countess reached out and pushed the wall with the tips of her fingers to reveal that it was in fact a door. It swung open with the ease of a silk cloth waved in the air and she passed through to the dim interior of a room. The door closed soundlessly behind her.

Ivan Ivanovitch continued, 'You are here tonight at the personal invitation of the Countess. You need not wonder how she knows of your bereavement, for this is simplicity itself and I will tell you; the spirits of your loved ones, newly passed over, are desperate to speak and she, a willing vessel, has been begged by them to contact you.'

There was an audible murmur of astonished distress from the people gathered in the hall. Sophia linked her arm through Mrs. Worthington's and was unsurprised to feel the other woman's body vibrating with tension.

Sophia whispered, 'I'm here to look after you, Mrs. Worthington. Please don't be anxious. But, if you don't think you can manage, we can leave now; if you think you can't...'

'No, I'll stay. I'll find the courage. I am glad you're here though.'

Ivan Ivanovitch stood in the alcove barring the way into the room. His head was bent thoughtfully onto his chest for some seconds until he looked up sharply and announced:

'If you will follow me – but in silence, my friends, in silence.'

He stood back and swept his arm into the darkened entrance; the door was opened by an unseen hand.

They were guided by Ivan Ivanovitch into the room beyond and found it enveloped in shadow; faint illumination came from small earthenware oil lamps placed in niches around the walls. The Countess herself was seated in a throne-like chair behind a huge circular table. This table, surrounded by eight seats, was bare of any covering, its pale wood glimmering in the soft light.

The last to enter were Sophia and Mrs Worthington and Sophia took the opportunity to examine her fellow visitors. There were two men who were alone and separate, one very elderly and slow and the other no older than herself, handsome, but grey with sadness, bowed with grief she thought. Then came two couples and in each case, Sophia could tell from their demeanour, that one was a husband with his mother and the other were a married couple of early middle age.

So, she wondered, *that would mean that five souls have wished to make contact through this woman. How did she know...?*

The door closed behind them; they were shown to their seats by Ivan Ivanovitch, and his murmured directions were strangely mesmerising. Sophia caught the sweet scent of basil on the air; a gentle stroking of the senses bringing peace and a welcoming calm for her, and she hoped something soothing for Mrs. Worthington. But she sensed other emotions churning about the room; there were spikes of anxiety intruding sharply, a swelling tide of grief and something else, something unforeseen; there was also a layer of anticipation.

Is it elation or unease? Is that it? Why? Who is feeling like that?

Ivan Ivanovitch slipped noiselessly behind the Countess's chair and stood silently surveying the room. She, with both hands outstretched and laid on the table in front, kept her head bowed, was the very personification of deep concentration tinged with expectancy. Sophia could sense the tension in the woman's body; the air quivered around her.

The stillness and the silence lengthened. The visitors stirred in their seats, glanced at each other. Sophia laid her hand on Mrs. Worthington's arm; she nodded slightly, and Sophia took that to mean she would cope, but the next minute there was a tremendous and piercing shriek; all the visitors jumped and variously gasped and cried out themselves, staring about them to discover the source of the noise.

Sophia felt the scream surround her, as though it had come from the very walls of the chamber. When it rang out, she had her attention on her companion, so that when she looked up once more, she was startled to see the Countess standing. Her arm outstretched, she pointed it at the young man who had come alone. Her eyes were closed. He jumped from his seat, and stood, twisting his hands together nervously.

'Is it me? Do you have a message for me? Oh, please tell me she'll speak to me. She must speak to me now.' His voice was high with emotion, sweat beaded his forehead and his face flushed deep red. He was well dressed in an immaculate linen suit with a silk shirt, his blond hair neatly barbered, his expression desolate.

The Countess did not move; her eyes were still closed as finally she spoke. Her voice was low and had a strong accent that Sophia could only guess was Russian.

'You did not care for her as you should have. She is angry. She cannot rest. You must make amends.' She chanted the words in a monotone, her voice ringing out, bouncing from the walls in repeated recrimination.

The man trembled. 'I tried, I tried. She's always angry. What can I do, what can I do to help her now?'

The reply was terse. 'You must find her daughter, her lost child. She begs this final favour; no, she *demands* this of you!'

Her eyes flew open, bored into his and he recoiled, gasping, 'Yes, yes, I will – anything.' He sat down heavily and held his head in his hands, sobbing breathily for some seconds before getting up slowly like a sleepwalker and going from the room.

There was the sound of the soft door closing.

At that the Countess sank down again, closed her eyes and began to breathe deeply and noisily. She took four measured breaths before opening her eyes wide to sweep them around the table, resting for seconds on each expectant countenance.

She spoke again. 'I have someone standing beside me who suffered greatly at her passing. She was in such pain until the glorious release.' Her voice now was gentle, consoling. 'She wishes her children to understand that she loves them still. Who will take this message from the other side? Who takes it?' she repeated and gazed up at the ceiling until a man answered.

'Yes, I will, of course. Emeline and Albert, our children. My wife, my Grace. Can she hear me? Can I speak to her?' the man murmured, his hands on the table held in fists. An older woman next to him put a hand on his shoulder.

'She knows what is in your mind, your heart. She hears you wherever you are, whatever you are doing. She is with you, her beloved. She thanks you for your care, your devotion, the way you held her tenderly to your bosom as she passed beyond the veil. She knows your dear heart is full of grief. I see her holding her head, in such pain. Ah me! This tells me of her affliction...' She cried as if in pain herself, held her own head, rocking backwards and forwards on her seat.

He interrupted, his voice desperate, 'Yes, yes, it is her. Her poor head. She was tormented by seizures.' His voice broke. The woman with him, passed him a handkerchief then using another she dabbed ineffectually at the steady stream of tears that coursed down her own face, but nothing stopped them.

It was then that Sophia recognised them both then; she had seen them only last week, part of a funeral cortège', belonging to another city undertaker. She had also seen an obituary in the Evening News that mentioned a mother of two and with all the details that made it this couple who were chief mourners. If she had all this information, reason told her, then so could the Countess Irena and her people. But more important to Sophia was that she also could feel the presence of the poor dead mother in the room and see the aura of deep and desperate grief that hung about those who mourned her; a heavy load for them to bear. So, for the time being Sophia resolved to keep her mind open about the power of the medium.

'Love is all,' the Countess whispered. Her head dropped to her breast and she appeared asleep. She even snored gently.

Suddenly the room was filled with the trilling of silvery bells and the fragrance of roses wove around them, refreshing, delighting.

The Countess spoke again, but this time her voice was altered. It was light and her accent English. 'Father, Father!' she cried.

There was a middle-aged couple sitting next to Sophia and as the medium spoke, they both cried out in pain.

'Father I cannot see you any longer. Father!' came the child-like voice once more; it was a pitiful sound, like that of someone lost.

The couple clasped each other and cried out, 'Where is she? Mary! Mary, we're here, my darling!'

The answer was quick and seemed to come from the other

side of the room, 'Here I am, here, Mother, here. Only look...'
This time the medium's lips had not moved.

Everyone turned to the sound. The scent of basil intensified and in that corner of the room, which was most deeply in gloom and having the door on that side shielded by a long dark curtain, they all saw that a delicate mist had formed. Most distressing yet delightful to the parents, this mist seemed to take on the form of a small figure in a long gown. It did not move from its position, but its form was stirred by the air currents in the room and seemed to pulse gently with unnatural energy.

Mrs. Worthington had her hand on Sophia's arm and at the child-like cry had gripped with such an intensity that Sophia had to gently lift it and put her own arm round her shoulders.

'I'm here,' she whispered to try and give comfort.

Sophia watched everyone carefully, particularly the suffering parents. They clasped each other desperately, unable to drag their eyes away from the apparition, unable to move their limbs, only to cry aloud and yearn. A dreadful cry issued form the lips of the mother and she fainted away, held on her seat only by her husband's arms. All eyes then flew to the Countess Irena; she groaned, a sound of deep sadness that faded as she slid gracefully forward to rest her arms and head on the table, mirroring the distress of the mother. Sophia could not have said, later, when the apparition disappeared because they were all intent on the grieving parents and the medium.

Sophia rose from her seat and offered the father some smelling salts, which he waved away without meeting her eyes, his own blurred by tears. His wife recovered and they looked long into each other's eyes, both crying silently. Sophia watched them but realising that this might appear intrusive, she was about to look away when she saw that the curtain that was drawn across the door moved very slightly. A second later the whole bottom of the curtain belled out just a little, as though disturbed by the draught of a door opening, and Sophia felt a surge of disappointment that the spirit of the child might need to use a door.

So, a cheap gimmick?

But before the thought developed further, the medium stirred and holding her hands to her head appeared for a time to be confused. Ivan Ivanovitch was quickly at her side; he stood behind her and taking hold of her hands lowered them gently and then himself proceeded to massage her temples until she regained her poise. She kept her eyes closed throughout. Ivan Ivanovitch reached round to an ornate table behind him and picked up a silver thurible. It must have been lit earlier because Sophia had seen curling tendrils of smoke creeping gently upwards. He swung it gently in the space around the Countess; exotic incense now filled the air.

All was silent for a short time. Even the heartbroken parents were quietened, clasped in each other's arms, faces hidden.

Sophia was unsurprised when she herself felt a presence in the room, a kind soul, a homely, comfortable person. No trickery here. The soul that had come was as real to Sophia as any other person in the room.

Suddenly the medium opened her eyes, fixed her gaze on a far distance known only to her and began to speak. This time hers was the voice of an old woman, an English woman.

'It was time, my dear,' she said. 'Come to me soonest, come to me. We have never been parted so long before. All is peace. All is peace.'

The old man, who had come alone, had given a little start when the voice was heard; Sophia watched both him and the medium throughout the speech. His expression was welcoming, attentive and benign and when the Countess stopped speaking and let her head slump down to her chest, he

139

merely bowed his own head, as though all his hopes were fulfilled; he was consoled, soothed.

Mrs. Worthington turned to give Sophia a slight smile and she knew she the mother longed to hear such comfort from Adeline's lips.

Sophia felt the old woman's spirit leave and watched her husband. He sat back with his eyes closed, his hands folded in his lap, his white head nodding gently and a smile upon his lips as though remembrances of joy flitted tenderly across his memory and something else, he now wore a look of happy belief.

This peace did not last; he was soon startled from his reverie, as were all the others, when the medium gave a shrill cry. It seemed to come from the very core of her being and rise, unstoppable. But stop it did. She flung her hands upwards, one round her chest and upper arm and one covering both her both her mouth and her nose. She kept it there even though her eyes bulged, her face paled, her body shook, and she began to retch and choke – seemingly by her own hand. Her other hand now clawed at the one over her mouth. Ivan Ivanovitch was instantly there and tried to pull her hands away, but suddenly, without his aid, her hands were flung behind her back. She bent her head to her shoulder, raising that shoulder up to her ear and winced as though in pain, tears streaming down her face. Then she was still. Sophia realised that Ivan Ivanovitch was as shocked as everyone else in the room at the sudden vile pantomime, but he covered his fear so smoothly that she was sure no one else noticed his response; the way he paled under his tan and licked his lips nervously, the look in his eyes.

Mrs Worthington gasped, began to breathe in short snatches and Sophia felt her shaking so she took the cold hands in her own and tried to chaff them a little, even as she watched the medium intently.

The colour which had suffused Irena Petrovna's face, now drained away leaving her sun-brown skin greyed, her features twitching. Her eyes focused, but slowly; she searched the faces of her visitors and quickly caught Sophia's eye and held it. There was a desperate question burning in them, *Who is it? Oh, what is happening?* but it was cut short. As everyone watched, her entire countenance changed once more, this time it was contorted into a mask of terror. Sophia recognised it; she had seen that look on the faces of two other women. The medium clawed at the neck of her robe; she appeared to find some revolting object tucked in there and snatched it out, tried to throw it from her, found herself unsuccessful and batted away an invisible hand as it returned the grotesque thing to her. She stood abruptly. The expression of profound horror remained carved on her features and everyone gasped to see her place her arms solemnly across her chest. She became a statue, an effigy.

Ivan Ivanovitch was still beside her. Sophia saw that he was as frightened and unprepared for this as the other people in the room. He stepped behind her, murmured something and tried to gently move her, a hand on each of her forearms. She was a breathing sculpture. He turned away, stood silently for a heartbeat. Sophia saw him pass a hand over his brow but when he turned to face them all, he had recovered a little of his poise.

'Irena Petrovna begs your indulgence,' he said quietly.

People began to shuffle, stand, murmur to each other. They seemed impatient to leave now. Ivan Ivanovitch stepped forward; arms outstretched in supplication, his expression begging their understanding. Sophia admired his quick perception and his quicker explanation.

'The energies of the spirit world have exhausted her. Her aura, it is now dimmed; she must seek the balm of silence and seclusion. She goes to her cell to meditate and I beg that you will forgive her; your own needs will not be neglected and, fear not, she will write to you soon, a personal condolence and message from your own loved ones who have passed over.'

He stepped back to the medium and this time when he tried to turn her away from the visitors, she obeyed. He had to shepherd her carefully because her body was stiff, and her upper body retained the awful formal death pose with arms across her breast. She stumbled several times and each time he whispered encouragement; the lights dimmed, and Sophia saw the curtain drawn aside and another hand appeared to help the afflicted woman out.

The look of dread did not leave her face and Sophia was in no doubt, the medium was shocked into this state by the same psychic experience that she herself had had. Perhaps this was the first extended and truly frightening psychic experience the Countess had ever had, for Sophia knew that much of her performance this evening had been fed by chance. And artifice. She knew the woman had sensed the presence of the old man's wife, as she herself had, and perhaps by telepathy had known that the young man wanted to find his wife's lost daughter. It may be that the child was from a previous marriage and had been neglected by her mother in this one. Guilt had a powerful presence and was easily telegraphed to other minds, as were the thousand physical clues people presented, unknown to themselves.

The other people in the room were quiet, apart from the odd cough or sniff, a clearing of the throat. But when Sophia turned to speak to her companion, she noticed with alarm that her face was drained of colour too. She was stunned and unable to speak. Everything about her said she had surmised the medium was re-enacting a part of her daughter's death.

But she doesn't want to say this in case that makes it more of a possibility, more real.

Sophia knew it was. And she knew that Adeline Worthington had reached out to her, Sophia, again, but she didn't yet know what to do.

Everyone in the room wore the same incredulous, dazed expression. They stood silently and waited as if in a trance themselves. The silence was so profound that when the tiny bells quavered once more, everyone started. The lights were restored a little, enough for the visitors to gather themselves and file out of the now opened door, and there in the hall waited the same maid with their garments, and there also was a fully restored Ivan Ivanovitch. He smiled composedly at each of them and murmured thanks, and also his firm promise of hearing from the Countess on the morrow.

Out in the heavy air of the summer evening, Mrs Worthington looked about her, bewildered and Sophia put her arm about her waist, just in time to prevent her stumbling. With each further step away from the house, the stricken woman had faltered until Sophia was supporting her entirely. Once outside the garden gates, she waved to her cabby and Patterson reached them just in time before she fainted; together they got her into the cab. She came back to her senses, patted Sophia's arm, said she needed to be quiet for a minute, yes, she would be alright.

Sophia asked Patterson to take them on a slow walk around any quiet area he knew of because her guest was in need of a little doze before the journey home. Indeed, she was right, and Mrs. Worthington lay back in the seat, closed her eyes, and by all Sophia could tell, did fall asleep, the sleep of utter exhaustion and grief. They drove around gently for a half hour until Sophia saw her stir and pass a hand across her brow, as she woke.

'Miss Kelley,' she murmured, 'My dear Miss Kelley, I think I have been asleep, but it's time I went home now,' she said. 'Oh, my child, my child,' she whispered. 'Why did this happen to you?'

A silence lengthened itself for a couple of minutes, broken by Mrs. Worthington. She gave a deep sigh and looked at Sophia quite calmly. 'Thank you for your care. Thank you.'

They drove back along Oxford Road, along the boundary of Whitworth Park as they had two hours earlier. The other woman relapsed into silence while Sophia looked out of the window as they drove; the light was hazy with heat, but she saw clearly enough across the park and was not altogether surprised to see some people she recognised. It was a middle-aged couple, both dressed in mourning, and they were laughing together, arms about each other's waists, she with her hat in her hand and her hair loose in the evening air, he looked down at her, jacket over his shoulder. It was the grief-stricken parents of the ghostly child summoned by the Countess.

Her father, she knew, was partly right in his opinion of the séance business.

As they neared the Worthington's home, Adeline's mother spoke again.

'But I didn't hear Adeline speak after all, did I? I wonder why? I hoped to. I so wanted to hear she was at peace. There was no comfort to be had for me, was there?' she asked plaintively. 'Those other poor people felt some ease though.'

She did not mention the last minutes of the séance before the stricken Countess was led away.

Sophia could offer nothing to soothe her, but Mrs. Worthington had been right about one thing. Even though much of the medium's performance had been theatrical and creative, there was some truth and there was much comfort for some of the bereaved. Perhaps that was what gave mediums like the Countess their value and their role and Sophia could not find it in herself to condemn them for this.

Mrs Worthington's daughter-in-law met them at the door and took care of her then.

Sophia was driven home, to think.

In peace and quiet.

Chapter 13

'Early one morning,
just as the sun was rising'
English folk song

ADELINE WORTHINGTON'S funeral was held two days later. It was another beautiful summer's morning. Mrs. Worthington, her son and his wife had been to see Adeline's body in the Chapel of Rest the day before and had stayed above two hours, but her father was too unwell to accompany them. All the time they were there Sophia was anxious to have the coffin back in the refrigerated storage room, because the sad fact was, despite the embalming and the ice, bodies were not lasting as they might in a more typical English summer.

It was a desperately poignant funeral attended by many friends and family. St Ann's Church was crowded, people spilled out into the square. Nat was there with two other policemen; all in their smartest uniforms to pay their respects. But Sophia was annoyed to see a group of obviously curious strangers, the sort of people she had seen often, who, hearing the deceased had had an unusual death, tagged on behind the mourners, following the cortege.

Watching the grief of others.

She wondered what they got from this voyeurism; was it a

feeling of relief that they were not so bereaved or that they themselves were alive and well, or did they enjoy the pain of others, the perverse excitement of a heart-breaking event?

What a strange phenomenon this is, this schadenfreude.

Perhaps it was curiosity about anything connected with a crime. She heard them talking among themselves about the way poor Adeline had been found; their facts were untrue, but sensational. She wanted to shout at them, 'Wrong, wrong, wrong!'

They exchanged lurid details, exaggerated distortions of the truth; that the poor girl had been found naked, surrounded with flowers, found in a cellar, found in the cemetery at midnight, had been hideously mutilated, like the Ripper's victims. They were hungry for the melodrama of a horrendous death, especially one of a young woman. They seemed to revel in the very idea of youth and innocence despoiled. She added a more generous idea; perhaps they wanted to see the monster who did this captured and destroyed so that they could feel safe. Who could really tell why they did this?

She also saw a small group of men at the back of the crowd; a couple of them had cameras – the news reporters, hot on the trail of gossip. She recognised one of the men with notebooks, Johnson of the Manchester Guardian. The cameramen were taking photographs of the cortege, one ran forward and called to the relatives and when they turned, he took their picture. Sophia dreaded to think what the caption might be.

Took, yes, that's the right word. The photographer took the family's worst moment and will show it to the world. It's a violation. How can they do it?

But one thing was certain, the press knew there was a killer abroad in the city and would jump on every tiny detail.

Maybe the killer will see the photograph in the paper and will feel…what? Triumph? Satisfaction?

Adeline's father did not attend the funeral. Sophia was told by Alice, who had it from one of the maids in the Worthington house that the master kept to his room and wept.

The day after the funeral and early in the morning, Sophia sat on a chair by the kitchen door and thought things over. She watched the day's work begin in the yard.

Since the séance, and especially after this funeral, she had found herself increasingly examining her own psychic experiences; lifelong they might be, but she wondered whether she was being merely intuitive, highly perceptive, or was she simply prey to her own very creative imagination. There had been times when she had had a telepathic experience, had known the thought that someone then went on to voice exactly in words. How good it would be to turn that gift on at will, but it didn't work like that, to know exactly what another person was thinking.

She went over the séance in her mind; the Countess Irena, if she was indeed a countess, had some psychic ability; she had sensed the soul of the old man's wife, as Sophia herself had, but there were other more practical questions Sophia forced herself to confront.

It's possible this woman is an incredibly talented actress and the whole event a play of some kind. It's also possible that she is the murderer herself or was somehow involved in the attack. I suppose she could have been an accidental witness, hidden from view. That would account for her knowing of the death and, more importantly, exactly how it happened, or how it happened as I saw it.

It was a lovely morning. The sky was blue, and the heat had not yet built up; there was a light breeze to move the columns of smoke away from the city. She usually enjoyed watching the yard awake, the sound of hooves on cobbles, the laughter and shouts of the men, the soft snickering of the horses as they waited to be harnessed or led away for their rest. But this morning she was deep in thought and couldn't savour the moment.

Did I imagine it? The Countess could have been told of the murder by someone else. How else could she imitate the struggle as she had? Maybe, armed with this information, she wanted to use it to extract money from the family by promising contact with Adeline on the other side, and then inventing bogus messages? A confidence trick?

But then she remembered that the medium's own lips had been quite blue tinged as she was led from the room; she was sweating and she shook so much her teeth chattered, even though her features were stretched in that ghoulish expression.

No, she decided, *I don't think it's a trick; no actress could invent such instant physical reactions. She had the same dreadful vision as I had; I know it. Yet she wasn't in contact with Adeline's body, as I was, so maybe she caught my own thoughts, made that link between our minds just for a short time. That frantic look she gave me...she seemed to know of me, my own connection to Adeline. Goodness knows, my mind was full of her during the séance. Maybe the shock she felt was because she had never had such a powerful psychic experience before? And she could have had all the other details of the poor girl's body from any number of people who saw her, but one thing no one knew of but myself and Father, until I told Nat, was the presence of the posy...she had tried to snatch an object from the front of her dress, had looked appalled...was it the posy? It was in the very forefront of my mind – my heart. And of course, the murderer knew of it.*

Then she recalled the laughing couple she had seen in the park on the way home with Mrs. Worthington; that same couple, who at the séance a short time ago, had been distraught when they were contacted by their dead child. The mother had fainted to see the apparition. They were frauds and they must surely be in the employ of this Countess.

However much Sophia tried to lessen the validity of the séance, and recognising that the medium had some psychic ability, she was nevertheless completely sure, sure that the woman had also been a vessel, and that Adeline Worthington's spirit had reached out to her as she had reached out to Sophia herself. She'd possessed the medium, making her parody the final terrible moments in her life in the same way Sophia had experienced. Could it be Adeline's spirit wanted to prompt Sophia into taking some action? Did she want revenge, or did she just want the murderer to be found and stopped before there were more victims?

Reason finally convinced her that the medium had reacted truthfully, in that at least, and she felt a great relief. That link from beyond the grave validated her own experience. But never before had her own clairvoyant visions been so important as in the case of a murder. It was a sobering thought, and she did not yet know what to do with the information.

Michel, the wounded surgeon, was another unsettling factor in her world, simply because they knew little of his character. His very presence, his dependence, his growing relationship with the men and her household and friends was made a little difficult because there was one person who did not like him, but she hoped that only she could detect the dislike Nat was fostering.

Arnold Kelley and Daughter, Undertakers of Distinction, continued to be busy, but as Sophia and her father often said, sometimes there are more deaths than normal, and normal times are always busy anyway. It was a growing city.

The day after Adeline Worthington's funeral saw business as brisk as usual; the whole yard was busy with the men, the horses and even this early, a newly arrived or departing wagon or two, everywhere movement, endeavour. Harry and Bert, the two drivers they employed, also collected the newly deceased and they had just returned with another client's body in the small, closed vehicle they kept for that purpose. In contrast to all the activity, the resident cats basked in the full sun on windowsills or the top of the surrounding yard wall; and the three watchdogs lay dozing in the shade. The night was their time on full duty.

Chapter 14

'Time's winged chariot hurrying near…'
Andrew Marvel

ALBERT SHOUTED from the harness room.

'Eddie, I told you to get them horses washed down. Gerra move on. They need their feed too, when you've done. They've work to do later.'

'I'm doin' it now, Boss! I know what t'do! And there's no need to tell me about feed!'

Albert turned to Ernie and Davy. 'When you've moved that vehicle, see to the harness for this afternoon. Make sure it's gleaming!'

'Aye, we know.'

'*Boss!*'

'Aye, Boss.'

Sophia listened to the familiar dialogue as she sat there in the pleasant shade of the kitchen door.

She'd already chatted with Albert. The horse with the abscess had recovered. The syringe was ideal. Could Albert have a couple more to keep in his medical box, for future use? Of course he could and Sophia said she'd send them over with Alice later. It was a moment of peace to sit and listen to the morning begin. It didn't last; Alice raced across the yard.

'You'd better come, Miss Sophia. They're 'aving a bit of a 'do', up there – all three of 'em. That Michel might be quiet, but he gives as good as he gets, I'll say that for 'im. And that new vicar, he were a one; right loud 'e were.'

'A 'bit of a 'do'. A knees-up, is it?'

'I'm only just saying…and you know what I mean, Miss.'

'Mmmm. I think I do…' Sophia marched off across the yard with Alice striding at her heels. 'What happened? Are they arguing or talking with long words?'

Alice was silent.

'What did they say to upset you?'

'Pardon me, Miss, but it's not them as upset me.'

Sophia stopped walking. 'What then?'

'You, Miss. I know you're the mistress and I should keep to me place, but I know long words, as y'call them, even if I don't choose to use 'em to speak proper! I can read anything. Me dad taught me when I were little. Said as 'ow girls can do better than boys in learning. This were because me brothers wouldn't read, and he valued it. We 'ad books in our house, and we was all members of the lending library.'

Sophia repressed a smile, but Alice noticed and stood with her hands straight down by her side and with her chin up, remaining silent.

Sophia felt shame, rise and flush her face. This was a familiar feeling lately.

'You're right, Alice. And I am sorry. You're a model for any young working woman, and as I am a working woman also, I'll take my lesson from you. Will you tell me what you heard? Let us walk on.'

'Thank you, Miss Sophia. Well, as I were saying, I know an argument when I hears one as well as I can tell chalk from cheese. They were all talking about God.'

'God?'

'Aye, Him up there.' Pointing heavenward. 'Him that 'as a

153

short name – God.'

Sophia grinned.

'They've been going at it for a bit now!'

'How do you know, Alice?'

'I heard them yellin' when I were passing the bottom of the stairs, so thinking someone were in trouble I went up a few steps to hear better,' she said. 'When I heard they was talking about God, I thought I'd better get you, because folk come to blows about God. Y'should 'av heard them lot at the Methodist Hall back 'ome!'

The raised voices in the loft were audible across the yard and Sophia ran up the stairs, followed by a curious Alice.

'I shall be able to confront whatever is there alone, Alice.'

'I'll just see you're alright, Miss.'

Sophia smiled at the girl. 'Come on then,' she said.

The loft door was ajar, and the men's voices were loud. Sophia held a finger to her lips and took a tiny step forward. Alice joined her by the door.

Michel was speaking, his voice sharp and strong, his accent more pronounced.

'I am a Christian. Of course I want to go to church. Sacré Dieu!'

'Indeed! St Ann's is not far, once you are well enough,' Reverend Knightly said, 'I could show you the way.'

Nat laughed softly and Sophia knew immediately that he was not amused and was about to be sarcastic.

'Church? Why would you bother to give thanks to a God who allowed this injury and this destitution, this destruction of your life?'

'Why is it that you assume I want to give thanks? Maybe it is that I want absolution for something.' Michel's voice was tight with emotion.

Alice and Sophia exchanged a quick puzzled look then lent forward to listen again.

'And do you? Have you done anything that warrants absolution? You know, for instance, that there is a murderer loose in the city. Do you know anything of this?'

Michel gave an angry shout and there was the sound of the wooden bed being moved a little.

'Let me help!' Reverend Knightly spoke quickly.

'I can manage, I thank you.'

Then came a cry from Michel. 'Arrhh! Dieu merci! What is this? You push me down like an animal. You dare?'

'You were getting too excited. You should calm yourself, man.' Nat's voice was firm, authoritative.

Reverend Knightly interrupted hotly, 'Sergeant have a care, for pity's sake! Michel, please stay on the bed now; your injury... have a care!'

'Reverend, I thank you, but I can answer for myself. And, Sergeant Roberts, I say this to you – I thank you for rescuing me and bringing me to safety and friends, yes friends now, even after so short a time. But I tell you also that you should keep these accusations so vile to yourself. I am no murderer. How could I be, such as I am now?'

Nat didn't bother to answer that question. 'I asked about...'

Sophia decided it was time she went in before the situation became any more heated. As she opened the door, she saw the three men were glaring at each other intently. They all spoke at once when they saw it was Sophia.

'Sophia, I wondered where you were.' Nat was in a familiar pose; he stood aggressively with arms folded across his chest, glaring down belligerently at Michel who sat on the edge of the cot.

Reverend Knightly had his hands on his hips, head thrust towards Nat in bullish challenge. For all his elegance of dress and his station; his face was red, his auburn hair adding even more fire. He relaxed his pose when he saw it was her.

'Ahh, Miss Kelley, I was passing by on my way back to church and...'

'Mademoiselle Kelley, I must ask ...' Michel held his injured arm yet looked as ready as the others for whatever was next in the confrontation.

She cut across all their exclamations. 'Well, good morning to you, although you all sound like boys scrapping in the school yard. Alice here was fearful for your safety...'

'No, I weren't, Miss; I thought as how it'd be me mopping up blood...'

'Mademoiselle Alice, I would never...'

'Nothing was further from my mind, I assure...'

Nat interrupted the others. 'I only suggested...' and in seconds they were shouting again. It was impossible to understand any of them in the babble of voices.

The women listened for a minute but eventually Sophia threw up her arms.

'Come on, Alice. I've better things to occupy me than listen to a brawl between overgrown babies. The dead are much less noisy.' She motioned to Alice to go before her down the stairs.

'Miss, let me stay and listen!'

'Come on, we've work to do, Alice. I don't even want to know why they are arguing like this.'

Alice ran across the yard to the main house kitchen, where the housekeeper would be waiting for her and Sophia walked briskly to the work kitchen. She resolved to leave the three men to whatever was disturbing them and get on with her own busy day. Thankfully, the kitchen was empty, and it was beautifully cool. She went to the sink and turned on the tap and held her hands under the blessedly cold water for a time and then splashed her face, dried herself on a towel.

She was just putting on her brown work pinafore when

Reverend Knightly came to the door and as she turned to greet him, she happened to glance across the yard. There was Nat, leaving without coming in to speak to her, striding across and pushing his way through the men and horses to the street entrance, all without a look in her direction.

Why is he so belligerent today? Something must have happened. He can't possibly think Michel had anything to do with the murder. An odd thing for him to say.

She watched Nat leave, forgetting her visitor for a moment. Then snatching her eyes from the yard gate, she said, 'Reverend Knightly, please come in, come in.'

David Knightly followed her gaze. 'Thank you.' There was a tiny pause before, obviously desperate to speak out he said, 'I shouldn't make a comment on the relationship between two people who intend to marry, but I...'

'Then don't do that,' she said pleasantly yet firmly. 'Come in.'

'No, you're right and please accept my apology.' His face was still red and although his clerical garb must be warm, she could tell that the heat in his face had come from temper as his eyes were still showing the emotion, but when she spoke there was an extra flush of embarrassment that spread up from his neck.

'I wanted to explain about the altercation. Now I'm mortified; forgive me,' he said but added, 'Even a clergyman can be goaded beyond endurance. We are human, not God incarnate, merely his messengers on Earth.'

'The shouting match? It upset you. One of the others upset you?'

'No, no, it would take a great deal to really disturb me.'

But you do look disturbed...

'No, one of them went out of their way to deliberately upset – no, antagonise the other.' He threw himself down onto a chair and began to unbutton his coat. 'Pardon me...I'm

157

beyond hot ...'

'You look as boiled as a lobster. Reverend Knightly, do take your coat off. Don't stand on ceremony in this weather. Some cold ginger beer?'

'Ahhh, I thank you, yes.' His coat was off in seconds and hung on the back of the chair.

She saw the dark sweat stained patches on his white linen shirt and thought with some little amusement, *So, a real human after all – not one of God's angels.* Aloud she said, 'Now what did Sergeant Roberts, Nat, say to stir the broth the wrong way? You see, I've guessed the troublemaker!' She laughed and saw it eased both his temper and his embarrassment. 'He is like a dog with a bone when there is a case to be solved.' *His tongue runs away with him.* She smiled inwardly at the irony.

'They argued about why someone would still believe in a god who allows murder and poverty, then they disagreed about what kind of comfort the church could offer. When you had gone, I had to defend God, and my calling, so both Michel and I were both ranged against Sergeant Roberts. He was furious with both of us.'

'Oh, dear me,' was her mild reply. She would see Nat later and find out what really bothered him so much about these two men.

'Miss Kelley, I'm sure he'll tell you himself.'

'He might do. But I won't be shocked by whatever Nat says. I expect it was something about Michel. Nat is a man with a big heart which he hides, but he seems to be a little suspicious of Michel, even though he and I were the ones to find him and bring him here.'

'Hmm, the Church offers alms solely on need, whether to Christians or those who follow another god, or go another way entirely.' He mopped his face with a handkerchief.

'Yes, of course, and if someone needs our help for a time and we become friends, then we're the fortunate ones; that's the bonus,' she said. She brought two glasses of ginger beer to the table and sat down opposite him.

He took a long drink, pressed the back of his hand to his mouth, laughed.

'That was good.' He took another drink. 'We Christians offer help freely, with no thought of our own reward, or any ongoing relationship after that, but in some societies the person whose life is saved feels he owes a great debt to the saviour and it must be discharged or the person is dishonoured. It is possible that Michel feels this, and Sergeant Roberts doesn't like it.'

'Nat's not the Saviour!' She raised her eyes heavenward and smiled behind the glass as she lifted it to drink.

'You're teasing me again!' He did not look offended. Reverend Williams would have upbraided her, but gently, for taking the Lord's name in vain.

'I am. But we've strayed from my question. Please tell me what you were all arguing about – David. May I call you that, even on so short an acquaintance? And please call me Sophia.'

'David, yes, use my given name, please. And thank you - Sophia. Our argument. It was about God, as it happens. Michel, who seems to be a man of strong emotions and great intelligence; said he would like to go to church. Sergeant Roberts asked why he would bother to give thanks to God who allowed this injury and this destitution, this destruction of his life.'

Reported truthfully! Aloud she said, 'That does sound like his opinion. He is ever confrontational.' She shook her head thoughtfully. *Many's the time he's told me he gets truthful answers that way. Playing the devil's advocate. Does he suspect something? Is he just fishing for information?*

Reverend Knightly said, 'I am always ready to debate, the

row was not the sergeant's sole blame.' He had finished his beer and rose to put on his coat. 'Time presses. I must go, and I thank you. Firstly, for the chance to speak with you and secondly for your welcome since I came to the parish. You have offered friendship and on a very practical, everyday level, and it's most welcome. We'll meet this afternoon, in church.'

'We will. And I enjoy the way you give the funeral service. Comfort and hope are so much better than fire and brimstone punishments awaiting the deceased sinner.'

He laughed. 'Thank you. But tell me, I'm curious, if it is not too impertinent, will you marry in church as the sergeant seems so against God?'

She did feel uncomfortable now, but not because of the question itself, but because she did not know what Nat wanted. *How odd that feels.*

'No, it's not impertinent, but we haven't made our plans yet. In any case, I don't believe he's against God in any way. And to change the subject, I must go and see if Michel needs anything, see how the wound fares. He seemed so much better and spoke of making himself useful to us, then finding a place to live and an occupation. I don't know if he can still practise as a   doctor – I mean with the injury he has sustained, but Dr Smith may be able to help him there perhaps.'

'Michel seems to be a man who has much to offer. On the matter of accommodation, there may be room at the vicarage for a lodger such as he, and I'll canvas Reverend Williams, but now, I must let you continue with your day.'

She smiled her thanks and he left, just as cook rang the dinner bell.

Where is Alice when she is needed? Cook will be looking for her, I'll be bound.

It was then that Alice made a timely appearance with broom in hand.

'Reverend Knightly have a lot to say, Miss?'

'Is this your business, Alice?' She glanced at the girl and couldn't help but grin.

'No, Miss, but I just wondered. Sergeant Roberts went off in a right huff. Jealous if you ask me!' she said as she put away the broom and took off her rough apron to exchange it for a cleaner one to wear when she served the meal. She was wearing a pale pink muslin blouse which Sophia had not seen before.

'Jealous? Of what?' Sophia was incredulous. *I have given this girl too much countenance* she decided.

'Well, I've seen how that monsoor looks at you and how the Reverend gazes; moonstruck, he is. He's proper handsome. I do like watching 'im in church. Like a dancer, he is, light on 'is feet. Takes me mind off what he's sayin'. Y'know Miss,' she continued, avoiding Sophia's eye, 'I like the look of that monsoor now. Lovely eyes and I like the colour of 'im too. It's right pretty.' She beamed at Sophia. 'Reminds me of me sweetheart – the one as died in a cave-in at Maypole Pit. He were black alright! If you're a miner, you're all black half your life!'

Sophia laughed at the dark humour favoured by so many people in the funeral business about deaths, terrible deaths, and by the grim humour of those people of mining communities where death and danger were daily companions. 'Is that a new blouse, Alice? I think it's your Sunday best. Perhaps *Monsieur Michel* likes the colour…'

'I wouldn't know, Miss. It's just cool,' Alice said.

Sophia opened her mouth to retort and scold Alice for a whole number of things, but before she could do so, Eddy came running across the yard to the kitchen. He was yelling as he ran.

'There's been another one, Miss Sophia. Someone's been killed again. A bloke says it were in the cathedral.'

Chapter 15

'For whom the bell tolls'
John Donne

SOPHIA RUSHED OUT into the bright day. Alice followed. They paused at the yard gate. Sophia looked left down the road leading to the cathedral close; she was uncertain why she had even come as far as the gate.

'Miss, where're y'going?'

Sophia shook her head, not understanding what was in her own mind, what she was doing other than feeling drawn to the scene of death, as if she didn't have enough of death every day. She began to walk slowly down the road, staring intently ahead, arms hanging by her sides. She still wore her brown pinafore.

'Y'never going for a look?'

Alice was shocked, Sophia knew, and that wasn't a common occurrence. She stopped in her tracks as she searched to find a reason.

'I've got to go and see for myself. I think that's it. We've both seen the other poor girls, Alice.' She pushed her hair away from her face. It was damp; the humidity was awful. 'This might be another one murdered as they were and it might be...oh, it might be someone I know – you might know her too. Sergeant Roberts told us that a girl was attacked the other day, near the cathedral; Jenny, Jenny Hargraves it was. But she got away. The sergeant was going to speak to her.'

'Never say that! Yes, I do I know her, Miss – well, only to say hello to. She sits in't cathedral garden of a dinner time.'

'I've just got to go and see for myself, see if it's her! You can go back. Really, I will be fine on my own. You've enough to do. Go on, Alice.'

'Miss Sophia, I'm staying right next to you.'

Of course Sophia knew she could go alone, but right at the back of her mind she suspected that seeing a murder victim newly dead, and in the place where it happened, might be a step too far, even for one well acquainted with the leavings of death.

Especially since I saw poor Adeline attacked.

And Alice, she'd been into the workroom often enough not to be upset or even curious about death; as she said herself, there were plenty of people dying in a mining town, and, as she often said 'In proper nasty ways too.' But she did wonder how Alice, or she herself would react if they saw a young woman presented in death, at the discovery scene of the crime, and in a bizarre ritualistic pose, by the murderer himself - exactly as he had intended her to be found. Nat had told her how it was for the first two victims, but he only had it from another police officer. In fact, she didn't yet know if it was another young woman, another to add to the pattern, as Nat would call it. Still, she felt compelled to go and see the place, and it seemed as though all of Manchester felt the same way.

'Look at that, Miss Sophia; flippin' great crowd of people with nowt else to do but gawp at some one else's troubles.'

'As I am…Oh, come on, if you must.'

'Well, I wasn't about to leave you on your own, Miss. What d'you take me for? And what would the master say? You going alone to see summat like that!'

They sped up, despite the searing temperatures and fairly raced along the pavement, Sophia felt the heat of the stones burning through the soles of her shoes. Alice felt nothing of the heat as she wore her work clogs. The pavement was full, and they were almost pushed into the road when suddenly, right next to them, a horse screamed and reared. Its crashing hooves would have caught Alice on the shoulder if Sophia hadn't turned at the first clattering of its hooves and managed to snatch her away in time.

They ran on, Sophia oblivious to the commotion behind as the horse overturned its cart and then itself was pulled over amid a tangle of leathers and wood. Screams and shouts and the clamour of hooves and wheels on the cobbles, iron crashing on stone, added to the din. Other noises filled her ears, filled her mind, the cacophony of hundreds of human feet, hundreds of voices. Crowds of people were pouring down Deansgate, heading for the cathedral. They filled the pavements and as the masses grew, they spilled out onto the road itself, forcing carriages, carts, wagons and an omnibus to halt, as they headed their way towards the scene of a shocking murder. The news had spread like wildfire.

Voices, voices, thrilled voices! Sophia tried to blank out the sound of them, high and loud as they speculated, exclaimed, and bellowed their fear, their excitement, their anticipation. This crowd was so much more alive and dangerous than the morbid curiosity seekers at the funeral. As she and Alice caught snatches of the talk, they exchanged looks. They heard talk of the notorious Jack the Ripper, of slashing and tearing, terror-filled hearts and unearthly screams heard in the dead of night.

Alice caught her sleeve. 'Miss Sophia, Has the Ripper come up 'ere? What do you think? Did Sergeant Roberts say owt?'

'No, he didn't.'

They had to force their way through the bodies. Sophia took

hold of Alice's hand.

The crowd was a creature, a ghastly, spitting, gurgling monster, its furious indignation growing because a killer stalked the city, as he had done in London, and was preying upon the flowers of womankind.

Hundreds of people swept to the front of the cathedral, surged round the sides too; there was no stopping the tide. At the front of the building, police officers were stationed near the immense gothic doors and a pair of them also stood guard at the small entrance. Closed carriages were parked nearby along with a couple of police vans; all waiting for something. It was an ominous scene to Sophia. The horses snorted and stared around with the whites of their eyes showing, hooves stamped anxiously, and their handlers stood by their heads, trying to gentle them. The crowd formed a deep ragged line facing the police, but held itself on a tight rein, desperate to leap forward.

'How're we going to get anywhere to see anything, Miss?'.

'Elbows and knees, Alice. Failing that, simply squeeze through.'

'Nothing lady-like then?'

Sophia didn't answer, just slipped between two large men whose bodies closed back together as if they were lips smacking with satisfaction after a bite of something tasty. Sophia glanced quickly over her shoulder, anxious about Alice, but when she saw her elbow a tall woman in the side then shoulder ram another one out of her way, as Nat did to the opposition in a game of rugby, she felt a surge of relief. The woman turned and swore roundly at the man behind her and a row broke out.

Sophia quickly scanned the front of the cathedral. There were several figures standing there and she was surprised to see among them her friend Reverend Williams of St Ann's, deep in conversation with the Dean of the cathedral. Both men wore their ecclesiastical robes as though they had been disturbed

165

whilst leading worship, and their expressions were serious; both were shaking their heads. They were soon met by a third man in clerical dress, Reverend Knightly. He came out of the cathedral by the small side door to join the others in urgent conference. She wondered what they knew about the victim.

Someone in the crowd yelled, 'Who's dead?'

Others joined him:

'Is it devil-worship?'

'Is there blood on the altar?'

'What's goin' on?'

''Ow many's dead in there?'

''As the killer got sanctuary then?'

'What're the police doin'?'

'Gerroff! Keep t'yerself.'

'Is it another poor girl - a working girl?'

'Come on, who is it?'

'Evening News here – Rogers - has the killer been caught?'

Behind all the shouting was a cackle of noise, some angry voices, a constant rumbling of talk, some laughter and a growing swell of psalm singing from a group on the Shambles side of the building.

Sophia glanced up at the giant edifice; there were hundreds and hundreds of pigeons lined up on the topmost ridges of the roofs, ordinary city pigeons, some on the tiny, decorated spires and window ledges.

She thought, '*It must be so cool way up there as they are, in the path of any little breeze, away from the press of the crowd. They must gaze up at that peerless peacock blue sky, oh how lovely, and know that whenever they wish they can open their wings and rise up heavenward, soar away to green fields. Tranquillity only a hundred yards away. There's evil down here; it's as though the city is writhing in torment. That's it – torment...*

She couldn't supress a shudder of fear as she dropped her eyes down again to the level of humanity. There were now about forty policemen assembled near the vans, all wearing grim, alert expressions. Suddenly all their heads were thrown up and to one side, listening to a command that Sophia couldn't hear clearly. They swiftly formed up a tight pack, shoulder to shoulder, truncheons held forward for use, their free arms going behind the man adjacent and grasping their belts firmly. On the next order they marched forward, nailed boots crashing like hooves, to meet the spectators face to face.

Once in place they drew out into a defensive line, arms held wide apart, truncheons in hand to force people back from the huge doors. But the crowd, being an unruly animal that disliked the control, surged forward, yelling indignantly. A small bulge of people got as far as the gathered clergymen, forcing the police line back against them. Sophia saw Reverend Williams pushed over, a flurry of white surplice flying upwards as he dropped from sight.

'No! It's Reverend Williams. Alice...'

She grabbed Alice's hand and together they fought their way through to the front. The people were only a foot away from the policemen, each side staring into each other's faces, combative, energised; the spectators yelling, spitting, swearing, the policemen silent, some grim, some grinning, all imperturbable. She and Alice were only chest height to the buttons on a constable's uniform. Sophia yanked at his sleeve to get his attention.

'Excuse me, can I pass? I know Reverend Williams, I need to help him,' she told him. She could see the old clergyman was being helped to sit up.

The constable, formal at first, yelled in her face:

'Get back there, go on! He'll be seen to alright, Miss. Go on, clear off! He won't need no one ...oh, Miss Kelley, didn't realise it were you for a minute there.'

Sophia recognised him as someone she'd seen with Nat.

'Yes! Thank Goodness it's you, Constable. Can you let us pass? The Reverend knows me well.'

'Aye, go on then.' He glanced about him, probably to see if his own sergeant were nearby to stop him. 'Slip under me arm – and you, Miss. Mind how y'go.' He winked at Alice who raised her eyebrows, eyes sparkling.

Seeing them allowed past the cordon there was a sound like a indignant cry from the people nearby.

"Old y'noise. The lady's here for the vicar. Gerroff! Step back. Back I said. Step back there. Back!'

Sophia and Alice ran quickly to the old man. He was being helped to sit up by Revered Knightly who knelt to support him.

'Miss Kelley, a welcome sight. You've no idea how welcome,' said Reverend Knightly. 'You can help? I must see the Dean, urgently. Alice too, welcome. But what brought you here? Don't worry; I'm glad you are for my friend's sake.' Then to the older man, a little louder, 'Reverend Williams, Miss Kelley's here to assist you.'

The old man looked up at her, smiled.

'I find I am a little better, but if I could be attended to the cathedral, there is a kind woman who makes tea, a friend, and I should be grateful for both. A terrible day, my boy.'

'It is indeed,' David Knightly agreed, turning to Sophia, wondered, 'But, Miss Kelley, what brings you out in this crowd, to this scene?' He sounded shocked.

'We heard of the murder and somehow we were drawn here because we have prepared the two others. Really I don't know what else made me come.'

Alice bobbed a curtsey. 'Pardon me, Sir, I came to see Miss Sophia didn't get into no trouble.'

David Knightly smiled broadly this time. 'I'm sure she's

grateful. I know I'm glad of both of you. May I leave Reverend Williams in your care?'

'Of course,' Sophia said.

He quickly joined the Dean who was speaking to two serious looking older men, one was a police inspector that Sophia guessed could be Inspector Bateman, Nat's superior officer, the other was unknown to her. When she turned back to the old clergyman, she saw that Alice had made him smile again, so together they helped him up and slowly walked him to the small door into the cathedral.

Inside it was calm, beautifully quiet and blessedly cool, all in contrast to the simmering atmosphere outside. Sophia felt the serenity of the ancient place of worship wash through her body. They all three stood perfectly still. There was incense and the scent of beeswax candles on the air; underlying that lay the dust of antiquity and the mingled odours of the people who had, only that morning, come here to worship. Worship before murder.

The light swam ocean-like through the building, changing as people outside interrupted its flow to dart past doorways and low windows; here in deep corners it was dove greyed, there in front of a window the flagstones were bejewelled as it coursed through the stained glass. On the high altar there were golden orbs of candlelight. A door opening in another area of the building allowed a beam of vivid light to cleave the muted colours in half, a gilded knife.

They were looking for a bench to sit on when they were approached by a brisk old woman who, by the way she looked at Reverend Williams, must be the friend he had spoken of.

''Ere, Reverend, this is a t'do, in't it? A murder right here in't cathedral itself,' she called. She swept towards them across the huge stone flags as though it were a skating rink, her feet

169

unseen beneath her over long skirt. She was a small and very thin person of more than sixty years. Her hair was white and coiled around her head in a thin plait that was crowned with a flattened felt hat of indeterminate design and colour.

'Wicked that is, proper wicked, and I'm told it's a young woman! Poor thing, I say, poor thing. And I just 'eard you'd had a tumble or summat. Them lot out there, them police constables should have been watching out for the likes of you! That's what I think.' She threw a piercing look up at Sophia. 'It's Miss Kelley, in't it? How do? I'm Mrs. Jenkins, Mary to friends.' She threw an appraising glance at Alice and added, 'What's y'name, love?'

'Alice, Mrs. Jenkins. I'm here with Miss Sophia.' The use of the titles seemed to please the older woman. Alice smiled politely and not for the first time, Sophia realised that she was an increasingly self-confident young woman, comfortably speaking with people of any calling, rarely embarrassed by status yet never disregarding it. She took people on their merits.

Quite a new woman of the times. It was a good thought on a black day.

Sophia suggested that Reverend Williams could do with a little care and rest and asked if Mrs. Jenkins would undertake the task; she was warmed by the woman's ready agreement.

'I'll 'ave 'im up and doing in a tick. We're old pals, me and the Reverend, aren't we?' She addressed the question to him, and he added that Mary was one of his parishioners and had buried three husbands and six children. 'So, yes, we are old friends, yes, yes.'

Mrs Jenkins laughed a little. 'I'm married to the church now. Come on Reverend, us old 'uns'll get some tea in the vestry.'

But Reverend Williams didn't move straight away. He clearly had something to say. He pointed a shaking hand at a bench in an alcove. 'A moment's rest will be worth a night's sleep. If you please...?' He leaned forward and staggered a couple of steps alone, but then smiled his acceptance of the arms held out to help.

His surplice is clean today and he hasn't had a drink; his words are clear too. It's early yet.

'But the poor young woman who is dead. May the Lord have mercy on her soul,' he murmured.

'Amen, Reverend, Amen,' Mrs Jenkins intoned.

Once seated he continued, 'I found her you know. It was strange because I thought at first that she was asleep or perhaps had felt faint and lay down to rest in the dimmed quietness, there in the Lady Chapel. But then it occurred to me that her extreme stillness could mean that she was a little unsettled in her mind...the way she was lying there, a ritual pose.'

Sophia shivered. She saw Alice's face drain of colour, but she remained calm and still.

'It's evil, Reverend,' Mrs Jenkins supplied.

The clergyman nodded, didn't contradict her.

Sophia felt cold inside. *This must be the same as the other murder. A third one.*

Reverend Williams hadn't finished.

'And because of the way she was displayed, as it were, I was reminded of an effigy on a tomb, a figure of inanimate stone, just like one of the many in this place who have lain here since the cathedral was built. It's medieval, you know – built in the year of our Lord, 1421. Yes, 'the ancient of days'. But I should have recognised straight away that the poor body was but the empty shell left when the soul has departed. Yes...' His head dipped and his chin rested on his chest, his eyes closed. He was so still for some long seconds that Sophia felt a stab of alarm. She saw the others did too.

'Reverend?' She patted his back gently; he rallied with an embarrassed smile on his lips.

'Did I succumb to the entreaties of Morpheus? Ah! It's almost refreshing.' He nodded his head a few times as if gathering his abandoned thoughts. 'Yes, I should have realised she was dead. I did not do so for several seconds, seconds that felt like hours. I stood transfixed. Death has been my companion these long years, but you see, the difference was that I wasn't expecting the young woman to be dead – and in such a pose and in such a place. Nor was I prepared for the expression on her face. Do you know, it was one of pure horror?' He looked at each of the listening women. 'Her pretty face distorted so cruelly.'

'Oh, my Lord!' Mrs Jenkins exclaimed.

'And she was so very pretty. I knew her well and that was part of the shock too...but the Lord will take her unto his bosom and keep her there in perpetuity...' A tear found its way down the folds of the old man's face; he didn't wipe it away.

'Amen, Reverend, Amen,' Mrs. Jenkins added.

Sophia felt a jolt of alarm. It must be Jenny. Her mouth felt dry; she dreaded to ask yet must.

'Who was she, Reverend Williams?'

He took both Sophia's hands in his and looked directly at her. 'It was poor Isabella Waterstone, my dear. I have a feeling you knew her.'

'Oh, yes, yes I did. But I thought it was Jenny, Jenny Hargraves.'

'My dear girl, I know her too. Why should you think it was her?'

Mrs Jenkins gasped. 'Oh, my Lord! I know Jenny Hargraves. Don't tell me summat's happened to her too?' She laid both hands on her chest, as if to sooth a troubled heart.

'There, there.' The Reverend Williams patted her shoulder.

Sophia told them both what she knew about Jenny being

attacked.

'Attacked? By whom? Perhaps the same person who did this evil thing today. Jenny was hurt?' he asked.

'Not that I heard, Reverend. But she must have been terrified.'

'Oh, I think so. I will visit her at home to offer what comfort I can. Her parents will help, but I've known her all her life too. I must go, yes – but later.'

Mr Jenkins tutted. 'Oh, Reverend, you'll need to be in your bed early after such a shock as you've 'ad. Yes, you should, I say.'

'Perhaps you're right, but poor Isabella. What comfort can I give the Waterstone family? You see, it was the first anniversary of her mother's death and Isabella came to the Lady Chapel to say a prayer and light a candle. I saw her yesterday morning and she told me of her intent. Then this fateful attack today. She had a good job you know; she was Supervisor of the whole Millinery Department at Kendal Milne and Co, a very exclusive shop. She had six young women under her charge.'

'Yes, I know.'

Alice said, 'I always went straight to Miss Waterstone when I had things to collect for Miss Kelley and whenever I go down Deansgate I always look at the hats in the window there. Look like sweeties they do. Oh, and the dresses, frothy and brilliant. The colours were so fine. All the windows was full of things, a fairyland I always think.'

Sophia glanced at Alice; something she had just said rang a bell. *What is it? What is it?*

But her attention was suddenly taken by a sigh from the old man. His hands were shaking, and he was flushed, despite the cool of the building and she saw Mrs Jenkins looking at them too. This was a new Reverend Williams that Sophia hadn't seen. Maybe she hadn't looked closely. The man looked ill; perhaps this was the cause of his normal slovenliness, his slurred speech, his seeming drunkenness. Today he looked different.

Mrs Jenkins patted his arm. 'Come along, Reverend and I'll get you sorted. You'll be doubly upset then, what with the poor girl and them lot out there slamming into you, knocking y'down like you was a sack of potatoes too. Fancy that. I said to the char woman, y'know, Maggie, I said, fancy them doing that and 'im not good on 'is feet, I said. Them feet of yours; they're always cold, aren't they? Any road, I've got a drop of something for your tea as'll buck you up no end. Come along then.'

They all helped him rise and the two elderly friends walked off slowly together, arms linked, speaking as low and as familiarly as an old married couple. Sophia's heart swelled, despite the events, and she thought of Nat and herself. Would they ever be like that?

'Miss!' Alice hissed, interrupting her muse. 'I think I can hear Sergeant Roberts. Look, with those people over in't Lady Chapel.'

Chapter 16

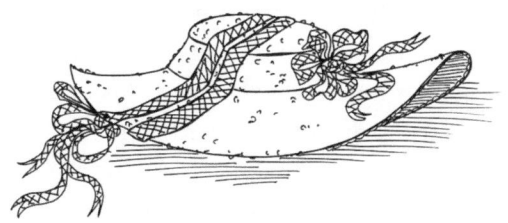

'Lie still, lie still, my breaking heart'
Christina Rossetti

'NAT? Sophia murmured. 'Oh poor, poor Isabella.'

Alice took the initiative.

'Poor thing, yes. She were lovely. But y'know, Miss, we just dashed down here, didn't we? We've not found out nothing yet, really,' she observed. 'She might not 'ave been murdered though. She might have had a seizure or something. My dad had a heart seizure; just dropped down dead, he did, holding onto 'is chest. We've listened to them gossips. They love a bad death. Come on, perhaps the Sergeant'll tell us summat proper.'

She took an encouraging step or two in the direction of the Lady Chapel, but Sophia caught her arm.

'Alice, the Reverend mentioned the expression on her face. Remember the other two girls?'

'Aye, I do. How could I forget, Miss?'

They made their way across the silent floor to the Lady Chapel. As they approached there was a buzz of noise that rose like a shaken wasp's nest. It was a business-like noise, men's voices, incensed, questioning, commenting, rising and falling with their emotions. There were also noises of heavy objects being moved, something metallic, wood, wheels. The huge building took hold of the noises and flung them from wall to wall in strident rhythm, alien echoes in such a place.

As the women rounded one of the giant pillars, a disturbing scene unfolded before them; there in the Lady Chapel was a hospital screen around something near the altar, incongruously medical in this place of worship. There was also a photographer's tripod and camera, a bag and some other cameras on a chair, wooden chests, chairs and several large men.

And Nat.

Nat looking straight at her, mouthing her name in disbelief.

She and Alice froze. Nat excused himself from the other men and strode towards them.

'Sophia, why are you here?' He demanded, but quietly. He flicked a glance at Alice, dismissing her from the question. 'What have you come for? We're trying to keep the curious away.' His voice was low, angry. 'And how did you get into the building?'

She put her hand on his arm. 'I'm not one of the idle thrill seekers; you know that,' she said, her voice contained. 'Davy came running into the yard and told us what had happened. It's Isabella Waterstone. I knew her.'

'I did too, sir,' Alice added. 'Anyway, I came to help Miss Sophia, in case she needed me.'

Nat glared at her.

It warmed Sophia to hear Alice's confident tones and she knew without looking that she would be standing boldly, her chin raised. Alice had said many a time that an angry policeman was nothing to an angry miner and she thought the sergeant was all noise, which had made Sophia laugh. A policeman could put you in prison, but an angry miner could put you in the hospital.

Nat didn't look at Alice now, he kept his eyes locked with Sophia's. He looked truly angry today, more than she had ever seen him.

'Well, Nat? It is Isabella isn't it?'

'It is,' he admitted.

Sophia was drenched with sadness – and fear. She trembled. Alice stepped closer, stroked her arm.

'Oh, Miss, that's right awful, that is.'

Nat rubbed a hand over his head and Sophia noticed, irrelevantly as one sometimes did at times of great emotion, the little things; his strong curls hardly moved under his hand.

Then she saw his anger drain; he flushed; his face softened.

Fear makes him hostile, as though it's an enemy to be beaten. Yet fear doesn't stop him facing up to anything, does it? Maybe that is true courage, knowing the danger but still going forward because you must.

'Sophia, I'm sorry.' His voice low, tender. 'You must go, love.' He turned to look Alice full in the face, a commanding gesture. 'Alice, take your mistress home. There is much yet to do here.'

Sophia laid her hand on his arm. 'No, Nat, let me see her.'

'I can't do that. I'm on duty and everything is official; you know that. My inspector's here too.' He took hold of both her hands in his, quickly raised them to his lips.

Alice interrupted, 'Sergeant, sir, we'll go then. Miss only wants a minute because she is an undertaker, as you know – well, I know you know. I mean, like as not she'll have to deal with the poor girl, as she did for the others.'

'Alice, don't overstep yourself,' he retorted and turned to her, his dark, fierce eyes upon her again.

'Yes, right sir, sorry.' She lowered her eyes, took a prudent step back.

He glanced behind at the Lady Chapel. They could all see that the photographer had set up his tripod and was taking photographs of something that seemed to be at a distance. There was a searing flash of light and a faint popping sound that, in the cathedral, reverberated like gunshot. A voice called from outside; the photographer looked up, as though recognising the summons. He took something from his camera, put it in one of his bags, then motioned to another man, possibly his assistant, to follow him and together they strolled out of the building. One of them had a small hand sized camera. Sophia noticed the two inspectors had also moved and were strolling slowly, deep in discussion, away from the chapel, towards the centre of the cathedral. She signalled this to Nat with her eyes and she saw his jaw clench, a sure sign that he was giving the notion some thought. He nodded agreement.

'Quickly then.'

In a heartbeat they crossed the nave. Nat opened the screen ready for Sophia to pass through and sent the two constables outside to help control the crowd.

'Wait over there, Alice. Tell us if anyone comes,' Nat said. She nodded and Sophia saw her move to a place where she could see the nave and the entrances.

Sophia and Nat slipped behind the screen. Everything was very still. A Milky Way of dust motes hung in the galaxy of coloured light streaming from the high windows. The altar itself was presently in shadow, and there, on the floor in front, Sophia saw that it was indeed, Isabella Waterstone who lay dead.

'Oh, Nat, it's as though she's some sort of offering,' she whispered, a catch in her throat.

'Yes. That's how I saw the scene.' His own voice was sombre.

'Reverend Williams found her I believe. How doubly sad; he knew her too.'

'It was he who sent the charwoman, Mrs Barton, out for a

constable. He said he wanted to get the woman out of the way before she saw the girl; it seems she had just lost her eldest daughter in childbirth. He and that old woman - a Mrs Jenkins, I think, draped an altar cloth over the body. But not much was disturbed by that, as far as I could tell.'

'Is she in exactly the same pose as the others were?'

'I didn't see them at the scene of their deaths, but I believe so. Look at her face.'

'Yes, the same expression as the others had. Terror. A dreadful death etched on her face.'

She had never told him about her psychic gifts, so of course she hadn't told him about her vision of Adeline's attack.

What would he say? How can I possibly explain that this is as much part of me as the colour of my hair or my skin? I was born like this. Will he understand the notion? He is so practical, so much a man that wants to see things with his own eyes, touch things, decide for himself.

They had known each other three years and were still exploring their relationship, learning more about themselves too. The latter wasn't always pleasant. It had taken them a year to realise they were in love and it had come as a shock to them, but a joyful shock. A complex relationship, often confrontational. Always passionate, always tender.

She frequently thought of it being like a train journey with many stations and wayside halts, delays for timetabling, halts for water or coal, logs on the line, landslides, snow or flooding and more and more passengers joining the train. The carriage she travelled in with Nat was luxurious, his company thrilling, and the passing countryside exhilarating, even if smoke sometimes blew in at the window and spoilt the view. There was no destination, just the lifelong journey.

I can't explain about the vision. Not now. Instead she asked:

'Nat, is there a posy?'

They stared at each other.

He said, 'You found the others tucked well down inside their bodices when they came to you?'

'Yes. But they had been to your police mortuary first,' she reminded him.

'That's true. And no, I didn't look down the bodice of this victim! We must leave things as they are now; the photographer has taken many pictures and I don't want to change anything in that evidence. The body will go to the mortuary soon. If she is brought to you to prepare and there is a posy, we will know a couple of things by that alone.'

Sophia gasped, saw the implications at once.

'That the people – the police doctor and his assistants at the Newton Street mortuary did not examine her carefully, did not remove her clothes or do a proper post-mortem examination. Or...'

'The posy was returned to its place...'

'For a reason.'

'For a reason.'

'What message will there be in poor Isabella's posy – assuming there is one?'

'I'm confident there will be,' he said quietly. 'In fact, I hope there will be so that you can find its message and we will have another clue about the mind of this killer. But the message...? I dread it.'

Sophia caught at his sleeve urgently. 'Nat, we must make a list of the main features, I mean the way she's laid out, what things are present here that were also there for the other poor girls.'

He was already taking his notebook from his pocket as she spoke. 'We should have women police officers because women always notice the tiny things.'

He dropped a kiss on the top of her head, and she replied with a ghost of a smile. Her attention was on Isabella's body, her eyes rapidly scanning what they could, what they could find without her having to disturb anything.

'The posy, we don't yet know about. But look,' she bent down near the head, 'only one earring. Like Adeline and Sally. I didn't notice with Sally, but Adeline Worthington had the tiny pinprick mark under her ear. Can I touch her ear? It's a little sore looking. Nothing else will be disturbed, I promise – the lightest of touches.'

'The ear only? Yes, go on, love.'

She crouched down and gently lifted the ear lobe, without moving the girl's head. 'Yes, there it is.'

Nat made another note in his book. 'The way she is displayed is apparently the same as it was for the other two, so I am informed; arms folded in this parody of an effigy, limbs straight, clothes straight and undamaged. And that expression of terror...it's startling.'

'Yes, yes, it is.'

'The clothes all these young women wore, they were clothes to be worn at an outing, not working dress, even for someone who worked in a smart department store,' he said. 'They were all attractive young women, prosperous too.'

'Yes. They all wore clothes to be proud of too. They were all dressed carefully. And, another thing, they were the clothes they left home in, not anything the killer dressed them in, which he might have done, I suppose. He seems interested in their dress - well, their whole appearance, as he straightens everything and gives them a posy. The families of both the others recognised the clothes and commented on them being amongst their daughters' best outfits. Another thing, Nat, the hair on both was unspoilt, as is Isabella's, look.' She paused as a thought came. 'Or he did their hair too.'

'Ahhh, maybe he did; you're right. I knew you'd see everything.'

There was a loud noise in the far side of the cathedral, a door closing, the sound amplified to a level that made them both aware that people might come at any time.

'You need to be going, love. Do you think the family will want you to handle the funeral?' He pulled her to him, looked down and kissed her gently before releasing her.

'We've acted for them before, her mother's funeral only last year, so they may well do. I hope so. Will you have to attend the post-mortem – or the examination, if the doctor doesn't require a full post- mortem?'

'No, I wouldn't usually be called on, but the Inspector might want to be there as this is the third murder, even though he wouldn't normally attend himself unless the circumstances of the death warranted it. The doctor would simply call him in if there were something of note, or put it in writing, perhaps talk to him later. Given what we know of the posies, all conditions at the police end should be the same as they were last time. Then if there is a person who has tampered with evidence such as the posy, they won't be put on their guard.'

'Will you tell your Inspector about the evidence we noticed?'

'Not yet. I need to think this through, get all the facts aligned in a logical order – then I will go to him. What I don't want to do is sound like one of the crowd yelling that the Ripper has moved up here. We'll keep everything to ourselves, love – for now.'

'And there she lies.'

The medical screens were rattled, Alice whispered, 'Miss Sophia! Miss! People are walking across the nave, heading this way! Three, no, four men.'

Nat acted quickly. He ushered Sophia and Alice to the side

door, called a constable over and told him to escort them back home, avoiding the crowds.

As they hurried down an alley, Alice whispered to Sophia, 'Miss, did I hear you talk about the Ripper?'

'No, no you didn't. Only that we don't want to add fuel to these stupid rumours of the Ripper,' she replied absently; her steps slowed, she stopped altogether, suddenly enlightened. 'A hat, Alice. That was it – what was on my mind when you were talking about the shop windows earlier. She worked in the Millinery Department; hats were her business, her delight. There was no hat there – in the chapel. The others had no hats. You mentioned it.'

'I did. No hats...? What does it mean?'

Chapter 17

'It was the worst of times'
Charles Dickens

'IT MEANS THAT someone has them; they're not simply lost,' Sophia said.

She glanced at the constable who was escorting them, smiled a little. 'I think we 'll be fine from here, thank you, constable. Perhaps you're needed back at the cathedral?'

'No, Miss. More than my hide's worth.' He grinned. 'Sergeant Roberts said to take you home and that's what I'm going to do – for you ladies, of course, and for me own safety. The sergeant's a tough one – but fair, mind.'

Both young women acknowledged the truth of his sentiments and quickened their pace. They were soon back at the yard, where all was bustling normality. The constable excused himself and hurried off.

'Only you and I left our posts then, Alice. I shall scold us both.'

'Can I get you some tea, Miss? Then you could tell me why these hats are getting you all het up. I mean, if you think it's right.'

Sophia nodded and Alice ran off to the yard kitchen while she checked the arrangements for the burial that afternoon.

A short while later she walked into the yard kitchen as the tea was being poured. Alice handed her a cup.

'I shall need to be getting changed soon, but just now, this is exactly what's needed.' She took a sip, sighed. 'I can't stop thinking about Isabella Waterstone. Sit down Alice, I'm not so strict a mistress, as you know."

Alice nodded, sat down. She cradled her own cup; the kitchen was comparatively cool and she shivered.

'What you were saying earlier, Miss, that you think the murderer took the hats. You mean it was like a keepsake – like some flowers a fella picks when you're out on a walk and you press them in a book, keep 'em 'til they go to dust?'

'Maybe that's it. Maybe he, whoever he is, has kept the hats for just that reason.'

'Oh, Miss Sophia, that makes it sound like he enjoyed it and wants to remember it.'

'Yes.'

They were both sobered by the idea.

Sophia filled up their cups. 'The families of the other two girls said they were wearing their best clothes when they left home but didn't mention missing hats when we exchanged the soiled clothes for their burial clothes.'

'No, you're right. Nobody mentioned it in my hearing. Hats though …I always like 'aving a look in the window of Kendal Milne's when they have hats there. They've a lovely display right now, when I come to think of it! Y'know, Miss, they're ever so tiny; it's the new style; just puffs of lace and feathers and a bit o' ribbon.'

Sophia caught her drift. 'And they are so small that someone could just push them…'

'…in a pocket or a bag or summat,' Alice finished for her.

'And just walk away as though the dead girl were nothing to do with you.'

'Left there, all laid out for her own funeral, like.'

'Yes,' Sophia murmured. 'And then they come here, and I lay them out in almost the same pose for that very thing – their own funeral. How weird, how bizarre.'

'Proper nasty, I call it.'

'I've some business to do; time is moving on. Things might straighten in my mind if I stop myself thinking for a while. Alice, you must be needed in the kitchen by now.'

She drank the last mouthful of tea and went quickly out to her workroom.

A heat haze shimmered over the tiles of the yard roofs. It was later in the afternoon, when the last of the funerals was done and the men in the yard were washing down the horses. The air was full of shrieks and laughter. The animals snorted, shaking off the excess; a rainbow arc of droplets flying all around to cause more hilarity.

What a welcome job on a day like this, Sophia thought. She looked forward to being cooler herself, as she was about to change from her black clothes into something lighter to finish the day's work, when there was a tap on the door of her bedroom.

It was the housekeeper.

'Pardon, Miss. There's a gentleman waiting for you. Very upset. A man, I think it's Mr Waterstone – 'im as is father to that poor girl today, down at the cathedral. Wants to see you, now, if you will. Very urgent he said. Oh, I forgot to mention, Miss, there's his daughter with him, the younger one, eh, dearie me, the only one now, I suppose. What are things coming to? I think she's called Christina, by the way.'

'Thank you. I'll come straight away. Can we have tea, please, Mrs Kittering?'

She ran lightly down and smoothed her hair before stepping

186

quietly into the Receiving Room. Always cool, the room was also welcomingly shaded from the glare of the sun as the building opposite cast a long shadow over the shop fronted window.

A man was pacing up and down, his hair stood up on his head, his clothes were all awry. His face, Sophia noticed with a pang of distress and pity, had a similar look of horror to that on the face of his murdered daughter. She knew him to be in middle age, yet since she had last seen him a year ago at his wife's funeral, he seemed to have aged another twenty years. His hair and skin were greyed by deep grief. Accompanying him was a young woman who sat quietly with bowed head on one of the visitors' chairs.

'Good afternoon, Mr Waterstone. How can I help y..'

He burst out, 'No one can help, no one at all – ever. And I beg you will not say how sorry you are. Such words are very painful to hear at the moment.'

She inclined her head. 'Please, step with me into the parlour where we can be more private.'

They followed her but even in the other, smaller, room he continued to pace up and down. Sophia sat down on the settee out of his way and indicated a chair for the young woman. They were just seated when there was a tap on the door and after Sophia had called, 'Come in,' Alice entered with the tea tray. Sophia saw her glance at the distracted father with compassion; they exchanged a look; Alice took her cue, bobbed a curtsey and left quickly.

Sophia went over to where the young woman sat and laid a hand on her shoulder.

'Can I get you some tea, Miss Waterstone?' she whispered.

'Christina; my name is Christina. Miss Waterstone was my sister's title, being the eldest. I don't want to take her place, yet.' She looked up at Sophia, her eyes brimming. 'But all the

187

same, yes, I think I would like some tea, please. I think it might do me some good, I mean if you think I should.'

It was difficult to avoid the man who paced out his grief in a staccato rhythm, but the tea was given. She sat next to Christina and before many seconds had passed, the bereft father stopped abruptly in front of them. His hands hung loosely, his shoulders slumped, his breathing was irregular and fast.

'I am almost at a loss, Miss Kelley,' he began but before she could make any comforting remark, he held up a hand. 'No. I beg you, no words. I said *almost*, only. My sole thought is to kill the man who has done this. I want to find him, somehow capture him and then take a very long time to kill him. I have been, just now, to the Police Mortuary at Newton Street, and I have done what no father should have to do, though many are forced by circumstance. I have had to identify the body of my daughter, my eldest child.' He choked down a sob, now clenched his fists until the knuckles were white.

Christina sipped her tea, eyes blank and staring ahead. 'I saw her too.' Another sip.

He continued, 'I saw her face. I want the face of her killer to wear that same terrible expression throughout the rest of time, through Purgatory and then on his journey straight to Hell where all the legions of Satan may deal him the most exquisite torments of that place to rend his soul as mine is.' His eyes wide and staring, held Sophia's. 'May the Archangel Michael capture his devil's heart as it leaves his body and pitch it straight into its punishment. Oh, how can God let this happen? How? She was all goodness, all kindness.'

Christina continued to sip her tea.

There was silence for a short time. He tried to breathe more steadily, failed. He looked near to collapse, and Sophia started to speak but his hand once again asked for her silence.

'They came running to the bank – *strangers*. It seems it was all over the building before my own under manager came to me. He came alone and told me the news. I did not know these people who brought it so swiftly. Everyone likes to bear bad news.' He squeezed his eyes shut, blew out a breath.

'I ran to the cathedral; oh, how I ran! Only round the corner, after all. They said she was in the chapel. I knew she was going there to light a candle for her mother. Those policemen, they would not let me see her there. Why not? I had the right. Who else? Everyone has seen her. There were crowds, crowds of people – there was *laughter* too. Why should the worst day of my child's life - of our lives...' He glanced at his other daughter. She sipped her tea. 'Why should it be their entertainment? Why would God allow this horror? Why was she killed, and like this - murdered?'

'Father, Father, please stop – for me, for a little while,' Christina whispered.

He took a ragged breath, nodded, laid his hand heavily on her shoulder then looked at Sophia.

'You wonder then, why I am here. I wish, of course, to arrange a burial for my child. She was with us, alive...only this morning, but...I want the arrangements made now, before I am incapable...'

His daughter interrupted. 'Miss Kelley, you arranged mother's funeral, only a year ago now.'

'I remember. It is the anniversary today.' Sophia's mouth was dry. She swallowed and turned to pour more tea, a distraction she hoped would bring a second of relief for Christina at least, and she herself was desperate for the drink. She had never before had someone in there who was so wild, frantic, furious in their grief. Dangerous even.

Mr Waterstone said, 'A year, one little year. Such a short passage of time in the whole of eternity but one that feels like eternity itself. Now another death to add to that abyss of time.'

'Father...' Christina tried again.

He did not heed her; his eyes saw only an infinity of sorrows. He said simply, 'She was going to light a candle for her mother,' he repeated. 'Just a candle.' His voice had dropped to a murmur.

'Sit down, Father, please.'

'I do not want another funeral.' He stopped pacing and looked down at the two women. 'I do not want her put in a box, lowered into the ground, buried under all that filthy soil, buried down there and left in the dark and the cold.' He threw back his head and howled, his arms clasped about his body in his pain. Christina rushed to him and wrapped her own arms around him, sobbing now.

The parlour door was opened. A tall figure entered smoothly, unobtrusively. Sophia's father. He took everything in at once.

'May I help?'

'Father, this is Mr Waterstone and his daughter.'

'My condolences, Mr Waterstone, Miss Waterstone. We are at your service,' Arnold said and on hearing the ritual words, the deep, assured voice, the grieving father and daughter seemed to slump a little.

Edward Waterstone took a deep breath and clasping his daughter's head very gently he pressed a kiss on her forehead and led her to her seat again.

'I'm sorry. I am not quite myself.' His voice was quieter now. 'You'll forgive me, Mr Kelley, Miss Kelley. I do not want to bury my child, yet I must. All that my daughter, Christina, and I are feeling, must be put aside for a short time while we do what must be done.' He stood up a little straighter.

'I don't want a big ceremony. I want no fuss and parade; there has been enough already today. I want a single horse and your plainest and best hearse but with no decorations. No embellishments or symbols would do her justice. Myself and my daughter will be the only mourners. She was everything to us and we will share her final parting with no-one but God. Therefore, I would like all to be quiet and private. My daughter will bring roses for her sister. She loved the ones in her garden, which was her joy and pride. We will go to St Ann's and Reverend Williams will read the funeral service and pray for her - her dear, dear soul. He loved her too.' His voice caught. He paused and collecting himself again, turned to Sophia.

'Miss Kelley I would like you to prepare Isabella yourself, if you will. Her sister will bring her clothes. Everything should be simple and quiet for her dignity.'

Sophia's father stood beside her. She said, 'Everything will be done exactly as you ask, Mr Waterstone. We will make all the arrangements to bring your daughter here today.'

Christina took her father's arm. 'Come, Father, Reverend Williams sent to say he would call before Evensong. Thank you, both.'

Sophia's father escorted them out.

Sophia sat down in the silence but not many minutes had passed before there was a quiet knock at and Christina Waterstone slid into the room, closing the door behind her.

'Miss Kelley, I must tell you something important before we leave.'

'Your father?'

'Mr Kelley has taken him into your kitchen, the one opening onto the yard and barred all others from entering. He said he would drive us home himself; he called for the brougham to be readied, and the blinds to be let down. I've just taken this chance to see you – I must.'

'Sit, please, sit. I am so sorry. Isabella was lovely, very lovely.'

'Yes,' Christina said. She covered her face and Sophia took her in her arms and held her until she was ready to speak.

'I have something of Isabella's that may help discover who killed her.'

Sophia was shocked. 'You have? What could it be?'

Christina had a handbag with her; it was made of tapestry in shades of ruby and magenta and was shaped like an envelope. Sophia had seen bags in this style in Kendal Milne's herself; they held more than the ordinary reticule and were used by businesswomen. She, like Alice loved to linger at the windows and gaze at the sumptuous displays, silk scarves, Indian shawls bejewelled with the colours of the East, sublime ball gowns that glittered in the sunlight, luxurious handbags fit to hold all the treasures of the world, not the simple daily treasures of a woman. The treasure in Christina's bag was a small leather-bound book.

'My sister, my darling Isabella, kept a diary and I thought you might show it to Sergeant Roberts. He was there when we were at the police station. He would know how it might help.'

'A diary...' Sophia breathed and took the book that was held out to her without thinking. She felt as though she had touched a live coal and her hand jerked so that the diary fell on the floor. A sprig of rosemary fell out of it.

There's rosemary for remembrance...

Sophia heard the words in her head, spoken by a woman's voice, a voice full of laughter and love. She saw a blue sky as though from the ground, lying on her back, and at the edge of her vision were long stalks of grass and wildflowers: meadowsweet billowing, buttercups aplenty, cornflower, clover, poppy. The air felt warm. She was not alone on the summer meadow bed.

A man's voice whispered, 'You know what buttercups say? *You are radiant with charms.*'

The woman's laughter, soft, happy. She murmured, 'Ah, the

language of the flowers; you know it so well. But I know a verse – Shakespeare, and although it's about marigolds and there are none here – I will get you some, my love, though this is from *A Winter's Tale* and we are living our summer story, are we not? Listen:

Here's flowers for you;
Hot lavender, mints, savory, marjoram;
The marigold that goes to bed wi' the sun,
And with him rises weeping; these are flower
Of middle summer, and I think they are given
To men of middle age. You're very welcome.

A cloud drifted across the blue sky above Sophia's head. The man's whispered reply was swift, indistinct, hard; like the hiss of a viper. He was angry suddenly.

Sophia found her breathing become difficult; in front of her face she saw a man's forearm wearing a fine blue cotton shirt sleeve, rolled up at the cuff. The back of the hand and the arm itself were covered in fine black hair. This was the arm in her visions. Her throat felt tight, she coughed, choked, felt a hand patting her back hard.

'Miss Kelley, Miss Kelley. Oh, what shall I do? Miss Kelley, are you all right?'

Sophia opened her eyes and saw Christina's face watching her anxiously.

'Oh, dear. Did I cry out? Just a dry throat – the weather.'

'You seemed to faint for just a second, then coughed and choked too.'

'I'm fine, I thank you.' She picked up her teacup and drank the rest of the tea cold. 'I didn't worry you, I hope? My throat is sometimes dry with this heat,' she lied.

'As long as you are all right. I expect the brougham may be ready soon. I must hurry. I read her diary. I went straight to her room when we returned home after...after we saw her. She has

193

only just left us – I know my action seems hasty today of all days, wrong. I know it's private, but it seemed to call out to me, as though her own voice spoke to me again, my poor sister. I so wished to hear her voice – and it's here in this little volume. Would you read it and if you think it useful, show it to Sergeant Roberts?'

She handed the small book to Sophia, who hesitated for a heartbeat before taking it, then feeling nothing unusual, allowed a relieved sigh to escaped quietly. She opened the diary and saw that it was filled with writing, a long sloping hand, carefully written and adorned with tiny sketches of flowers, hills, trees, hearts, initials entwined.

Her private thoughts. She never thought someone else would read them. But her words may tell me what she was like. I knew her a little, but not about her hopes and dreams. Christina's right: there may be something that points to her killer; she may have written about a man.

'Christina, your poor sister has only just died – today – yet you bring this to me now. Why?'

'I am frightened. I know there's something in it, but I can't puzzle it out just now, Father needs me by his side today of all days, and I may not get another chance to see you. I took a chance to catch you alone.' She touched the diary gently with her hand, stroked it.

'I saw a change come over her. She was never secretive but has been so lately. And she has been quite reckless, wilful, you might say. But this is only since our mother died. Isabella was talking of the future and of a dream house she might be mistress of – one of those big villas in Altrincham. When she went out this morning...' Tears sprang to her eyes and she dashed them away quickly. 'Only this morning, she was happy, dressed to go on an outing; it was her day off. She was flushed, radiant. I feel she went straight to her death and that this outing had something to do with it.'

'What hat did she wear?'

'Pardon me? Her hat? How has her hat …?'

Sophia interrupted, grasped the other woman's hands. 'It may be important, but I cannot tell you yet. Please trust me, Christina.'

The girl paused a second, holding Sophia's eye, until with a little shake of the head, she said, 'Very well, I will trust you, of course. She wore a tiny straw bonnet, the size of a doll's hat, full of silk flowers and trailing ribbon. It was jaunty, frivolous. Hats were her passion.'

'Thank you. I will keep this book safe and read it tonight. I will send my carriage for her poor body. Now that you have given me instructions to act for you, the police will allow her to be moved straight away. I will take the greatest care, do not worry.'

The young woman thanked her solemnly and left to join her father.

Chapter 18

'But thinking makes it so…'
Shakespeare - Hamlet

LATE THAT AFTERNOON the day's funerals were done; there had been three, two of them children. The men had brought Isabella Waterstone's body from the cathedral straight to the workroom and it should have been lying, as Sophia always imagined the dead to do, in a brief peace before the body was prepared for its funeral. But this body looked anything but peaceful. She drew back the sheet covering it and felt the up-draught of cool air from the ice blocks beneath the table. Rigor mortis had begun its changes.

Is there a posy? The question had tormented her all day, along with the assertion, *There will be.* Eventually she decided this was so, and she was so confident of this that the absolute certainty was chilling in itself. *What will it say? Oh, God, if only you, God, could tell me, explain why this is happening?*

Isabella was in the same pose that Sophia had seen in the morning; arms crossed over her breast and her final expression fixed and full of torment. No one had attempted to uncross her arms or close her poor eyes.

Can I see underneath her bodice? I can't move her limbs now without causing some damage and I want to be able to handle her properly when rigor is over.

She bent down and, lifting the fabric of the neckline she found that she was right; she could just see the edges of petals and leaves and using her long-handled forceps she was able to draw the posy out cautiously without damaging it.

'There.'

She took the tiny, pretty thing over to her bench, where she placed it with deliberate care. She stood back and stared. It was no bigger than the palm of her hand.

'What's here then?' she murmured.' She looked at the deep green foliage, just enough to provide a fitting background for the flowers; all tied tastefully with a white ribbon. She picked it up. All the elements were fresh, as though picked that morning. 'Ah, Monkshood. A tiny spray.' *Such an elegant shade of blue. Almost like lapis lazuli, exquisite, yet this flower signifies the approach of a dangerous foe.*

Sophia shuddered. *A foe – indeed. Isabella met hers. And what's this? Oleander – all parts are poisonous, and this too is lovely to look at. That deep frosty pink. But its message is 'beware.' And here – 'jealousy' in that jaunty little French marigold.*

The flowers themselves aren't evil but here, together, and for this purpose, they are the very essence of a murder's vile mind. These little plants speak, and we hear the message. 'For there's nothing either good or bad but thinking makes it so.' Hamlet – the old man, Polonius, I think. It's true.

She dropped the posy on the bench, sat on her tall stool.

The message here. Beware of jealousy, a dangerous foe approaches. But she is beyond all foes now – so who was this message intended for? Did the killer show the poor girls their posy before he killed them or is the message for those who will see their body after death? Who is it should beware then?

Her eye fell on the little leather-bound diary that she had put

197

at the back of the workbench. When Christina Waterstone had left to join her father, Sophia had gone straight to the work-room and had placed the little volume on her workbench, pushed to the very back. Her fingers tingled with the feel of it, her mind was still full of the scene in the meadow that she had witnessed when she first touched it.

Now I'm connected to Isabella too, as I am to Adeline. I feel as though I'm being urged by them to do something more positive than simply be witness to their torment. No one knows about all this but me.

'And there your poor body lies, Isabella,' she murmured. 'Dare I read your diary?

She turned to look at the book. She could not pull away her eyes, her hand strayed across the surface and the instant she laid a finger on the cover she was jolted back in time, into Isabella's final moments of life.

She smelt the incense and the dust, felt the cool air in the Lady Chapel sooth her grieving mind – no, not hers, Isabella's mind. The light in there was diffuse, soft colours were brushed across the floor and the altar. Later, when the sun moved round the building, the colours lent by the stained glass would sharpen to vibrant life. She heard soft voices singing, a gentle hymn at the other side of the building; caught the urgent sounds of the city that strayed through an open door somewhere, but she was within a bubble of gentle quietness, there in the chapel. Sophia looked down and saw a candle in her hands, beeswax by the scent. It felt warm and softening.

'I'd better light it quickly.' She placed it on the stand. 'For you, Mother.'

She held a single white rose too; the flower was almost open, and she lay it gently, on its own glossy leaves, at the foot of the altar.

She turned her head quickly. There was the sound of

footsteps moving slowly across the floor behind her, but Sophia felt no surge of panic in Isabella, or even curiosity, rather she felt that the presence of this person was expected, welcomed. Hands were laid gently on her shoulders, a caress, and Isabella lifted a shoulder, leaned her cheek down to touch the hand, return the greeting, content to remain kneeling, her eyes closed.

'My love.' A man's voice, light, anonymous in quality.

He patted her shoulder and walked away slowly to the back of the chapel. Isabella remained at the foot of the altar to kneel there; hands clasped together. Sophia felt the tears run slowly down her cheek as the girl prayed, and after a little while she heard again the same familiar measured footsteps walk slowly to the kneeling girl.

'You came back, my love.' Isabella said. This time, as she stood, ready to turn round into the arms of the man, one of those arms circled her chest, pinning her arms in place, facing away from him. The other hand went over her mouth and nose. Sophia's breath caught in her throat.

'Miss! Wake up, Miss!'

Sophia felt herself shaken, none too gently, tried to pull something off her face, wriggled violently, desperate to break away from the strength and the threat of that arm holding her, the shock of that arm holding her in that way.

'Miss, you've got to wake up, you'll fall over else. Come on, Miss!' Alice said urgently.

'Yes, yes, I'm coming...' Sophia muttered and then jumped violently as she felt water dashed in her face. She shook her head, pulled her palms down her face trying to wipe away the wet. Opened her eyes.

'Alice? What...?'

'Miss, I'm sorry but I had to do it; you were having a nightmare or summat. Here's the towel.'

'Do what, Alice? You had to do *what?* Why am I wet?' She took the towel, confused.

'I had to throw water on you; you were all mussed up. I think you were 'aving a nightmare about the sergeant.'

She saw that Alice held an empty water glass in her hand. Hadn't it been there on the bench?

'What?'

'You were calling him "My love", but then your face was all scared – like those poor girls. I was frightened for you, Miss.'

'It wasn't him, not Nat. I couldn't see who it was, but it wasn't Nat.'

'Who, then? Nightmare's is like that, though. Here, sit down again. I'll get you another glass of water, shall I? Here you go,' she said as she helped her mistress to her stool.

Sophia nodded, shakily, sat down and drank the whole of glassful that Alice handed her. Her eye fell on the small leather covered book that she had dropped on the floor and she took a deep breath before bending to retrieve it, hesitated before finally touching it.

Nothing this time! Thank Goodness.

'What's that, Miss Sophia?'

'It's Isabella Waterstone's diary.'

'*No!*'

'Her sister came back before they left and gave it to me. She wants Sergeant Roberts to read it – and me too. She thinks her sister was behaving unlike herself for some time before she died, and she thinks there might be a clue in here.'

'About the bloke what did it?' Alice finished.

'Maybe. Yes.'

'Miss, can I ask: why are you so upset? Is it just being woke up from a nightmare? Or is it these murders? I mean, I know it's terrible, but you deal with death all the time.'

Sophia looked at her, considering what to say. *Trust. Yes.* 'I can trust you, Alice.' It was a statement.

'Well, I 'ope so, Miss. You saved me after all, from a life of… well, summat bad anyway.'

'Sit down a minute, Alice. I need to tell you about something, and I have an idea you will understand and be able to give me some advice.'

'Me? What do I know?'

'Life, Alice. You've seen a lot in your life, a lot of horrible things. And you've come through them unscathed.'

'I wouldn't say that, Miss. I've still got the scars from when *he* beat me – and all the rest, y'know…. I'll not even say 'is name; he's part of me past. Well, if it's summat terrible you're worried over, y'know I'm not nesh. Don't fret, Miss Sophia, I can stand hearing owt.'

Sophia took hold of Alice's hand, looked at her closely. 'You had the courage to take a chance and escape from that life. I'll never forget Father's face when you jumped out of that coffin. It was like one of those pantomime horrors that everyone laughs at.' Sophia had to smile at the bizarre reminiscence.

Alice returned the smile, but with a wry grimace.

'More to fear from the living than the dead. The old mistress were always kind to me. It were she as took me from the pit-head and put me to be housemaid. Anyway, she were proper thin and I wasn't that squashed in there with her. I'd have done owt to escape …'

'You did!'

Now Alice was inside a crystal memory.

'I were jolted terrible by that wagon on the road from Wigan to Hindley and then that train ride, all the noise in that freight wagon. Still, the old mistress wanted to be buried in her hometown. I would have been dead meself soon if I'd stayed without her being there. He's master at the Colliery, now old Mr Barkley is gone too. Eldest son, he is. I'll spit on his grave when he dies, that I will.'

'I'll go with you, Alice. You've been a great asset to the business here.'

'Thank you, Miss, I'm glad. You've given me a home and a job. You got me meeting all sorts of people. I'm a different person now, thanks to you, Miss. There's not many folk would listen to a girl as jumps out of a coffin where she's been a stowaway – or give her a job. If I can help you with anything, I will. Is it something important?' Alice asked.

'I think you may understand what I'm going to tell you because you have lived through some strange events – one especially weird, bizarre event!' She smiled. 'And you can still see things clearly,' she said, slowly.

'Miss Sophia, I'm good at secrets and I'll believe anything at all that you tell me. I'll do my best to help if I can.'

Sophia told Alice about her gift and about the visions she had had.

Alice listened attentively, not interrupting, a calm expression on her face. When she'd finished, Sophia took in a deep breath.

'Alice, would you make us some tea and that'll give us both time to come to terms with what I've told you. It'll change things, having two minds on the problem.'

'I will, Miss.'

She went to do so and while she was gone Sophia moved Isabella's body to one of the body storage rooms. The new trolley with wheels made it easy. When the tea was made and a cup taken, Sophia turned to Alice.

'What I wanted to talk about was, not so much about the nature of my gift, but whether I should tell Sergeant Roberts about it.'

'He doesn't know?'

'No. I don't know what he'd think of it.'

'No, you won't; not until you ask, Miss. You *have* got a gift

202

and because these poor women have been murdered, and you know something about it, it's real urgent that you find out who's done it before any more of 'em get killed. And the sergeant's right, they all have a look of you. It must be someone local as knows where they work and such. The sergeant's official, and he can talk to people when he wants, find out things, so you might help him do his job better if he knows them other things from your visions. He'll want what's best for you too, I reckon.

'Yes, You're right, Alice.'

'And I'm not shocked, Miss. Talk about spirits and such is something I know about. There was a woman called Francis Faraway – well, that's what they called her, at 'ome. She was a medium and she were right good. She knew things other people didn't, about things they were thinking or what happened a long way away. She could give messages from people who'd died. Y'could tell they were real because it were only once in a while she did it and she took no money. Thing was, she always came up with summat really personal that only the wife or husband might know.'

'I think I need to read the diary and then talk to Nat. You've helped me make up my own mind, Alice. I can't show you the diary…'

'Oh, no, Miss. I wouldn't expect it. Miss Waterstone said for you to read it. It's personal, i'n't it?'

'I'll do it now then, before I start thinking too much.'

Alice turned to go, but Sophia saw her eyes rest on the little posy on the bench. She stretched out a hand to pick it up.

'No, don't, Alice, no.'

'Sorry, Miss I only…' the girl began.

Sophia picked up the posy herself. 'It's that I don't want you to be tainted by this thing; it's something designed to do harm,' she said and paused, undecided for a time, then suddenly making up her mind she said, 'No, I have trusted you so far, I know I can trust you in this, Alice.'

'What is it?' Alice asked, staring, mesmerised at the small thing in Sophia's hand.

Sophia explained about the posies and where and how they had been found. Alice listened patiently and when Sophia asked her what she thought she replied:

'It's evil, that's what it is. But I think the message is for them poor women first. I think 'e'd show it to them before 'e killed them, God rest their souls; told 'em what it meant, but before that I think 'e shoved it down their bodices to shame them some more and last of all it's a message for someone who finds the body.'

'But who? How would the killer know who would find the body and look down there too?'

'I heard she, Miss Waterstone, I mean, was took to the police station to that Dr Johnson? Did he find it then?'

'No, or he would have said, surely.'

Alice thought for a minute before adding, 'Perhaps I should tell you, Miss, the lads say that that doctor's a drunkard. Always worse for wear and short of money to pay for it too. And another thing, 'e 'as a sick kiddie what needs to go somewhere special. And he's got other nasty habits what need money to pay for them. Maybe someone paid 'im to look the other way – or not look at all, even. People do, Miss.'

Sophia considered the idea, nodded slowly. 'Very compelling ideas. But who would pay him and why? And if someone else were intended as the recipient of the message, how would the killer know if they received it?'

'That posy needs thinking about.' Alice tidied the tea things and stood, ready to go. 'Was there anything else you wanted, Miss? I'll be needed to 'elp Mrs Kittering now.'

'Alice, thank you.'

The girl paused by the door. 'Miss Sophia, can I say that I won't try and get above meself because of what you told me. I mean, I know my place and I won't presume. I mean I am trying to better meself, with your help, but you're still the mistress and I respect you.'

She left and Sophia was moved, her throat tightened.

She breathed deeply, tried to clear her mind, welcomed any guidance from benevolent spirits and then she opened the little diary at random, just let it fall open.

It was an entry from two days ago.

My dear, dear boy – for so he is. Past his middle years yet such a child. He was so disappointed to not see me tomorrow. Professional matters would detain him. Urgent business in the city. If only he would tell me what they are. I know nothing about his work save that it is so very important. And he is well regarded in the world. His clothes are so fine – his housekeeper looks after him well. I'll keep her on when we are married. Only think, our secret is soon to be known. He'll tell his sister tonight, he says. Her health is good and happy news will not prostrate her now. I long to tell Father and Christina. We are to live in Altrincham, a lovely suburb. So near to Tatton Park which was heaven when we visited. Christina will come to stay, he says. She shall have the pick of the warehouses for her wedding clothes. He wants me to wear pure silk, cream silk and Brussels lace. But the veil and hat are for me to fashion as I am the expert, he says. I can't even begin to think what I'll have. Something glorious. Thank goodness leg-o-mutton sleeves are no longer the mode and bustles are out of favour too. He hates both styles. And he says he wants me to veil my beauty a little when we are out in the world. He would share it with no one. I am his alone, for ever.

Sophia closed the book. '*I am his alone.*' *This is what she believed. What was the final betrayal like? Oh, her last moment.*

Chapter 19

'An ever-fixed mark...'
Shakespeare: Sonnet 116

A SULTRY EVENING began to steal into the city; the air was heavy with moisture and crackled with anticipation. People were saying a storm was on the way as clouds began to gather in a sky unblemished for weeks. Sophia had persuaded Nat to walk with her to the cathedral as the Bishop himself was to hold a re-consecration of the Lady Chapel that evening. Reverend Williams and Reverend Knightly were to take part. The place was to be cleansed without delay.

'Such a day, Nat, love. I've never had such a horrendous day,' she said.

'It's almost over and as you are with me this will be the abiding memory to wash away the rest – at least when we're alone again after this service.' He smiled, confident.

Will he feel like that later, when I have told him everything? What will he think of me?

'How long will the service last?' he asked.

'I don't know. I've never been to such a ceremony before. Poor Isabella. How can prayers wash away all the evil done today in that chapel?'

'Prayer is powerful, we're told. I believe it too. You do, don't you?'

Sophia glanced up at him. 'I do, yes, but I wasn't sure about you. We haven't talked about church or our beliefs much,' she said. She felt sticky and she was uncomfortable all over, apart from being drenched with anxiety too.

How to tell him about the visions.

She said, 'I think it's probably a formal ritual, one with all the majesty and solemnity of the cathedral will make everyone feel that the evil is cleansed, banished, exactly as Mrs Jenkins and Mrs Barton washed the floor. You know they stayed until the body was removed and then they've been there hours polishing and dusting, finding new flowers too. They're worn to a frazzle but anxious to listen to the service.'

He said, 'I hear Mr Waterstone is to attend with his younger daughter.'

'Yes,' she said slowly. 'You know he wants the funeral to be entirely private and very, very modest. Only the two of them as her mourners.'

'I would feel the same.' His voice was heavy with sadness.

They were near the ancient stone gatehouse of Chethams; few people were around. She pulled gently on his arm to make him stand still a minute. He wore a light jacket in deference to the solemnity of the occasion and was very warm. She wore a cotton crocheted shawl and a petite, subdued straw boater, a formal skirt and blouse instead of one of her lighter muslin dresses. Despite that, she was more than warm, almost feverish with anticipation of his reaction.

Sophia paused, irresolute, a flood of unease surged through her as she simply blurted out what was on her mind.

'I have something I need to tell you, something especially important.'

Her voice was so serious and the fact that she was visibly trembling made Nat gasp with shock.

'What? What is it, Sophia? You worry me now. Are you

hurt?' he demanded.

'No, no, not at all.'

'Is something wrong with your father? Have you upset someone?' He stared at her.

'Me? More you...'

He ignored her. 'Does it concern us, our relationship?' he asked; he licked his lips. His voice was stern, and some people would have judged it threatening, yet she heard the panic in it.

Her expression was confirmation enough for him before she added, 'It may, yes, it may affect it,' she told him, her voice now so tremulous that he pulled her round to face him, glowered down into her face.

'It's that oily clergyman, isn't it? You are drawn to him! He of the newly laundered shirts and brushed suits. He with the smooth manners and clean hands, that's it, isn't it? I knew I didn't trust him.' He had flushed deep red.

Sophia threw back her head and laughed, more with hysteria than amusement.

'You are a daft one, Nat. Or, as Reverend Knightly might say, *you are quite absurd*. No, I don't want to tell you of my sudden and irresistible passion for David Knightly, scar or no. And no, it's not the interesting French surgeon either. There is no other man but you, be easy. Anyway, I think Alice has an eye for Michel, thinks his colour is, *right pretty*'

He grimaced. 'Alice? She's just a housemaid.'

It was Sophia's turn to be shocked.

'You're outrageous. She's a young woman who is being educated and has turned her own life away from poverty, and, I might add, by her own courage and labour. And by the way, Michel, although he's a surgeon, he's now an injured and maimed vagrant with no means of support, so on those terms, Alice is above his station. You're not quite as liberal as you like to think you are, Nat. It's no wonder most people think the police are thugs!'

She felt fury heating her own face now. She was angered by him, by everything that had happened that day and suddenly found herself crying, silently, with tears coursing down her face. Her throat was painful with emotion, although which emotion she hardly knew - horror, fear, anger, love, sadness. Her nose ran, her eyes were tear-blinded, she shook silently. Her lips were compressed tightly to keep a sob within.

He didn't answer directly, he simply took a large handkerchief from his jacket pocket and wiped her face with it. Then he took her arm through his, covering her hand with his own.

'Come on,' he said, 'Come, this way.' He walked her away from the ancient arch, onward to the cathedral until they were on the shaded side where there was a little garden and a bench. It was cooler there than in the open and there was no one about. He coaxed her gently to a seat.

'Now what did you want to tell me? Don't tell me you've changed your mind about marrying me or I shall take you to the Irwell, or the Irk, that foul sewer - only back there by Hanging Bridge - and pitch you in headfirst.'

'Now, that's why people are wary of the police; the inclination to violence,' she muttered and sniffed as she wiped her own face with the handkerchief.

'Tell me then. I'll listen and not interrupt until you've finished.'

She felt his own arm tremble as she laid a hand on it to thank him.

'This may sound incredible, Nat, especially as I haven't told you of it before, but you need to know about it because it is concerned with the murders – at least at present with the murders, but not normally.'

He stiffened. 'You've information and haven't told me. What

can it be?' he exclaimed.

'You said you'd listen.'

He nodded, was very still.

'I'm worried what you'll do when I tell you.'

'Don't be frightened. I'll never hurt you and I'll still love you – I hope.'

'I hope you're serious in that. Well, Father knows of my gift...'

'From whom? What gift? Is it from the clergyman? He is wealthy.' He was ready to find his panic and grow it into a temper again; he surged to his feet.

'Be calm, Nat. Sit down, sit down, love.'

He did not answer. She could feel his tension and his own fear, and her heart melted to see him slump then like a small boy, shoulders bowed, hands loose between his knees, his expression building to a new level of wrath, ready for a life changing hurt.

She closed her eyes for a second, then began, speaking slowly.

'Since I was a small child, I've been able to see things others cannot: hear people's thoughts at times, know that something was going to happen before the event. And no, I can't hear your thoughts at will; it's not under my control in that way. Sometimes I can see in my mind's eye what has happened to a person by touching them or an object they owned. It is a sort of waking dream that encloses me in their life for a brief period. In short, I have the gift of clairvoyance. I'm a medium.'

She looked at him intently as she spoke, her eyes searching his face for signs of his thoughts. This was one time she desperately needed to hear those thoughts.

'You still love me and will marry me? This is the only, the sole thing that is of importance to me,' was what he asked when she was quiet, but did not turn his face to hers, as though fearing to see an unwelcome answer before she voiced it. 'Nothing else matters at all.'

'I'd marry you this very evening if it were possible. I will love you always,' she answered simply and from the very bottom of her heart.

Nat drew her into his arms and kissed her passionately, her eyes, lips, neck, every part of her face. Different emotions chased across his own face, dread, relief, desire. He crushed her to his chest as though they stood facing a chasm and she was in danger of being swept away by a hurricane of dread leaving him alone and howling into the winds of fate.

She had to thump his shoulder to get him to release her.

'You don't mind?' she gasped. 'About this, all of this?'

'So you are a medium; I've heard of this ability before – quite often, now I think of it. Strange we haven't talked about it really. No, I do not mind; how could I?' He cupped her face with his hands. 'I learned one of Shakespeare's sonnets at the grammar school; this part of it is what I feel, Sophia...'

He held her eyes with his as he spoke the words of the sonnet; and she heard his voice, not declaiming, nor arch and fatuous, but in his own everyday honest tones say:

'"Love is not love, which alters when it alteration finds, or bends with the remover to remove. O no! it is an ever-fixed mark that looks on tempests and is never shaken; it is the star to every wand'ring bark." You are that star for me. Will you marry me next week, or as soon as I can get the licence and the church arranged? Here, in the cathedral. Would that be possible?'

'Yes, and it might.'

He threw himself back on the bench, dragged his palms down his face, exhaled noisily. She saw his throat working as those his strong feelings boiled inside. He turned to look into her eyes, long and deeply. 'Now the world can come at me, strip me of everything, abuse me, turn me away, as long as I have you, Sophia.'

'You are strangely romantic tonight,' she said wonderingly.

His voice trembled with sincerity and simplicity when he said, 'This is how I feel with you, you alone. Always.' Then on a lighter note he added, 'Sometimes I'm forced to disguise the emotion – it wouldn't be acceptable at Newton Street Nick.'

They smiled at each other; eyes still locked. Her soul was satisfied.

All was soothing silence between them for a little while, as they listened to their own hearts, to the buzz of the city, the bubbling of the pigeons as they came in to roost high on the soot-blackened cathedral spires and roofs.

He spoke first.

'Tell me then, what is it like to be a medium then, love? I've heard some things said about this. These things, these visions, the people in them – are they what we call ghosts? You know, as in books or the pantomime, floating figures, mists and such.'

She scowled at him. 'No, I don't see phantoms...no and no mists, ever.' Her lip began to tremble, her throat tightened, how to describe it? 'If you have a dream, a powerful one that you remember when you wake, it's a little like that except that I hear everything and remember it all because it's as though I'm there. I'm experiencing the emotions or pain of the people in the vision. I can sense smells and feel heat or cold, other sensations; bright light or fog would affect my eyes as it would the people in the vision. It's as though I'm there in another place for a short time.'

He put his arm round her shoulder, offered the big handkerchief again.

'No howling dogs and wailing phantoms then?'

'No...' she said, her voice flat.

'Sophia, I'm only teasing. Find some humour, laugh a little, call me a clod.' His voice was warm now.

'You *are* a clod,' she said, managing a smile at last.

The sky was darkening, and the faint stirrings of a wind swept the myriad scents of the city flying through the noisome alleys and under bridges. It spiralled around the towers and trees, catching up dust and dirt in its wake; all the flotsam and filth was stirred to life after the long baking days of stillness. The heat was as bad as ever and the clouds gathering above the chimney smoke rolled onward.

Nat cleared his voice. 'We must go in soon, my dear,' he said as he looked at his pocket watch. 'It'll soon be time. But before we do, what made you want to tell me about your gift now, and so urgently? You think this is so significant that you mithered yourself almost sick before you could break it to me?'

'Yes, it is,' she said. 'Because I've seen things that are part of the murders.'

'What? You've seen…what? What is it? Tell me!' He was shocked, loud. His eyes examined her face closely to gauge whether she exaggerated but her manner was validation of how serious she was.

'I'm trying to gather the words…'

'Tell me! Please.'

He took hold of her arms, stared intently into eyes. 'What have you seen, love?'

'I'm used to my gift, but I know it'll be hard for you to believe, but you must, Nat, you must.'

Carefully, with much halting and searching for adequate words, she described the visions she had had for each of the girls, how they made her feel, the impressions on all her senses, especially smell and touch. She'd had no visions of the first victim's ordeal, nor from Jenny Hargraves who was attacked.

He thought through the information carefully.

'And she escaped the killer's clutches. I'll try to get permission to interview her as soon as I can. Nothing has been done yet. She may tell us something. But why hasn't she been spoken to before now?' He turned away, thoughts racing across his countenance. 'Love, you'll need to explain more if you feel you can. I know nothing of things like this other than what you've told me, the odd bit of gossip and the music hall séances you see advertised on billboards. Now you tell me you've seen things to do with the murders, will you describe more of how you felt, where you were when it happened, how it began and what you were doing? Was anyone else there in the room with you?'

Leaves, burnt to a crisp, raced across the browned grass as the wind strengthened, and she watched them while she gathered her thoughts carefully. The small trees in the garden softly undulating in the wind shook their parched leaves noisily and sounded to her almost like hand bells, as though they were shaken by tired Morris Dancers after a long afternoon's capering.

What odd things race through the mind at the wrong timed, she thought.

'I told you; I feel I am the person. And I can be anywhere, alone or with others. I experience the whole atmosphere: sights, sounds, touch, smell. I see nothing else around me, save that vision that comes to me somehow, in this case, through the eyes or as I feel, from the very spirit of the dead girls.

'They did not then see their killer?'

'No, I didn't see him through their eyes, but I guessed they knew him quite well. And I have a sense that the two victims whose deaths I have felt, keep a need within themselves to protect the man. It is too strange, but it's as though they feel he didn't mean to do it. I think they are in the habit of secrecy with regard to him, and even after death it is hard to break such a pattern.'

'I see,' was all he said.

She fell silent. *Does he really believe me or is it that he mistrusts the way I know these things?*

Nat said, 'I find it hard to imagine such a vision, yet I must. I must. I believe in you though.'

She was a little mollified.

'There are things I saw that you and I confirmed with our eyes and there are things only I saw in my vision, but when I tell you, you'll realise there's truth in it. And there's something else your policeman's mind, your detective mind, will relish much more. I've been given Isabella's diary...'

'Her diary! My Lord! My Good Lord, woman!'

'... by her sister. She asks that you and I read it because she thinks it'll have clues as to the murder's identity.'

'His name? Does she say his name?'

'Christina says not.'

His face fell. 'Perhaps it was too much to expect.' He smiled.

'Yes, we'll look at it later. We must go now. Oh, Nat this ceremony; it'll be so important for everyone's sake, but more especially for Isabella and her family.'

She stood, took his hands, tugged him up too. 'But one more thing, love – did anyone find a single white rose at the altar? It was in my vision; I saw Isabella herself leave it there for her mother. Perhaps it came to be under her body?'

'Yes, yes. I believe there was. Yes. I was there when your men came for her. I picked it up and thinking it had been forgotten by someone, I just placed it on the altar. It was somehow undamaged and fresh, heavily scented. See, you are making a florist of me! And a believer in your gift.'

He took her hand, kissed it.

'Could the rose be put where she intended it? It was for her mother. The killer didn't bring it.'

'We can see to that. We must go.'

They had only to walk round the corner of the building to get to the chapel, but in that short time, they had to shield their faces from the dusty swell and brush themselves off in the porch. The air was changing outdoors.

Chapter 20

'We walk in the light'
The New Testament: John : Ch 1 : v 7

THE CATHEDRAL was cool and dim. As Nat and Sophia entered, they heard voices raised in song, a low melodic harmony, a gentle hymn, a prayer for Evensong. It was the cathedral choristers who sang, unaccompanied by any instruments. Their voices climbed effortlessly to the highest point of the vaulted ceiling.

They are all here to bless the chapel anew, purify it. But for such a reason. How must her father and sister feel?

The choristers were in stately procession behind the crucifer, he who carried the processional cross, and their slow, measured walk and the swaying movement of their long white surplices in the gloom lent them a heavenly aspect. The verger followed and they preceded the Bishop and other clergy, all in most sacred vestments, resplendent with celebratory gold and blue embroidery, the blue in honour of Mary, Mother of Jesus. All walked with bowed heads, hands clasped in prayer. The scent of beeswax and incense accompanied them, flowed around them in benediction.

Sophia saw Mr Waterstone and Christina as soon as she and Nat entered the building. They wore black and were shadows

218

on the same stone bench earlier occupied by Reverend Williams. As Sophia approached with Nat, they looked up, recognised the dreaded moment had come upon them and silently, with heavy steps encumbered by grief, they joined the procession. They spoke not a word, nor looked to left or right.

The Lady Chapel glowed; no detritus of horror remained. Sophia knew that Mrs Jenkins and the charwoman had worked tirelessly all afternoon and she noticed them both, these two goodly women standing reverently at the very back, close together. Both had found something black to wear, a scarf round a faded blue hat for Mrs Jenkins, an armband of the same stuff for Mrs Barton. Outside the sky was almost hidden by the lowering clouds, but the chapel was illuminated, gilded richly by many candles. And there on the altar was the statue of Mary, flanked by two giant candles in gold candlesticks. That evening there was a strange and numinous beauty in the ancient place of worship that filled Sophia with awe.

Oh, and there is the rose. Sophia it saw with a surge of gratitude for Nat. *There at the feet of the holiest of mothers.*

The small chapel was full, the clergy, the few connected people like the Waterstones, she and Nat and the good women. It was a solemn ceremony filled with power and mystery, led by the Bishop and served by the lesser clergy, including Reverend Williams. Sophia watched her old friend.

He is full of sorrow, and tired too. But how determined, how sure of himself.

The choir sang, 'Abide with me,' softly at first and rising to its joyous crescendo. Their voices rang pure and true and as the final notes hummed on the air, the candle flames caught the emotion and trembled themselves. A profound silence followed. The Bishop stepped forward from the altar, spread his arms wide and struck his mitre on the ground three times in a trinity of sound that became thunder as it echoed throughout the entire building from its vaulted arches to its stone floor. In a voice confident of victory, he spoke the new prayer to banish evil, calling on St Michael, the Archangel:

'*Blessed Michael, archangel, defend us in the hour of conflict. Be our safeguard against the wickedness and snares of the devil (may God restrain him, we humbly pray): and do thou, O Prince of the heavenly host, by the power of God thrust Satan down to hell and with him those other wicked spirits who wander through the world for the ruin of souls. Amen.*'

He turned to the server who held the silver aspersorium, the vessel that contained Holy Water, and Sophia saw him take a long and very deep breath, saw him square his shoulders and lift his head.

He faced the congregation, his face ablaze with Holy purpose; he was tasked to purify all and as he lifted the aspergillum to sprinkle the Holy Water on the altar and the four corners of the chapel, his voice rang out, calling on those there to lift their voices and their hearts to glorify the Lord God and his blessed servant, Mary, mother of Jesus.

He moved from place to place, praying aloud the re-consecration and dedication. Finally, he came softly to where Mr Waterstone and his daughter stood and they both knelt while he laid a hand on each of their heads in turn and blessed them.

The Bishop returned to the altar and held his arms wide, head bowed in prayer and as he stood thus, a boy chorister stepped forward alone and in his pure voice sang, 'Ave Maria'.

As the last note rose to heaven, the ceremony was finally ended, and the clergy processed from the chapel. The choristers followed, and sang softly as they walked, the hymn, 'Mother dearest, Mother fairest'.

There was a stillness in the congregation before anyone stirred and it seemed as though there was almost a reluctance to break the spiritual spell. But leave they did, slowly, in small groups. Only the bereaved family lingered by the altar in silent prayer, arms around each other. Nat and Sophia left them to their grief. She chanced to look back over her shoulder and saw Christina pointing out the rose to her father who clearly recognised it as one from Isabella's garden; he put his hands to his face, sobbed anew. The candles burnt strongly and lent a kindly light to the poignant scene while outside there was the first ominous deep rumble of thunder.

Sophia looked up at Nat and realised something.

'You didn't have time to put the rose there, did you?'

He was about to answer when they were interrupted by a woman's voice. It was Maggie Barton, the charwoman who was walking out with Mrs Jenkins and had chanced to hear.

'Begging pardon, Miss, it were me. I saw it there on the floor when everything was gone. Me and Mary 'ere was cleaning. I put it there for my daughter as passed away last week through childbirth. I didn't think the young woman as died here would mind somehow. I 'ope I done no wrong.'

'No, I don't think she would mind at all. She was truly kind, don't worry. She'd brought the rose for her own mother and was no stranger to grief, Mrs Barton. I've not had the chance to say how sorry I am to hear about your daughter,' Sophia said, and the women fell into a conversation while Nat strolled on slowly.

Just as she and the women were taking leave of each other, Sophia saw Reverend Knightly approaching, head bowed and still wearing his vestments. He looked wholly at one with his surroundings, a man of the church. Each time she had glanced at him during the service, she had noticed how very absorbed he was, his face glowed, his hands trembled in the urgency of his prayer. Every fibre of his being was invested in his belief. This evening, she too had felt surrounded by the presence of

God in the Lady Chapel, but when she attended church at other times in the course of her work, she experienced no special emotions and feeling the contrast, her faith was renewed. Her visions sometimes alarmed her, often surprised her but never, even when they showed the terrible events recently, did she feel they were anything other than God given. She had a gift that could be used for good purpose; of that she was sure.

Her eyes roamed the cathedral as she walked over to meet Reverend Knightly.

There's Nat, all the way over there. Is that Inspector Bateman? It must be. They look very intent. Perhaps Nat is relaying the information about the two young women.

She smiled as Reverend Knightly approached. Over his shoulder she could see that a third man had joined Nat and his Inspector.

Surely that's Dr Smith? Too tall? No, it is him. I hadn't realised how big he is, similar in size to Nat. He's joining them; they're interested in what he's saying. Maybe he noticed something on the bodies that Dr Johnson missed.

Her attention was taken by David Knightly.

'Miss Kelley – Sophia. It is good to see you here tonight and after such a day,' he said. He was quiet and serious.

'I wanted to be here; it's a special place for me, as for many. I also came to see the place reconsecrated, cleansed - because of poor Isabella, of course.'

He nodded; hands still clasped before him in clerical stance. He was solemn.

'Murder. The worst sin. Sometimes a man is killed out of fear for one's own safety, or by accident, but this is beyond anything I've experienced before. You see, I've led a sheltered life, as I told you. Reverend Williams has been asked to read the funeral service because he knows the family well. I'm told they want only him. They would like her buried in our churchyard and the Bishop has given permission in this special case. It's but a small cemetery as you know.'

'And her father's asked us to handle the funeral. She herself lies in my workroom,' Sophia told him.

'Is that so? Reverend Williams will be comforted by that. The poor man is unwell tonight but insisted he play his part in the re-consecration. I have just sent him back to the vicarage with two reliable young men – choristers, and in a cab. It is not so far back to St Ann's Place yet much too far for him to walk, I think.'

'That was kind.'

He continued, 'He's very anxious to read the service for poor Miss Waterstone; it's of the greatest importance to him, but I'll be there to offer my support - in the background only.'

She told him of Mr Waterstone's instructions about the funeral.

'How tragic a death for anyone, let alone a young woman in the prime of her life. I can take Reverend Williams to speak to the family if it would be of comfort, but we'll have to see how well he recovers from this day itself. I'd arrange a cab, of course. This has been a great blow to the old man. Do not worry, I mean no disrespect and even in so short an acquaintance with him, living under the same roof, I can see his sincerity and his great talent as a priest.'

'I've known him all my life, it seems. But have you a doctor nearby in case he needs it?' she wondered, not knowing who the vicarage called on at such times.

'We shall soon have. I perhaps overstep myself when I tell you that your guest, Michel, a doctor, as you know, will soon be leaving you, because the Reverend Williams joins with me in offering him lodging at the vicarage.'

'Ahhh,'

'He hopes to find some useful medical employment too. I believe your good Dr Smith can use him in a suitable capacity; but in the meantime, as he heals and regains his fitness, he'll be on hand to help our old friend.' He winced. 'I meant no pun about the hand! I am not thinking clearly. He will advise and use his knowledge. Michel intends to speak to you and Mr Kelley himself, and I know how much he feels indebted to you.' He looked closely at her, searching her face for some sign of disappointment or offence.

'I'm not offended, worry not, David,' she said, returning the smile that lit his face when she said his Christian name. 'It's as well and I'm glad for all parties; I think the men are a little in awe of Michel's learning and experience in the world, that is, apart from Albert, our Yard Manager and Head Groom. It appears he's a dark horse, excuse my pun there, and has travelled the world like Michel, speaks French fluently too. But it will be good for Michel to move somewhere less rowdy and busy, and I hope he can help Reverend Williams.'

Her eyes flew to a figure looming out of the darkness that was gathering behind her companion.

'Ah, here's Nat.'

Reverend Knightly turned around quickly. His expression was a little guarded, she thought but wasn't surprised given that Nat was rushing towards them like a charging bull. Nat's own expression was as mysterious as the light had become in the cathedral. He was in haste. He was stopped in his rush as there came a mighty rumble of thunder that was so deep and lasted so long that everyone in the building halted what they were doing to look heavenward yet for purely earthly reasons. It sounded as though the ancient place were tumbling down around them.

'Sophia...' Nat shouted but was halted again as, before the last tremor of the thunder had ceased, fierce lightning cracked the air all around them, filling the building, plunging the whole of their consciousness into a light as intense as the centre of the sun.

Sophia fell to the ground in fear, her arms wrapped over her head and felt someone throw themselves over her protectively. It was David Knightly. No one could see clearly; the lightning had blinded them for long seconds. She fought to lift David's robes from over her face where they had been flung. They had served to protect her eyes and she saw, in a single agonising glimpse, that Nat was some little distance away. Blood streamed down his face. He was standing very still. Small lumps of stone and plaster had fallen, she thought from the low arch above him, and dust coated his shoulders. He swayed.

Another massive boom of thunder shook the building, the city, and it seemed to her, the whole world. With it, another explosion of lightning to rend the evening air and this time everyone in the cathedral heard it strike and heard quite clearly the following avalanche of masonry – something close by had been hit.

At last she threw off the robe that pinned her down. 'Nat!' she screamed, trying to rise.

'Stay here. I'll cover you!' David Knightly shouted. He pulled her arm and being unbalanced she fell backwards onto him.

Nat ran past her and David and to the door near the Lady Chapel. He didn't seem to see her; he was intent on something else. The sound of falling stone came from that side of the building.

The air was full of screams. The two dreaded twins of thunder lightning assaulted the city once more.

Then rain.

Louder than the thunder it came, beating down on the roofs, the filthy pavements, the drying rivers, the scorched trees and the people themselves. Rain. It beat a never-ending tattoo, plummeting down as though a million taps, pumps, waterfalls were trying to flatten the city and wash it away. The downpour hit the pavements and surged straight up again, creating a boiling mist a yard high.

More thunder hit ears that throbbed with pain; more lightning seared vision still blurred from the first flash. But the storm was moving further away every minute, mile by mile and instead of filling the cathedral with primeval white light, each receding flash now streamed through every window at once, whatever side of the building it graced; every piece of stained glass shone in its glory, instead of displaying its riches only when the sun directly allowed it.

Sophia struggled to her feet, away from David's arms and stood up looking after Nat. The last she saw of him was his silhouette in the open door, the deluging rain before him, his body bent ready to spring forward. When the next crash of thunder sounded, and lightning filled her sight, he was gone.

Amid the shouts and frightened screams that now took the place of the thunder in the cathedral, she heard a faint rhythmic sound getting slightly louder with each beat. Her ears felt as though they were pressed full of wool, and as it became a little louder, she realised that was because it was coming nearer and recognised it as running footsteps. Before she could turn to find who it might be, and to what purpose this speed, Dr Smith streaked past her. He flew through the same door where Nat had been.

What can it be? Have they discovered something? Oh, Nat, but you're hurt.

Chapter 21

'Words, words, words'
Shakespeare - Hamlet

THE CITY WAS IN CHAOS. Sophia could see it and hear, but dimly, some of it within the cathedral and some of what was happening outside. Most of that she heard later.

Horses screamed, carts and cabs were overturned as the petrified animals tried to escape the fury from above. A man was run over by a tram in Market Street as the horses bolted; they eventually came to a halt near the Infirmary. The city rivers were boiling brown broth and one, the Irk, found itself so full of debris that its way under the road near Hanging Ditch was soon blocked. The water level rose and rose almost to the underside of the bridge before the source of such extra volume was exhausted and the levels were stable for a while.

The torrential rain persisted for an hour, lessening to a heavy shower as the storm moved south easterly to the Peak District. The aftermath was everywhere. Filthy streams washed down any sloping ground in the city making people lose their footing and fall, then to be rolled over and over by others who tripped across them in the rush to get out of the water. Small booths and carts that had latterly been full of pies, sausages or hot potatoes and other such casual foods were destroyed in the deluge. Their owners ran around lamenting, but joyful dogs raced everywhere, barking, splashing in the water or stealing the bounty of food before it washed away.

Gin palaces and beer houses lost all their customers as soon as the deluge began; they rushed outside to dance in the rain and spill their drinks, so welcome was the rain after weeks of heatwave. People screamed their excitement, laughed and shouted hysterically, or bellowed their pain, terror and anger. It depended on how they were affected by the vast amount of water. One man, wearing a greyed sheet that had escaped its washing line, draped it around himself and getting his legs tangled, fell over the parapet of the Victoria Bridge to drown in the Irwell before anyone had the wit to save him.

Inside the cathedral there was superficial damage to a window; the plaster work and some stone ornamenting, that which had hit Nat, was shaken loose. The worst of it was that people inside had been deafened by the proximity of the thunder and lightning and many didn't regain their hearing until several hours later. Lightning had struck close by, causing much damage to a five-storey warehouse near the cathedral and a mill chimney on the other side of the Victoria Bridge.

All this Sophia saw for herself or heard of later that evening and the saga continued for days afterwards when she met different people. In the cathedral itself, immediately after the first fury of the storm, people milled around, badly shaken, especially those who had been at the service in the Lady Chapel. For most of them, the occasion for the service had been traumatic and emotional enough without Nature's dreadful after blow.

Not long after Nat ran out, Sophia noticed the Waterstones by the entrance to the Lady Chapel; the girl was in her father's arms, her head on his breast. She was strangely quiet, yet her father wore an expression of such fierce exultation that at first shocked Sophia, but as they remained so still in the midst of this storm of panic, she suddenly understood completely the depth of their grief.

They have lost Isabella. Storms are nothing.

She patted Reverend Knightly's arm lightly, nodded her head in the direction of the grieving family, searching his eyes to see that he understood her message. He had and with bowed head and crossing himself his lips moved in a silent prayer.

'Are you unhurt?' he asked, at first she assumed it was in his normal voice, and then when she mimed that she could not hear, he was forced to shout and she to reply in the same way, so that they ended up laughing at the deafness they both experienced.

The Waterstones had gone when she next looked that way and when Reverend Knightly saw the direction of her gaze, he shrugged his shoulders.

'Home. They have gone home,' he mouthed slowly and distinctly.

Sophia smiled at his antics then remembered that he had many mills in the parish and guessed that this was his attempt to ape the mill hands' speech. There was such a volume of noise in the mills that the hands were no strangers to deafness and consequently became adept at the me-mawing he had attempted. He was new to the skill.

'Did you see Nat run out? Nat and Dr Smith?' She had to raise her voice and speak slowly, trying to copy his delivery.

He had not, but then, by unspoken agreement, they both began to look to other people in the building to see if any needed help. There were surprisingly many people milling around, some who may have come in from the rain, some who were there for their own religious purpose and those from the service in the Lady Chapel. None seemed to need help; there were no physical casualties, only people who were shocked and temporarily deafened, as they both were.

'Shall I take you home, Miss Kelley?' he asked, formally, 'As Sergeant Roberts is perhaps on police business.'

It didn't occur to her later that she had welcomed his help in a dangerous situation – she who prided herself on her independence.

How independent and professional I am! she thought with no small dose of irony.

She and David Knightly used a mixture of lip reading, mime and me-mawing to communicate. She wanted to return home, to see how things stood with everyone, her father especially. She worried about the horses, the building, Nat's whereabouts. The curate went to change out of his vestments; both themselves and several other people who had been near them when the building was shaken were covered in a fine layer of plaster dust, as Nat had been.

But where is he? Why rush out like that?

Her fertile imagination caused an anxious few minutes as she created situations in her mind where Nat was lying hurt somewhere in the city, but thankfully for her, before they grew wings and flew, her nightmarish thoughts were disturbed by a tall policeman.

This must be Inspector Bateman then. What news? Oh, Nat.

He introduced himself; it was. Their conversation was difficult because he was forced to shout, and she tried to direct the sound better by cupping her hand to her ear. It seemed Nat had pointed her out and the inspector wanted to tell her that Nat had been sent to search for someone, a suspect. They had had intelligence of a man they wanted to speak to who had just been seen, before the storm. He would say no more. He asked if she were alright and offered to take her home, but just then,

Reverend Knightly returned, and they parted politely.

Not as curmudgeonly as Nat would have me think.

There were signs of storm damage everywhere as they walked the short distance back home. People were running, calling to each other, trying to clear up the mess. The runnels down the centre of the smaller streets were cleaned out by the volume of water, their foul tangled slurry gone for a time. Gone too were the lines and lines of daily washing strung across alleys and tenements. Clothes and other items were plastered on top of roofs, laid out flat on the streets or clogging up the rivers and ditches. Devastation for some.

What will home be like? Is Father all right?

They said their farewells at the yard gate.

'Reverend Williams will be in need of some comforting talk, I expect,' she said. 'At least he will be able to hear you as he wasn't in the cathedral for that fury of a noise. My ears seem more normal now, as are yours, I suppose?'

'Indeed they are. And yes, he'll want to talk; I think he's been lonely for some time. Most evenings we talk for an hour or so, and with great interest on my part. He's a man of deep philosophical ideas. Still, I'll be there within ten minutes, barring further storms, man-made or natural.'

The rain had stopped by the time they arrived. A fitful sun attempted to dry up the remains of the storm and the temperature rose steadily once more. The undertakers' yard was a mess. She looked around in dismay at the hay and straw that covered everything, and she knew only too well how easily that happened if there was a strong wind and one of the lads had dropped an armful. But this was a large amount, and it was not that simple in explanation. One of the doors of the barn had come off its hinges, she guessed, by banging in the storm. All was drenched in the porch of the great barn, but it would soon dry again in the building heat. More pressing was the sight of the small van they used to collect bodies. It lay on its side and the shafts broken.

Thank Goodness no horse is lying between the shafts, at least I hope there was not.

A couple of the yard lads were scurrying about, picking up tiles, brushing debris, fetching water. She was thankful to hear only the usual level of noise from the stable block; there was no sound of horses banging, no distressed whinnying or snorting. She rushed over and met Albert coming out and he read the anxiety in her face.

'Ah, Miss – not to worry, all well as ends well.'

'Any hurt?'

'Aye, just the one. Captain was being led into his stall when yon sky fell in and he reared up. Coming down he smashed his near side fore into the partition – went straight through – and that's good thick ash wood. But he 'as good big feet, well shod.'

'Not broken?' she gasped out, her face suddenly feeling parched of blood. She held her hands tight over her face.

'Nay, but the partition is. He's cut the foreleg bad, no tendons damaged as I can tell, is all. He's walking fine on it.'

'Show me,' she demanded and strode ahead of him to the stables.

All the other lads were in there to see the horses settled, grooming or quietly stroking them.

'They've all been in enough storms, they have, and it's not so bad out in't fields – natural like, but that one were summat else, Miss,' Ernie told her, tugging his cap. 'Good job it were in the evening, when day's work were done!'

The other lads and the horses all lifted their heads at her entrance and variously nodded heads or smiled, snickered. She was shown the leg. Albert's expertise was clear to see.

'I expect you stitched that when it was newly done,' she said, 'and he wasn't feeling it. I doubt it will leave a scar, even on hair as fine as his. Good boy, good old boy,' she added, stroking the horse's nose. He'd bent it round to nudge her back as she examined his leg.

'He never felt a thing, our Davy here was a kissin' 'is nose and feeding 'im knobs o'sugar like they was carrots.'

'Miss,' called Davy from the end of the line of stalls, 'I never, Miss. Captain just likes me well enough. I have the touch. He'll do owt for me.'

Albert threw a derisive glance at the lad and gave Captain a pat.

'Miss Sophia, all's well on't yard. Master Arnold is in the yard kitchen if y'want him. And y'may want to know – a note's come for you – just.'

She ran across to the kitchen. Alice was pouring tea for her father.

'Oh, Miss Sophia, I am glad to see you're fine. I'll pour you some too,' she said.

'My dearie! You're alright?' her father asked.

'Yes, thank you. But I lost Nat when the lightning struck. We were in the cathedral. It was such a, such terrible noise...'

'Lost, Miss?' Alice gasped, her voice quivering. She looked at her master, who shook his head and drew out a piece of paper.

He shook his head at Alice.

'No, not lost like that, but I've news of him, dearie,' he said, turning to Sophia and handing her the paper.

He stood and drew out a chair, led her to it. Alice brought the tea.

'It's addressed to both of us and is from Dr Smith,' he told her.

'He was there. He ran out after Nat. What can have happened?' She snatched the note read quickly once then again slowly and aloud.

'It says…

Dear Mr Kelley, Miss Kelley,

I have news that may alarm you, but not for long, I trust. I have had Sergeant Roberts taken to the vicarage of St Ann's. Unfortunately he collapsed near there whilst pursuing a suspect. I beg that you will not alarm yourself when I tell you that he fell to the pavement becoming unconscious on impact. I had followed him on the same urgent errand and as a consequence, I was directly on hand to render aid. Again, I beg that you are calm; he has a head wound which I have treated and is not of a nature to excite undue anxiety on the part of a medical man. He is put to bed and I shall remain with him until the Reverend Knightly returns, for at present there are only the elderly housekeeper, a couple of other servants and of course, Reverend Williams here. He, poor soul, is indisposed after the exertion of the service this evening.

Be assured of my utmost vigilance in the matter of Sergeant Roberts's recovery.

I am, ever respectfully

James Smith.'

She dropped the note, nudged her arm on the table and knocked off the tea.

'Oh, Father!'

Alice ran to clear up and her father pulled Sophia up into an embrace, saying to the girl:

'Run across to the stable, Alice, and ask Albert to ready the gig with - let me think, Crimson, yes, she's rested.'

To Sophia he said, 'We'll go and see him now. Will that suffice? He's with a doctor – and one we know and trust.'

'Yes, yes, thank you, Father. Alice…'

Alice handed her a shawl. 'Here, Miss, you'll need this. Yes, Master, I'm going across now!'

He grimaced a little. 'That girl!'

She ran to the door then stopped short.

'Oh, pardon me, Monsoor!' she exclaimed, then, 'Steady there, you'll fall. Here, let me. I'm a strong un.'

Michel was in the doorway. Alice pushed herself under his uninjured arm and held him up as he slumped.

'Are you hurt?' Sophia cried, 'The storm, you were hurt?'

Michel turned and smiled at Alice, gently extricated himself from her support.

'Thank you, Mademoiselle. I merely slipped. My balance, it is not good yet.'

'Alice, the gig – quickly,' Sophia said, and Alice flew off with an expression of some regret.

Sophia's father turned to the injured man.

'Are you in need of something? Alice will get you whatever it is, but we must speed on our way. We go to the vicarage at St Ann's where Sergeant Roberts has been taken – injured. You'll excuse us…' he said, in some embarrassment at dismissing him, Sophia thought.

Michel was alarmed. 'I can be of use to you? I am a doctor. I would like to help, you understand, to help one who brought me here.'

Sophia saw the appeal in his face but could not delay. 'Michel, Dr Bonaventure, thank you, but Dr Smith is there as we speak, and we must hurry. Thank you for being so kind.'

They left with all haste.

Chapter 22

'With storms around and fears before'
Emily Brontë

WHEN THEY ARRIVED at the vicarage the sky was darkening, but this time with the night and not a storm.

'Father, look!' Sophia said. Her voice was a shaken whisper. 'There in the cemetery. 'Are they ghosts? What am I seeing?'

She pointed a trembling hand to shapes in the few trees, which to someone not distraught would have looked, as they indeed were, like bed sheets blown by the wind and now hanging in the branches in awful semblance of phantoms. The remaining wind sensed her fear and blew their trailing arms in bizarre imitation of bodily movement.

Her father had to guide her to the door; she was weak with fear by then.

'You're distracted, overwrought – come now! A strange day, my dearie. Come, Nat may be awake now,' he said.

They went in.

One of the new servants at the vicarage had met them when they arrived.

'Dr Smith asked that I look out for you, Sir, Miss,' the man said, explaining his vigilance.

Crimson and the gig had been left in his care.

They were met by Reverend Knightly in his shirt sleeves. Straight away his eyes found Sophia's and, with a rapidity and sensitivity she was coming to know, he reassured her, saying:

'Don't worry, he's in bed and very deeply asleep, not unconscious any longer. The doctor gave him something to make it so. He woke for a few minutes and complained of a severe headache, and Dr Smith thought that sleep would cure that. The sergeant recognised us and knew where he'd been when we questioned him, so it was felt that there was no hurt to his brain or his reason. The doctor then had to leave but expressed a wish that I reassure you that the sergeant will recover by morning.'

'Ah. Where is he? I must go to him. Where is he?' She asked, her expression pleading.

'Miss Kelley, Sophia, this way,' he said with alacrity. 'He's in good hands, don't worry.'

'Come, Father.'

'I am, my dear. I'm right with you.'

They followed the curate upstairs and to a bedroom at the back. It was a large house of the Georgian period and the window reached almost to the ceiling, but nothing was to be seen from there as its shutters were closed against the noise outside and the gathering night. The floors were bare oak boards but scrubbed clean and a bright worsted rug lay at the side of the bed. All basked in the soft glow from a pair of oil lamps; the vicarage was still very much in the Georgian period and did not have even the established modern device of gas lighting.

Sophia rushed over to the side of the bed and looked down, searching Nat's unconscious face for signs of hurt.

'Father, he's very pale. Too pale for mere sleep, do you think? The blood's been cleaned up.'

She turned his head, lifting the bandage a little to peer closely

237

at the wound.

'Dr Smith has stitched it well.' She sat down on the edge of the bed. 'All is as it should be yet…yet…it's Nat, Father.'

Her father dropped a heavy hand on her shoulder.

'I know, dearie,' he said quietly and then stepped to the other side of the bed.

There were no curtains or drapes; it was a four- poster in plain style and looked as though it might have been in the house since it was built and polished every week since.

Her father reached over the sleeping man and gently raised his eyelids, then put his palm over Nat's heart to feel its rhythm.

'He sleeps, lovie. The pupils in his eyes look the same; remember when the old washerwomen collapsed, Dr Smith himself said he could tell she had had a stroke because one of the eyes was completely black. Now Nat's heart beats quite steadily under my hand, and that can only be to the good, though I'm no doctor. Indeed, Dr Smith wouldn't have given him any drugs else. How came he by this cut on the forehead? D'you know?'

'Some bits of masonry fell from one of the arches in the cathedral, during the storm. He was just below the place.'

Nat, love. What are you thinking now? Do you see me in your mind? How I wish I could call up my gift at will and see what happened to you this evening.

'He's very still,' she said, quietly, glancing round at both the other men. 'Why is that?'

Reverend Knightly said, 'He sleeps deeply, and I think it's necessarily so. I believe it's not unheard of when there has been a head injury and the good doctor did give him a mild drug of some kind to prolong that rest for his mind - rest from the pain of the injury. I'll sit up with him tonight. I'll bring a chair up here as easy as anything.'

Her father answered, 'No, no. It'll be my duty, after all, he'll one day be my son-in-law.'

'Father, I'll stay. Will you take Crimson home and call for me early in the morning? We've much work to do tomorrow.'

'My dear! No, not unchaperoned.' He was very firm, but kindly.

'Oh, Father! To stand on ceremony at such a time.'

Reverend Knightly came between them, her father now a little frustrated and Sophia white with anguish.

'Shall you both stay? I can get Brown to return your horse and vehicle back to the yard. He's worked with horses before and may be trusted. If you, Mr Kelley, can help me, we can bring chairs enough up here. The vicarage has a new consignment of easier chairs than it had previously. I don't say *easy* chairs, but comfortable enough.'

His light manner, competent and thoughtful, gave her a little comfort; she thanked him.

'Yes, a solution. Thank you, that will do nicely. Sophia, I think we have a friend in Reverend Knightly.'

'We are already friends, and friends call me David,' he said.

Her father clapped the younger man on the back. 'David, then. Eh, my dear?' he added, appealing to Sophia.

She heard this too but did not reply. She was looking intently at Nat. His chest was bare, and the covers pulled up to his waist. Her mind, entirely intent on Nat, caught her up and spun her away in a memory.

Since the day, last summer, when they had swum in the moorland reservoir – it was called Anglezarke, she remembered, since that day she had almost forgotten how heavily muscled he was, and how dark his hair. His chest was covered in a dense mat of dark curls and his forearms with the same colour but straighter hair. He had combed her own long hair with his fingers until it had dried in the sun. He'd said it felt like sunshine, the colour and the texture of sunshine, glistening, warm, alive. Anglezarke, a strange, hard name for an achingly lovely place, high up on the moors near Bolton. Down in the valley, the town's mills had belched smoke as freely as at home, but up there, all was heavenly.

She was restored to the present when her father rubbed her shoulder.

'Sophia, lovie, he looks asleep,' he reassured her.

She was able to smile up at him and then looking back at the sleeping figure, she concentrated on his breathing until she was convinced it was steadiness itself. She watched his nostrils move slightly as he inhaled, willed the next breath to be drawn in too, and slipped into a whirlpool of remembrance once more.

The air was filled with the warm living scent of the heather, purple heather, growing in abundance this year, Nat had said. *The partridge will do well, and the pheasant too,* she thought, as lost in this recollection as in any of her clairvoyant visions. *Nat loves his birds; up here he sees so many, not like the pigeons at home, filthy from the soot, poor things. And the little house sparrows; up here he says they're washed clean, living like natural birds, not vermin. What've we seen today? The peregrine, soaring near the sun, so wild and intense when they dive. Then the lapwings; that melancholy call; oh, such music. An upland wilderness. He's got that list of the birds he wants to study: hen harrier, curlew, golden plover, red grouse; names filling the mind with earthy poetry. We'll come here again - often. Bolton Station from Victoria, not too far, a short cab ride to the start of the moorland path - a public house called The Moorgate.*

She saw herself lying on the soft bank of heather. She had lain back and turned her head to gaze under the bushes into the miniature world below and in the spaces between banks.

There were tiny dog violets, nestling down in the damper ground, bird's foot trefoil, so sun yellow, and the mosses, minuscule forests of intricate perfection. All giving off a rich bloom of scent that made her head swim.

And Nat, he had so wanted to show her this place he loved, so far away from the grime and energy of the city. They'd brought a picnic in his knapsack and ate it in the lee of a stone wall that enclosed a rough meadow. A skylark sang high above them, sheep cropped the short grass close by and were unconcerned by the visitors.

'Sophia, dearie,' her father said gently, rousing her again. 'You're tired, come and sit down.'

She had been immersed in the memory of the summer's day. Her head swam with tiredness, but she did as he suggested and stood, a little stiffly, ready to move to the offered chair, swayed.

'She's quite overwrought, I'm afraid,' she heard her father say, as if he were some way in the distance.

'I'm here, Nat, love. I'm still here,' she told the sleeping figure.

She bent to stroke his forearm, a caress, and as she did, an intense lethargy overtook her. She sat down heavily on the edge of the bed, quite overcome with fatigue and unable to stay upright, then slumped over onto her side, across Nat's feet.

She could not move. This had become of late, eerily familiar. Panic filled her mind; an arm was clasped tightly round her neck. There was that smell! She struggled. A forearm, a bare forearm, black hair on it, moved before her eyes. There was danger all around. Nat was there. Why him? He was running, pounding along, his face set and determined and try as she might she could not tell whether he was running away from her or towards her. All she knew

241

was that her heart ached dreadfully. Then before her eyes she saw a glistening object, a drop of fluid. It hung suspended from something and it quivered rhythmically. She knew instinctively that it moved in time with the beat of the killer's heart. The droplet hung from the needle of the hypodermic. What was she seeing? Was it Adeline's murder again? Was the danger for Nat himself?

'No, no,' she screamed.

'Sophia, wake up, my dear. Sophia!' her father's voice.

'Has she fainted?'

'Exhaustion, I think, David.'

'Come, we'll get her on this chair. Here's a footstool.'

She heard Reverend Knightly's voice, then she knew she was lifted off the bed and onto the chair, positioned comfortably, covered with a shawl. A familiar hand and voice now.

'She'll be better for some sleep, lad.'

'I think you're right.'

Sophia had felt herself leave the vision, the reminder of a sacred purpose – and now allowed herself to dive deeply into that surging wave of physical and emotional exhaustion, her limbs slack, her mind dull – and blessedly empty.

The room was lighter when she awoke, morning; and it was empty but for her and Nat. She struggled to focus her eyes and was rubbing them when a voice made her start.

'You're awake, at last,' he said. He was sitting up awkwardly and looked ill. 'I didn't want to wake you. Have you been here long? I saw you the instant I woke. I thought I was dreaming then, seeing you here.'

Sophia rose and moved stiffly to the bed. She sat gently on the edge and put her arms around him.

'Nat, love. I've been here all night, of course, since you were brought here.'

'Where am I?'

She told him and he grimaced. 'Don't tell me that your new friend has been my nursemaid!'

The face he pulled stretched his wound and he winced in agony this time, held his head in his hands.

'Be quiet and calm yourself, love, you were hurt. Don't you remember?'

He managed to whisper, 'Yes, yes. But the storm...?'

'It's over and looks to be as hot as ever,' she answered, glancing behind at the window shutters; there were no curtains. Light streamed around the edges, begging, demanding to be allowed into the room. She went over and started to open them, but the bar of sunlight that just an inch of opening allowed into the room cut through the shade like a knife. There was a sharp cry from Nat.

'Oh, my head!' he cried. This time she thought the voice was unlike his; she had never known him in such pain before.

The shutter was quickly closed, and she helped him to lie down again and waited while the pain subsided. He held her hand and squeezed it so hard that she had to cry out herself.

'Nat, be still, be still. There, there,' she crooned, stroking his face softly, felt the unaccustomed bristles of the night beard.

They were quiet for some minutes.

'What happened to me, love?' he asked when he opened his eyes at last.

She absorbed every tiny detail of his face. 'You look a little better now.'

He gestured to be helped up again and as she struggled, she continued:

'You were hit by some falling masonry in the cathedral; at least I think it was that – you were surrounded by the debris when I saw you, dust on your shoulders and blood on your face. It was during the thunder and lightning – yesterday now. Then you ran off, right past me on some errand for Inspector Bateman. He came to me and explained and the next I heard of you was from Dr Smith who followed you out. He says you collapsed in the square outside – St Ann's that is. He brought you in here and Reverend Knightly and he put you to bed. We had a note from the doctor so…does this sound familiar to you?'

'I feel as though I know this, but it swims in the back of my mind somehow.' He screwed up his eyes, as though recollection could be forced out. It took only a minute or so for his mind to clear and he explained:

'The Inspector sent me to follow up some information. A man had been seen attempting to molest a girl, a young woman, here around the back of St Ann's Place.'

'How did you know this?'

'The doctor, Smith – he came running into the cathedral with some news. It seems far fetched now – whimsical. The details are coming back to me.'

'Will you drink this, love? It'll refresh you.' Her eyes sparkled as she handed a glass of water from the small cupboard at the side of the bed. 'I'm sure the exceedingly kind Reverend Knightly left it here for just that purpose,' she said mischievously.

'Hmmph.' He drank, sank back on the pillows. 'My head feels as though I were twirling on a roundabout or the helter-skelter at the fair.'

'Dr Smith gave you some drug for the pain, perhaps you need another dose.'

'Smith. Yes. He came to the cathedral. I've said that, haven't I?'

His voice lacked its usual vigour; she could see it was an effort to talk, though he continued, haltingly.

'Smith said that a man known to him, a vagrant he comes

across from time to time, had seen an older man accosting a young woman around the back of St Ann's. She was being held against her will, struggling, an arm round her neck. No one else would help, they were all in panic through the storm. The man, the informant, was almost at the cathedral when he saw the doctor and bade him get the police. He knew several officers were already there for the service.' He paused, screwed up his face, as though willing his voice to carry on. 'It's clear now. It's coming back to me; the man was sickly and wouldn't have been able to rescue the woman alone. No one else was around. It was so much in keeping with the murders that we thought it was just such another.'

She listened, but in some disbelief.

'It's a very complicated tale, don't you think so?'

'I did, but the doctor said his informant was very believable and had nothing to gain by telling what he saw. I was sent immediately by the Inspector. There's nothing else I remember other than falling...'

'Love, you're hurt, but you'll recover with rest.'

'Rest with me...come here,' he said, held out his hand, held her eyes.

'No. I'll not! You'll not distract me from my task. I'm going downstairs to find someone, anyone in this cavernous house, and I'll get food for you and water to wash – you smell, Nat, especially badly. I'm staying here today to look after you. The business can go on without me.'

'But what'll we do all day, just here in this room?' He smiled and then winced as it pulled his wound.

'We'll read Isabella's diary. Yes, I'm serious. I haven't told anyone else I have it, only Christina knows of course, ah – and Alice. She's completely trustworthy, Nat.'

'Alice? The diary...' Nat's voice, she was pleased to notice, held his usual sneering disbelief when she spoke of Alice.

She was gone from the room before he could say anything else and finding the kitchen eventually, she discovered it was eight o'clock and the household was busy. Mrs Jenkins was there in the kitchen with the housekeeper.

'Well, Miss Kelley, how's the Sergeant? What a t'do! Y'see I've been told all, never fret,' she said, wiping her hands on a large coarse apron. 'I'm 'ere to work, if that's bothering you. Reverend Knightly 'as given me a job, helping Mrs Biggs 'ere. I'm right glad of the money too. And I've a bed and my own bit of the garret, private like. Save me being under me daughter's feet. I allus liked me independence – as Reverend Williams says."

Reverend Knightly is a regular hero in time of need, she thought caustically, then wondered why she felt so vitriolic when he was a truly good man and he had welcomed Nat here. She was pleased for the old woman's good fortune and marvelled at the way the new vicar had arranged things, even providing the money for all. *A Christian, a real Christian then,* she decided somewhat ruefully this time. *Nat needs me to be his heroine though.* This thought uppermost, she was soon organised herself.

I'll send a note to Father. I must stay here today...ah, but the diary's at home. No, I'll go instead of sending - wait until Nat has had some food. If I go back home this evening, then I'll be in good time to prepare Isabella's body for the chapel tomorrow. Her father and Christina will be coming then. The temperature dropped with the storm but it's rising again; she must be prepared today.

The housekeeper had asked Mrs Jenkins to make a tray for Sophia to take upstairs: warm muffins, butter, jam and of course, tea. She presented it with a flourish.

'A proper feast. There y'are.'

Mrs Biggs told Sophia that she had put a fresh towel and

some ladies' soap in the bathroom on the landing next to where Nat lay. She would follow with some hot water.

'I must look dishevelled. Thank you, thank you both.'

Nat managed but little food, feeling weak and nauseous. Once her ablutions were complete, she sponged Nat's face, which is all he would allow and promising to be no more than an hour, Sophia took her leave. She was in the hallway, explaining what she intended to Reverend Knightly, who had come from the study to speak to her, when there was a knock at the front door. He opened it himself and there before her were her own maid, Alice, and the wounded Michel.

Well, I see the cat has got the cream…'

'Welcome Monsieur le Docteur, welcome,' said Reverend Knightly. 'We have a patient for you already.'

'Ah, the good sergeant. I have been told by my friend, Monsieur Kelley. Mademoiselle Kelley, my regrets at this accident.'

He was wearing a suit of her father's clothes and they appeared incredibly old fashioned on the younger man. He'd shaved and looked fresher in the face because of it, although she saw he had dark shadows beneath his eyes. She smiled her welcome willingly.

'I never thought to see anyone step into my father's shoes,' she said, gesturing with her eyes at his outfit, and adding a greeting to Alice – raised eyebrows. The girl smiled radiantly and added her reason for being there at all:

'Excuse me, Miss Sophia, the Master asked me to come with Monsoor, to show him the way.' She curtseyed becomingly.

Cheeky little madam, she thought fondly.

She turned to Michel, saying, 'What a good arrangement has been made for you. I heard of it yesterday. No, no…' she began when he started to apologise for not telling her in person.

He said, 'Bien sûr, it is that I will see you in this vicarage often and can thank you daily. And I am to help the good Dr Smith – in some things, to earn my place here.'

He really is a pleasant man she thought, assuring him she would see them all again in an hour and, taking Alice with her, she walked off briskly.

Chapter 23

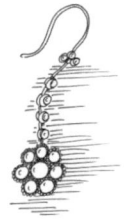

'The little things are
infinitely the most important'
Sir Arthur Conan Doyle

ALICE REGALED HER all the way back with what she had learned about, 'Monsoor Michel'.

'Y'know, Miss, he speaks to me as if I'm the same as him, the same class, I mean. He says as how there's all sorts of different peoples in the world and they are all human. Never mind the colour or where they come from, how much money they've got, they can all get the typhoid!'

'Typhoid?'

'He means that anyone can get ill and bodies are all the same to germs. Germs know no class, they are – let me see, what were it 'e said? Ah – *they are the very essence of equality*, he says.'

With a quick glance at Alice, Sophia said, 'I think you have a good ear for the sound of accents, Alice.' She added playfully, 'I expect he has a lovely wife in Orléans…'

Alice was unperturbed at Sophia's suggestion. 'He says not, Miss Sophia, as I asked him that one!'

'Really? How did you word the question?' She was very, very curious. This maid of hers had hidden talents.

Alice smiled, 'I just started off asking him about his home,

249

where he lived, who else was there, like brothers and sisters. He got talking; glad to 'ave someone to listen as the lads up in the loft were making fun all the time – not Albert though. Said 'e spoke French to 'im. So, the wife would have been mentioned, if there were one. Anyway, 'e has three brothers. One is a captain on a ship going to the West Indies, one's a priest in't Catholic Church. The last one, the youngest, Pierre, helps his dad in the pharmacist shop – like 'ere. He says France is a bit like it is 'ere.'

Sophia was astounded at what she had learned. 'How did he become a ship's surgeon then? He said he went to the university in Paris, the Sorbonne.'

Alice's steps were light and bouncy, despite her clogs and Sophia saw how she held up her head, feeling well and... *What? Admired? Could it be? I'll watch my little girl here. If a friend is wanted, I am she.*

Alice answered readily. 'We had a long talk, Miss – now don't fret, in the yard kitchen, after you and the master had gone. The door were left open so anyone could 'ave come in and heard nothing bad. He were worried. Anyway, he thinks the sergeant doesn't like 'im. I told him 'e was probably right, but he'd come round soon enough. When he were at home he wanted to see the world, see all the people of different colours and kinds. They 'ave such a lot of different folk in Orléans, and he wanted to see the places they come from. So, he joined a ship as the surgeon to keep up with 'is medicine before settling to be a doctor back in Orléans.'

Sophia stopped in her tracks. People on the now busy street, pushed past, muttering angrily.

She said, 'You can certainly root out secrets, Alice. Did he ask about you, your background and such?'

'Aye, 'e did, but I only told him the bits I wanted 'im to know. Then we got on to talking about the service last night, at the cathedral and the poor dead woman and all. We both said as 'ow we'd have like to have gone but couldn't. That got us onto churches and he said 'is brother, the priest, upped and went to Rome, to the place they call the Vatican, to 'elp in the services with the head of all the Catholic churches in the world, the Pope, they call him. Michel's not a Catholic. Me own Dad didn't hold with them, said they had too much perfume in church and dressed up everything with too many prayers. Give 'im a plain-speaking God, he said. He were a Methody.'

'Michel? First names now?'

'He said so. Mind you, I do like 'im calling me 'Mamsel Alice. Anyway, Miss, why I'm tellin' this is because he went talkin' about the West Indies and spiritualists and summat called voodoo where they get visions and folk see ghosts and make spells. They send curses to them as they don't like, and some drop down dead with fright, 'e said. Sounds a bit like All Hallow's Eve to me, Miss Sophia. He said as how there're Christian churches in France what have healing services and summon spirits. And they cure some of the people too. I didn't tell him nothing about what you said to me, Miss. I know you'll believe me.'

Sophia said simply, 'I do.' They carried on walking; she was needed at the yard and then must get back to Nat.

'Anyway, 'e says the lads were talking, our yard lads, I mean, and they were saying that it's all over the city about a famous hypnotist – that's one of me long words, Miss.' She grinned at Sophia. 'He's coming to the Palace Theatre. But the thing is, the lads've heard about another one that's puttin' on his show at the small places like beer cellars, public houses and working men's halls. He's been putting young girls in one of them trances and makin' them do things – y'know.'

Sophia raised eyebrows in surprise. 'Go on.' She began to feel her heart beating, faster, faster.

'Well, I were thinkin' that maybe whoever killed them poor girls *hypnotised* them.'

'That's proper clever, Alice.'

'Oh, Miss Sophia, you're mockin' me. That's unfair!'

Her expression was hurt and seeing it was genuine, Sophia was instantly sorry for her tactlessness.

'Oh, it is. I am mocking. I'm sorry Alice. How could I? I shouldn't have said that. But it *is* clever. Very clever, putting all those facts together that you heard in different places and then realising they all came together to make a new, more important idea. I'm sorry. I hold you in more respect than that.'

Now Alice stopped dead. 'Me? Oh, Miss. I'm proper touched, no, 'ang on a minute – I am overcome with gratitude.'

'Now who's mocking?' Sophia smiled broadly. She could hardly wait to tell Nat.

'But Miss, you haven't said how the sergeant is doing.'

'You were too busy telling me of your interesting conversation with Michel!'

'True, Miss. But, how is he?' she asked.

They had arrived at the yard gate. All was bustling and movement.

Sophia smiled at Alice, saying, 'Dr Smith was able to stitch up the head cut very well and has given him some painkiller, as you heard last night. He seems more like himself now, but I am going to spend the rest of the day with him and return this evening to prepare Isabella Waterstone. I'm going to read the diary and one reason I came back was to get it.'

'Will you be changing your clothes, Miss? Only the laundry makes its second collection today and the water is already on the boil for y'delicates. I do them special, not with anything else. I never trust that laundry with owt very special.'

'Alice, how do you stay so cheerful? You sound as though

you relish the opportunity of bettering what Ridgeway's Laundry does.'

'Miss, it's clean work and when I get all your fine frills and laces up, I know I can make them beautiful again. It's a bit of a craft, if you like. Anyway, Miss, anyone not 'aving to work at pithead just needs to be thankful for owt. And I'm right grateful to be where I am.'

'Yes, I also – I mean I'm grateful to have you here.'

They walked on.

'Alice, do you know the storm blew people's washing all over the city. I think we'll have some bedding that we can well spare. Find what excess sheets we have that are good and might be useful and then ask Reverend Williams who in their parish might need them. I expect Mrs Jenkins can help. We met her yesterday, remember? That can be your task today. And ask Mrs Kittering to release you for a couple of hours.'

Alice sighed. 'Them people who've lost washing'll never get it back. Dirty they might be but sheets cost money to replace. And keeping sheets clean costs money to heat the water and that means coal. They've never enough to keep warm in cold weather. Some o'them poor folk in the tenements might 'ave jobs but they need their money for food, for all them kiddies they 'ave. I think there'll be plenty as'll need sheets and stuff.'

'Yes, you're right. See what you can do, Alice. Now to find my father.'

'Thank you, Miss,' the girl said.

Sophia saw her father in the barn speaking to Albert and he came across to meet her, asked about Nat and her plans. After she had explained what she intended regarding Isabella's preparation and mentioned the job she had given Alice, he smiled affectionately.

'You've organised things well, my girl.' He kissed her on the top of her head. 'Are you going back now? You're not to go alone until this killer is found; yes, I know you value your independence,' he added quickly when she opened her mouth to speak, 'but you must see how dangerous it could be for you – the likeness; I fear it, my dear. And don't worry about anything in the workroom, I'll ensure that the poor girl's body is kept cold, never fear.'

She turned in that direction saying, 'I will just get something from there before I change, and I'll see you later, Father.'

The workroom was blessedly chilly at this time of the day and she anticipated the cool air with pleasure, but when she did enter, she was immediately confronted by a sensation of intrusion on the air. She stood, rooted to the spot, casting her eyes all around, and felt herself grow cold within as she detected the tiniest thread of that dreaded scent drift past her nostrils. It was the scent of that substance underneath the victims' fingernails, the scent she had sensed when deep in the visions of their deaths – the scent of the killer.

These feelings, these waves of fear, lasted but a short time, and she forced her mind to push them away so that she could concentrate on the task in hand. But before she did, she went straight to the cold storage room to take a look at Isabella's body.

'I'll be back this evening and then I'll do my utmost to make you look as beautiful again for your poor family,' she told her.

Returning to the main room she paused. 'Now, where *is* her diary?' she murmured to herself as she searched through the items collected on the back bench. *The flower press was next to it last night, then I put it back in the cupboard and left the diary over....*

She moved everything off the workbench and put it back in its place, opened all the cupboards and drawers, looked under the benches, all of them; moved methodically round the room until she had searched every corner, every nook and cranny.

'Where, where?' she muttered, panicking and now leaving logical method behind to open and close cupboards at random.

She searched everywhere once more. Then she called Alice, using the workroom bell that connected to the housekeeper's room where she could be found.

As she turned back into the room, she caught the scent again, the strange, unpleasant scent. It hung in the air like a calling card.

Has he been here, here in my workroom?

Then it was gone, and she could only smell those things that were familiar in her workroom.

'Impossible,' she said aloud, 'The lost things must be here, no one could have got in,' she told herself firmly.

A third search was made and this time it included going into the cold storage room and searching round the folds of Isabella's skirts and underneath her body to discover whether she'd simply put the things there out of sight or for greater security.

I may have done. What if I did? The times are so strange that I could have done anything. I've been so worried about Nat.'

There was a knock and Alice bobbed her head round the door.

'Yes, Miss?'

'Alice,' she began calmly, 'Did you come in here last night? Did you move anything or show anything, perhaps, to Michel?'

'No, Miss. I wouldn't do that,' the girl answered quietly.

'Are you sure? I will not be angry,' she said, although her voice, she could tell, was becoming tight and too firm.

'Miss, beg pardon, but I'm sure I didn't. I'm not a liar,' Alice said, with firm dignity, her chin up in her characteristic confident stance.

Sophia felt as though the finest Toledo blade had been slipped between her ribs, and very slowly and with precision, into her heart - then twisted. She slumped back against the work bench, then slowly slid down, her back to it, until she was sitting on the floor with her legs stretched out, her arms limp at her sides, in an attitude of dreadful shock.

'Miss, Whatever's the matter? Are y'poorly?' Alice cried, dashing to Sophia's side and bending down. 'Let me 'elp you up. Come on. You're not y'self. All this talk's not like you. You're just not y'self.'

She dragged Sophia to her feet and pushed her onto a chair.

'What's happened? Something has,' Alice said, a touch of panic in her own voice.

She didn't respond. Sophia felt Alice shake her by the shoulders. Again, Sophia could not move or answer.

'Miss, is it the sergeant? Has summat 'appened to him?' Alice demanded.

Sophia shook her head, put her hands over her mouth, felt her eyes lose their focus as she searched her mind for possibilities.

'Have y'lost summat, Miss? Is that it?' Alice tried again, bending close to Sophia's face and speaking very clearly and slowly.

This time she was able to nod so Alice ran to the sink, got a glass down and filling it with water, she took it to her and helped her sip it. When it was obvious she'd had enough, Alice asked:

'What's missing? Is it something t'do with this killing?'

Sophia turned her face to Alice and with fear slipping an arm round her throat, she forced herself to answer.

'Oh Alice, the diary is missing and so is my little flower press with the three posies in it.'

'No! Missing? How could they?' she cried, sceptical, Then stood silent and staring not nothing. 'Don't say that!' she whispered now, sat back on her heels; her own hand flew up to cover her mouth. 'No!'

Sophia was suddenly thirsty and she gulped down the rest of the water, then wiped her face with the edge of her skirt.

Alice got up, and pointing at the skirt, in an attempt to lighten the air, she said:

'Mother'd clip me one round the ear for doing summat like that, muckying up a skirt as someone else has to wash. I'll forgive you though.'

'Alice I'm sorry for doubting you. I doubted my own eyes. I don't know what this means.'

'This door's never locked, Miss. Anyone could come in here.'

'Only if they had access to the yard, and the dogs are out at night. *I know* I saw the posies and the diary before I went to the service yesterday evening. The yard would have been busy then, and someone could have slipped in, perhaps. It is only locked later on and the dogs let out.'

Alice added, 'There're always people about, so a stranger would've been spotted. The dogs are around in the day too. They know everyone.' She paused. 'Now I think on, Albert said as 'ow they were all slow off the mark this morning. Now that's not like them, especially that Bertie. He never sleeps.'

Sophia remembered the hypodermic and thought if someone had access to drugs for that then why not drugs that could dope a dog? She told Alice.

'Well, I never. That could be so. What can you do now, Miss? What'll the sergeant say?'

Sophia jumped to her feet with a cry. 'Oh, I should be back there now. Nat will wonder what I'm about. I need to talk to him about this.'

'I'll come, Miss, see if you've got everything you'll need today. The Master says as how you mustn't go out alone – in case...I'll ask cook for something for the sergeant too, shall I? And don't you worry, things'll turn out alright. The sergeant will be better when you get back and he'll help stop this killer, mark my words.'

Sophia paused in her panicked flight. She said, 'Oh Alice, sometimes you sound old as the hills. Please help, yes. You've been a wonder.'

'Thank you, Miss. Me grandmother said as 'ow I were born thirty three, yet I'm only nineteen now!'

Ten minutes later Sophia and Alice were on her way back to the vicarage. The day had turned muggy, the sky was not to be seen and a blanket of cloud pushed the smoke relentlessly down onto the city streets so that they had to clear their throats continually. Other people were doing the same, bumping into each other in their annoyance at the smog and the heat. The humidity was another contributing factor to make her short journey slow. By the time they got there Sophia was drenched in sweat and exhausted. Alice was a little less ragged, but she had not the same worries. The weight on Sophia's mind of what had been taken – no, stolen, was almost too much.

The killer must have known I had those things which means he knows how vital they can be as evidence against him. And because he knows I had them - how he knew I cannot think - then he knows me. He knows that Nat and I have discovered what he's done. He knows where I am, what I do – who I am. Is Nat right about the resemblance between me and the poor girls? Am I vulnerable? But what I can't understand is why he wanted to kill them in the first place. What had they done to him? What have I? If I knew who it was – aye that's the thing - if I knew that then perhaps I would discover some sort of a reason for this death and torment. Well, it would be reason for him, but then someone who can do this is not reasonable, is not sane.

Standing outside the door of the vicarage, Sophia was feeling considerably worse, despondent and fearful and lacking all her usual self-confidence, the very trait she prided herself on having.

She rang the bell and being sure someone would answer it swiftly, had her legs poised to step forward and into the hall, but it took two more rings before a maid, another of the new servants, answered.

'It's Miss Kelley is it?' she asked, and that being confirmed, she added, 'I was told to send you straight up as Sergeant Roberts has taken a turn for the worst.'

Chapter 24

'The accents of despair'
Lord Byron

THE MAID BECAME INVISIBLE, Sophia hardly felt her presence as she leapt past and took the stairs bounding like a gazelle in fear of its life – as indeed she was. He was all to her. Her sole impulse was to be at his side. She burst into the room where he lay and with no thought of who else was there; she saw no one; she threw herself to her knees at the side of the bed and beheld a sight that froze her heart.

Death beckons him!

He was hot, very hot, sweat poured down his face, such a rugged face. His eyes were unclear, bleary, dimmed and wildly moving in every direction but seeing nothing.

He can't see me. Can he hear?

'Nat, I'm here. Nat can you hear me? Nat, love...'

His curls were plastered onto his head, and his arms were strangely quivering. Tremors raced the length of his body and he groaned, a deep and alien sound. A spasm shook him, and it was then she heard another voice, a doctor perhaps.

'Miss Kelley, please stand back a moment. I must aid him. Please stand back.'

The voice of the doctor was familiar. Dr Smith? Hands were

laid on her shoulders, a man's hands that tried to move her aside.

She could not move, nor would she turn to see the speaker, she could only watch Nat's body, his poor body, curling up on itself. Did he have stomach cramps?

A small hand was laid on her arm.

'Come on, come over here a minute, dear,' said Mrs Jenkins. 'Let the doctor 'ave a bit of room. Come on, up we get.'

She felt herself pulled to her feet and she stumbled back, guided by the old woman, all the while keeping her eyes on the form on the bed. The room smelt stale. Surely it hadn't earlier? She hadn't been gone that long, why the sudden and devastating change?

'What's happening to him?' she found herself whispering, rather she felt the sound in her throat, as though she heard someone else speaking the words. Her whole being was with Nat. He groaned again, so heart wrenching a sound that she cried out aloud herself, feeling his agony. His face was contorted in a rictus of pain and she stretched out her hands to him, but Mrs Jenkins was surprisingly strong for such a small person; she was restrained.

'What is it?' she cried again. 'What's happening to him? Someone please tell me.'

The old woman put an arm about her shoulders and answered gently:

'It's some sort of fever, the doctor 'ere says. Come on sudden like, after you'd gone, dearie. The sergeant's a strong one mind. Strong as a bull he is.'

Someone cleared their throat and at last Sophia's attention turned to the other person in the room. Yes, it was a familiar voice and presence, Dr Smith.

'Ah, Dr Smith. What is this? What's happening to him? You must know,' she whispered still, unable to trust her voice to take on any higher note lest she howl her misery.

'Indeed I do,' he told her and his own voice was so normal in tone, so confident that she felt a tiny droplet of relief.

He continued, as he bent and lifted Nat's head to press a small glass to his lips, 'This will make a difference. I have given him aspirin in a syrup, to help bring down the temperature. He suffers merely a fever brought on by the excessive heat, the head injury and the... how shall I describe and give the correct flavour to that extraordinary time – the varied excitement of yesterday.'

Incredulity rose in Sophia's breast like an avenging angel, until she recollected the doctor's inclination to employ irony when describing anything of importance. Normally she accepted it as part of his personality, today she felt hurt. She swallowed the retort and focused her eyes hungrily on Nat's face.

Nat turned his head away from the glass, spluttered and seemed to choke on the trickle of amber liquid that the doctor was urging him to swallow. But it was a very small amount and was soon done, he swallowed.

'There, man, this will do you some good,' the doctor murmured as he lay Nat's head down again.

He shook his head, saying, 'An imbroglio of the first order. The good sergeant laid as low as a beast even while he is on the trail, like the good bloodhound he is, of this fearsome slayer.'

That comment shocked Sophia to the core. What did he know of Nat's activities? She swallowed, stood paralysed, was at a loss for words to ask.

The doctor seemed to read her mind.

'My dear Miss Kelley, your expression betrays you. You wonder how I know he is bent on discovering the fiend who stalks the city?

He read my mind? Did I allow it?

The doctor enlightened her. 'It was Inspector Bateman. We are acquainted through Newton Street Police Station. On occasions I go there to add aid post-mortems or to treat suspects if my colleague, Dr Johnson is unavailable. I am afraid I was inadvertently the cause of the sergeant having to overextend himself last evening, as he raced after a possible suspect.'

Her mind cleared.

'Ah, yes,' she managed to say. 'I heard about it. And I saw you at the cathedral, speaking to the sergeant and his inspector - of course.'

Dr Smith smiled. Inclined his head politely and began to pack his bag, giving all the signs of imminent departure.

Sophia gasped, frightened anew. 'You're leaving him, doctor? What shall we do? What will happen?'

He stepped across the room to her and laid a friendly hand on her arm, smiled reassuringly down at her.

'For a couple of hours, no more, my dear, dear Miss Kelley. I have another patient who very much needs my urgent care. Fear not. The sergeant is in no immediate danger. Although he strains and shivers, the best you can do is help to lower his temperature, which I can tell is already responding. I have also given him a little sleeping draught,' he said, drawing her over to the bed. 'See, he breathes more steadily. If you and the good Mrs Jenkins could help, the sergeant would benefit from cool compresses and a bed bath,' he began and then embarrassment flooded his face and he appeared to remember she was a young woman and although engaged, this might be inappropriate, he finished, 'at least washing the chest and back would suffice to continue his cooling.'

He gave a short bow, by way of apology and putting on his hat he left quietly, quietly as a ghost because Sophia heard nothing but the sound of Nat's breathing. She flew to the bed,

263

felt his forehead.

'Mrs Jenkins, will you get the water? And Reverend Williams, how is he after he terrible events yesterday – forgive me for not enquiring earlier.'

'God willing, Miss, a little more 'imself, but mornings is not good for him, it seems. He feels dizzy and that, needs 'is cup of tea, Mrs Biggs says. I'll get the water right now. Your sergeant needs cooling down, doctor's right.'

She left bustling.

Sophia put her face next to Nat's, murmured close to his ear:

'Nat, love, can you hear me? I wonder; why can't I have the use of my gift when it's needed so much? If only I could read your mind,'

His disturbing movements had quietened and as she watched, his breathing slowed, and she saw he did indeed sleep. She lay her head on the pillow next to his, her own hands holding the one large one of his that lay still, so still on the bed at his side.

Her own mind was in turmoil, thoughts, feelings, all wallowing in the dense mire of a panic. What could be done? Who could do better than Dr Smith? She should, she must draw courage and trust, believe, hope all would be well.

There was a knock at the door, and she started violently at the shock of so commonplace a noise.

A voice called, 'It is I, Michel. I may enter, Mademoiselle Kelley?'

'Please, Michel, please come in,' she called, feeling relief at the sound of his voice.

Michel – a doctor too. Perhaps he may help.

He looked so different; she saw that instantly. He looked like a gentleman. He had changed clothes since she had seen him earlier. Instead of her father's old-fashioned leavings, he now wore well-made trews, light weight leather boots and a cambric shirt of palest blue, open at the neck. There was a waist coat of grey linen that displayed his broad shoulders and neck. She could still see the ravages of pain and hunger on his features, but it was an interesting face, an intelligent one. Even the sleeve of his missing arm was neatly pinned up and he wore a linen sling, doubtless to take the strain off the upper arm and remind him to protect and restrict its use. He was of a strong build and the clothes looked as if they had been made especially for him. Sophia's assessing glance did not escape Michel, and he said, by way of explanation:

'Reverend Knightly gave me these, his clothes, so that I might feel more myself,' he said. 'We are of a size together. The monsieur, your father is a bigger man than I and the clothes, they were warm for this weather, I think. But this house is cool I find. I told Reverend Knightly that I would repay him for the clothes, but he would hear nothing of my promises. I am much in debt since I was found beneath that bridge, and for my life, more than anything.'

She smiled, held fast to Nat's arm. 'And you, Michel, how does your arm feel? It's still but newly injured.'

'Ah, I find, Miss Kelley, that a quiet mind does much to help healing. I myself am a man who is calm. I feel myself in a safe place and I have not done that for many weeks before I came here, to your house and now here at the vicarage. My arm, it was tended well, and the good Dr Smith will look at it tomorrow, he says. The dressing, will be changed then, but I feel the heat gone from it and I shall heal.'

He stepped nearer and taking a chair said, by way of explanation of his action, 'The Reverend Williams, he said I must, how did he say? *make myself a home.*'

'At home – make yourself *at* home, we say.'

'Ah. Thank you. These English idioms can be the trip up.'

She smiled only, did not correct him this time. Sophia found

265

him easy company, approachable, soothing. Nat slept on steadily; his hand was hot in hers and the sweat still glistened lightly on his chest. Michel might be a doctor, but Sophia had not yet discovered how learned or experienced he might be.

'Michel, Dr Bonaventure, what do you think of this fever of Nat's? Tell me plainly, please.'

'Michel is my name, no formality between us, I beg. Both you and the good Sergeant Roberts will always have a hold on my heart; my gratitude, it will be great. As a doctor, what do I think? Hmmm.' He stood, saying, 'You permit I take the pulse?'

He nodded at the hand she was holding, and she put it gently on the bed and leaned back out of the way. He took hold of Nat's wrist positioned his fingers to feel the pulse.

'I am thankful that fate took my left arm and not my right one. It would be awkward to learn anew how to feel for the pulse and other delicate things with an arm and hand unused to the action.'

He held Nat's wrist for a while then laid it down and felt for the pulse under his jaw, as if to check he was right, then he straightened up and gazed intently at the sleeping figure. Sophia moved slightly, began to say something, but Michel held a finger to his lips.

'Shhh!' Another short time elapsed before he stood back and resumed his chair.

'Do not worry, I beg of you. Me, I listen to his heart at the two main pulse points. The heart it is steady. It is fast, yes, like a trotting horse, but it does not gallop and of the utmost importance, it does not jump around here and there. I admit that it did do this earlier but now it is steady and strong. He is hot, yes, but the weather it is hot and also he has an injury to the head. This I saw many times on board ship. The men, things hit them. They fall ill of fevers all the time, especially if they drink the water of wherever we are moored. These things

266

I know of; I am - how do you express it? I am the expert with fevers and other ailments of sailors.'

He leaned forward and lifted each of Nat's eye lids in turn.

'And the pupils are equal, the brain has not had the shock extraordinaire,' he told her, and he put his hand gently on her shoulder, his expression reassuring and calmly smiling.

Even a gentle smile is dazzling against his dark skin. Smiling seems to be something he does often. How much better he looks now, only a few hours later. He feels settled, safe. It makes a difference.

He said, 'I do not wish you to worry; know always that I can be of help when Dr Smith is not here.'

Sophia felt her body ease just a little; his words were encouraging, gave her hope.

'Mrs Jenkins is fetching water so that we can wipe him down and use a cold compress to help cool him,' she told him.

He nodded approval. 'Good, good, that is the thing.'

Footsteps sounded outside on the landing, heavy clumping footsteps, voices approaching and followed by a knock at the door. Michel was up quickly to open it. There was Mrs Jenkins with a small bucket of water and some cloths, and behind her, bright interest lighting her face, was Alice. She carried two large buckets of steaming water.

Michel was all concern.

'Mademoiselle Alice, Madame Jenkins, let me to help,' he cried, 'I am not so injured that I cannot.'

'No. Please. Michel, I can't let you!' cried Alice, turning her shoulder away from him, as if she imagined he could snatch the buckets from her. 'You need to rest, get y'strength.'

He smiled his acquiescence. 'For one more day I will do this, this convalescence, and then, Mademoiselle Alice, I am a man again. I cannot let you do what I can do easier. And it is needed that I strengthen my one arm, gain my balance to walk

267

properly.'

Mrs Jenkins cast a look over her shoulder. 'Never you mind, my good sir, that lass is a strong one. She'll be a good help here; I can tell you. Aye, she'll do!' She hurried over to the washstand, poured the water into the bowl and ewer, arranged things busily.

Sophia was alert. 'Alice, you are not needed at home? The washing, you mentioned?'

'No, Miss Sophia, the master said I was to stay and help you here, at least for today and to walk home with you. He said so, before we left. He doesn't want you to go alone.'

'Very well, as you say, Alice,' Sophia said, feeling quite unable to argue.

Fear perched on her shoulders and with intrusive, arctic fingers, caressed her neck.

The mundane interrupted the larger emotions with ease when Mrs. Jenkins plonked a smaller bowl of cold water down by the side of the bed.

'Here, y'are, Miss Kelley, dip that cloth in there and keep laying it on his head. Don't let it get warm now, keep it cold, dear, wipe it round 'is neck and over his face. He'll not wake, mark me. I know what I'm on about, done a lot of nursing people in me time. You going, dear?' She addressed Michel who had risen and was moving to the door.

'Indeed, Madame, I go and I will speak to the Reverend Williams, see if he needs some more of your strong tea.'

'I expect he will, that he will. He's a thirsty one today,' she said and when he'd gone, she continued a theme that from her expression, had been foremost on her mind. 'Me first husband had dark skin. Nice, he was, proper nice. Died of the typhoid. We lived in Liverpool when we wed, down near the docks as 'e were a sailor from far off climes.'

It was said casually but the old woman became quiet as she

bustled, holding hands with her memories.

Sophia sat by the head of the bed and simply did as she was bid. She could no more have lifted up Nat's sleeping form that she could fly to the moon. Her strength seemed to have seeped out of her body and she imagined it pooled about her feet with the water she dribbled from her cloth. The shock had prostrated her for the moment. She did not even feel a shiver of jealousy as the other women lifted and wiped his body. She smiled inwardly though as Mrs Jenkins firmly tucked a sheet around Nat's hips, slapping away Alice's hand as she was about to fling it back.

'Sorry, Mrs Jenkins, just I'm used to helpin' scrub me brothers and me dad, when they came up from the pit. No one's that nesh in Wigan – leastways, miners aren't!'

'That's alright, love, I know 'e's wearing drawers but the sergeant 'ere needs a bit of dignity even if 'e is asleep.'

'Maybe you're right though, the sergeant wouldn't like it. I'm sorry.'

The job was soon finished and as the two prepared to take the things back to the kitchens, Alice gave a sudden exclamation.

'Oh, Miss, I clear forgot! I bumped into Jenny Hargraves on the way here.'

Mrs Jenkins added to her news bulletin. 'Oh, right? I saw her mother down the street this mornin,' but 'ad no time to spare for a chat. How's she doing, love?'

Sophia searched Alice's countenance for bad news, found it clear.

'Did you speak to her?'

'I did, Miss. She's feeling better since the attack. Not a bit nervous, even though, she says 'erself, that the city is abuzz with the talk of the killer. In all the papers now. You'll never guess, Miss, it turns out that she knew the fella what attacked her. He'd been after her for a wife when they lived out at

Glossop; seems his family was friends of Jenny's. He'd followed when the Hargraves moved here. Has a job as a drayman for Boddington's Brewery now. He's been pestering her summat shockin' these past couple of weeks.'

Sophia listened intently, knowing that Alice would not divulge anything in front of Mrs Jenkins, that they wanted kept to themselves for the moment. All the same she listened for any discreet bits of knowledge the girl had gleaned.

Alice continued, 'So, he followed her about, waiting for 'er outside the Assurance Office she works at, Phoenix it is, and he were there every day when she finished work, trying to get her attention, walk her home and all that romantic stuff. His work must knock off earlier. The *attack*, as was reported, was only reported because she never saw the bloke. She were shocked, as y'would be. A man put his arm about her shoulder, and without turning, or looking she says she just lamped 'im; swung 'er bag and hit him in the face, then ran like the 'ounds of 'ell were a chasing her.'

Mrs Jenkins was all ears. 'What then, love? How did the police come to busy themselves with the goings on?' She was rightly curious. 'Was 'e the killer then?'

'No. It were 'im, Peter's his name, the man as fancies her. She said 'erself as how she were hysterical. She ran into the arms of a policeman and told 'er tale and 'e raised the alarm; people had seen the fella and told the police what he looked like. The story spread and grew a lot I hear. Later that night, the drayman, Peter, comes to 'er house and brings flowers. He had a big bruise on 'is face and were proper sorry and polite. She were relieved to know it were innocent like and not the proper killer, I mean. Her father asked him in, and all is forgiven, she's walking out wi' 'im. Jenny's father went to the police and cleared him. Said it were a mistake.'

'Well,' commented Mrs Jenkins.

'She's a lovely looking girl, Miss Sophia, and she does have a look of you; same build, same colouring, likes hats too.'

She and Sophia exchanged knowing glances and the two women took their leave.

Sophia was glad of the news but had longed for them to go. They were alone again, she and Nat.

'Nat, are you asleep?' she whispered.

His brow twitched; the muscles of his cheek tightened. He mumbled something, a growl, an oath? She couldn't be sure.

'Speak to me, love. It's Sophia, your own darling.

His body was cooler now and cleansed; his skin was smooth, and she recognised the familiar scent of it that she would know anywhere. Laying her head gently on his chest, she heard the very steady beat of his heart. She was comforted, until he groaned once more, in anger, not pain, and then, as she listened, she heard his heartbeat increase until it fairly pounded.

'Shhh, Nat, quiet there. Everything is well. Hush, love.'

He seemed to become calmer at the sound of her voice but then he gave her a shock.

'No!' he shouted. His eyes were closed. He slept on.

The surprise of him speaking at all, let alone such an exclamation, made her jump up and she stared, saw his face working as some inner tumult fired him.

Does he dream? Is it a nightmare? Perhaps the medicine the doctor gave him?

He shouted again, 'No, you will not!'

This time his body tensed all along its length. Sophia laid her hands on his chest, an unconscious effort to sooth his heart and this time, the instant her skin met his, she felt a jolt in the very core of her being, and her vision darkened.

She knew she must rub her eyes, strain to see what was

there, there in the darkness. For she was in total darkness and in a strange place. There was a human presence close; her skin prickled with the proximity. She felt breath on her neck, the smell of sweat, male sweat. Comfort - it was Nat's. But he was fearful and angry. She could feel her body straining against some force, the muscles in her arms bunched and her torso tensed. Were they together – she and Nat? But where?

She raised her arms feeling a frantic need to defend herself. But from what? From whom? Faint shapes coalesced around the edges of her vision; they were blushed with a grey blue light which blended into shifting silhouettes. They were in a shadow land, a liminal space. She must push, strain, free herself. Her arms felt powerful and she raised them to thrust away from something. There was enough light to see them now, but they were not her arms that were raised before her eyes - they were Nat's! Who else but she should recognise them, the familiar arms of her beloved?

Her shoulders ached with strain, but whose shoulders? Nat's? She was fearful of the answer. Where was Nat? She shuddered. Then realisation dawned; she was experiencing Nat's vision, his unconscious, delirious vision.

As she saw that this was her role, Nat cried out again, a mighty shout.

'No, you will not, devil. Away!'

The shadows formed substance and became men's bodies grappling. She recognised Nat's arms and shoulders; he wore no shirt; everything about the opponent was unclear save one thing - he gripped a syringe in his fist and Nat had his wrist in an iron wrench. There were terror-filled screams and angry voices, devoid of all humanity, swimming about the two men, and in her clairvoyant state, they appeared as glittering ribbons, sharp and pliant as whips.

'Nat!' she heard herself cry as she saw the syringe fly in the air.

She woke with a start.

Her eyes met his; he had woken.

'Sophia!' He panted as though after a great exertion.

She fell on his chest, sobbed with relief to hear his voice, his coherent voice.

She felt arms go about her, but this time there was no vision; it was Nat who held her to his heart.

'How did you come to be here? I'm in bed, I think. Am I ill?' he whispered into her hair. 'In bed? Not at my lodgings. Where?'

The knock on his head must have hurt his brain. I have heard of this before.

He shook his head. So once more she explained what had happened the night before and reminded him of the injury he sustained at the cathedral.

'It came about that our own Dr Smith was at hand to help you and he gave you something to make you sleep. You were a little feverish, the bump on your head. You'll have a scar like the Reverend Knightly – but not as big, and it will be hidden by your hair.'

His voice was quiet but gaining strength as he spoke. 'Ah, well, I will be in good company. You have a penchant for men with battle scars?' There was a small twinkle in his eye as he watched her reaction.

'Now I know you are conscious. Yes, I do,' she teased, glad to be able to do so.

'I think he gained his scar when the patisserie chef at home threw a knife at him for stealing sweeties.'

She laughed at his sarcasm, kissed him, exclaiming, 'You're entirely yourself, feeling rightly jealous of the handsome curate. I was beyond the bounds of fear when you were fevered.'

She lay down her head next to his, face to face and whispered, 'Oh and you will be pleased to know that Michel, our other friendly doctor is now removed here to the vicarage and has offered to tend you in Dr Smith's absence.'

'I am in hell – now I know it. Both of them?' He tormented her unmercifully. 'And Smith, so helpful and kind...well, to you at least. He's more forthright with me. I feel he is a ladies' man.' He paused, looked anxious. 'He has an eye for you, love. And here am I, laid up like a babe.'

'Now I know you've had a knock on the head; you're hallucinating.'

'Not so much – but still. How long does Smith think I will be like this? I feel low, weak. It's an alien sensation.'

She sat upright, shook her head, her hair had fallen from all its pins and tumbled around her shoulders. 'I don't yet know.'

He tried to lift his hand to caress the hair, but he had to let it drop onto the bed; the effort seemed too much.

'Nat, love, you'll be weak at first, but rest today, and your strength will soon return, tenfold.'

He had turned his face away.

He is ashamed, unused to this state.

'I must be better tomorrow. There's much to do – this killer.'

She moved his face back with her hand, kissed him, smoothed his chest tenderly, her fingers slipping between the curls there.

'Water, Nat, here's some, drink, feel better,' she said in a brighter tone than her heart tended.

She managed to lift his head and he took some sips from the glass.

'Last night – Dr Smith said he'd been told a woman was being attacked in St Ann's Place. The Inspector sent me to look...'

'I heard about it.'

'Smith says the three victims had all been suffocated, Doctor Johnson told him. He mentioned that Johnson was a strange shy man and hadn't removed the women's clothes, his excuse being it would be unseemly as the cause of death was so obvious.' Nat did not sound convinced by the reason he had been given.

'Ah, that tells me he trusts Dr Johnson, did not look for himself, but then, there would be no reason for him to be there at Newton Street, unless Doctor Johnson was absent.'

Nat nodded, winced.

He's still in much pain, poor idiot. What will he feel when he learns about the theft?

She must tell him her pressing news.

'I need to tell you what has happened in the space of less than a day since you were injured. There is some good news, but the worst thing is we also have a setback, love.'

His eyes were alert on the instant. He listened without interruption as she explained about the missing posies, the diary and the news of Jenny Hargraves.

She added, 'At least she cannot be counted as the victim of a failed attack.'

He answered with a single nod.

He made a huge effort and managed to turn himself over slightly so that he could look at her. His expression showed his fears had multiplied, had become legion.

'Don't you see, my own darling? This means you're in direct danger. The killer knows you, knows you had the evidence.' He fell back. 'He knows you!' He groaned.

'Yes,' was all she could say. Her heart was full; fear flooded her veins.

Nat's face cleared a little. 'Will you go and speak to Inspector Bateman - and Inspector Caminada, if you can? Will you ask them to come and see me here and then we can lay out all we know to them? I can do nothing on my own account at the present.'

'I'll try.'

I can't tell them about my gift. They'd think me one of the army of charlatans. What little can I tell them?

There was a knock at the door and when she called that whoever it was could enter, Reverend Knightly stepped into the room. His expression was grave.

Chapter 25

'So do not fear'
The Old Testament: Isaiah Ch 41: v 10

'AH, SERGEANT ROBERTS, I was told you were unconscious. I'm glad to see you awake and perhaps, feeling better?' Reverend Knightly said, pleasantly, his gravity soon clearing when he saw Nat was awake.

Nat turned his head slightly and answered, 'No.'

Sophia added quickly, seeing the slight, but hastily hidden surprise on Reverend Knightly's face:

'He has just woken up, David, and didn't know where he was for a time, even though he was told this morning. His mind was jumbled like a bag of old clothes.'

Nat's eyes bored into hers, he scowled.

Reverend Knightly was undeterred.

'Ah, I recognise that feeling. I meet it each morning. But this morning, the vicarage has been so full of people and so busy that I've not had the time to indulge myself in my own morose musings. Michel has joined us here and, at this very minute, is being consulted by Reverend Williams because the poor old man feels a little unwell today. He is always so thirsty in the mornings and Michel tells me he has an idea of what ails him.'

'It must comfort him, as a doctor, to be able to help someone once more – in a medical matter, I mean,' Sophia said.

'As ever, Sophia, you are right. He said so himself, not five minutes ago and moreover, Dr Smith has some work for him that does not require both hands. Of course, Michel is not physically strong yet.'

Nat had listened to the conversation without comment until this point and now he turned himself slowly and addressed the curate.

'It embarrasses me to be in the same state too and because of that I must thank you; it seems. I'm told you came to my aid last night and for that and this bed, I'm truly grateful. I wouldn't have you think me as rude always, as I have been recently.'

Sophia tried to keep the surprise from her expression, but Nat noticed.

'Ah, Sophia, assure Reverend Knightly that my surly behaviour is not common with me but comes from fear of this killer.'

She eyed him narrowly.

'Don't ask me that, love. I can't be false to a man of the church. Reverend Knightly, David, the sergeant is always this surly, which is why I'll marry him to effect a cure. Each morning he'll wake and be puzzled and maybe even anxious about what I intend to do that day that doesn't involve him in a dilemma of any kind. It'll cure his ill temper.'

The curate laughed, Nat sank back on his pillow, closed his eyes in exasperation.

'Don't worry, Sophia, I hold nothing against anyone. Sergeant Roberts, no need of any words. You are most welcome to our care.'

Sophia watched Nat open his eyes, nod his thanks, but thoughtfully.

He is ever slow to trust, but that may be the legacy of his job.

278

People dissemble, lie, and deceive.

Reverend Knightly was relaxed, hands in his pockets.

He asked Nat, 'I wonder, do you have need of anything? I'm confident that we can find whatever that might be to aid your comfort and recovery. I can even arrange for a nurse.'

Nat shook his head. 'Sophia will, I hope, be at my side some of the time, but she's a few errands to do today and I think she'll be needed at the business to arrange an important matter. So, I thank you, but no nurse is needed. I feel as though I'll manage if I can just rest quietly. '

Sophia stood. 'Shall I try opening the shutter again? Can you bear just a little light so that you can see where you are?' she asked and as he lifted a hand in agreement. She went to the window and opened the shutter slightly on the shadowed side, away from the sun's present position. She caught Nat's eye; it was alright.

For the past few minutes, the noise outside in St Ann's Alley, beyond the graveyard, had been growing and she craned forward to see what was happening below.

'Oh, look, there is a Doom Seller outside; that's what I call these advertising men. One of them, *Repent your sins,* is being pushed along by the other sandwich board men. Poor man. But no, he has kicked one of the others; not so poor a man then. They will come to more blows before long. And there is *Drink is the scourge of the working classes* being jostled by *Hendricks Gin.'*

The curate joined her at the window, laughter in his tone.

'Ah, your man has one of my favourite Old Testament quotes; Revelations 12:12 *Woe to the inhabitants of the earth and the sea! For the devil is come down unto you, having great wrath, because he knoweth that he hath but a short time.'*

David was grinning broadly as he declaimed, but Sophia turned from the window; suddenly the diversion had soured.

Dismay clothed her.

'This is what has happened, isn't it? Those poor murdered women are but the result of the devil's work in our city.'

Reverend Knightly was standing next to her and the light shone gently on him through the dusty glass. She suddenly recognised that she experienced an overriding sense of familiarity and safety whenever she was with this man.

His aura is golden, he radiates comfort and compassion. That may be why he feels familiar and good, because I have always been used to such treatment. I have never been in mortal danger.

'Sophia,' he said gently, 'Another favourite of mine is Isaiah 41:10 *So do not fear for I am with you, do not be dismayed for I am your God.* And I am sure the police are going to stop this particular devil before he takes another poor victim. I expect you're confident of that, are you not, Sergeant Roberts?' He turned around.

'Not yet, Reverend Knightly. I'm laid low right in the middle of the investigation and although I'm a mere sergeant, I need to be involved because of the connection to Sophia; that's my main focus of engagement. This couldn't have happened at a worst time. I must be on my feet tomorrow and back to my station.'

He began to struggle to lift himself up in the bed and both Sophia and the curate rushed to help.

'What do you try to do now? What are you going to do if you sit up like this?' she chided him. 'Why not sleep a little?

'I don't want to sleep any more. I don't know what else I want but I feel more like a man if I am upright.'

David Knightly offered to fetch him a newspaper, 'If that will help occupy your mind perhaps.'

The offer was accepted and once the door closed, Nat looked at Sophia and said:

'I'll be all right for a time, please, love, do that errand for me. Go to Newton Street and try to see Inspector Bateman, ask him to come and see me if he will. It is not usual by any means for one of his men to ask him to visit like this, just because of an injury. But a word of warning; he is of a strangely changeable temper, and often precious about his own status as well as about his men, as I explained before. But maybe, because of the connection between you and the victims, he may agree to come. If we both explain and outline the clues we have discovered and the missing ones, of course, then he might agree to assign more men to the case and not only that, but he could also have someone assigned to guard you when I'm unavailable.

She agreed and said she would take a cab across the city.

'Take that ferocious *pit lass* with you, she can be as staunch a bodyguard as many a man. I'd not have you go out alone until this killer is caught.'

This made Sophia laugh until she saw how pale he had gone with the effort of such a long speech.

'I hate to leave you alone in this state. You're too impassioned to recover without someone to keep you still. Will you promise to stay in this bed until I return?'

He promised.

'Then rest quietly,' she said and kissed him on the lips, as ever.

She had no sooner finished speaking than Reverend Knightly returned with a newspaper he had got from downstairs. Having extracted a promise from him that someone would be with Nat at all times until she returned, she went to the door.

'I'll read the newspaper to the sergeant, if that will suit?' David looked the enquiry at Nat, who, to her surprise, nodded. David added, 'The Manchester Guardian, a good read, produced here in this fine city! And if we tire of that, I have the

Mercury – also a Mancunian rag.'

Nat grunted his farewell to her. Sophia laughed as she left in search of Alice, her eyes locked with his, and with the curate's last words in her ears.

'We shall get along together, so do not fear. Go in peace.'

Sophia collected Alice and they set out in a cab found for them by Brown, the new manservant at the vicarage. It was a difficult journey across the heated city; the roads were blocked in many places with the crowds of people on foot and horse-drawn vehicles of every size and shape from the ungainly omnibuses and the massive drays of the breweries to the tiny cabs and delivery vans. This was the usual traffic of the big city but today tempers rose; there were fights, shouting, screams of people and horses. Smoke hung everywhere in the windless air and the temperature remained high. With empty roads and on foot, the journey would have taken about fifteen minutes, as it was it took a gruelling hour and both women were drained of energy when they alighted the cab in Newton Street.

They wore light cotton skirts and blouses, but these were now stained with sweat. Both of them were glad of the muslin shawls they had brought for the sake of some formality as they served to hide the worst stains of travelling. They hastily tidied each other up, smoothing hair, straightening the summer hats; Alice had a little straw boater with pink paper flowers on the rim; Sophia's was a pale blue wide-rimmed straw; both were limp with the heat and humidity.

'We look a sorry sight to sue for an interview with an important policeman!' Sophia's tone was heavy with cynicism, but Alice opted for frank description.

'No, Miss, excuse me (Michel says *pardonnez-moi*) sorry to disagree, but we look like a couple of working girls out on a daytime extravaganza!'

Sophia burst into laughter and they both stood outside the police station helpless with their merriment until, the happy emotion quite spent, it morphed into fear.

Sophia wiped the tears that had gathered ready to spill.

'It's bizarre; everything in the world is turned on its head, Alice.'

Alice dashed away the little moisture from her own eyes.

'We're just hysterical, Miss. Many's the time me own mother would have thrown a bucket of cold water over me and me brothers for getting in such a state. If there were a horse trough nearby right now, I'd stick me head in!'

'Oh, Bliss!' Sophia remarked with some feeling. 'But,' she said, 'my serious errand calls. Come on.'

She glanced up at the carved stone portico above the main doors, and at the huge windows to either side. It was an imposing building. Nat worked here. He was responsible for the constables on his watch as they paced their beats in this vibrant city, would know to each minute exactly where they would be at that time. Policemen were passing in and out of the doors, some alone or in pairs, some manhandling their prisoners, men and women who had been brought on foot. Others were brought to the station in the closed van, the Black Maria, which in reality was a prison cell on wheels. As they passed the entrance to disgorge their cargo in the yard behind, the sound of the horses' hooves on the cobbles, the yelling of the prisoners and the clanging of the wheels made a deafening cacophony.

They hesitated at the door; a police constable stopped and spoke to them. He stood very close to Alice and his familiarity angered Sophia at once.

'Alright there, love?' he asked casually of Alice.

'Here to see the Inspector, if it's anything to do with the likes of you!' she answered pertly.

The man hadn't noticed Sophia who was ahead of the maid and continued speaking to Alice in the same vein:

'And what would the likes of *you* be doing for him, I wonder? You can see me instead – anytime, love,' he sniggered.

Sophia swung to face him. 'Pardon me, I think that has gone far enough. I'd ask you not to speak in such a way to my maid, thank you constable,' she snapped and looked pointedly at the number on his collar. 'Three, five, six, I see. I'll be mentioning that to the Inspector and to Sergeant Roberts. Please step aside, I'd like to go in. Come Alice.'

'Sorry, madam, my mistake.' The man's face had undergone a change from leer to fear as she spoke, and now he leapt aside as the women swept past him.

Inside, the entrance was dominated by a huge mahogany counter with which to serve the enquiring public and criminals alike. All the area of the entrance and its corridors were painted a dark green and the floor was tiled. A serviceable space. Barred doors led off this entrance and there were rows of benches against a wall. Behind the desk, and writing in a huge bound ledger, was a sergeant, an older man than Nat, ponderous, powerful, a nonpareil of experience. His uniform was the same as Nat's, but indoors here, the three stripes on his sleeves were strangely vivid against the dark fabric and surroundings. Imposing, authoritative.

Sophia approached the desk and introduced herself, explaining that Nat was injured.

'Ah, Miss Kelley, good day. It's good of you to come, but we have already had word from Dr Smith. I believe the sergeant was taken to St Ann's vicarage. How's he doing, if I might ask?' the desk sergeant said.

She gave him a brief account and told him how she had information from Nat for Inspector Bateman, asked if she might see him.

'Always busy, Miss Kelley. See what I can do, though – as it's you.' He called to a constable to watch the desk and strode away down the corridor. His passage was nothing short of momentous, prisoners on benches cringed away or spat when he passed, his men stood up respectfully.

Nat must be like this man in many ways. He has a presence.

The sergeant was soon back and threw out his arm in a gentleman-like gesture that showed they were to follow. Alice hadn't spoken at all. Sophia was thankful she was taking her role of lady's maid so seriously as he ushered them into the inspector's office.

It was furnished with a grand dark oak desk and file cabinets, a glass fronted bookcase; a busy, important space that said, 'I cannot deal with trifles.' Notwithstanding he had a small nosegay in a tiny china pot on his desk; they were lilac Sweet William. The man himself was an impressive figure as she had noticed when they met at the cathedral. She had found him polite enough then, but now she saw that he took great care about his person and thought a great deal about himself too. His uniform looked new, buttons, chains, buckles and medals shone dazzlingly, his boots were glossy and his dark brown moustaches splendid, curving round his cheeks to meet his sideburns. He was a fashionable policeman.

He greeted Sophia courteously and although they had spoken briefly on the evening of the storm, he seemed to have forgotten.

The inspector indicated with a careless sweep of the hand that whoever wished to sit, might do so. Sophia did, but Alice bobbed a curtsey and moved to stand behind her chair.

'My dear Miss Kelley, I appreciate this call. Is there something I can do for you?' he asked, still standing and of necessity, looking down at her.

She explained that Nat had important evidence he wished to unfold directly to the Inspector and that she had information herself. Sergeant Roberts wondered if the inspector had time to call on him today at St Ann's vicarage. He was confined to bed by his injury.

'Well, my dear Miss Kelley, I am regretful, desolate indeed, but I cannot arrange police matters in such a way and at the behest of my officers' friends and associates.' His tone was soothing, polite. 'I feel it would be more fitting for the sergeant to report to me when he is fit and well and we shall see what he wishes to say. Time enough then.'

Sophia raised her eyebrows slightly.

'And, I might add, I wonder what a person such as yourself can have to do with sordid murder, all too common in our city. You cannot have any personal knowledge of the incidents, surely?' he said, his voice quiet, yet astonished.

'Of course not, but I do ha...'

'Pardon me, Miss Kelley, I do find it unseemly that a woman could be interested in this matter.' He was almost bewildered.

She stood. 'It is because I am a woman, Inspector Bateman; women have been murdered, professional women, as am I. That leads me to have a personal interest in the progress of the case. Apart from that, my fiancé, Sergeant Roberts asked me to bring his message myself to emphasise the urgency of the matter. He is very ill.'

'He urges me?' he enquired softly, almost menacingly, she decided.

He continued smoothly, 'Miss Kelley, *the case* as you designate it is actually three separate murders. It was assumed at first that they were connected. I do counsel caution when faced with mass hysteria. As a result of this we have many public order incidents in our city at the moment, and I am very much afraid we may have to have The Riot Act read. But, my dear young woman, we are not in London. So, do not fear. The Ripper does not stalk our streets. Perhaps one should beware of reading too many of these lurid stories in the newspapers.' He smiled, showing his strangely white teeth and then continued in a brisk voice, 'Now, do tell Sergeant Roberts that I will certainly see him when he returns to duty.' His tone throughout the interview had been polite, firm and chiding. He walked from behind his splendid desk and opened his office door.

Sophia felt Alice bristle near her shoulder.

If only Nat were not a sergeant here, I would delight in tearing this man apart with a few well placed and razor keen remarks on his person and behaviour.

He held out his hand as she moved to sweep past and convention and more importantly, Nat's position, forced her to take it fleetingly.

The touch was electric. The image was merely seconds long; she had no sensation of swimming or entry into another's world, as she had had recently with the other visions. This time she saw a man – Inspector Bateman himself, on his knees in front of a second man. His hands were tied behind his back, his head was bowed, he was soaking wet and, on the floor, an empty bucket lay on its side. The inspector was naked, she could see his ribs. The other man was laughing.

Sophia dropped his hand as quickly as thought, walked quickly out of his room and out of the station.

She had to stand and breathe calmly to dispel the image. Alice nudged her arm.

'Miss Sophia, are you alright?'

The man has a secret, something he delights in. An odious secret. He is pleased with himself.

'Don't say any more, Alice. There is nothing you are thinking that I haven't already thought.'

'I know, Miss, but, pardon me, in your head, did you use the sort of words a Wigan miner would be right proud of when having a barney with an overseer and not caring if he were sacked?'

Sophia laughed and laughed.

They decided to walk back as it would be less tiring than taking a cab.

Chapter 26

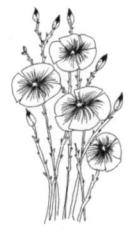

'The gentle rain from heaven'
Shakespeare: The merchant of Venice

THE STORM RAIN had had no lightening effect on the city other than to drown everything temporarily. The mud and mess created in that short and dramatic time had dried hard, becoming unearthly sculptures that surged up from the pavement with outstretched talons to tear at women's skirts, or leered around corners and set children screaming with excitement. Many of the messes were less creative and merely tripped people up. But clouds were gathering above the smoke and many hopeful forecasts were for more rain before long. A strange wish in Manchester, but this had been an unusual year for weather.

By the time Sophia and Alice arrived at the vicarage it was midday. Michel was in the hall when the door was opened.

'Ah, you return. I have been sitting with the good sergeant a while. He has been worried,' he told them, leading the way upstairs for Sophia. Alice had bobbed him a curtsey and tripped lightly downstairs to the kitchens.

Michel climbed the stairs carefully, grasping the bannister.

He must surely still be in pain, much pain, but what effort he puts into his recovery. A man of courage, decidedly. But where does he draw it from? Many would have wallowed in self pity after the trauma he has undergone. Yet, he's kind, gentlemanly - ah, and how is Nat? This last thought came as they approached the door of his room.

He did not look any more himself, but this did not trouble her unduly as he had had no rest during her absence. Apparently first David and then Michel had kept him company. Perhaps they were now better acquainted and to her surprise he did motion for Michel to stay when he would have left them alone. Perhaps…perhaps they would become friends. Who knows?

She described the meeting at the police station but both men were unsurprised.

Nat said, his temper growing as he warmed to his theme:

'There are many men, many in the Force who are like that, especially about professional women. The inspector is arrogant and yet he holds a position of power, hopes to wield more. He would be superintendent when the present man leaves. But to treat you as of no account! What was he thinking? I'll put him right, the snivelling fop. He cares more about the shape of his whiskers than he does about the law. And he says there are three unconnected murders. Blind! Conceited idiot. He wouldn't have treated you so if I had been there. I would crush his perfumed throat the second he tried to belittle you, patronise *you!*'

Michel stepped to the bed. 'Be calm, mon ami! It is not good for the heart to be so agitated. Rest, rest. It is needed. C'est un cochon. He is worse, a chauvinist! There are men like that here in England, but men are more respectful of women in La Belle France.' He spoke with fiery spirit.

How Alice would enjoy hearing this!

She said, 'We must forget him. We have more important people to speak to. Now I'm just thankful we haven't told him anything crucial. Nat, would Inspector Caminada have the same attitude do you think? Have you had much to do with him?'

'No, 'I've not, but he's a fine reputation, well respected by the men. I'm told he is as unlike my own inspector as a blancmange is to a side of beef.'

'Mademoiselle Kelley, perhaps to speed matters in this terrible case, the sergeant and you should play the same game to reach the goal in good time? In this instance use a man of influence to contact this Inspector Caminada.'

'In good time? You mean before the killer strikes again?' Nat said. He pulled himself more upright, painfully, slowly; shook his head quickly when she went to help.

'No, I can manage, love. I can manage.'

Michel continued. 'The Reverend Knightly is a man, how do I say? of charm, and he is of the upper classes in this country. In France, we are more egalitarian, no? Here, Reverend Knightly would be the one to win the prize for allure and persuasion. There is another word…ah, urbane, he is urbane.'

Sophia said he was right and Nat was soon convinced, and, despite his earlier antipathy, he also seemed to be finding the curate more agreeable.

He said, 'Yes, his newly laundered shirt and brushed coat will impress anyone. He speaks prettily too.'

'Nat! Thankfully, I can see you are in jest about his outfit…'

'I was not!'

'… but do you think he would undertake this office? It's more than ever vital that we get some help, isn't it?' she said, and her lip quivered. It was unlike her and she knew Nat would notice.

Michel was puzzled.

'Mon ami, if you speak to this man, who is not your inspector – I am a stranger here, is that what is allowed on such a matter and in your police force?'

To Sophia's practised eye, Nat's expression registered several emotions: fury, consideration, decision; fury at the way she had been received, consideration of his own rank, his career and the decision that it could not matter as much as the value he placed on her, not simply her person and image, but her life. There was a killer in the city who was preying on women like her – women who looked very much like her.

He kept his eyes locked on hers as he said, 'No, Michel, it is not commonly allowed, yet from what I have heard of this inspector in the detective division, he pays little heed to convention. I'll take the risk. I must!'

'Bravo, I also would do that which you have decided.'

Nat held out his hand to Sophia.

'Love, you have work of your own this evening; that I know, and it is a task that will not wait yet can be done by no one else. Will you enquire whether Reverend Knightly is here and ask him if he would come up as Michel and I have had an idea that only he can help with?'

He was there and he came and agreed to find the man and deliver the message with urgency.   When he and Michel had gone from the room Nat urged Sophia to go home, he would feel more settled and would sleep knowing she was preparing Isabella's body in good time.

Yes, his head was still so sore, but a kiss would be as balm from heaven, so it was given, and she left with Alice.

Outside the city had a new feel; the air was surely cooler stirred by a slight breeze. Sophia watched other people as they made their way home and she noticed that they walked a little faster, appeared less harassed. They were almost home when a young man walked quickly up behind them and fell into step next to Sophia.

'Excuse me, Miss Kelley, isn't it?' he demanded.

Sophia glanced at him.

'Do I know you?'

'Matthew Morris, 'The Courier'. Just wanted to ask how you are.' He had a notebook in his hand. He was confident, ordinary to look at, wore a serious expression and kept pace with them as though he intended to have his answer.

'I don't know you, so I don't think this is your business. Now if you don't mind...' She made a dismissive gesture with her hand, but he ignored it.

He persisted. 'Miss Kelley, you're in the Undertaking business but how does it feel to deal with murder victims? There was a third one yesterday. How did she die? What did she look like? The police have given the public no details and they deserve to know.'

'Go away, whoever you are!' she answered curtly and walked faster. 'That's awful – what you said. Awful!'

Alice was less polite and pushed between him and Sophia.

'Sod off! Go on, before I call for a policeman. Go on, just bugger off,' she shouted.

The city was noisy, and her voice didn't cause any shocked stares.

'Nice lady's maid, Miss Kelley. Got a name, love?' he glanced at Alice, pencil poised, adding, 'Was it like the Ripper victims, Miss Kelley?

Alice turned to him, still walking and slapped his hand hard upwards so that his notebook flew up and rolled down the street.

'Come on, Miss!' she cried and they both ran, flying into the yard and into Albert's path.

'Albert!' she gasped and once she had told him about the news reporter, he and Eddie went outside to find him. When they returned a little later, they announced that he hadn't managed to outrun them and probably wouldn't trouble her again.

She was furious about the reporter; all he wanted were sensational details to write a lurid story. It was also frightening that she could be pursued like that as though she was involved with the deaths, was an integral part of the latest murder story.

But with those visions, I am involved, very much inside their story...

'Albert, show me the horses. I need something normal to think of.'

Alice went off to see to her work. Albert sent Davy to watch the road outside the yard for any more nosy passers-by then he joined her.

'The air's lightened a bit, Miss Sophia, but the horses're not fooled – no, not they. There is some more weather in the air. They're not saying another thunderstorm, it's just that I can feel 'em relaxing a little, liftin' their nostrils to taste the air. They're lifting their legs a bit snappier too. Y'know what I mean, don't you, Miss.'

She smiled at him as they walked over to the stable block, feeling a little better.

'You know I do. Maybe this blessed heat will go at last. I can't bear it much longer. Look,' she exclaimed, pointing to wall by the yard kitchen where her pots of Busy Lizzie and geranium stood. 'Just look, even the flowers are looking forward to a respite – they're desperate.'

The Busy Lizzie, so fond of heat, had wilted, their heads bowed as if awaiting a drink. The geraniums were more stalwart and merely delivered more buds among the browned petals.

'I must tend them first and then I'm to prepare poor Isabella Waterstone for the viewing tomorrow.'

Sophia took a feed scoop and half filled it with grain then she and Albert walked the length of the stalls inside the block, stroking each horse in turn as they rested. Each one bent its head to her and nudged her for the expected treat, a palm full of grain, which she gave with a fond word for each. The ponies, only a pair today, were in the loose box at the end of the row and they pushed each other to get to the door and raise their noses up.

'Steady, steady,' she chided them fondly, 'Here.' She reached her hand over the door so that they could take their treat from her palm.

Albert sighed heavily. 'Isabella Waterstone, poor young woman. All the city talks of her; word got out because she was in the cathedral. It were in the Evening News and the Mercury too.' He shook his head, his face showing disgust. 'Now then, Miss Sophia, about the Waterstone funeral, I thought we'd use Duchess for the hearse, as they want one horse only and the plainest of our hearses and Butler Boy with Samson for the brougham. Just the one following vehicle I hear from Arnold,' he said, 'But two in hand because it lends more dignity. There will be four to carry and one would do it well enough, but not for this funeral.'

'Yes, and a plain pall over the coffin, the best we have, the silk. Her sister will carry roses for her, no other flowers, and the blinds down in the brougham. She is to be buried in St. Ann's graveyard, by permission of the Bishop, and it is to be at night – nine o'clock.'

'Aye, special, that is. That's right and proper,' he said. 'There's fewer crowds at that time and they're bound to be folk wanting to gawp. We'd better keep an eye out for them reporters too. Can't have them interrupting a funeral.'

There were one or two other matters about the yard to talk over, then Albert moved off down the row to speak to Ernie at the end. Sophia stayed in the stables moving along the stalls, talking and petting each horse again. As she got nearer the

295

men, she caught snatches of their conversation which held her attention when she heard names she knew.

Ernie said, 'It were the station blacksmith what had it from one of the charwomen. Definitely that Dr Johnson. He were sellin' it to some other well-to-do fella.'

'How d'you know it were being sold, lad?' Albert enquired.

'She saw money, paper money.'

'Well, don't tell no one else. Probably all gossip and you're turning into an old granny, yackin' all day. Any road get Duke and Duchess ready. Southgate's to be buried, two o'clock. Right?'

'Right, right. I heard,' Ernie answered as he walked away.

When he'd gone, Sophia caught up with Albert.

'What was that all about then?' she wanted to know.

'It were gossip, Miss Sophia, as you well know.' He busied himself with checking the harness buckles were properly polished.

'Well, Albert, I'm asking for a particular reason as I was at the station today. I've never seen this Doctor Johnson though. I went to give Inspector Bateman a message from Nat..'

'Oh, yes? How is 'e, then? The sergeant I mean. Something like, yet?' He stopped and looked carefully at her.

She shook her head. 'Not yet, strangely weak and kept in bed by Dr Smith. He said it's common after a head injury. Now that Michel has moved to the vicarage, he's there to tend to Nat also. They seem to be getting on.'

'I quite took to the Frenchman meself y'know. I think it helped him, me knowing the language. You went to Newton Street, you say?' he prompted her.

'Yes, you dark horse. What other talents have you, I wonder? I had to see the Inspector because Nat wanted to speak to him urgently, but he declined to be asked by his underlings and especially not through a woman. He was politely yet very effectively rude.'

'Aye, I've heard what he's like, but gossip again. Mind, with my own eyes I've seen him going in a cellar, down near the new dock warehouses, one night when I were bringing the horses back late from the meadows. And y'need not ask what goes on there, as I'll not tell you, Miss. I'll tell the sergeant when I see him, if it helps any way. I'm meaning to say that Inspector Bateman isn't one to trust in my opinion.'

I saw him. Inspector Bateman. Nat thinks him proud and tied to his career. He respected him as a policeman, until I told him about this morning's meeting. Will I tell Nat what I saw? No, not yet. I can't decide that yet.'

She patted Albert on the shoulder fondly. 'I'll be going back to the vicarage tonight, when I have finished the preparations. I'm worried about Nat you know.'

Albert grinned. 'He's not so delicate that lad, never worry. You can give 'im my best, if y'like.'

As she walked across the yard she breathed in the familiar smells, not now subdued by the heat; the smell of burnt hoof as the blacksmith shod one of the horses, the scent of soap and steam from the wash house, the earthiness of the muck heap, cooking food on the air, sweat, coal smoke, pipe smoke drifting through the gate as someone walked past, and the faint hint of formaldehyde they used in the workroom. A patchwork of scents that were this place alone.

Even in the space of an hour the air was fresher, the temperature must have plummeted. She looked up at the sky, saw fast white clouds just beyond the drifting smog.

'Rain? Wonderful, if so.'

She watered her plants, rain or no, they were parched, next she went to the kitchen in search of a cup of tea, urgently needed. She was soon in her workroom.

It was cool and calm in there. They had three other clients in the storage room, but the priority was to be Isabella. In Sophia's absence, Christina had delivered clothes for her to be buried in and there was beauty in their simplicity; a plain print dress, white leather slippers, a silver locket and a fine lace fischu. Modesty. Homeliness.

Sophia dressed herself for work, her long sleeved pinafore, rubber apron and long rubber gloves. She had pinned her hair high on her head and tied a scarf over it too for the cool air to cool her neck. She paused before beginning; this was the third victim of a sadistic killer, whatever that inspector might say, she knew only too well the truth.

She washed Isabella's hair carefully; it dried quickly with brisk towelling. The same golden colour as her own, but less curling. Her body was washed, then Sophia began to inject the embalming fluid; the whole process taking a couple of hours. All was cleansed and finished meticulously. She was then to be dressed in her burial garments. Only a few touches remained; her nails to be trimmed and buffed, her hair arranged as Sophia had seen it in life and her face given a tiny touch of colour with the cosmetics kept for that purpose. Then all was done.

Once the Southgate funeral was over her father came into the workroom.

'You are tired, my dearie,' he said, sitting on the tall stool as she cleaned up.

'Oh, yes, Father; I didn't sleep well in the vicarage chair.'

'I hear that Nat is talking and eating a little toast. Reverend Knightly officiated at the funeral this afternoon. Will you content yourself to be taken to see Nat, then brought back to your own bed? Tomorrow sees fit to be as busy as today,' he said, taking the tools from her and putting them in the sink. 'That can be done later.'

'I'll do it now, Father. Things get left otherwise – until they're needed urgently.'

He smiled at her insistence.

As she worked, she told him how Nat was to ask David to carry his request for a meeting to the detective, Inspector Caminada. Had he heard the outcome? He had not and he was thoroughly angered to hear of her treatment by Inspector Bateman.

Everything was cleared away. Together they placed her body in the lined coffin and took it on the trolley to the Chapel of Rest. It would be there in case the father and daughter should come earlier than expected.

The coffin was placed on the bier, candles were lit. Outside the sky had darkened and the golden candlelight caressed the dead girl's face. She lay all clothed in white, hands clasped on her breast, a sculpture of youth defeated.

'I'll stay a minute, Father. Go on without me, will you?' Sophia asked.

'Ah, yes, my dearie. I'll be in the house kitchen; surely there must be food by now.'

When he was gone, all was serenely quiet and peaceful. Sophia felt herself quite subdued in the presence of this poor girl's body, lying there to wait the tears of her family.

After a time, her ears caught a mouse-like pattering on the window glass and she saw that the added glitter on the stained-glass images came from raindrops, tapping gently then slowly winding their way down.

When she was little, her mother sometimes said that soft rain after the heat of summer was balm to the soul, saying it was tears from heaven, tears of joy because they were the water of life.

Tears of joy...

She felt her heart was sore.

Chapter 27

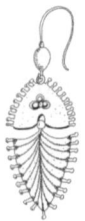

'Something wicked this way comes...'
Shakespeare: Macbeth

WITH HER FATHER as chaperone, Sophia returned to the vicarage. It had been raining for about an hour, although the early evening streets were busy as usual. Yet everywhere looked and felt different; the wind was brisk and warm, the heat was not yet chased away, but it was possible to get glimpses of the sky between the clouds and the chimney smoke.

Her father left her with Nat, having made his own greeting. He went in search of Reverend Williams, to chat in comfort for once, instead of restricting their talk to brief snatches by gravesides or in the vestry. Nat was sitting up but looked no better to her keen eye. He said he could not eat; his throat ached as though he had been punched or strangled, he said, and he fancied he could see two of her, he said - but that was no bad thing. And, he said, he felt nauseous all the time.

'But otherwise, love, do you enjoy your stay at the vicarage, even in this weakened state?' she teased.

'I am overcome with sleepiness or I would demonstrate to you just how weakened I am now,' he replied, gloomily, only a little of the old spark to his eye.

'Your drowsiness will soon be lifted; I am here to cheer you and make you feel better,' she told him, moving to sit on the bed.

'How will you do that?'

'Talking, love. You are too weak for even a kiss on the cheek.'

He lay back with a groan, but his face cleared as he remembered what matters pressed.

'You're right, love. Your pet curate fulfilled the errand, by the way. Inspector Caminada has agreed to come here in the morning. It's a great honour and I'm confident that he'll hear what we have to say and act on it. Rivalries'll work in our favour here because he and Bateman are daggers drawn most times – so there need be no fear of any communication between them.'

'Thank Goodness. You're pleased?'

'I am. I've been more than worried because of the theft. But the other Waterstone daughter, have you seen her since then?'

'I haven't, but she'll be coming to view her sister in the Chapel of Rest tomorrow. You're thinking as I do, that she might remember something from the diary?'

He smiled, pulled himself up from where he had slid. 'I am, yes. But more importantly, you're with someone at all times, love?'

He groaned suddenly.

'Cramp, my legs, arms,' he mumbled.

She rubbed them for him until it eased, tucked him up again.

'Never go anywhere alone,' he said.

Of course, she assured him she was taking care.

'The only people I see alone are clients or their deceased relatives, but at other times I'm with people who I've known and worked with for a long time, and I'm safe with them; don't worry. Now it's time you slept and certainly time I did. Father insists that I go home to my bed; I think he'll tuck me in.'

Nat grinned. 'One day, Sophia...'

'A bedtime story is what I can offer you now,' she told him as she rearranged the pillows and covers on his bed. He lay passive.

Unlike himself. Nat.

'It's part of our story, the one we weave together each time we meet, a thread each day. We'll retell this story when we are old and grey. The thread I'm thinking of was last summer when the weather was wild and really more English than this year. The colour of the thread was lilac grey – that's for the colour of the sky and the sea - and from that you may guess I'm going to remind you of our journey to the coast, to Blackpool.'

Nat smiled. She continued, her tone that of a storyteller. He'd tease her about that later, she knew.

'The train, a gargantuan iron monster belching steam and smoke, took us prisoner in a dungeon of rock and steel and bore us quickly away. At the end of the line we were freed, thrown out alone, for the beast's belly was empty of other passengers.'

He interrupted, 'They had more sense than to go on this journey.'

'Nat, we enjoyed it! We walked all along that beach – the tide had hidden itself a million miles out – in Ireland, I think! And we were well buffeted and wetted for our pains but oh, how we enjoyed it.'

'We did, love,' he murmured, sinking back on his pillows, his eyes relaxing and softening.

She continued, her eyes holding his, waiting for his to droop and close.

'We strolled on the wet sand, hard as city pavements and knobbly as cobbled streets, crunched our way through the litter of dried seaweed and shells and bottles too, left at the last winter. We toiled up the steps against the wind, up to the pier, had to hold onto our coats to stop them being ripped off by the angry gusts, but we ran the length of the pier, out to sea, our footsteps like drumbeats of an invading army...'

'Invading army...' he scoffed.

'Hush love, I am weaving a tale.'

'Scheherazarde. You are she.' He sank further down.

'And I will return the next night to tell another...but this one ended with a silver locket bought at the little shop on the pier and with a concert at the Pavilion. We hummed tunelessly all the way back to the railway station.'

'With fish and chips to eat...' His voice was scarcely a murmur.

He sleeps. So tired. Why is it? I'll ask Doctor Smith when he comes. Should the injury to his head cause this sleepiness? How long will it last?

'Sleep well, love,' she whispered, kissed him on the lips and went gently from the room.

In the hallway she met her father who was coming in search of her. Both Reverends Knightly and Williams and Michel saw them off. They would all meet again tomorrow.

The rain persisted. When they returned to the yard, Alice was waiting anxiously, hoping they would soon come because Christina Waterstone was in the Chapel of Rest, come unexpectedly and wanting to see Sophia.

She hurried there and found the girl sitting still and tearless by her sister's bier. She was unworried by the delay in seeing Sophia, wanting to see her sister's body alone without her father. His grief was heavy, and Christina said she wanted to remember good and beautiful times with Isabella.

'Christina, but you're wet! Did you not have a coat or an umbrella?' Sophia wanted to know. The girl's dress hung limp and damp and her hair glistened with water.

'I don't care, Miss Kelley. I'm young and strong, and I'll not get a cold from this little wetting. Isabella would have loved to run and splash in the rain, if only she could. When I saw it rained at last, I had to come here and see her, tell her about it. Do you understand?'

Sophia did, she understood perfectly the need to stave off the final parting by pretending it need not happen.

'Can I get you a shawl, now you're here? You may get a chill and tomorrow you'll be needed, greatly needed,' she said, and rang the small bell that would bring Alice.

She soon answered it and a shawl was fetched, accepted, and drawn gratefully around the girl's thin shoulders. A shiver ran down her frame now that she had the shawl, as though she realised suddenly how much her body had wanted it. Minutes later Alice returned with a tea tray. She put it down silently and went.

Christina looked full at Sophia.

'Isabella looks beautiful – here. It's a strange place. We came here to see our mother, and now here am I, alone. Father doesn't know I'm even out of the house – and here. He's in his room. We'll both come tomorrow, in the morning, as the funeral is to be at sunset Father says. Reverend Williams said it will be the quietest time at that end of the city and around the churchyard.'

'It will, and it will be peaceful. Perhaps it will be as though she is going to bed,' Sophia suggested.

Christina nodded. 'Perhaps.'

Sophia poured her some tea and Christina was shivering as she took it. She wrapped her hands round the cup, sipped gratefully. Sophia came to sit next to her, took her hand.

'There's something you need to know, something quite dangerous in many ways – but dangerous to me, don't fear for yourself.'

The girl was more alert now. 'Miss Kelley, what is it?'

'The diary, Isabella's diary has been stolen from my workroom, and some other things too, but the diary is the most important of all because it can only have been stolen by someone who knows the value ...'

'...of what is written in it, you mean,' Christina finished. She stared into Sophia's eyes. 'What other things were taken, something of my sister's?'

'No, no. I cannot tell you exactly, but they are not as important as the diary. And I can't tell you because Sergeant Roberts is handling this with another policeman. Please accept my explanation.'

'But is your workroom open to anyone to visit?'

No, only people who are regularly seen here. Could someone have run in?

'No, it's not and that is the biggest worry, I'll own. It means someone knew I had it and where it might be.'

'I know I told no one of the diary but someone wicked knows *you*, Miss Kelly,' Christina said, her hand flew to her mouth, her eyes became wide with fear, tears started from them. 'You have a look of my sister too. Oh, Miss Kelley, please take care. Poor Isabella,' she said and turning to Sophia she flung her arms about her and cried.

She held the girl until the moment passed. Christina turned to look at the body in the coffin.

'She is safe at least,' she said.

Sophia wiped the girl's eyes with her own handkerchief.

'Sergeant Roberts wants me to ask you if you remember anything from the diary. You say you only read it on the day she was killed, can you bring anything to mind that you read at such a dreadful time?'

Christina thought carefully.

'I think I may – a little.'

Sophia's heart gave a leap of hope.

Christina began, 'Some of what I keep in my mind is just unconnected facts that felt strange to read. For instance, she wrote that he wouldn't allow her to take him into Kendal Milne's to shop; she said he was shy. Perhaps she wanted to show him off to the other assistants on the shop floor. I work there in the offices, as a typist you know. Maybe he didn't want me to see them together.'

She paused to gather more details to mind. She said she remembered some things because they were special trips, and she, Christina, had not done anything like that with a man – someone she was walking out with, that is. Apparently, Isabella had been taken to Liverpool on the train and she had been to an art gallery there, a grand place, the Walker Art Gallery. She had wanted to go to the museum and the library too, but he had hurried them away suddenly, saying they would miss the train – Lime Street Station, that was it. Very grand, she said in her diary. Once they had gone to Knutsford to see where the author, Elizabeth Gaskell had spent part of her childhood and they picnicked in a meadow there. Curiously, he only took her out into the city here when it was dark; he said found crowds and the night lights exciting.

Christina looked at her sister's body. 'Issy, I do miss you, but I must tell someone of these things. I shall go mad otherwise.'

Sophia said, 'I'll listen to you. I'm so sorry you miss her. Poor Isabella.'

The girl blew her nose, wiped her eyes. 'I remember something bizarre. She wrote that he promised to take her to a theatre one night (I hadn't heard of it so it mustn't be a popular one), to see a man who could hypnotise people and make them do odd things. It was very peculiar to see this in writing, and she must have thought it so herself to record it in her diary, but I also have a feeling she was very excited about it; he told her she would be surprised to see who the hypnotist was.'

'I heard some gossip about a hypnotist going round the small theatres and halls.'

Christina didn't seem to have heard her, she was lost in her own reflections, confused also.

'They must have been out on these jaunts several times, yet we at home knew nothing of it – or him. Issy and I had our own rooms and father always works late in his study, so neither he nor I could have heard her leave. But what shocks me is that my bright, normally truthful sister could be so devious.'

'You said your father wouldn't have approved of her seeing anyone?' Sophia asked.

Christina managed a small smile.

'He is not like some fathers who want to keep their children at home for selfish reasons. He simply wants to keep us safe, especially since our mother died and it's since then that he has come to think that we all live on a knife's edge. Isabella wrote somewhere that the man was older than her. Father wouldn't have accepted that, and he talked many times of much older men preying on young women, especially younger women with money – he is a bank manager you know, and perhaps came across this in his business. It was distasteful to him. I think he saw that she became restless and then reckless after mother died. Oh, she was still loving and kind, but there was something that lit a fire in her eyes, and I know Father noticed.'

Sophia shook her head. 'Who is he? What does he look like?' she wondered and then she looked at Isabella's body and heard her voice quite clearly...

Christina also shook her head in disbelief about all that had happened. She sat quietly and contemplative, her head bowed because she was not aware of anything but the silence and the sputtering of the tall candles.

But Sophia heard Isabella:

'So handsome, so tall and distinguished. I sound like a schoolgirl describing a beau, but people always say this of him, and they respect him. Why wouldn't they? He does a great service. I'm to assist him when we are married, because I'm used to management. He said I'll help him get to the top of the profession.' She sighed. 'His hair, so thick but well cut, dark like his beard. It's so very distinguished, beautifully sculpted like one of those paintings of the old masters – the Flemish ones, I think. He's strong too and he lifted me so easily over the stile that day...'

Isabella quietened. Sophia's mind became still.

'Miss Kelley,' Christina said, touching her arm, 'Miss Kelley, are you alright? you must be tired; you look so drained. I will go now.'

She was about to show Christina out, when the girl stopped her abruptly.

'Oh, Miss Kelley, I'd forgotten something. It may be unimportant, but it upset us - rather, it upset Father. For my own part it made me angry, angry to my core. When we were taken to the police station to identify Isabella, the doctor there, I can't remember his name, he seemed to behave strangely, as though he were drunk and he didn't listen to anyone, merely moved about haphazardly. He slurred his speech and he even *smiled* a little. I wanted to hit him. There was my sister...there on that table... and he smiled!' Her body shook with that same anger until she took hold of herself and was able to continue. 'It wasn't right. You'll tell the sergeant? I think that's important.' She turned again, 'You'll tell the sergeant?' she repeated.

Sophia promised. She got one of the lads to find a cab for her, insisting she, Sophia, paid for it.

'You'll soon be home, you're very tired too,' she said but Christina answered:

'I am tired to death – oh, that is wrong isn't it? But I am tired of death. And I miss my sister.'

Sophia went to bed but found all she could think about was what she had now learned about the killer.

She woke next day unrefreshed and heavy.

Chapter 28

'The better part of valour is discretion'
Shakespeare: Henry IV part 1

IT WAS FIVE O'CLOCK. Sophia could hear the yard awakening and the sounds from the street beyond vied with them as usual. Iron shod wheels and hooves crashed heavily along the cobbled streets. People called to each other. There were shouts of the early vendors selling milk, fruit 'up from the country'. She usually laughed at their cry because the vendors she saw regularly were never in the country and their goods were got at the fruit market, fresh from Victoria Station. Factory hooters sounded and competed with the distant whistles of the early train departures.

She fell back to sleep, this time a deep sleep, the sleep of exhaustion and mental chaos. When she awoke it was eight o'clock. She felt a need to see Nat, a great need. If he was unlike himself it was because there was something wrong. He surely should have made a recovery by now. She opened the curtains and threw up the sash, groaned when she felt the air.

Warm again. It's too much. At least it may be a little cooler for the funeral tonight, although we haven't had to bury anyone in darkness before. It was good of Reverend Williams to suggest that time. If anyone gets wind of it and they know

*she is one of the victims, there may be people coming to gawp,
as Albert says. Worse still – the newspapers. I must see Nat. I'll
go now while it's quieter on the streets, if it ever is so.*

She dressed quickly and in light clothes once more, had tea
and called Alice, who was delighted to accompany her. They
walked; the temperature was cooler in the back streets than on
the main roads just then.

Sophia carried a basket of foods, both for the men at the
vicarage and for Nat, small things she knew he liked, hoping to
tempt his appetite. Alice carried sheets and other bedding to
ease the laundry load on the vicarage and some of them for the
charity basket.

'How's the sergeant, Miss? Is he getting better? On the right
side yet?' Alice asked as they kept up their fast-paced walk.

'No, not yet; not as well as I thought he should. Michel is on
hand though. That's a comfort.'

Alice brightened. 'He *is* a nice man, don't you think, Miss?'

'You know, I think he is. How lucky we found him when we
did, he'd have died otherwise. Will he stay here in Manchester
long, I wonder? Perhaps he'll want to travel back to Orléans
when he is well. '

'Dr Smith says he has something Michel can do, some
medical thing, not needing two arms. Mind, he's still injured,
isn't he? He's a tough one, but the arm must be that sore.
Anyway, I think he'll like it here and I reckon he'll stay on.'
Alice smiled broadly to herself. Skipped a couple of steps.

Sophia threw her a swift look. 'Alice?' she asked with
meaning well beyond the single word.

'Yes, Miss Sophia?

'What is on your mind, imp?'

'Nothing, Miss,' she said. 'It's just that he's so kind. I think we
can be proper good friends. He says we speak the same
language, and before you scoff, Miss, he meant the language of

our souls.' She was wholly serious.

'Sophia stopped in her tracks. 'Souls? He said that?'

Oh Alice. Are you caught by the handsome Frenchman? But she's so young and my responsibility. Vulnerable despite her hard exterior. Is he trustworthy? Is she mistaking his friendliness and his extravagant turn of phrase for a different emotion? Romance?

Aloud she said, 'Alice, I want you to be careful in this friendship. Let it grow very slowly, if it is to grow. I know you have seen a different sort of life to the one I have, but I am older and more importantly I'm your mistress, I must look out for you and advise. I don't want harm to come to my little wild spark.'

'Oh, Miss Sophia.' Alice was certain of herself here, Sophia could tell by her tone. 'Thank you but never fret. I know my own station and I were taught early on how to look after myself, even if I was caught by the young master. But he were a different kettle o'fish, so to speak. It's harder to look after y'heart though, don't you think? Any road, I'm not looking to Michel to hold my heart. I just like him.'

They walked on.

'It is. You're a wise girl for your age but take care and tell me if anything goes amiss. And now that you have struck a bright romantic note to the day – make it musical – orchestral even and tell me something from Wigan that will entertain me – make me laugh. It feels like I've not laughed properly for an age with all this death and disaster and weeping, so much weeping and sorrow. Dig deep in your memory, but not too deeply as we'll be there in ten minutes.'

Alice brightened, heaved her basket onto the other arm as she wove past some people carrying rolled up rugs on their shoulders. That manoeuvre was no sooner completed than she had to avoid a man pushing a handcart full of rags and on the pavement, where he shouldn't have been. Next they both had to take a dangerous detour across a couple of planks that spanned a gigantic hole in their way; it was full of workmen who were digging deeper than man's height and beside it were heaped soil piles and pipes.

'A single miner could've had that hole ten men deep in an hour!'

'A miner can do anything according to you! They're the strongest, toughest, handsomest, most adept at swearing, blackest men on the face of the Earth,' Sophia teased, but Alice merely smiled.

Even at so early an hour, the city was awake and had started its day as it meant to go on. A barrel organ and its grinder took up more space round the corner, his jaunty tune competing with shouts and traffic noise. Other people were forced to surge around each obstacle too and the way was tortuous. People, gaudy and hot in their bright clothes, swinging skirts, striding legs, dogs on leashes, clumsily loaded baskets that disgorged goods and shopping. Here and there darted filthy children selling anything from bunches of watercress to tiny books of matches, some stealing what they could, food or valuables.

Alice ran a few steps to catch Sophia up.

'Miss, I've remembered something to make y'laugh. It were when I were a pit-head lass. Some places called 'em pit brow wenches, but whatever we was called, we were a bold bunch, I should say! We were out in all weathers, all day, with nowt but a bit of singing to warm us – well, that and our jackbit (what you call dinner, Miss) oh, and a tin pot of cold tea. Every one of us with bulging arm muscles and the blackest 'ands this side of the pit itself – *up top,* as they say.'

A pause when they detoured around an impromptu sale; a man was standing on a box enlightening a small crowd about the properties of a bottle of medicine, which he held; it would cure most things – anything – heart break, dyspepsia or broken bones.

Sophia and Alice came together again, and the tale was taken up again.

'We used to stand under a canvas shelter of a sort, on a platform, so as to reach the moving belt. Anyway, on that came the coal in all sizes and we 'ad to sort it. Biggest lumps were already taken off t'the furnaces and to go to the mills in wagons. We 'ad to pick out the rocks and sling 'em and sort the coal with great big sieves. They were a weight; I think me arms stretched. We had to use a shovel to sling the coal into wagons too.'

Sophia interrupted. 'Well, that's the lesson in how industry progresses. I'm not moved to laugh yet.'

'I'm getting to it, Miss. It seems that rich gentlemen had a fancy within them to watch us workin' and some of 'em came all the way from London to watch.'

'Watch what?'

'Watch us lasses at work – all bending and stretching and bulging. Seems men liked to see the trews we wore, showing off y'legs. But to me they made y'legs look like tree trunks, what with the knee shields and patches and muck.'

Sophia wondered, 'Bulging?'

'Backsides and bosoms, Miss, begging pardon.'

Sophia laughed long at this and when she was almost recovered Alice continued:

'Most o'the girls were big as many a man too. Every mine in Wigan had 'em. But what I'm coming to is that the local photographer in Wigan, and many a one from other cities, used to come and take photographs of us. And they sold 'em as picture postcards.'

'Pictures of you?'

'Yes, Miss. We had to pose in our working clothes, with a

sieve or a shovel, sometimes against trees to look countrified. I did one where I had to stand leaning on a coal wagon, on't railway line. "Smile at me love," the photographer'd say – but I never did. Used to do me best scowl.'

Sophia wiped her eyes with the back of her hand. 'So you were an artist's model, in a way?'

'I suppose so, but with all me clothes on. I wouldn't do nothing wrong like that, I can tell you. Me dad would have burnt the photographer's shop to the ground if there were anything immoral like. Seems the photographer liked me because I were much smaller than the other lasses; he paid 10 shillings for three poses. Very good money. And d'you know what he had printed underneath me picture? *Though she be but little, she is fierce.* That's William Shakespeare that is.' Alice's voice held much pride, Sophia noticed.

She plied Alice with more questions about the poses and who bought the postcards, how popular they were. Did she have them to show now? No – her father burnt them instead of the photographer's shop or the man himself, though he made fair to do that too.

'Miss, the newspapers in London and here were saying it was indecent, the way we was dressed, but it was what were needed on the job – like you have your black outfits. They spoke of it in the parliament too and Lord Crawford stuck up for us. He's the one as owns Haigh Hall and all the land and most of the coal thereabouts. He wrote in the paper himself, If I can remember, he said us pit girls were not immoral and our clothing, "the inheritance of their mothers and grandmothers", were only objected to by "ignorant prudes, who, if left alone would probably put a 'frill' round the ankles of their kitchen table". Have I cheered you up, Miss?'

'Yes, I am. The very idea of the kitchen table...' Sophia laughed.

How very strange, the things people find amusing or in this case, just plain saucy. Ah, I wonder if Alice knows anything about this other strange thing?

But Alice had something entirely different on her mind.

'Speaking of Lord Crawford, Miss; I used to walk out with one of his grooms – senior groom he were and I've 'ad a letter from him – well, a couple of letters really…three.'

'You dark horse, Alice. Well?'

'Well, the thing is, erm, well, he wants to write to me regular like, and take me out. Is it alright if I do, Miss? On me day off – he could get a train to Victoria and we could have a walk or tea, or something.'

'Of course, Alice, of course. We need something good to happen here. If you decide you're going to be very good friends, then he can come to the yard and see the horses, as he's a horseman too.'

'Ooo, Miss, thank you. That'll be grand, really it will. And he'll love it.'

'His name, this young man?'

'Will, Miss. I mean William, William Martin.'

'William. Hmm. By the way, have you heard any more of our men's gossip about the hypnotist? They're worse than a band of chattering sparrows.'

'Why d'you ask, Miss? – if I may be so bold…' She smiled broadly.

'Very bold, Alice! It's just that I was talking to Christina Waterstone last evening. She remembered a great deal from the diary. I suppose after such as shock as a sister's terrible murder, your senses might be overwrought either to blank everything from your mind or, as it seems with her to make it especially retentive. She says that Isabella mentions the prospect of being taken to a hypnotist show. She thinks it must be at a small theatre or other place as she had never heard of it.'

'Ah, yes,' Alice said brightly. 'I did hear the lads talking. They were planning, but only the younger lot, to go and see summat that sounded very sassy – the hypnotist who calls 'imself Monsoor Maurice. It's to be on at the Rose and Crown, down Deansgate, tomorrow night at nine o'clock. Why, Miss?'

'I want to go and see who this man is. It feels critical, it feels like the key to all. You'll have to come with me.'

'Oh no, Miss, you're a lady. It's a rough place, I believe. I wouldn't go myself.'

'Then we must dress up like the sort of women who would go.'

'Miss I reckon only lower-class women and street walkers go there.'

'Can you find the sort of clothes we'd need – as a poorer working woman, mind, something more respectable. The pawn shops perhaps? Have you the skill to disguise us? I think I can speak the type of language they do; I've heard it when out with Nat, when we have passed by people, I mean.'

Alice pondered the problem, walked slower, her eyes troubled. It had already taken them longer to get near St Ann's Square than they planned, due to the busy crowds.

'Miss, can I say – I think it'd be proper dangerous.' Alice was hesitant. 'What would the sergeant say?'

Sophia interrupted. 'I won't need to tell him. A pair of respectable working women would be safe enough, surely?'

'I don't know, Miss. Maybe. You know best, I'm sure.'

'Hmmmm. That's settled then. The clothes? I'll give you money, of course.'

Alice's expression was still worried. 'Oh, Miss Sophia, even at the pawn shop on Water Street, I'd need as much as ten or fifteen shillings.'

They made their plans.

By the time they reached St Ann's Square, Sophia owned

herself better in spirits and when they turned into St Ann's Place, Alice ran up the steps to ring the vicarage bell feeling she had done what she was asked. Sophia smiled at her anxious glance, nodded.

They were met by the open door of the vicarage, the gifts were accepted by Reverend Knightly and before he could say anything other than a greeting, Alice was off to take the food and laundry to the kitchens, and Sophia had run lightly upstairs. She'd been told that Dr Smith was attending Nat at the moment and that Michel was there also. It was with a lighter heart than she had had for many days that she stepped unawares into the room.

Both the doctors were leaning over Nat's bed. He was flat on his back and Michel was saying:

'Pardon, but the breathing, it is made easier for the patient with a temperature if he sits up, The lungs, they need to expand so, his heart will steady also.' His tone was respectful to the other doctor. 'I see this onboard ship and in the hospital for the poor in Orléans. There are many fevers.'

Dr Smith stood upright when he heard the door open. 'Ah, Miss Kelley.'

He stepped aside and she saw with a stab to her own heart, that Nat looked very ill. His head moved restlessly from side to side, he was flushed once more, his limbs trembled. She could see the pillows were wet. Was it a fever?

'No! No. I though he was better. What has happened?'

His eyes are open, no – closed again! He's barely awake.

Dr Smith shook his head a little, his expression guarded.

'Nothing but a small relapse, my dear Miss Kelley. Do not worry. He has a sore throat and is feverish – a bad cold, nothing more.'

Michel added, 'But the breathing is depressed, and he is

318

nervous, restless like a bag of frogs. Mon ami, Dr Smith, indulge me. Allow him to sit up. And we should place the pillow so that his head is a *little* back to open the throat, n'est-ce pas? Do but try him sitting, I beg of you.'

Dr Smith assented, but reluctantly, she thought. Perhaps he resented interference. She did not care; Nat came before his feelings.

'Please try, Dr Smith. We can always lie him back again if this does not ease him.' Her voice had taken on a pleading note and it annoyed her. She needed to be firm.

He paused a beat before answering:

'You are right. Indeed. We will see if his breathing improves and try to get this temperature down,' he said. He touched her shoulder lightly. 'Do not worry. You need to be strong.'

Nat's the strong one.

As though sensing her thought he groaned, thrashed his head on the pillow, tried to open his eyes. Sophia felt terror rising within like a beast against the bars of a cage. She forced herself to be calmer, looked at Michel and saw that he empathised. He pointed to his injured arm and then with a sorrowful inclination of his head and a wholly Gallic shrug, he gave her to understand that he could not help turn Nat's unconscious form. She hastened to the bedside.

'I can help, Dr Smith,' she murmured.

He glanced at Michel and with an apologetic bow of his own head at him, he smiled acceptance at her.

Together they managed it well.

I'm used to handling bodies. But his body and in such a state! God help me – and Nat.

She bit her lip and turning to Dr Smith, her expression now all practicality, she asked:

'How long before we know if this position is good, doctor?' she asked aloud; inwardly she screamed *Save him. God save him. Breathe well, love. Wake up properly, speak.*

Michel answered for the other man, smiling, 'Almost immediately.'

Dr Smith graciously acknowledged him with a bow.

They watched as, over a few minutes, his breathing eased, but only a little. It seemed shallow to Sophia. Dr Smith said he would call for some water and cloths as before and once summoned, Alice and Mrs Jenkins responded quickly. The women spent the next hour sponging and cooling Nat's hot body. During that time, he moaned and muttered, tried to grasp the hands that were helping him, but seemed incapable of resisting too strongly. Eventually he responded and he was able to recognise Sophia and managed to squeeze her hands with his own.

Feverfew would be good for him to sip. It's a powerful herb for reducing heat, she thought; aloud she asked, 'If only there were some feverfew growing somewhere nearby. It's such a good remedy. I've none at home, but maybe...'

Mrs Jenkins said quickly, 'I do know, Miss Kelley, blessed if I don't. There's some growin' down near the river on that waste ground by the old munitions factory. I can slip over there in a trice.'

Sophia brightened. 'But it's a long way. No, Alice can go.'

Alice was up in a second. 'I can, Miss; save Mrs Jenkins's legs.'

The older woman answered, 'Now, now. My legs is fine. I can skip down there alright, but come if y'like, love.'

Dr Smith added, 'Yes, indeed, the herb will be useful as an infusion and I will give him a mild sedative which he can take for some sleep. These fevers can drain energy very effectively.' He addressed Michel. 'My friend, you were right. I take my hat off to you. We will keep him upright until the fever has subsided altogether.'

Michel murmured, 'De rien, mon ami.'

Alice was clearing up materials with Mrs Jenkins, but Sophia saw her mouthing, 'De rien,' to herself several times. They were quickly gone.

Michel and Dr Smith crossed over to the window at a signal from the latter and engaged in medical talk from what Sophia could overhear; but she paid little attention because Nat's eyes were open and they were more alert; he was looking at her. She quickly went to sit on the bedside and continued to wipe his forehead with the freshly drawn cold water. It had been replaced from the ewer on the washstand and fresh towels added to the wooden rail.

'Much better, my love,' he managed to whisper.

'Nat, a little relapse, that is all. I thought you were improving?' Tears started and rolled down her cheeks.

'Now, now. I'll get better.'

He raised his hand shakily and brushed the tears away with his fingers and she caught hold of them and kissed the very tips. Her heart was full and threatened to overflow once more. She must do something; perhaps talking about urgent practical matters would help her guard her emotions from him. He must feel none of her despair. His skin was blotchy and reddened on his arms and face, going down his chest too. She wouldn't mentioned this yet.

'Love, you need a shave! You feel like a rough brick! I'll send Alice to do the office for you.'

'You'll send Alice back down the mine! I'll not stand the very thought of her with a blade near my throat – that *wench* is too vigorous for me.'

Sophia laughed but it stopped short when she remembered something.

'Oh my! Inspector Caminada? When is he expected?' she asked.

'I think around noon, love. You'll stay? I'm weak at the

moment; I might forget something.'

The doctors finished conferring and Dr Smith said he had many calls and promised to come again that evening, but early. In the meantime, he was confident Michel could handle any needs. It was arranged that she should stay and see the infusion made and spend the afternoon here. She could give the sleeping draught when Nat was ready for it, they said, and left.

His breathing is better, he is lucid and cooler. That's good, I think, but I'm no doctor.

The feverfew was harvested and brought to the vicarage, made into an infusion which Nat affirmed did his throat good too. Mrs Jenkins maintained that it was the honey that she added to the drink; it was the best thing for a sore throat, and she had three husbands to prove that.

When the good woman's back was turned, Alice mouthed at Sophia, 'All dead!' drawing a finger across her throat. Sophia felt the bubble of laughter rise in her throat, but when she looked at Nat it morphed into a smothered sob because he had two days' growth of his strong beard, which he normally liked to shave twice a day. He hadn't mentioned it.

Alice and Mrs Jenkins set about to tidy up the room in the expectation of the important visitor. It was big and cool, thankfully for Nat's condition. The sun had moved round to the other side of the building, so they opened the shutters and threw up the window. No sooner was that done than the noise of the city intruded, but as it didn't seem to disturb Nat, it was left alone.

The marble top of the washstand was cleaned, the water replenished again, soap and towels straightened. The bed sheets were straightened, and the quilt carefully folded and laid across the blanket press at the end. A fire was ready laid in the grate of a fine marble fireplace and Sophia wondered what sort of person had this bedroom when it was new. The wallpaper was faded damask roses which she liked and then wondered what Nat would like when they were married. The pretty thought was fleeting. The mantle and two solitary candlesticks were polished, the oil lamp filled, and a shine given to its brass base. Cushions on the *easier* chairs, so described by Reverend Knightly, were plumped and shaken. It was a comfortable room.

Noon and the visitor arrived, shown up by a suitably awed Alice because Inspector Caminada was an imposing figure. He was tall, swarthy in complexion with a dark, neat beard and moustache, short dark hair parted neatly in the centre. His clothes were well cut and even in the heatwave he wore a dark suit of clothes and a tie. He was pleasant, personable.

'No, Roberts, don't stir. You're unwell. This is not like you, from what I hear,' the inspector said and shook hands with an embarrassed Nat. Sophia was introduced and he bowed over her hand.

The formality and strangeness of the greetings done; they spoke of the reason for his call.

'Sergeant, your own inspector – Bateman, isn't it? You've approached him, I hope. The chain of command is important.'

Nat's voice was quiet, his manner subdued, but he was clear and insistent that he had proceeded entirely as the rules of his uniform dictated. He affirmed that he had followed orders to the letter, but that because of the evidence he and Sophia had collected, he was convinced that she was in very present danger and he would do anything to protect her. His own inspector had declined to listen to Miss Kelley or any so-called evidence, declined to visit and hear in person what had been discovered, so he had willingly risked his career by going behind his back and requesting this meeting. The speech left him exhausted.

'Miss Kelley, may I ask your connection to these murders, other than being affianced to the sergeant here?'

His voice was rounded, deep, his manner forthright and penetrating. She found no difficulty explaining her role which was, in the main, professional and together she and Nat outlined the clues they had discovered, some by happenstance, others because of her contact with the bodies, but not, of course, her clairvoyance. Being the chosen undertaker, she was face to face with the evidence as it presented itself: all three victims were similar in appearance and indeed so was she to them. The formality of the victims' pose, the expression of their faces, the missing earring and the hat, the pinprick mark under the ear and finally the chilling discovery of the posies - by her alone, were all the same for each victim. To the best of their knowledge, none of these things were discovered at the police mortuary.

'And I have the knowledge of flower lore to read the message these posies contain. I've written them down for you, Inspector Caminada,' she told him and drew a sheet of paper from her handbag, gave it to him.

He read them first to himself and then aloud, his tone disbelieving.

'There is Sally Hepplestone, who was the first victim. The posy left with her was made up of the daisy, which is for innocence, the nettle representing pain and the forget-me-not, which is for hope and optimism, apart from the commonly known message of remembrance.' He looked up from the paper and blew out his cheeks in disbelief. 'Now for the interpretation, the reading of the combined notes from each flower into a message.' He looked separately at both of them, his expression infinitely sad. 'Together they say, *remember the pain of this innocent,* or, as you say, Miss Kelley, they could have another message entirely; *hope must bring pain for the innocent.'*

Sophia said, 'And it has, hasn't it? Brought pain.'

'Indeed,' he agreed, sombre and looked down to read about the second posy.

'This was left with the second victim, a Miss Adeline Worthington. It was made up of honeysuckle, which I see represents affectionate devotion, and also carnation, purple carnation. I know this particular colour symbolises many negatives: antipathy, capriciousness, changeability, unreliability and a whimsical nature. You note that this can all be contained under the term *coquetry.* I don't believe I have ever seen a purple carnation...'

'A white, newly cut bloom has been put in water containing a purple dye, such as ink,' Sophia told him. 'The cut end is dyed too.'

'Ah, is that so? And back to the list, there is deep blue periwinkle which for centuries has symbolised death and was woven into garlands for condemned criminals in times past. I see.'

Nat raise himself up in his bed. 'Sir, the message in this is even more disturbing.'

The inspector nodded, read on.

'The meaning could be that devotion has been distorted by coquetry. The colour purple is used in mourning, so that makes the final message one of death. I see you note down, Miss Kelley, that the periwinkle confirms it, making the meaning, *this coquetry has led to your death.'*

'Yes, I think that's the message. Inspector Caminada, this final posy was the one left with Isabella Waterstone, the third victim, who was killed in the cathedral,' Sophia said.

He continued, 'Ahhh. This one has monkshood, which even I know is poisonous – aconite, I believe - and I see it signifies the approach of a dangerous foe. Then, oleander, of which *all* of its parts are poisonous! Good Lord above! Its message being beware, and finally, the French marigold which is for jealousy, of all things. Who would have known that? So, the message is *beware of jealousy, a dangerous foe approaches.'*

He folded up the paper slowly, his expression thoughtful. When he put it in his notebook, wrapped the strap around that and put it in his pocket, it was as though he were putting the evil messages out of view, out of mind for the time being.

'Miss Kelley, this reading takes great skill and knowledge. I've seen some sights, but these simple messages chill my marrow.'

She dipped her head. A simple acknowledgment.

Nat had lain back, tired after the first flurry of talk. Sophia then explained about the diary of the last victim and, how it had come into her possession and how, tragically that and the posies had been stolen. The only other evidence was from the sister of this woman who could remember much of what was written in the diary. No, there was no name mentioned, nor was there any concrete description. All was secretive.

Nat licked his dry lips, tried to swallow and after Sophia had given him some water to wet his mouth, he was able to speak and add, 'This theft means that my fiancée is known to the killer, sir. It's as though she has been targeted to receive this information. This is what terrifies me.'

Inspector Caminada agreed; she could tell by the way interest and professional respect flared in his eye. All was laid before him. He had listened most carefully and had made notes too.

Nat was restless but he wanted to continue; there was more he could add, was desperate to add. He felt his throat, drew his hand over brow. This time Sophia gave him more of the herb drink and cooled his brow; he was relieved a little so she called for Alice to make more and to make tea for the inspector so that Nat would have time to recover.

The little interlude refreshed Nat as much as the Indian tea, which he also drank.

He needs as much to drink as he can take; he has surely lost much fluid from his body with this fever. He looks more himself right now, but perhaps it's the talk of evidence with another policeman. Look, he is sitting up better. How much he wants to impress this inspector. She gazed at Nat tenderly.

'Sir, I was recently in London on an errand for my division, to see about the control of riotous crowds. But while I was there, I met Inspector Reid...'

'Did you now!'

'We had a rapport straight away. He spoke to me about the Whitechapel Butcher, the so-called Ripper case, very freely, once he knew of my interest in detection, and he showed me the photographs.'

The inspector sat forward, keen to hear what Nat said, adding, 'I also have met him and seen the dreadful images. An interesting man...'

Nat described what Inspector Reid had told him about the concepts of repeated behaviour patterns and of signature features common to some murderers. These murderers commit several similar killings in different places and times almost in a series.'

'And you have identified all these things here, in Manchester. You've done well indeed, sergeant and I understand your need to protect Miss Kelley; you are right,' he said. He turned to look at Sophia. 'Miss Kelley, your own extensive contribution to the case is invaluable, quite invaluable. I'll give this some careful thought overnight and with your permission I'll return tomorrow early in the morning and we'll discuss what we can do. In the meantime, I'll assign two of my very best detectives to shadow Miss Kelley. I agree, she could well be in the eye of the murderer. And I realise you both know this, but Miss Kelley is also a professional woman and I am guessing from what I have been told, that you are of an age with the victims and also you enjoy the same marital status, being yet unmarried. I do not worry you too much, madam?'

'No, you don't, but there is one difference in that I have a fiancé and the other young women didn't. Perhaps that difference is some protection for me?' she supposed but he shook his head gravely.

'That I don't know, but we'll take no chances.'

'I'm grateful, and I have other people with me at all times here too.'

'I'll send my men within the next hour, but you'll not see them – be assured of their presence though.'

He rose to leave, thanked Nat for alerting him and Sophia for the hospitality, and for that of the vicarage too – she would pass this on? She would.

As he opened the door he turned to Nat and said, 'Roberts, you have the makings of a fine detective. It's a gift you know. If Bateman rejects you, he's a fool and I'll hope to be the winner in the exchange. You'd work for me?'

'I would. I thank you, Sir,' Nat said. His voice was weaker now after the exertion of the past hour.

Alice was sent for to show him out. He was gone.

Sophia returned to Nat's side.

'I'm so weary, love,' he said, and fell asleep propped upright on the pillows, no need of the sedative the doctor had left. She stayed with him.

What would the inspector make of my own special gift? I'll not tell him. Nat won't, that I am sure of. But shall I tell Nat about the excursion planned by Alice and me tomorrow? Will that help, in his present state? I think not! We'll be safe enough – and now we'll have our own detectives – hidden protection indeed.

328

Chapter 29

'Away into the silent land'

Christina Rossetti

ISABELLA WATERSTONE'S funeral was to be held at nine o'clock. This was the time when a lull was felt in the energy of the city's entertainments, coming between the early evening revellers going home and the more determined late-night ones coming out to play.

The weather had been changeable in the day; one minute it was blazing hot and then next, with a rush of wind, clouds bowled across the sky dodging the plumes of smoke from the unsleeping furnaces, making the temperature plummet.

Sophia's father told her that the Waterstones, father and daughter, had visited the Chapel of Rest that morning, as arranged, and had stayed for two hours. They had wanted nothing but to be left alone with Isabella, and when they eventually emerged, quite exhausted and wan, he had driven them home himself and made sure they got into the house, into the care of the housekeeper there. It was the least he could do, he said, and Sophia kissed him.

Towards early evening, the sun had disappeared behind a curtain of cloud and smoke. There was a light flurry of rain, but the heat grew and as the hour approached for the funeral, between them they gave birth to a swelling mist that prowled about the city, melding walls and pavements into a soft grey universe. Streetlights and windows became blurred stars; the remnants of the almost set sun coloured the mists in ochre and gold. The effect was to deaden all sound; the usual cacophony of the evening city was only heard through thick woollen mufflers, as though at a great distance, far across the world. And above everything, the air vibrated with smoky earthiness.

Sophia had left Nat in the late afternoon, secure in the care of Michel and David, yet still she wondered how they would get along together when she wasn't there to referee. Indeed, she was quite pushed to imagine how they would do together once Nat was restored to his full strength and determination, and she admitted to herself – his unique energy.

But as things stand, that's what I long for - for him to return to his usual passionate and opinionated self.

At half past eight that evening, everything was ready for the sad ceremony; Sophia and her father were in professional mien, smart, respectful, sombre. No one was to attend the funeral but the two mourners and the clergy, but there were practical matters necessary in order to make this privacy a reality; vehicles were needed and did not drive themselves, pall bearers must carry the coffin hither and thither. Everything must roll out as smoothly as was humanly possible.

Isabella's coffin was draped in a plain black silk pall and without flowers to adorn it, as instructed. All the horses gleamed like polished jet, their stately presence needing no other ornament on this occasion. Six quiet black clothed bearers were in attendance and walked three at each side of the hearse, driven by Albert. It was their plainest vehicle and pulled by a single horse, as they wanted. Sophia and her father sat in the coachman's seat of the brougham, with two horses in hand, which was to carry the family. Sophia tucked a stray lock of hair under the dense net that she wore to contain it. She repositioned the hat veil over her face, tweaked her jacket straight.

It was in silence that they left the yard and made their way across the city to Isabella's home. Once there, her father and sister took their places inside the vehicle for the short journey to St Ann's, Isabella's last journey. The hearse preceded them with Sophia now walking on foot to lead this slower and more ceremonial procession, as was the custom.

The city was indeed hushed at that time, made more so by the enveloping mists that undulated and rolled like a tranquil sea. Even the clash of horses' hooves and the roll of carriage wheels was dulled. They saw few people. No passing bell was rung, and the only lights in the church were the candles on the altar, those on the chancel steps and those at the entrance to the aisle. Outside, the double rows of arched windows seemed in darkness, but the lower ones to the front of the church showed a little welcoming homely light.

The cortège arrived at the porticoed entrance where Reverend Williams waited to greet them, and the curate stood at his elbow to support him. The older man had been much distressed by Isabella's death and a little unwell since the storm, yet he was determined to read the service for her; it was his final tribute to a girl he had known all her life, he said.

The hour was come; the mourners stepped from the brougham and took their place at the church door with mute gravity; Christina held a small bunch of roses that were so fresh that Sophia guessed had been picked that evening, just before they were wanted.

As though aware of the occasion, the city sounds in the square receded when the coffin was unloaded and lifted to the shoulders of the pall bearers; the whole tableau existed in a grey kingdom as they took the first pace forward to begin their stately procession. No one spoke. Sophia's eye fell on the churchyard; that very instant a veil of mist moved as though a soft hand had lifted it and she glimpsed the ready grave awaiting its occupant; a heartbeat later it was hidden once more, and she stepped forward to follow the mourners.

The two clergymen led the way inside; Reverend Williams lifted his head and as they passed the threshold, he intoned the greeting.

'We receive the body of our sister, Isabella and give it into God's care. "And God shall wipe away all tears from their eyes; and there shall be no more death, neither sorrow, nor crying, neither shall there be any more pain: for the former things are passed away".' His voice was thin but clear, and full of sorrow.

The clergymen paced forward; their black robes swayed from side to side in a gentle rhythm matched by the steps of the pall bearers. The two mourners followed with their small, unwilling steps, arms around each other, their faces gazed ahead, but who knew their thoughts? Sophia grieved for them, felt every pang of sorrow for the ordeal they now suffered. There was no hymn, only the sound of footsteps to accompany Isabella to the chancel where her coffin was laid on its lonely bier. Unwanted now, the bearers melted into the distance. Her father remained outside by the brougham, silent in attendance, on guard, and the hearse, which was no longer needed, was taken away by Albert.

Sophia herself slipped like a shadow into the back of the church. At the entrance to the aisle ahead she saw blushes of soft light in the dark interior; the chancel candles and those that graced the altar, radiated mellow calm, the flames tall and unwavering. Not so for Reverend Williams. He hesitated on the steps, began to fall but the curate was close by and caught him in time, kept him steady and gently guided him to a seat in the choir. Sophia saw with a pang of sympathy, that he was unable to go on, saw him shake his head, lift his hand in supplication – would Reverend Knightly kindly do this? He would. The older man slumped back on the seat; eyes closed.

The ceremony did not falter; Reverend Knightly's presence was solace, his voice balm.

"'I am the resurrection and the life,' sayeth the Lord. "He that believeth in me, though he were dead, yet shall he live: And whosoever liveth and believeth in me shall never die.'"

The father and daughter looked up as he spoke, recognizing the change, and Sophia also saw their acceptance; Christina allowed her gaze to linger a little longer than her father's, but then, as he did, she returned to her own prayers.

"'Blessed are they that mourn: for they shall be comforted.'"

The funeral service was read with dignity and in the full majesty of The Word. When it came time for the committal, the pall bearers appeared, and once more in silence the coffin was borne aloft, this time to the graveside. The mist had not dispersed; it festooned the gravestones and monuments, weaving sadly around the statue of a guarding angel that stood near the waiting grave. There was no sound, even the eternal music of the stars was hushed. Shadows loomed in and out of the mist and formed a ghostly congregation, but whether they were real people or phantasms, no one could guess.

Reverend Knightly took his position quietly by the graveside with his head bowed and his prayer book in hand. He had helped the old clergyman out at his insistence, and he sat himself very gratefully on a stone bench against the church wall where Sophia joined him. The coffin was in place and the bearers ready to lower it.

The beautiful voice of the younger clergyman spoke the words of the committal so quietly, with all gentleness, but without losing any of their grandeur.

"'Forasmuch as it hath pleased Almighty God of his great mercy to take unto himself the soul of our dear sister here departed, we therefore commit her body to the ground; earth to earth, ashes to ashes, dust to dust; in sure and certain hope of the Resurrection to eternal life, through our Lord Jesus Christ; who shall ...'"

The coffin was lowered, the bearers left. Christina recognised the time was come and she stepped slowly forward; a single sob escaped her as she placed the bouquet of roses at the head of the grave and in that enclosed place, the scent rose up from them and banished the earthiness.

It was done.

The mourners stood at the graveside, looking down into the maw. Sophia knew this was the awful moment when they realised that now the ceremonies were over, the loved one was gone at last, the coffin in its final place. It was Reverend Williams who approached them at this time, this sad limbo in their lives. Reverend Knightly helped him rise and gave him his arm to help him walk. He joined them like a fond parent; they looked up; their faces fixed in a look of blank incomprehension and like the fond parent he comforted them, took their hands in his and blessed them most sincerely.

hey remained standing forlornly enough, as is the common scene at a new graveside. The mist embraced them until they seemed to float above the grave itself. Isabella was with them; Sophia felt it as surely as if the dead girl had greeted her.

It was time to go. She followed behind the clergymen when they made their way to the vestry, but they were all suddenly halted by an unexpected trill of sound, clear and bright and strange. They and the mourners looked all around, puzzled, wondering. It was Christina, there at the graveside, that noticed the singer first and pointed upwards; everyone followed her direction and saw that there, high up on the edge of the church roof, sat a robin. It was this little creature that filled the air around it with the most breath-taking and melodious song.

Reverend Williams understood immediately.

'Ah, a night robin! It is known sometimes to happen, these small creatures are trumpeting their territory, but God, of his mercy, and knowing of its beauty to our human ears, transforms it into a song of comfort and remembered joy.'

The night-time and all the watchers were gifted yet another glorious chorus.

The old man's eyes shone, and his voice grew stronger as he remembered the robin's legend.

'It is also sent to show God's love and protection here for us now, just as the little brown bird did who flew to sit on the end of Our Lord's manger in Bethlehem. That small thing stayed in that spot to shield the baby's face from the blaze of the fire and his breast feathers were scorched by the heat. For ever after he has proudly worn that colour on his breast as God's thanks.'

The bird sang lustily and while he did, all movement was arrested in the dark churchyard. There was some little light shed from the windows near the altar, enough to show the location of the new grave, but Reverend Knightly had anticipated further need as the evening lengthened, and he retrieved a storm lantern he'd placed out there earlier. When he opened its window to let out the light, the bird finished its work, and it was then that Christina and Edward Waterstone drew themselves away and along the path from the grave. The robin was gone in a flurry.

Sophia led them to where the brougham waited, and they were soon taken home. No one spoke.

On the drive home, she and her father were quiet for a while but then she decided there were things he must know of before any more time passed; she told him about the meeting with Inspector Caminada and his decision to set two of his detectives to watch her. He was glad of it, he said, heartily glad. Had she seen sign of them?

'I thought I saw shadows in the mist, but perhaps that's all they were.'

He grunted his concern.

'Perhaps...but Nat was right that you are too like the poor dead victims to be free of care. I welcome anything to keep you safe. This inspector, he was more attentive than the other?'

'He was and Nat was relieved by that. I'll stay with him tomorrow; he should be getting better by then.' She hadn't yet told her father about the thefts, which she now remedied.

He was aghast, more worried by this than anything else he had heard in the past few minutes of conversation.

'Someone got into the yard? Past the dogs? How can that be? I'm blowed. No! Someone must have a legitimate reason for being there – but everyone who does, knows each other person, at least by sight. I'll have to think carefully about this.'

The mist began to clear, and he urged the horses into a gentle trot. When they reached the yard, Sophia dismounted and looking up saw that for once the stars were visible and, what's more, a fine west wind was chasing away the smoke and clouds.

Chapter 30

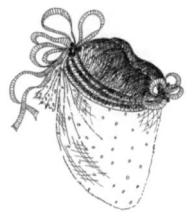

'Women are naturally secretive'
Sir Arthur Conan Doyle

SOPHIA WOKE next day slightly more rested that she had done recently. The sad funeral was done, and Nat was somewhat improved, and he was gratified by the interview with Inspector Caminada.

He feels so helpless at the moment, and he is in many ways. He puts great store by this inspector; I hope he's justified. The visit certainly helped his spirits. He comes again early this morning. I didn't see his detectives last evening... but surely that's the way it should be?

When she met her father at breakfast, he suggested that he could take much of her work, so that she was free to be with Nat for the day.

'Your safety's my main concern, as always my dearie, but at this time, until this killer is found and stopped you must be guarded so well,' he told her. 'These detectives – you've spotted them?'

'No, and I wonder if I shall? I've never been the object of such surveillance before – at least I think not. I suppose that we must simply trust that they're there.'

By half past eight that morning she was on her way to the vicarage, along with Alice. The humid weather continued, but the mists from the previous evening had dispersed over night. They walked and met with the same traffic on roads and pavements as the day before, but this time, Sophia allowed herself to feel a little more buoyant; not only had they made steps to discover the killer, but she and Alice were to go on a discovery mission that evening.

Alice voiced her thoughts.

'Miss, I've been out this morning to the pawn shop, and I've got us some very fine things; we'll look a treat.'

'I don't want to look like a street walker.'

'No Miss, 'course not! Me neither. I think we should look like ordinary working women, a bit modest like, tired with hard work and a bit grubby like we've no soap to our names, but out to enjoy ourselves for an hour. That'll be the ticket.'

Sophia added, 'You're right, we mustn't be noticed, but blend into the background. We don't want anyone to accost us. Do not be too pretty, my girl!' she admonished Alice. 'We don't want some oaf carrying you off.'

'Like to see 'im try. Anyway, pretty's not that important, Miss, it won't matter what y'face looks like if a man's after one thing!' Alice was down to earth as ever.

'Alice!' Sophia said, her voice suitably shocked but her face wearing the excitement she had bubbling within.

Why am I feeling this? It's dangerous, deceitful; I haven't told Father. Is that what I want – fear? Do I crave the thrill? Isabella's diary mentioned the promise of this spectacle and the gossip says this person makes people do things against their will. They spoke of it as entertaining. Is that it? Am I morbidly curious about what happens, like everyone else? But will the killer be there in the crowd? He promised to take Isabella; will he now go alone and revel in the memories of her death?

She so rarely did anything out of the ordinary that she forced these fears to the farthest reach of her mind until this almost-adventure took on a lighter aspect. Alice insisted on humming the latest music hall song, *Ta ra ra boom de ay,* and their steps moved in time. The walk to the vicarage seemed lively and short but lurking in her heart she felt the thread of doubt uncoil and start its progress.

It was Tuesday so the Trading Floor was soon to open at the Royal Exchange in St Ann's Square and businessmen were arriving by the hundreds, all smartly dressed with their long frock coats, their top hats and their appetites craving business and money. They streamed through the classical portico, loud, eager. The whole square was packed, and they had to push their way through the crowds and round to the vicarage.

Once they had gained the door, they knocked for admittance and as they waited, Sophia, mindful of being too sure of his recovery yesterday, only to see him worse, quickly schooled herself and prayed for good news as the door was flung open.

It was Michel. 'Bonjour, bonjour, mes demoiselles.'

His welcoming gesture was wholly Gallic, as he stood aside, smiling – brilliantly, Sophia thought. She caught sight of an answering and becoming blush on Alice's cheeks, before she dashed away to the kitchens. Her clogs beat a happy rhythm on the hall tiles.

'How is Nat this morning, Michel?' was what Sophia wanted to know.

'Ah, something of the same, I regret, Mademoiselle Sophia.'

'No! I thought he seemed more settled yesterday.' Her heart was stabbed with dread.

He told her Nat had been uncomfortable in the night, he was still nauseous and had stomach cramps, leg cramps and his heart was too irregular for Michel's liking.

'The cramps are unusual for the head injury and for a bad cold, such as Dr Smith suggested. There is a strange lethargy also, and I will think about these symptoms. This illness is a puzzle to me.'

As they reached the landing, Michel made his excuses and said he would join them later, if he may? She was grateful for his tact and on entering his room, she flew to the bed. Nat turned his head to face her and she saw tears gather in his eyes and she threw her arms about his neck.

'Nat, love, I thought you'd be better. I told myself you were. Oh, I've neglected you, left you alone.'

He dashed a hand over his eyes to wipe them.

'No, you have not neglected me. Sit up. There,' he said as she moved. 'You had the funeral last evening. It went as they wanted it? he asked.

'As smoothly as you'd want if your world ended. All was dignified. The mist kept people away. It was very private and may, eventually, be some little comfort to them.'

She passed him a glass of water when he pointed at it. He drank thirstily.

'I feel so weak. Michel says I am a medical conundrum.'

'What does Dr Smith say?' she asked.

'Mmmm, Smith, always the dandy doctor. Well, he says it is normal and gives me medicine for the pain – my head throbs, but this medicine seems ineffective on that score.'

'I'll stay with you now and Alice can fetch up all the good things I've brought for you to eat. And maybe you should try to stand and walk a little in the room to get your muscles working again. Lying in bed makes everything forget how to move, so I'm told. Even a few days can make a difference to one used to being active, as you are.'

There was a knock at the door then, and when Michel entered

Sophia enlisted his help straight away. He was only too ready to agree with her but said Nat should try to stretch his arms and legs on the bed first, feel confident in that movement before attempting to stand. If the cramps attacked – then they would fight them!

'Eh bien, mon ami, I will be here or David, to catch you if you make the fall.'

Nat scowled and she was surprised when Michel laughed.

They have become better acquainted with one another I see.

She joined in the laughter. 'Nat, you will be well soon and then you can laugh with us.'

'And I will!' he told them, relaxing enough to smile at least. 'Ah – the news, Michel!' he said and then struggled to sit up properly.

'I'm so short of breath…'

As they helped him, he continued, between grunts of discomfort, 'Tell her of the diagnosis you have made. It's a miracle, Sophia, love, wait until you hear this – and no, it isn't about me…'

'Ah, you will be filled with the English fervour when I tell to you this tale.' He smiled broadly then. 'It is this; a French doctor, but alas not I – if only it was I, this doctor he solved a great mystery! He was Doctor Bouchardat and an army physician at the time of my country's great conflict with Prussia.'

Nat interrupted. 'Sophia, Reverend Williams is ill, and not in his cups, as we thought. Michel thinks he knows the cause.' He yawned, looked drowsy. 'Tell her of the diagnosis you have made. It's a miracle, Sophia, love, just wait…' he repeated; his voice was weak.

'Sleep, mon ami, you are tired again,' Michel advised, and turned to Sophia to finish the tale as Nat did indeed slip into a doze. 'You have heard of Diabetes Mellitus?'

'Is that what they call the Sugar Sickness?'

'Yes, I believe so, but in the Middle Ages, here they call it the *Pissing Evil*, you know the term – ah, but it is impolite for a lady!' He looked abashed and gently slapped the heel of his hand to his forehead, another of his armoury of Gallic gestures that she thought charming.

'Yes, but I know of it – no matter, Michel. What of the illness? Is it this that Reverend Williams has?'

'I think so. He is tired all the time, so thirsty, he passes water a great deal, he eats of the sugary things - the bon-bons, and his water, it smells sweet. These are the symptoms of Diabetes.'

She frowned a little, intrigued. 'And your French doctor, what did he find?'

'The soldiers, in this war, had but little food, and that was of the ordinary kind, no bon-bons or things heavy with sugar. Those with the diabetes improved their health. The doctor knew because the *water taster,* he who worked for the good doctor, he found the water of such men, no longer sweet. So, the doctor said that eat less was the cure – and no sweet foods. None at all.'

'And your Doctor Bouchardat discovered it? Will this help Reverend Williams?' she wanted to know.

'I think so. I have told this to him, and he is most grateful. I will help him improve himself, become a little healthier, he will feel better. If I can help him in this, I have paid the debt I owe, but a little; he has offered me a home here.'

Sophia regarded him thoughtfully.

'You have a question Mademoiselle?' he wondered pleasantly.

'Yes, It's that you seem a little like a police detective, searching out clues. Is that what it is to discover what illness a person is prey to?' she asked him.

'Mademoiselle, it is,' he said. 'For our good friend, the Reverend, it is regrettable that we do not have the medicine, the cure. But a *strict* diet, as I said, will be of great help. He will feel well once more.'

'I'm so glad, Michel, so glad. He's a kind man. And you, yourself are kind to interest yourself in his problems.'

'I could do no other.'

'A man like you could not; you are a true healer. And please call me Sophia, we are good friends now, surely.'

They shook hands warmly, afterwards Michel lifting hers to his lips in continental fashion. Apparently shaking hands was a British custom, not widely adopted in Europe, so their gestures were a meld of the two.

Nat stirred; his doze being briefly snatched. Michel said his sleep had been like this; it was one of the clues he was trying to piece into the solution to Nat's present unwell state. Yes, he was in agreement with Dr Smith, but wanted to keep his other thoughts to himself for the time being.

Nat coughed; he was awake again. They helped him sit up more comfortably and when he had had a drink, Sophia asked him about Inspector Caminada. Had he visited yet?

'My mind is so woolly, love,' he said, 'He came very early, saying he wanted to get things in progress. Michel brought him up, didn't you?'

Michel made a dramatic play of remembering, threw his forefinger up. 'Ah, yes. I have been the imbecile, mon ami. Yes, I should have told you Sophia, Mademoiselle, but we spoke of medical things and I…I forgot. Je suis désolé.'

Nat grinned. 'He means he is sorry, love. Imbecile is the same in French and English. You see, I speak the language now!'

'Well, speak English and tell me what the inspector says.'

Nat continued, 'He wanted to know what the time interval was between each victim's death. I said I thought it was about a week; is that so?'

'I think so. Why is this important?' She was worried by this. Her mind raced.

If this is a part of the murderer's way of operating, and the spacing between events is almost regular, then it's about a week since Isabella Waterstone died.

Nat rubbed his face vigorously, shook his head. 'Michel, mon ami, some water if you please. I must be clear headed, though I feel like sleeping for a year.'

The water was brought and a glassful drunk; Nat shook himself again. 'The notion is, amongst those who study the way such murderers work, (ha, work, as though it is a profession) the notion is that they feel the urge to kill, they satisfy this urge, this hunger, and are satiated. A time elapses, they feel the need once more and so on.'

I was right…about a week…

Michel brought a chair for himself to the bed. Sophia was sitting on the bed, next to Nat.

'Go on, my friend…' he encouraged. 'You see, I speak English to encourage you!'

'He has sent his detectives to interview all three families this morning, to discover from them whether their daughters were behaving any differently from normal, any change of habits, behaviour, dress.' He took a pause. 'He wonders if the first two victims kept a diary as did Isabella Waterstone. He is also sending men to their places of work to interview their friends and associates; their behaviour at work may have altered. Were they excited; did they look as though they kept a secret that thrilled them?'

'He is very thorough,' Sophia said, thoughtfully.

'Lie back now, mon ami, lie back. You have told the tale,' Michel interjected kindly. With a hand on his shoulder, he urged Nat to move back onto the pillows. He had bent forward in his eagerness.

'The final command of the inspector, love, is that they should increase surveillance on you. Have you seen his detectives?'

'Father asked me. No, I haven't. Perhaps they change hats and false beards at each street corner.'

'Perhaps it is so!' Michel agreed so readily she wondered if she had hit on the very thing and resolved to be more observant and vigilant when she saw any men as she went about her business.

Michel left them then. He had some work to do for Dr Smith; he was to write out instructions for the pharmacist for several of the doctor's patients; it would save him time and done by a fellow physician, would be accurate. Michel was pleased to be professionally useful.

Several times during the rest of the day, when she wasn't wholly taken up with caring for Nat, Sophia went to the landing windows at the front of the vicarage and looked through Nat's bedroom window too, to see if she saw any men who seemed always to be hanging about. She did not.

They must be young men to be of any use if physical aid were needed. No, they cannot be old and decrepit like that beggar over there. He's one legged – the crutch would be in the way! Nor can it be the hot potato man? His equipment is too clumsy.

Nat slept a great deal, but she managed to help him wash and shave and take some little food, despite the sickly feeling. He also tried to exercise himself as Michel suggested, but he fell back often, out of breath with his heart fluttering strangely, Michel said.

Alice had been up and down with things required in the sickroom but when she and Sophia met in the hall to go home at six o'clock, she appeared to Sophia to be thoroughly gratified with her own day.

'You must be tired with all the running about Alice.'

'Thank you, but no, Miss. I was busy washing all the rags I got from the pawn shop. I told Mrs Jenkins and Mrs Biggs that they was for someone I knew, so I hope that was the right thing to do. The stuff soon dried in the heat out in the yard. Michel kept us busy in the kitchen, advising on cooking and crackin' jokes – French ones. They wasn't funny but it's the sound of 'is voice that makes y'laugh along with 'im and that smile…Mrs Biggs and Mrs Jenkins was swooning.'

'He's so much better, isn't he? The arm, does he guard it?'

'Eh, yes, he banged it on a cupboard and fair doubled up. But – gritted 'is teeth, soon got over it.'

They were marching along at a fast pace, the air cooler and the sky clearer than it had been for days, but nevertheless, they were very hot when they arrived at the yard. The horses were being fed and bedded; all was as it should be at that time of day.

'Can I ask, Miss, what did he master say about going out tonight.'

'Ah, that presented a difficulty, I'll own. He wouldn't approve of me going to such an event, yet I need to go. Something tells me it's vital I see what happens. But I was saved from the outright lie – though still lying by omission, when Father said he was going to spend the evening with an old friend of his, newly widowed. He lives in Chorlton so he's going by cab, Tommy Patterson's, and he'll wait for him all evening. There, I am my own mistress.'

Sophia told Alice to bring the clothes to the workroom, where they would don their disguises, at eight o'clock. In order to leave the yard without exciting suspicion in anyone looking, they would wear the light cloaks Alice had found in the pawn shop until they were near the pub and then they would dump them in an alley. Someone would find and use them. Cloaks were no longer in fashion, but who cared when you had nothing.

'Miss, d'you think them detectives'll follow us?'

'I think I'd be glad of them in case anything untoward happens.'

Unease sat cold in her stomach, despite the anticipation of dressing up. That would actually be fun.

'Untoward. I hope there's nothing.' Alice's eyes held a momentary disquiet, but she was full of pent- up energy.

'We need to be invisible – remember? We are simply going to see what this man's like, and only because it was mentioned in Isabella's diary. And I want to find out what he does; does he really mesmerise people against their will? Is it a hoax or has he some real power?'

'Miss Sophia, pardon me, but do y'mean the sort of power like in your gift, seeing things that've happened?' Alice asked.

'I don't know, I really don't. I just feel compelled to go and see this man – almost as though he's called me...'

'Now, don't say that, Miss!'

Sophia laughed this off by flinging up the collection of clothes and catching the first thing that came to hand. It was a dull grey knitted shawl. They spent an entertaining time dressing, Alice advising on the presentation and wearing of different garments.

'Miss Sophia, no working woman out for an hour or two would drape her woolly shawl so elegantly. Y'not going to the Palace Theatre for that Gilbert and Sullivan.'

Alice proceeded to wrap it round Sophia's shoulders, cross the ends over in front and tucked the ends in the back of her waistband. She tutted as she worked. She tied a cotton scarf over Sophia's hair.

'To hide it, being so bright. In y'mind, Miss, you're a

washerwoman, and the steam makes it a mess. Here, let me just pop that cap on top. There.'

Alice wore a striped skirt that was originally red and black, but with much wear and washing was now pink and grey. She had a dark green blouse under a small black cotton jacket, nipped at the waist. Her own vivid hair was scraped back in a tight bun low on her neck and on top she wore a flat straw boater that unravelled at the edges. Sophia was similarly dressed in washed out blues, with a flat cap on her head, the peak pulled low over her brow. Alice used Sophia's cosmetics to apply some rouge deliberately badly to each of their cheeks, before which she wisely greyed their faces and necks, with a little soot; they needed to give the appearance of being unwashed – apart from their water-reddened hands as they were washerwomen. They rubbed a little rouge on their hands and forearms to achieve that effect.

'We look like we can't afford to eat!' Sophia said, looking at herself in a hand mirror.

'Miss, but we can afford to 'ave a half o'the best Boddingtons though.'

It was half past eight; the cloaks were soon on and they made their way stealthily across the yard; Alice had found them canvas boots, so they went in silence. They were almost at the gate, Sophia having petted the dogs before they made too much noise, when a voice accosted them from the open door of the feed room. It was Albert.

'Good evening, Miss Sophia!' he called, his voice deliberately arch and polite, and she knew from old acquaintance that he was about to offer advice she didn't relish.

'Going somewhere nice, Miss? Would you like me to get the brougham ready?'

She stopped, sighed, whispered, 'Alice, he'll want to know all.'

Alice murmured her reply. 'Might 'ave to tell 'im, else he'll follow us I reckon.'

Sophia nodded.

They stepped over to the feed room. The air was redolent with the scent of horse feed cooking. It was linseed boiling in the huge copper kettle they kept for the purpose. All the horse feed was kept in this room in massive metal vats, safe from rodents.

'I love this smell, Albert. Linseed oil really makes the horses' coats shine, keeps the bloom well,' she commented, stroking one of the cats that made its bed in there, watching for the odd rodent venturing a meal of spilled feed. She knew Albert wouldn't be easily distracted. 'As to the brougham, no thank you, we'll be walking.'

'Oh, yes?' he queried, his face a studied blank, and his careless tone spoke a determination to know all, as they had suspected.

'Well, I have to go and see something tonight, that I don't want my father to know of yet. It's on Nat's behalf. We're going to see a hypnotist at the Rose and Crown on Deansgate.'

Then he was aghast.

'The Rose and...*that Hypnotist?*' He paused, stood head down with hands on his hips, shaking his head in disbelief. 'Eh, Miss Sophia, if you're set on going there – and I know you're never willingly dissuaded from what you've set your mind on, I'll be coming with you. I can't think what the sergeant'd want with a hypnotist I thought he mesmerised people himself, just with 'is eyes - like one of them basilisks.'

Sophia glared, irritated.

Undeterred he continued blithely, 'By the by, I never thought to see you in clothes like that, Miss. This one 'ere,' he indicated Alice with a nod, 'will get you in bother!' He diluted the insult with a grimace at Alice. She merely raised her eyebrows.

Sophia was quick to halt him before he carried out his offer of accompanying them. That would never do.

'No, no need, no need at all,' she said and, inevitably and with great reluctance told him about Inspector Caminada and the detectives he had assigned to her watch. 'And, Albert, you can't leave the linseed to boil. You know the lads'll not cook it as you do. I'll tell father myself when I see him, so do not bother yourself, but thank you for wanting to help me.'

Albert held up his hands in surrender. She and Alice walked quickly out of the wicket.

Chapter 31

'The devil is come down unto you'
The Old Testament: Revelations 12:12

IT WAS A MILD EVENING to begin with, balmy in temperature with a light wind that dispersed the smoke and clouds occasionally and allowed a full moon to peep shyly out. The humidity of earlier in the day had melted away, and the ground underfoot was so dry that they walked easily in their second-hand boots. Late-night crowds surged into the city, and Sophia and Alice in their worn clothes were soon invisible to any watcher, dimmed as they were amid the more flamboyant dress of other revellers. When they neared the end of Deansgate, where they were headed, the colour of the crowds changed to well-washed hues and older clothes; that end of town held the dens and hostelries of the working classes.

They walked casually; arms linked together like any working women bent on an unaccustomed evening out and they smiled and looked all around, murmuring their conversation.

'Watch for anything unusual, Alice. I don't even know what it is, but I feel followed. Do you?'

'What, apart from the crowds, y'mean? No, not really, Miss.'

'Maybe the detectives are even now on our track. They can't

go home for the night, they must have a night shift, which Nat did when he was a constable.'

'Maybe them two women over there are detectives in disguise,' she said and nodded over the road where two old women sat on the pavement. 'Like in them stories about Sherlock Holmes. He dressed up as an old woman, a right crone, and no one knew it was 'im.'

'You've read them?'

'Me dad got them out of the library, Wigan Library; he liked to read 'em to us.'

'Ah. Maybe you're right about the old women. You know, I might like to know where these detectives are. I'm beginning to feel this was a mistake'

'No, Miss, why...'

'Shhhh, Alice. Let me think a moment, please.'

She felt tense, a peculiar sensation.

What do I hope to discover tonight? Am I fascinated by the power of a hypnotist – assuming it is real power and not simply a trick? I am, yes. Do I want to know who the hypnotist is? Yes, because he is mentioned in the diary and people are gossiping about him. How will that be of any benefit to me? It won't. Am I more settled now? No.

They walked on in silence.

What do I want to see, want to know? Be honest with yourself. I want to see if the killer is there.

She felt cold.

But how would I know him?

The air changed.

I won't know him.

A long low wind came racing up behind them, travelling along the street at such speed it dragged their skirts forward as it passed and pushed them along as though urging them not to be late.

But he will know me...

Music, shouting and singing burst from public houses they passed, and the smell of tobacco smoke, ale and sawdust was strong on the air. It billowed forth whenever the doors swung open, only to be snatched by the wind to join its curbless flow and give way to another stream of smells, the acrid scent of urine and sewage from the gutters and alleys.

They walked past the dark entrance to a large courtyard of tenements and heard a dog howling from somewhere inside the gloom; the mournful and deep note surely issued from a large dog and caught on the wind, persisted in following them for many minutes.

'That's what I call...' Alice began, but Sophia interrupted:

'Eerie?'

'No, Miss – I call that a dog without 'is dinner or wanting to be let off 'is chain.'

Sophia laughed; Alice made her laugh, the girl had a gift for stating reality, cutting though nonsense, spreading cheer.

Thank Goodness I brought Alice. Otherwise, I'd be caught up in evil presentiment.

They soon arrived at the Rose and Crown and found it packed to the rafters; the doors were propped open, the energy and noise spilled out onto the pavement. It was a large public house, calling itself a hotel, having rooms for rent and accommodating travelling salesmen and other business gentlemen or articled tradesmen, but 'Hawkers, tinkers and beggars need not apply.' Still, it was situated in the more disreputable end of town.

'Look, Miss, they 'ave a proper stage. And look at the posters everywhere,' Alice said, unable to resist excitement.

Sophia caught a glimpse through the doors and saw a raised platform at the end of a large room. There was an upright piano next to the stage; a man sat by it; his legs crossed comfortably as he smoked in silence, head thrown back, one arm up, holding a cigarillo. In front of this were assorted tables with people ranged round them and the whole cauldron -like mass bubbled with anticipation; heads were thrown back in laughter, arms raised gesticulating, drinks lifted. It looked as though there were almost a hundred people in there. There were benches and stools aplenty near the back and barrels as tables too. All along one side of the room there were troughs against the wall for beer glasses.

A giant mahogany bar stretched all along one side of the room, its entire top was black marble and behind this, and rising to the ceiling, grew carved mahogany shelving, resplendent with glittering mirrors and shelves crowded with myriad colours of spirits bottles. The walls inside and outside were decorated liberally with posters advertising events on the 'stage', including prominently:

MONSIEUR MAURICE
Mesmerist Extraordinaire!
The Greatest Phenomenon of the age
Mystery upon Mystery
Wonder follows Wonder
This VERY night and for ONE night only
Be prepared to be Astounded, Enthralled, Entertained
Tickets: Best: 3s, back: 2s, standing: 6d

Sophia and Alice discussed the pricing and decided that the sixpennies would be the best location for anonymity. These standing positions were at the back of the room and they noticed with relief that they were near the door in case escape was necessary; they quickly found themselves a suitable place by an iron pillar with no one behind them. They got glasses of ale, as befitted the tastes of working women, leaned their backs against the pillar and surveyed the room casually; what they saw was a loud, smoky, seething mass of people out to enjoy themselves. No one seemed to think them out of place, they had blended in and other than a couple of younger men nudging and winking at them, they were ignored, immersed in the audience.

S ophia looked around surreptitiously, absorbing the detail, not even imagining what might happen as the night drew on, she just focused on the intriguing new sensation of being in a different life entirely. This wasn't her world, but it was fascinating. The floor was beer sodden and its early sprinkling of sawdust was by this time, a brown mush. Spittoons leaned drunkenly; one was kicked over and disgorged its reeking contents under the feet of a serving girl who slipped dramatically and threw the beer jugs she carried over her head. Roars of laughter accompanied her screams of protest. The air itself was heavy with the stench of bad tobacco and brandy and all was squalid deterioration from the chipped paint work to the grime encrusted lamp shades. But it was seething with life.

Her surveillance was interrupted by the pianist. Unobserved by most, he had turned to his instrument and suddenly struck a loud and forceful chord that rumbled on and on and caused the roomful of people to variously shriek, laugh or toss their drinks up in shock. This appeared to be the signal for the entertainment to begin; everyone seemed to expect it and they drummed their heels on the floor, slapped the tabletops and cheered.

There was a second rumbling of piano chords and simultaneously a man entered the room from the side. He bounded onto the stage with huge aplomb, strode to the very centre and flung up both his arms. The effect was immediate silence. He as a strange figure; every feature seemed emphatically shaped or coloured. He was dressed in immaculate evening wear, was of advanced years, carried a heavy mane of white hair and extravagant whiskers. Most importantly he possessed a searing energy in his very glance. The room held its breath.

He spoke in deep and quietly thrilling tones.

'Ladies,' sniggers from many of the audience, 'and gentlemen...'

A woman at the front yelled in scandalized tones, 'I do 'ope they're not!'

Much laughter from the room.

The Master of Ceremonies, for this is who he was, put an elegant finger to his lips. The audience attended obediently.

His voice rose just a little with each utterance:

'Ladies, gentlemen, others...(applause) welcome, welcome! The evening before you is one such as will furnish your fireside family tales for a lifetime. Elegant emotions, intricate imaginings, obnoxious obscurities will meld with the deliciously vulgar and entirely commonplace.'

The audience obliged by demonstrating unified gasps and various cries and screeches as the speech required.

'Furthermore, you will cry, you will weep, you will shriek and exclaim at the instrumental invention that accompanies all.'

At this point the pianist gave vent to a trill of the entire keyboard, stood, bowed and was applauded loudly.

Now once more, the resplendent figure on the stage held up his hands for silence. It was given. His expression was grave.

'Alas, tonight, my friends, my good friends - the terpsichorean transcendence, the acrobatic convolutions, the rippling revolutions of Madame Mimi's Belles is to be denied us...'

A man bawled from the back, 'I only came to see 'em mesmerised!'

Others booed and stamped.

'I hear you groan…' the Master rumbled.

They groaned.

'I see you mourn.'

They wailed.

'But stay…' He banged the gavel he held on the top of the table next to him. 'Greater sights await you: sights magnificent, (bang) sights marvellous, (bang) sights monumental, (bang) and mesmeric!'

'Ooooo!' they cooed as a body.

Alice whispered to Sophia, 'Isn't it exciting, Miss? I've never been to one of these dos before.'

'No more have I, Alice.'

Sophia saw Alice catch sight of something; she stood up a little straighter, craning her neck to see.

'Miss Sophia – don't look right now, but in a minute; over near the stage there's a couple of ladies, proper ladies, sitting by the front, to the left there, near that small door. Very nice clothes, Miss. Too nice, if you ask me.'

Sophia moved herself so that she could see the women more clearly.

'You're right, and they do look a little overdressed. Maybe they know someone in charge who has got them good seats and I should think they'll be chaperoned too. There are three of them, can you see? But I think one is a maid; look, she sits on the outside and is a little less confident; her hat is a plain straw yet the other two are fancy little confections…' Her voice trailed off.

She and Alice exchanged looks.

The brief talk between them had been of seconds' duration and the Master of Ceremonies stood with head bowed and arms raised waiting for silence from the whole audience so that he might continue. Sophia gently pushed Alice further into the shadowy area behind the pillar, where they were out of sight of most of the room.

'Let's listen,' was all she whispered.

The pianist set up a grand introductory rumble, a crescendo of expectant notes and a final booming chord that called for silence more effectively than voice. The room held its breath, the Master of Ceremonies stepped to the side of the stage and gesturing across it as in welcome, he began his introduction of the evening's star turn.

'Admiration and astonishment will fill your mind with equal parts of mystery, magic and mesmeric manifestation! Here, tonight, our guest, Monsieur Maurice, fresh from the stages of Paris, France, will work his alchemy. Wonder will run hard on wonder. But, to work his enchantment he will look to you, friends, to provide him with suitably sensitive subjects, those of you who are courageous enough to bare their inner souls and pit them against the power of his mesmeric charms. He invites the brave among you to try!'

There was not a sound in the room; all glasses, chairs, coughs and scratchings were still as the audience absorbed this.

'Tonight, in defiance of the laws of man and decency, your friends will perform acts you never thought to see...'

There were jeers and screeches aplenty at this.

'Get goin' then!'

'Let's be seein' it!'

''Ere, our John's ripe for owt!'

The piano sent up another chord, this time low and eerie. The stage was filled with purple mist, and the bellows used to produce this could be heard clearly by all, and all ignored it for their eyes were on that same mist as the anticipatory chords rose in volume.

A final crash of those chords and the mesmerist was there before them, appearing out of the mist and greeted by the screams and clapping of the audience. They cheered. Monsieur Maurice stood tall and with outstretched arms he seemed to gather the whole room to him. He wore a black mask over his eyes; it was studied with brilliants and flashed darkly when light caught it, and he was broad about the shoulders, this image being enhanced by a fantastic opera cloak, black lined with red satin. He wore a black beard, long and parted in the centre and waxed to two devilish points, as were the ends of his moustaches. And he wore evening dress embellished by a fantastically embroidered waistcoat.

It is him!

Sophia drew in her breath sharply; she felt a thump in the very centre of her chest, a spear thrust of dread into her heart. Simultaneously a single picture appeared in her mind's eye as though a curtain had been opened then snatched shut immediately. It was the vision of Inspector Bateman crouched on the ground humiliated, peering upwards at his tormentor, yet this time, the naked man was smiling, laughing...

Him? Is it him? I didn't feel fear, when I met him did I? Just disgust...

'Alice,' she hissed into the girl's ear, 'It's him – the hypnotist is the one. I knew I had to come here tonight, but I never thought I would see him in person.'

But is it him or the other unseen man?

Alice was astounded, couldn't answer for a minute as she kept her eyes on the man on the stage.

'Oh, Miss, are you sure? Are you really sure?' Her usually confident tones were subdued and frightened.

'No, not of who he is, but yes, I feel it. It is him.'

They were bent close, whispering. No one seemed to notice them, their attention was on the stage where the mesmerist had brought a young man. The audience was laughing.

'What shall we do, Miss?' Alice had turned pale, her hand

shook.

'Alice, don't be frightened, we are surrounded by people and nowhere near him.'

Alice shook her head. 'I think we should go, Miss. Perhaps we can get one of them detectives to follow him.'

'We don't know who *they* are, do we?' Sophia pointed out. 'I'd like to stay a little while to see what he does. Perhaps the sound of his voice or his mannerisms might give me a clue.'

'Yes, Miss, I'm not leaving you.'

'Good.'

They turned to watch the performance. A young man was on stage and was standing on one leg, bending forward with his arms out for balance and he was rock steady. The mesmerist beckoned to another young man who was being pushed up onto the stage by his friends as the audience hooted and laughed.

The young man gave in sheepishly and once on the stage was told to sit on a stool there.

Monsieur Maurice spoke. His voice was deep, soft and had a French accent. Sophia focused on each note, searching for some recognition to spark.

He said to the young man on the stool:

'Look at me, young man, look most carefully, look. Look at my mask and see only the lights playing across it, playing, playing. Watch the colours dance and weave before your eyes. Watch, watch, watch.'

All the while he spoke, he paced slowly backwards and forwards in front of the subject, always keeping his face turned to him. The gas lights above him and the candle lit footlights made the brilliants on his mask glint and dance.

He stopped suddenly, snapped his fingers in front of the man's eyes and got no response. At this he turned to the audience and smiled slightly; they gasped. Whilst facing the room and away from the subject he told him in a voice that was crisp and carrying, monotone and mesmerising:

'I am your master; my commands you will obey until I say otherwise. You must answer yes.'

'Yes,' the man mumbled slowly.

'You are released form my power when I slap my glove to your shoulder, your shoulder alone.'

He removed one glove and raised it in the air, bringing it down with a resounding slap on the palm of his other hand. On the uncovered hand there was a signet ring on the little finger and the stone on it caught the light, making it flash just once.

Sophia grabbed Alice's arm.

'I've seen that ring somewhere. Do you recognise it?'

Alice watched his hands moving as he replaced his glove.

'I don't think so, Miss, but I didn't see clearly.'

'Alice, it's someone I've seen recently. I'm sure of it.'

Alice stepped back a pace.

'Oh, Miss, let's leave now, if you know him – *he* knows you. He might see you.'

'He wouldn't recognise me in my disguise - surely. No, I must stay and watch how he moves about; people can't often disguise little things. You know, habits like a certain hand gesture, tweaking their ear, rubbing the end of their nose – things like that.'

Sophia had been convinced since she decided to come to the performance that she would not be in any real danger; fear moved around her, certainly, and she knew danger was present, she even believed this was the killer, but she felt as though she were inside a bubble, something similar to a huge soap bubble, a bubble of invulnerability. She would be safe.

The performance continued for three quarters of the next hour. The man on the stool joined his friend to balance on one leg, a plump older woman came next and put her hat on the head of one. She was then told to kiss them both, which she did with vigorous lip smacking that had the audience doubled up with hilarity. Various other people came to the stage, the first ones were released by the slap of the glove, but Sophia did not glimpse the ring again, much to her annoyance. The other subjects performed a variety of ridiculous acts; dancing, jumping like the barrel organ monkeys so often seen in the city, barking like dogs, women threw up their skirts to show their drawers, men cried like babies and put their thumbs in their mouths. The performance was received with huge approval. Beer flowed like a river.

Suddenly, the mesmerist released everyone from the stage and announced his need for refreshment.

'I need to gather my strengths, my friends; the best performance of the night is yet to come. Au revoir.'

As he spoke these words, the bellows started up and the stage filled with mist once more. He drew his cloak about his shoulders and stepped backwards into it, was swallowed amid its swirling clouds.

But they were not quite deserted. Onto the stage bounded a wonderfully colourful pair, a man and a woman. He wore a top hat and tails and ginger whiskers, she a most extravagant frilled outfit full of flounces and feathers and striped stockings. They serenaded the audience with *Ta-ra-ra- bum-de-ay, After the ball was over, Daisy, Daisy* and many others. The crowd joined in all the choruses and cheered until the Master waved them off the stage.

The interval had begun.

'Pies over 'ere!' yelled a voice nearby.

'Cockles, straight from Blackpool!' called another.

'Getcher oysters, better'en cockles!'

People stood, moved about, the noise and laughter rose.

A man approached Alice, staggering and laughing.

'I've got a beer for you, y'lit-tle cracker!'

'Push off!' she snarled in his face and shoved him back with both hands, whereupon his friends caught him as he fell and dragged him off; all of them hugely enjoying themselves.

Alice darted behind the pillar to look at something then finding it she caught Sophia's eye, who had not lost sight of her, and beckoned.

'Miss, one of them well dressed women 'as got up and gone. I saw her. She went really quick round the back of the stage. The other two are standing up looking for 'er.'

The big room was awash with noise and beer. Try as she might Sophia could see nothing of the women.

'Come on, Alice, we'll follow her through that door...'

She suddenly found herself caught round the waist and heard Alice's outraged screech, as she too was grabbed.

A familiar voice said in her ear, 'No, you won't Miss. You need to leave! Both of you!'

Sophia's head flew round to see the speaker.

'Albert!'

Chapter 32

'All smiles stopped together'
Robert Browning

HE PULLED THEM towards the door, both of them surprised into acquiescence. But when Sophia craned round and saw his face was thunderous, she was so shocked that it stopped her from pulling away, as she had begun to do, and then protesting at his manner, his treatment and his being there at all.

They had almost reached the door when their progress was halted in a frightening and unexpected way. Two men, who had minutes before been rolling drunkenly against another of the big pillars, cuffing each other and giggling, were suddenly sober and had taken the place of the women at Albert's side. The difference was that they now held his arms, one each and Sophia and Alice were free.

Sophia was suddenly indignant on Albert's behalf.

'Let him go this instant. Who are you? What do you think you're doing?' she snapped, forgetting her disguise in a rush of feeling for Albert. 'Let go, I said.'

Alice was less polite. "Ere, get yer 'ands off 'im,' she snarled and drawing back her foot she kicked the nearest of the attackers in the shins, and grabbed the back of the other's coat and tried to drag it down his arms to make him lose his hold.

The man who had been kicked roared in pain but did not let go of Albert who struggled with all his strength and was not silent in his captivity.

'Bloody 'ell. What's going on? I'll bloody 'ave you, see if I don't.' He struggled, tried head butting one, missed, tried kicking but could not find a target; they were both much bigger, broader and younger than him, tough though he was. He gave vent to his frustration and shame in swearing colourfully.

No one nearby paid any attention to the disturbance; such events were not uncommon in that establishment.

All the while the two men who attacked Albert were struggling to hold the much slimmer and older man and were both grunting, puffing and made comments such as:

'Steady, granddad; you'll do yerself an injury.'

'Quieten down, y'not bloody dead yet.'

'Keep still, y'stupid old bugger!'

Sophia and Alice attacked a man each, grabbing their arms, pulling coats, hair, but were stunned when one of them hissed:

'Miss Kelley, we're here to help. Let go.'

The other snatched Alice with one of his hands and dragging her close, growled in her ear:

'You need to keep civil, Miss, we're policemen. Now stand back!'

The whole skirmish was ended in an instant. Albert stood still; the men didn't lessen their grip and Sophia seeing this, told them they would all be quiet, and that Albert was her Yard Manager and Head Groom. This was a misunderstanding and that he was just going to escort them home.

'Please let him go.' She kept her voice quiet, hoping not to attract notice from anyone else.

However, the men kept hold of him and casually moved

themselves and Albert to the far corner of the room. One hooked an arm round the older man's neck in a friendly fashion. Sophia followed and didn't notice that Alice had slipped away. No one else in the place was paying them any attention, they looked to be a group with something to talk over, that was all.

The older of the two said, 'Miss Kelley, we know who he is, we were sent by Inspector Caminada. We've been watching your yard for a couple of days now, following you, as ordered.'

Both Sophia and Albert said they hadn't noticed them, and the younger man told them that was the idea.

'We change our clothes often, a scarf, a wig, a coat, a   barrow – it makes a difference.'

They were then both dressed like dockers in nankeen trousers of great age, collarless shirts, dark waistcoats, scarves knotted round the neck and unmemorable hair plastered down with water for the occasion of a night out.

Sophia felt foolish. Nat might find out she had attacked her detectives – and in such a place, although she told herself again that she did intend to tell him about the hypnotist when the time was right.

'Albert, I'm sorry you've been treated badly after you came to get me for my own good – I know that. No, don't say anything. These men are who they say, I've no doubt and I thank them,' she said, glancing at them and asked coldly:

'If you knew who this man is, why take hold of him here?'

The elder answered, 'Miss Kelley, it looked suspicious to other people here, to have you taken out struggling by an angry old bloke. As two younger men, it looks better if we rescued you, as if we were interested in you – begging pardon. You don't look like one of the regulars, even though you're wearing old clothes. You look like a lady being mishandled by a wrong un. Sorry, mate,' he grinned at Albert.

'Just looking after my mistress – mate,' Albert told him plainly. 'You can let me go now and I won't retaliate. One to one you'd have had trouble holding me,' he told them.

'That so?' the younger said.

Albert ignored him.

Suddenly a door slammed shut at the back of the premises. The wind had risen, and dust and dirt blew inside the main doorway in a wild gust. Leaves, straw, litter and any manner of grit filled the air, causing the group by the pillar to dust off their faces, clear eyes, the men to spit out debris.

Sophia looked through the open doors and saw that the street was unusually dark, saw a gas light across the road flickering and then go out. Snuffed by the wind? Someone on a bicycle was blown clean off it; the machine bounced over him. People ran down the street in groups, shielding faces against the blast, their clothes dragged out behind them or pulled before them depending on the direction they went. And channelled by the open door, the noise of the wind rose and fell, for the group nearby sometimes drowning the shouts of the revellers within. At the front of the building loose-fitting window sashes rattled urgently, importantly, drums beating the advance, and as the wind tore past it blew a continuous bugle calls, screeching howls issuing through every gap in the building.

Sophia, Albert and the detectives all moved together as of one mind, to a more sheltered place near the pillar where she and Alice had stood.

'Now you have established that I am coming to no harm and I do thank you for your vigilance, may I go home with my man here?' Sophia asked. 'And my maid...' she added, suddenly aware that Alice had been absent for a few minutes. 'Alice, where...' She looked around anxiously. 'She's gone. Albert, she's gone. What's she up to?'

The elder detective said in a low voice to the other, 'Joe, go and find her, will you?'

The man, Joe, went without another word, threading his way through the crowd, and the remaining one spoke to Sophia and Albert.

'Miss Kelley, he'll find her never fear. You, Rogerson – yes, I know your name; stay with your mistress if I have to move away. Don't leave her for anything.'

'I don't need you to tell me that – mate. Anyroad, what d'they call you?'

'Detective Sergeant is all you need to know, but for Miss Kelley's sake, it's Sam Whitely,' he said, looking now at Sophia and then adding, 'Detective Sergeant Samuel Whitely in case you need to tell Sergeant Roberts, Miss.'

She nodded thanks but was suddenly worried into distraction by the way Alice had vanished.

That girl thinks she's strong enough for anything. Has she got into some trouble? Why disappear like that?

The man hadn't been gone a minute when there was a terrible scream from the back of the room, backstage. It was so loud that it cut through the raucous noise of the place and froze everyone in terror for, what seemed like an age. Then, almost as a body, people rose from their seats and began exclaiming at once.

'What the 'ell were that?'

'Murder, murder!'

'Who is it?'

'The Ripper's come!'

Many of the men had rushed to the entrance that led back-stage, shoving people and chairs, tables, everything out of their way with their big, thrusting, powerful bodies that were stopped at the entrance by a single man. He was tall, broad shouldered, young and dressed as a docker.

'Stop there! Police!' he bawled at the top of his voice, which was loud enough to quieten people for a minute. He held up a card and although Sophia couldn't see it clearly, she knew it would be his warrant card, as he was the other detective, Joe.

'Stand still. Stand still there. Do not leave the building. Its surrounded by now and you'll be arrested. There's been an accident and you must sit back down. Don't make it worse! Sit down I said! Do as y'told there!'

Sam Whitely, the detective with Sophia, stepped forward at their end of the room, shoved a couple of men back who were dodging for the front door.

'Police! Sit down! Don't move,' he shouted in their faces and then to the room in general, 'Sit down, the lot of you!'

There was the sound of a police whistle blown just outside the front door and seconds later heavy footsteps could be heard crashing towards the public house. It was two uniformed policemen who came blasting furiously through the entrance bringing the wind, dirt, rubbish of all kinds and the roar of the gathering gale. They slammed the door shut and instantly the loose window sashes found a deeper note to wail.

The crowd was fearful and drunk. Sergeant Whitely grabbed Albert's arm.

'Don't leave her side.'

Then he turned to two old women who materialised from nowhere and said, 'Walker, Peterson, both stay here and guard these two.' He quickly pushed his way through the crowd to the back of the room where Sophia saw him confer with his partner.

The two old women nodded, and Sophia saw that one of them held a police whistle, which was quickly stowed up the holder's sleeve. They were dressed shabbily like costermongers, their heads wrapped round with scarves and every bit of their persons layered like a barrow load of rags. Filthy boots poked out from beneath skirts Sophia would not have used to wipe up the foulest dirt. She was sure they both had stubble on their chins.

'Very lovely!' Albert sneered.

'Shut y'face,' one of them hissed. 'We're doing a job here.'

Sophia said, 'You're detectives too?' she whispered, but even that level of noise caused the other one to place a finger on lips blackened with grime.

Sophia's arm was held by a dirty clawed hand; it was surprisingly strong and warm. A deep voice spoke in her ear; it was a man's voice.

'Miss Kelley, we're both detectives. Tell your man to behave because it'd spoil our disguise if an old crone were seen to punch him in the face. Sorry, Miss, but we must be vigilant. It seems something very serious has happened.'

She looked at Albert, whispering still, 'Albert, we must do as they say. I'm very much afraid it's happened again...'

'Oh, Miss, don't say that,' he murmured, then turning abruptly he threw a contemptuous look at the crones. 'You both blokes then?'

They nodded.

Albert said, 'Bloody buggerin' 'ell. Pardon, Miss Sophia.'

The wind was a constant dirge in the background as if a tempest were brewing outdoors – indoors too. The room was raucous with speculation. More policemen arrived, poured into the place, and stood around the walls, sticks ready if anyone attempted to leave. The tension grew, people grumbled, the noise became the growl of a caged animal; glasses smashed, there were shouts and falling furniture, scream and oaths. All the policemen could do was to keep the crowd in the room by threat and blow. Shouts from outside could be heard when the noise indoors fell for a second; the vagabonds and night idlers were hammering on the windows to get in and join the excitement.

Sophia was now at the very back with Albert and the two detectives, still in their characters. They said they might pick up some information if they remained undetected, someone might speak unguardedly.

'Albert,' she whispered, 'Where's Alice? It couldn't be her, could it?'

He shook his head firmly. 'No, no.'

It was then that the door to the backstage area opened and Detective Sergeant Whitely came out and without a word to anyone shoved his way purposefully round the edge of the room towards them. The people seated around, whether on chairs, benches or on the floor tried to accost him, shouting to him to tell them who was murdered, what was happening, but he said nothing, and the uniformed constables pushed and hacked at any that tried to leave or move about.

He came up to Sophia and the disguised detectives stood and jostled each other, arguing loudly, Sophia thought, to detract from him speaking to her. A uniformed constable joined the mock argument.

Sergeant Whitely said, 'Miss Kelley, don't be alarmed, but your maid, Alice Kemp, is round the back of the stage and she's in need of you. I'm going to take you round through the front door so as not to excite the rabble.'

Sophia was rapidly terrified. 'What's happened to her? Is she hurt?'

'No, Miss, shocked only. I'm aware that you know about the killings, Inspector Caminada briefed me and my team.'

'You haven't asked why I've come here.'

'No, Miss, not my place just now, but maybe later I'll need to know.'

'I think I've met the man who is on stage tonight, the hypnotist...' she began but he stopped her with a hand quickly held up.

'Please, not now.'

They had been talking quietly and their voices could not be overheard in the buzz filling the room, even so, he lowered his further, saying, 'That's just it, Miss, he's disappeared, and your maid saw him, met him, so to speak. Come along, please and we'll go to her. I'll just take your arm a bit roughly…'

He hurried her up and out of the door before Albert could react and all she could do was mouth, 'Stay there,' at him as she was pulled through the door.

The sergeant apologised for handling her like he had, but he explained that seeing her leave without that charade might rouse up the rabble to want to follow. Someone would always see what you did, he said. They needed to keep things very quiet and private backstage. He took her quickly round the outside of the building and were soon in the alley. They both had to use their arms to shield their faces from the furious blast of the wind; litter of all sorts whirled in the air, funnelled down the back alley; the noise of the city was doused by the wind. The streetlights on the road flickered and flamed; there was no light in the back alleys, but that shed from the windows at the back of the public house and other buildings. Past the police guards they hurried, through the yard gate, past the policeman at the door and inside the back of the building.

He opened the door to the backstage room for her, and she could see there were two policemen in there, with Alice…and the body of a woman on an ancient chaise longue.

Chapter 33

'Because he knoweth
that he hath but a short time'
The Old Testament: Revelations 12:12

SOPHIA WALKED IN AND was met with a wall of dread. The emotions whipping about the room were so strong and violent that she reeled back and fell against Sergeant Whitely who was close behind.

'Steady Miss Kelley, steady. Take your time there,' he murmured.

But she couldn't move, but stood shaking, trying to get her breath.

'Just take your time. It's alright,' said the sergeant. 'There's nothing to be afraid of now.'

But for her the air was redolent with destruction, terror, death and something else that she couldn't identify for a time, but it was a persistent scent and soon showed itself in her mind as the scent of triumph. The killer had left the imprint of his jubilation everywhere and it filled her mind as surely as if he had planted a seed.

She felt herself led into the room and gently pushed down onto a chair near the door. She couldn't speak.

All I've had for weeks is this horror at every turn. The visions that have come to me, the feelings I've experienced have all been to do with these murders. Yes, I've remembered wonderful things that have happened, had visions from my own memory, but the truly clairvoyant visions have all been of devastation, ruin, anguish, fear. Evil. All is evil.

She started suddenly at the sound of a familiar voice.

'Miss Sophia, can you hear me?' It was Alice, her voice forlorn.

She was sitting on the chair right next to her, beside the inner door. Sophia wheeled around to face her and saw immediately that she was upset, and this was so unusual in itself that the realisation gave her a physical jolt, relieved her from her tormenting thoughts.

'Alice, Alice. I'm here now,' she told her and threw her arms round the girl. Alice sobbed, just one breathy sob and then stood and straightened herself, tried to push her hair from her eyes and straighten it because it looked as though it had been dragged out of its pins; it was lying in abundant confusion on her shoulders. Her straw hat lay crushed on the floor at her feet.

'I'm right as rain now, Miss. Oh, Miss Sophia, when you was speaking to that detective bloke, I were looking at them women, y'know, the ladylike ones up front. Well, there was only two of 'em – the maid and the other ladylike one and they seemed real worried, stood up and staring all round, looking for the other. She was nowhere to be seen – the third one. I just had a thought about that fella, that Monsoor Maurice, about whether she were with him, so I came back here to see what I could and I saw...' She nodded at the body. 'This... this...like the cathedral.'

Her voice was tense, close to hysteria, Sophia felt. This was too much for the girl, she may have seen many bodies but to be the one to discover a dreadful murder and so soon after all the others they'd dealt with, was beyond the resilience of anyone, brought up in a mining town or not.

Sophia had stood when Alice did, but now Sergeant Whitely motioned for Sophia to sit and drew Alice gently by the arm to the chair she had left. Then he looked about the room and his eye fell on a couple of theatrical looking robes.

'You two,' he said to the policemen on guard there, and indicated with gestures for them to help cover the body with these things. Which they did, carefully, quietly.

Then he sent them out of the room, shut the door after them.

'Miss Kelley and, erm, Alice is it?' he asked. Alice nodded. 'I want to ask your maid a few questions while her impressions are fresh...'

Sophia nodded but Alice gasped indignantly, 'Fresh, bloody *fresh?* They'll never be fresh again...' She threw her hands over her face.

'No,' he said, 'Look I'm sorry. Just tell me what happened, would you?'

Alice wiped her eyes roughly, as though she were ashamed to give in to tears.

Poor little Alice, always wanting to be so tough...

The girl sniffed and looked assessingly at him and then at Sophia.

'I crept in 'ere very quiet, just opened the door a crack, no one else was near...but when I looked in, I saw ...' She pointed a shaking hand at the shrouded body. 'And then, the hypnotist bloke.'

Sophia and Sergeant Whitely, both spoke at once.

'You saw who he is?

'What did he do? Who is he?' Sophia clenched her nails into her palms. 'Could you tell?'

'No, he were dressed up and with that mask on.'

The policeman crouched down in front of her chair, saying quietly and seriously, 'Any details will be worth their weight in gold; anything at all. What did you do then?'

'He turned and saw me at the door and before I could say owt, he was next to me and grabbed me by the hair, pulled me in; shut the door, locked it too. I 'eard the key turn. I thought I were next...'

Sophia stirred, bent forward, whispered gently, 'Go on.'

'He just flung me on the floor there, aimed a kick at me, but I rolled over in time and jumped up. I tried to kick out at him – nearly got 'im too, but he punched me in the middle of me chest and I were winded right enough. Then he said I were *an interfering slut*. He went to her, the poor woman then. She were lying there, dead – like them others, I could see that well enough from the floor; he stood and looked down, smiling, like 'e was proud and then he went out by that door there, quick as lightning.'

She looked up at the ceiling, her lips tightly compressed, holding in her emotion, as though to get her story told as quickly as possible.

She threw a swift, significant glance at Sophia, saying:

'When he grabbed me, I could smell 'is cologne, or soap he'd used or summat. It were on his skin, Miss. I'd know it again, that I would.'

Sophia nodded slightly.

'Go on. When he left, what then?' the sergeant asked.

'The wind got in when he opened the door and all the muck blew in me face so I couldn't see nothing. When I got it cleared, I pulled meself up and went to see if she were really dead – felt near 'er throat – y'know Miss, like the doctor does?'

Sophia took hold of her hand, squeezed. 'Then what?'

'She were definitely dead, but I knew it anyroad. Then I felt something filling me up inside and I just screamed and screamed me head off. I just couldn't stop it, Miss. And I'm sorry Miss, for leaving you out there with them lot.'

'It was you we heard then. Quietened the whole place,' Sergeant Whitely told her, smiling grimly.

She flicked a disbelieving glance at the policeman.

He added hastily, 'You've done well, Alice. You've been brave I'd say. I could say you were foolish to come in, especially as you knew about the other murders from your place of work and from Miss Kelley here. You suspected the young woman, the victim, might be back here and might be in some danger. So, on the whole, I'd say brave. Not many women would have tried to fight back either.'

Alice dropped her head, was silent. Sophia said, 'Thank you, Sergeant.'

He stood up. 'Miss Kelley, I'm sending a message to Inspector Caminada. He'll want to see this scene as it is. We need to question some of the people in the audience, the landlord and others who may know who this Monsieur Maurice really is, where he's come from. And we need to take the other ladies who were with the victim somewhere private to break the news and then get them home, inform family and so on.'

'Thank you,' she said.

He continued, this time more firmly, 'I'll get a cab and I'd like you to go home with Rogerson and my two 'lady' detectives, if you don't mind. Don't worry, they can hang on the back or run after you. They'll do a quick change of appearance before that, if I know them. You are still to be guarded at all times, and now your maid here has been seen by the killer, she will need the same watchful attention.'

He did all that he had promised and in an hour Sophia and Alice were home. She sent Alice straight to bed and had Mrs Kittering see that she was given hot water, fresh clothes, tea, food, a hot water bottle and anything she needed. The older woman was very shocked by even the barest outline of events that Sophia gave her.

Her father returned later and had been given some of the facts and now, by his request they were taking a little brandy, alone by the fire in their sitting room; Sophia had also bathed and wore her bed robe and a warm shawl. The room was on the shaded side of the building and was always cool away from the fire despite the summer heat. All was as comfortable as it could be, just like a normal night - to begin with.

'Sophia, my dear,' her father said, but then stopped, took some brandy.

He was in his accustomed chair near the fire and the warm glow lent him a brighter aspect than his features told. She saw him begin to speak, then frown and hold back, as though trying to find the words.

'Father, what is it?'

He started up. His expression astonished. 'What is it? What is it?' He stood abruptly, strode across the room, anger in every step. 'What is it?' he snapped, bending down to her and looking full in her face, searching her features.

'Why do you not know? That's what I ask, Sophia.' He threw himself back in his chair, then leaned to the fire and assaulted the coal until it sparked and spat. 'But I'll tell you – I see I'll have to, at long last. In a short while, a police van will arrive bringing the remains of yet another murder victim, another young woman in the prime of her life, a professional young woman, one who is unmarried, one living and working in Manchester. All of these things apply to *you*. But there's more. Tonight's victim, as with, the other three, bears a remarkable resemblance to *you*, even if it's only the colour of her hair and her stature. Furthermore, *you* were within yards of her when she was done to death brutally by this devil.'

378

'Father…'

'No, say nothing, nothing. You'll listen to me – grown up or not!'

She was silent.

'I went out this evening thinking you'd be here at home, only to find the opposite was the case from Ernie. He told me that Albert had followed you (thank Goodness for a man of sense), and that you, along with Alice, were in some disguise. I couldn't believe him when he said you'd gone to one of the most vulgar establishments in the city, to see this hypnotist. All this I had from a lad who works for us and not from my daughter herself, the woman who runs this very prosperous business with aplomb.'

'Father I need to tell…'

'No, there's no need.' He held up his hand briefly, continuing, 'I guessed something may happen because Nat and I spoke of Isabella Waterstone's stolen diary. You see I do have facts at my disposal, because he told me, when I called in this morning, that the sister had remembered some of the more startling entries and that one mentioned a hypnotist. I take it this is the one our own men were gossiping about. I think you then assumed the hypnotist was involved in her death and because you are arrogant - no do not protest at all!' he added as she began to interrupt, 'because you are arrogant you decided you would go and expose yourself, actively put yourself in danger – because what could there be but danger? And you were proved right. Another woman fell victim and your maid was attacked.'

His face was dark, his hands trembled with anger.

Sophia sat very still, only the sudden stream of tears she couldn't repress moved.

'I'll tell you bluntly, my dear, that it will be a short time before he takes another victim, if the pattern of other killers of this kind are to be remembered. What terrifies me is that he is dangerously close to you. Alice has seen him, and of course he was probably disguised, but more significantly, he has seen Alice. I expect Nat knows nothing of this exploit?'

She shook her head.

He sat down heavily, threw the last of his brandy back in one movement and refilled his glass.

'You have been naive, Sophia. You think because you see death daily and are familiar with it, even with these terrible slayings, that you are invulnerable and that it won't happen to you. But when you meet death, its sting is gone. The deceased, however he appears, is not suffering, not speaking, nor does he take any action. You meet the bereaved all the time, and we know how they differ in their reaction to death, displaying elation or needing consolation, either way a time of heightened emotions, not everyday intercourse. You spend all your time at the business, only occasionally walking out with Nat.'

He rose from his chair to mend the fire properly and patted Sophia on the shoulder. Her tears streamed faster.

'But my dear, my fault as a father is that I have cocooned you here in this business and been glad to see your skills grow, so glad of the partnership, especially when your mother passed away. Part of the result has been that you know nothing of the wider world and the ways of mankind. Nat meets death in very different forms, sees violent death delivered to innocents on a whim or violently between criminals in a fight, or at the plotting of some murderer. He sees the lonely man expiring in a sewer, the baby breathing its last on its mother's breast in a dark, rat filled alley, or lying in a ditch alone. He searches out the killers fresh from their deeds, the common criminals about their desperate petty business, the clever crooks who live in wealthy mansions. He speaks to the victims of these crimes too, hears how they suffer longer, go on suffering into the future. He travels about the city and the country, meets other people in his calling, meets every kind of person in his search for the truth.'

He fell quiet. Sophia wiped her face and went over to him, knelt, and put her head on his knee as she did when she was a child and he rested a hand on her shoulders, patted her gently.

'Father, I'm sorry. I've let you down tonight. I wish heartily that I hadn't gone, but I don't think it would have ended differently for the poor woman. I can see that I've let myself down in many ways; I've tried to do what I thought was for the very best, but I've made some dreadful mistakes, especially since these killings started. But the truth, you spoke of it now; there is something else I need to tell you that affects me and affects the killings a great deal.'

She lifted her head to look at him but remained at his knee as she told him of her clairvoyant visions connected to these murders, of the horror she saw, the emotions she experienced, the things that she did because of this growing knowledge.'

'Father, there's not another person whose opinion and knowledge I respect more because you have known me all my life from the first moment. We grew closer when Mother passed away, but I feel her with me all the time, each day as though she watches over me. I've never had a vision of her, and I think it's because she is simply part of me and of you.'

'Lovie, you are my only child, and you are dear. When you started to tell me these things just now, I despaired because as you know I have always called this thing, this clairvoyance, foolish and counterfeit. Your mother, ah, your mother…she had this gift, as you know, and her mother too. It was as common to them as meeting real people. She didn't want me to discourage you because she wanted to watch the way you approached the gift yourself and not interfere in its growth, wanted you to choose how to use it. I was always the practical one, the mundane, the man of the grindstone, but she lifted up

381

her eyes and her soul to realms others cannot see, and if truth be told, wanted to know existed, however much they denounced them. That was me. You know I hate the charlatans who prey on people, and that's because they are thieves in a way, stealing emotions, memories, making false ones, preying on the weak. Your mother was a true sensitive, as you are, and I know you won't ever be a charlatan.'

He stood and drew her up into an embrace.

'It's late, lovie, you are very, very tired. One thing I will add, is why, knowing exactly what had happened to these poor women, why did you still put yourself in danger by going tonight? And I'll answer for you. You think it won't happen to you. And I hope to God it doesn't come anywhere near that! Never be so complaisant again my dear, my only child. Never!' He kissed her, looked down into her eyes, patted her back. 'Very well then. In the morning we will talk again, and I'd like to visit Nat with you. There are things to talk over.' He took out his handkerchief, wiped his nose, his eyes. 'You will marry him?'

'Of course. Soon I think.'

'Good, he said you would. Lovie, I'd like you to take some time on holiday from the business, a month or two at least and I want you to go and visit places, meet people, have a rest from death. Take time to think and to decide whether you want the undertaking business to continue to be your life when you are married. I'm hearty enough to manage on my own and if I can't then I'll get help, take on a junior undertaker.'

'I think I'd like that, Father, I really think I would – just the time to have a break, I mean. I love the work we do though. I want to carry on.'

'Well, that's good enough for the moment, my dear. And I wanted to tell you that my gift to you and Nat will be the wedding trip, anywhere in the whole world.'

She smiled for the first time in hours.

There was a loud ring on the outside bell. They both started.

'Ahh, the police, I expect. I was told as much – a message from this top man, Inspector Caminada.'

It was midnight. Her father answered the door and she heard him sending people round to the yard gate. He then went to rouse Albert and a couple of the lads. She heard Sergeant Whitely's voice.

Sophia decided to stay where she was and curled up in her chair, partly for desperate tiredness and exhaustion and also for the sheer comfort and safety at the end of a bad day.

When her father returned, he told her that the victim's body had been brought to them and not the police mortuary on Inspector Caminada's instruction. They had handled the others and he wanted a continuity of approach. They could see that she had died from suffocation clearly enough. Apparently, Inspector Caminada had specially requested that Sophia deal with this personally in the morning. The victim was Celia Gardiner, and she was the personal assistant to the head of an insurance firm here in the city. She had all the characteristics of the other victims. Sophia was to look for a message, the sergeant said, to confirm this was the work of the same killer. The victim's family had been informed and had given permission for her to be brought to Kelley's, but they were desperate to view her body there as soon as they could. The victim's friend and the maid had accompanied her to see the hypnotist because she told them he was her secret admirer, disguised as the performer. They had identified her at the scene of the crime; both had fainted.

Her father told her, 'My dear, this young woman was laid out in exactly the same way as the others and she has an earring missing.'

'Ah, I saw her, but I did not go up to her. Does she have a hat, Father? I didn't notice that either, because there was so much confusion. But what I did see was that mask of terror.'

'Ahh, yes. But as to the hat, I don't believe so, my dear. She is the fourth, as you are aware. Sophia, I can't allow you to go anywhere alone now and if Nat weren't ill, he'd make you safe, I have no doubt. You'll be fine when you are here on our own premises and when you visit the vicarage, but otherwise I will have you watched myself and there are the detectives that I believe are to guard you also.'

'We're not safe from this yet, are we?'

'Not yet, my dear.'

Chapter 34

'Another blue day'
Thomas Carlyle

SOPHIA WENT EARLY to the workroom; the family of the victim would want to see her today because they hadn't been allowed to last night, much as they begged. She prepared the workroom, collecting everything she would need all before she brought the body from the cool storage. She hadn't even looked out of her window with any interest this morning. It was as though she needed somehow to make amends to the woman, Celia Gardiner, for being nearby when she was killed, for even knowing about the way each victim was murdered and how they were treated by the killer.

Will there be a posy? There will. The message this time…and for whom? The family, the police; a taunt for them, as Nat says? The killer has been in here, right inside my workroom and stolen the diary and the other posies. It must certainly be no other than he who did this. And if he knows who I am, where I am, and that I'll prepare the bodies, then is the posy for…me…?

She was frozen in fear; it could have been ten seconds; it could have been an hour. Her mind was blank during this time and when she finally became aware of herself, she thought:

No, it can't be for me. Remember what Alice imagined. She thought he might use it as a final hurt for the poor victims, to show it to them as he held them captive, boasting, and explaining in terrible detail if they didn't know the language of flowers – not everyone does, that final awful truth about his feelings for them; so that they understand the weight of the betrayal, felt the pain.'

She gathered her resolve and brought out Celia Gardiner's body, gently drew back the covering cloth and looked down at her.

Her expression – Oh, the same!

She had only seen the woman across the room the night before, and she had seen enough of her dead face to recognise even at the little distance, that it was riven with horror, but here under the harsh lights it was in shocking clarity and the fear in her eyes was intense. Sophia shuddered.

She's a little like me, they all were, but I don't dress like these poor women did; they're all very fashionable and were dressed for an outing. I go on so few outings that I don't even have clothes that are so lovely. Dare I search for the posy?

Her hands trembled as she pulled back the low neck of the silk dress and slowly bent down to peer cautiously.

It's there.

She laid her hand on the young woman's shoulder, a silent apology for the intrusion, sorrow at her dreadful death. Using her long forceps, she drew the posy out, carried it to the workbench, away from the victim – forever.

He was the last person to touch this.

She threw a cloth over the posy, turned away from it and smoothed down her apron.

I've to prepare Celia for her family first; Father said they were to come later this morning. I'll prepare her for burial tomorrow. Look, one earring, beautiful silver with amethyst.

386

I'll take it to Nat for the inspector; it'll be evidence. Didn't he tell me the inspector was going to see the other three families and ask for the earrings as evidence? I wonder if he told them that the missing one was probably kept by killer or did he say it was merely lost – to save their feelings? After all, we don't know the killer took them, likely as it seems.

She folded her arms, stood away from the table, reluctant to begin, nevertheless planning.

The first thing is to try to alter her expression, smooth out those scars of terror. She'll need a little colour and I'll straighten her hair. It's loosened, but I suppose the killer didn't have time to arrange it as he did for the other women. No, Alice disturbed him. He'd taken a gamble – it was audacious, awful.

She trembled.

Her hands. Does she have that substance under her nails, as the others did? His skin...

She shuddered, took a breath, steeled herself to lift one of Celia's hands. Her nails were nicely polished, so pretty. She looked closely at the underside of her nails and found under all of them, as she expected, some grey matter; she bent and sniffed cautiously.

That's it.

Steeling herself, she breathed in the scent again.

There's a sour note. Sweat, I think. Dirty skin too. Something else on the edge of my memory. Is it a hint of cologne? A man's cologne. Yes. Where do I know it from?

She couldn't think.

She put the hand down and began her work then, deliberately keeping her mind on the work instead of screaming at the phantasm of horror that stood silently beside her, watching. It took her the best part of the next hour to arrange Celia's appearance to disguise as much of the means of her death as she could, and then, finally satisfied, she had the body moved to the Chapel of Rest. She would do the final preparation for her funeral next day.

Her steps dragged as she returned hesitantly to the posy. What would the message be? Throwing back the cloth, she confronted it, held it up to the light. Sophia recognised each flower and knew the meaning instantly as if the killer had spoken the words in her ear, close to her ear.

Buttercups for childishness. An orange lily; this for hatred, pride and disdain. Columbine, light blue; its message is folly.

She turned the little posy around in her fingertips, held it up in front of her eyes to speak its message.

Ah, so obvious a meaning: I have my pride, I reject your childishness, I disdain this relationship as folly. He taunted poor Celia with this and then killed her mercilessly – all those people in the other room of the Rose and Crown, oblivious – as we were too.

She couldn't breathe, her throat was tight, tears welled up and ran down her cheeks and all that she wanted to do was to get the thing out of sight. She snatched an old tin from one of the cupboards, pushed the posy inside but struggled to close the lid, almost bending the weak little hinges in her desperate haste to have it hidden. She'd take it to Nat this morning, along with the earring, both for Inspector Caminada's attention.

Sophia took off her apron, washed her face, collected what she needed for Nat, eventually found her hat and putting the tin and the earring in her handbag, she went in search of her father.

He should be ready to go to the vicarage now and she found him in the yard talking to Dr Smith. The wind had not dropped from the previous night and the air was filled with bits of hay, dust and other debris, floating in the seconds of calm, swirling up in the next gust, then skimming along the ground. They were standing by the kennels and both with their backs to the wind, discussing dogs. The doctor had his hand on the head of one of the watch dogs, the other hand fed the big creature a tit-bit. When Sophia joined them, the discussion seemed to be about what sort of dog was suitable for a child of ten, one of the doctor's daughters. Apparently all four of his daughters were under ten years, so his wife must be quite young. They'd never met his family. Dogs took the stage and all three discussed the merits of King Charles spaniels, whippets, and small rough terriers such as a Parson Jack Russell.

'Perhaps the little girl might like to choose for herself, Doctor?' Sophia suggested and he smiled, and he looked so different that Sophia was surprised, not as old as he seemed. It was not often he smiled as they usually met in some dire circumstance or another, such as a funeral, a death, an accident.

'Indeed, I'll take your advice. My wife would like a very small dog that will not take much room; that is the prime consideration.' He patted his pocket, felt whatever he wanted in one and smiled again. 'Well, it's blustery today and very strange when combined with this unusual warmth. Were you going somewhere?' he asked them, glancing back and forth at each of them.

Her father explained where they were going and asked the doctor in turn if he had called on them for any special purpose.

'In fact, I did. I heard about the latest murder, from my colleague, Dr Johnson at Newton Street. I was told that the victim was brought straight here from the scene of death. This is unheard of; no doctor to certify her dead?' he said, his expression now serious.

Sophia said, 'I believe there was a doctor locally who did the office and the detective in charge of this case asked specifically that she be brought here as we have prepared the others. He simply wanted a continuity. He's called Inspector Caminada, a well-known detective here, it seems.'

Dr Smith nodded, 'Ah, yes, I can understand the need for continuity. Erm, professionally, you understand, I'd be interested to know the cause of death for this poor woman?'

Sophia's father explained plainly and briefly that Inspector Caminada asked them not to speak of the case to anyone, fellow professional or not; he was sorry as he knew the doctor was discretion itself. He shrugged apologetically and the doctor nodded his understanding.

'Correct as ever, my dear Mr Kelley. Well, I also called because I wondered if there was anything I could do, not knowing that the victim had already been certified for the Coroner. But all is as it should be, and I might have known that would be the case.' He paused, looked pensive. 'The vicarage? I intended to visit myself this morning and speak to Dr Bonaventure about a medical matter, and of course to look in at my patient.' He gave a strange, embarrassed little bow to Sophia. 'Might I put myself and my cab at your service? You know I employ a cab for my daily rounds? I keep it on all day – the same driver always and the vehicle and horses are of the highest quality. I find it more economical that keeping a vehicle of my own. Could I be of help, to either of you, both of you?'

Sophia smiled, glanced at her father.

He said, 'Now you mention it, doctor, it would be useful if I could stay on the yard to deal with a piece of business that has arisen. I don't want my daughter to go anywhere alone until this killer is found, you understand?'

'I do, indeed; I have four daughters of my own.'

Her father continued, 'If you could escort Sophia, then I'll follow in an hour. My dear, is this acceptable?'

Although they'd known him for a few years, she had never been alone with the doctor before, but he was a family man.

She was mildly surprised to feel this reluctance to be alone with someone she only knew professionally, but what was she thinking? She wanted to go to Nat as soon as humanly possible.

'Of course, thank you. I am ready as soon as you like, Dr Smith.'

The doctor gave her his hand to helped her into the cab; it was surprisingly firm and strong. Did doctors have to have soft, weak and gentle hands?

How silly I am today.

Once they were seated, he opened the windows on both sides because the day, though still windy, was becoming hot once more and he seemed solicitous of her comfort. They travelled in easy silence for the first part of the way, and Sophia was glad of it. Naturally she looked forward to seeing Nat, but all her senses were numbed by the events of last night and now, this very morning, to be face to face, and intimately so with the victim, assured once more that this was the work of the same monster who stalked the city – it was too much. She felt quite disoriented.

Noise tumbled in through the windows, filling the cab, the rumble of wheels on the market carts, the ritual, incomprehensible bellow of newspaper boys on street corners, arms full of The Manchester Guardian, The Observer, The Times, The Mercury. There was the rustling sweep of the wind as it buffeted the cab, shrieks of women with hair dragged loose, laughter from some urchins chasing a hat. A myriad rich and varied smells swept in too, the greasy billows of steam from the several little eating houses, the riper scent of horse droppings, coal smoke – despite the day, the stench of a huge bin of rotten vegetables from a back alley.

All is as it usually is in town, she thought, then allowed her mind to swim in blankness, her body swaying with the movement of the carriage.

It was a short way to the vicarage in St Ann's Place, but the traffic was predictably heavy, and the journey took more than the usual ten minutes. They were almost there when, as they turned a corner, the gusty wind flew through the cab, from one window, across the passengers and out of the next, blowing Sophia's straw hat clean off. She managed to snatch it before the wind stole it away.

'Well caught, Miss Kelley, but don't you ladies anchor your hats with pins and such?' the doctor wondered, with a polite smile.

'I do, usually, but I see I forgot today. The wind's so strong when it's channelled through a small space like this,' she answered, holding the hat in her hands for fear of a repeat of the event.

The wind gathered strength, fairly wailed through the narrow window openings then raced down an alley, moaning drearily.

'Well, at least it is a serviceable hat with a bit of substance. These tiny feather and fluff concoctions some ladies favour would have been out of the window in a trice! My wife cannot buy enough of those – every colour, every shape! Charming!' he commented. 'There they perch enticingly like birds about to take flight.'

How poetic. I've never heard him speak like this.

He continued, glancing at her from time to time:

'One could almost build cages for them, fearing they would fly away! Do you not favour them, Miss Kelley? I've never seen you in anything other than your straw hat here, or your funereal top hat and veil; very smart.'

Clouds were blown rapidly across the sun, the wind whistled and screamed.

She said, 'I've never tried one, but, who knows, one day I may have a need.'

'Ah, a special event perhaps?' He was strangely coy.

'No, no, not at the moment.'

'The sergeant and you?' he prompted.

'Oh yes, but not just yet.'

I don't think I've ever spoken to him about personal things before. What's the matter with him? More importantly what's the matter with Nat?

'Doctor, the sergeant, may I ask how you think he's doing? His illness seems to have gone on for a longer time than I expected for someone who was hit on the head. What do you think?' she said, anxious to divert the conversation to practical matters.

She saw his body straighten; his face took on his usual, recognisable mask of the doctor with a medical puzzle.

'I do think it is an unusual case.' He paused as if to arrange his diagnosis. 'But an injury to the head is always difficult. We cannot ascertain how much damage there was to his brain. It's a delicate structure and can be thrown about inside the hard case of the skull. This is often observed in post-mortems following a great head trauma; the brain looks bruised and damaged, tissue often appearing almost liquified, a great deal of blood, naturally. And I always think…'

'Doctor…' she stammered weakly. This was too much after the events of the past hours.

He gave her a penetrating look.

'Oh, Miss Kelley, my apologies. I was crass and unfeeling. What possessed me to go into such detail about someone so close to you? Please forgive me.'

He moved around quickly in his seat, to almost face her and she thought for a moment that he would snatch up her hand.

Please don't. No sympathy, please. I can't stand it!

Thankfully he continued in his normal tone, 'You ask how he is, and I answer, he is still a little unwell, but recovering. I am confident. My only concern is his heart and the unusual palpitations, but I am giving him some medication to steady it. No, do not fear anew…indeed, I want to consult with Dr Bonaventure this very morning, about his medication. How fortuitous that he has come among us, having studied at the Sorbonne for so long and being under their famous professors. He has knowledge of the most modern research on medication for many of the major ailments. Sergeant Roberts will soon be up, but not for a few more days. Now have I set your mind at ease?'

'Thank you, yes.'

He glanced away from her to look out of the window and saw where they were.

'Ah, we have arrived,' he said. He stooped to lift his leather bag and gave a small exclamation. 'What's this, by your foot, Miss Kelley?' He picked something up. 'Good Lord, an earring, valuable too.'

He held up for her inspection a jet earring, a long lozenge shape set to dandle in a gold filigree lattice.

She held out one hand while the other went to touch each of her ears; both actions were instinctive even though she knew she didn't own it. She remembered, as she felt them, that today she wore the garnet and gold clusters, fashioned like flowers.

He looked puzzled.

'It must have been left in here by another passenger. Although I hire it exclusively for my professional hours, the cabbie is free to take other fares in the evenings. I'll give it to him, later. He may well remember the lady who wore it. Here, allow me,' he said, as he leapt out and offered her his hand.

Before she could take it, Reverend Knightly was by the cab too.

'I saw you arrive. Good morning, Sophia, doctor' he greeted them, a little subdued, Sophia noticed.

She caught his arm. 'Nat, he's alright?'

He gave her a reassuring smile. 'Yes, yes, of course. Did I alarm you in some way?'

'You look worried.'

'It's just the latest dreadful murder has distressed us all,' he said, leading the way indoors.

'Indeed, shocking, appalling,' Dr Smith added.

The two men stood aside to allow Sophia to enter.

Oh, what is that scent? That scent...

The thought passed through her mind as she was interrupted by Michel.

He advanced swiftly towards them from the back regions of the house, smiling a welcome.

'Ah, Sophia. At last you are arrived! Dr Smith, we will speak in a little while, bien sûr. Excuse me.'

He immediately led her upstairs, chatting about the latest contretemps he and Nat had enjoyed, about horses, of all things - commonplace enough, but she was diverted from her puzzling impression in the entrance. She heard Dr Smith and Reverend Knightly talking in an animated fashion as they disappeared into Reverend Williams's study.

Nat was awake and propped up in bed but when he saw her, he held out his arms and she went straight to him. When she turned her head, Michel left them alone.

'Love, how are you?' he asked. 'You looked washed out, why is that?'

'You know about the murder last night?'

'I do.'

He'd heard about it from several people and she was able to correct some details and add more.

'How do you know all these details, hmm? Why am I

suspicious, love?'

'That's because you are a policeman and question everyone, but I suppose it's also because you know me well and can see it in my face,' she said, sick at heart and ashamed. She told him everything about the ill-starred excursion by herself and Alice.

'And you went knowing, thanks to Alice's reasoning, that there might be a possibility of the murderer being there because of this hypnotism link? Is that right?'

'It is. But I think she's right, he may have hypnotised his victims. We know Isabella Waterstone kept his name a secret, even in her own diary. And the visions I had, from the souls of those girls, they didn't show me his face or any clue to his identity.'

He grabbed her arm, used her as a prop to pull himself up and looked exhausted by the effort. He wiped his brow on the back of his hand, scowled at her.

'Nevertheless, all that information could have been given to Inspector Caminada to deal with – perhaps not the bit about the visions, but the diary and the fact that the families knew nothing, none of them knew of an admirer. You just decided to put yourself right in the path of danger, in the path of *evil.* Why?' His voice was taut.

'Why? I don't know why. I just felt drawn to see him…' She swallowed; tears filled her eyes. 'and I was right, tragically…'

He stared hard at her. 'Did you have one of these visions, these clairvoyant visions, when you were there?'

'No, not then, I didn't, but I knew it was him, the hypnotist - as soon as he came on stage. I didn't recognise his voice, but I think it was disguised; I didn't recognise any mannerisms or movements, nothing. But it was him. It was as though my psyche recognised him.'

'Hmmm.'

'You don't believe me?'

'I do, that's the trouble. I'm just terrified he also recognised you. If someone – him, we assume, stole those things from the workroom, we decided he knows you because otherwise how would he discover you had those things in the workroom? Last night you might have been disguised as a washer woman, or whatever it was, but he would recognise your bearing, your face. I'm guessing you didn't try to alter them yourself? No. And don't forget he was very close to Alice, that warrior woman – no, I am not being flippant!' he said quickly as she was about to interrupt. 'Alice was face to face with Death, Sophia, and if she hadn't struck out and made a noise, Death may have won. That could have been you if you hadn't been stopped by the detective officers.'

'Yes,' she said, 'I know you're right and I can't imagine how he'll be caught, and this terrible march of Death stopped.'

He drew her into his arms, saying, 'Inspector Caminada has many men on the case now. He'll be finding out everything he can from the landlord of the Rose and Crown. I expect to hear from him today.'

She told him about the feelings she'd had last night and again this morning, how she had become heavy with sadness to deal so soon with the aftermath of the death, and this one the fourth.

'Oh, Nat, what's happening?'

'Well, you survived the event, so at this time I won't be angry with you, but I'm shocked you thought to do this.'

'Father has said that and more, so much more, and he's angrier than you. He's coming along later; I came chaperoned by Dr Smith who's downstairs speaking to both the reverends. He said he was coming here this morning to talk on a professional matter with Michel.'

'Is the doctor coming up to see me afterwards?'

'I guess so, love. Why?'

'Oh, no reason other than I want to keep you to myself; I want everyone to stay away,' he said and patted the bed beside him. 'No one is here, come and lie beside me. I'll pretend I am asleep if anyone comes so they'll think there's no impropriety. I am so tired still.'

'Have you eaten?'

'Felt sick. Stomach cramps too.'

They lay quietly for a short while until they heard steps coming along the landing, so Sophia got up and straightened Nat's bedding.

'Still can't breathe that well, love. What I need is a trip to the moors again. I need fresh air. Can you open the window?' he asked.

She rose to go to the window when there was a knock at the door and Michel entered.

'Ah, mon ami, you look worried now. Has Mademoiselle Sophia upset you?' he asked smilingly.

'No, no, I feel tired, weary,' Nat answered.

'Time for the painkiller perhaps, mon ami? The good doctor is downstairs and will visit you later.'

Nat mumbled and turned over.

When Sophia bent to look closer, she was surprised.

'He's fast asleep. Goodness. So quickly,' she murmured and pulled the sheet up over his shoulders.

Michel put a hand on her arm. 'He is exhausted. Sleep is good. Are you to stay in here with him?'

'I will, thank you.'

'I will speak to the doctor downstairs then.'

He left quietly and Sophia went to open the window a little, then sat in one of the chairs to watch Nat sleep.

Chapter 35

'Into the valley of Death'
Alfred Lord Tennyson

SOPHIA WAS no sooner in the chair than she fell into a fitful doze. An occasional snore or two from Nat nudged her to consciousness for a second but then she fell back into the waves of a turbulent theme: images of syringes, Nat's face drenched in sweat, the mesmerist throwing his arms up in triumph, the graveyard filled with mists and coffins piled high, with no one to bury them. All this with noise and scents that whirled around her: the bellowing of the crowd that night, a foul miasma over rubbish in an alley, the city racket, screams, hoofbeats, the smell of the killer's skin.

A soft tap at the door brought her to her senses. It broke through the chaos of her thoughts like an axe through matchwood. She quickly opened the door to find Alice on the threshold with her arms completely full of bedding.

'Please Miss, the master told me to bring you this stuff 'e thought you forgot. Oh, and your handbag was left in that cab what the doctor uses. The cabbie were waiting outside when I came and 'e shouted for me,' she said.

This was not the usual Alice, sparking with energy and joy, this was a subdued one, heavy with the horrors she had witnessed and endured the night before. Her eyes were deep shadowed, her hair loose in its fastenings and her skin, tired and dull. But deep within, embers smouldered; this was the respite after a battle and fires were being stoked, forces marshalled; Sophia knew it as much as she felt it herself.

She drew her maid into the room and to the window, away from the bed where Nat lay asleep.

'How are you feeling, Alice?'

'Not too bright, Miss, thank you for askin', but I'll be alright soon. Can I ask how you are, Miss Sophia? I heard you had to get the poor woman ready for her viewing this morning. It must 'ave been hard, that,' Alice said, putting the laundry down on a chest. 'Your handbag, Miss. It's right heavy too,' she said taking the bag off her arm where she held it in the crook of her elbow.

'Ah, fancy me leaving it. There are two very important things in there for the sergeant, evidence. I have another posy and an earring.'

'Oh, no!'

'The message is terrible. I'll tell the sergeant first, Alice. I can't bear to say it just now. I'm tired.'

'Yes, Miss, of course. Can I get you summat?'

'No, thank you. I'll doze until the sergeant wakes. I'll be fine in this chair,' she said, yawning.

Alice bobbed one of her curtseys, which made Sophia smile, then just as she reached the door, she paused, remembering something.

'Oh Miss, I forgot to tell you summat a bit strange. That cabbie, the one the doctor hires to take 'im round, well he says that the doctor lives in Chorlton in an apartment...'

'What?'

''E said the traffic were busy on Oxford Road even at seven o'clock this morning when the doctor was called out. I said why were you down there and 'e says, because I came that road from Chorlton, where the doc lives; one of them big 'ouses what's split into apartments for working people. Big enough for one, 'e says. Grand, for one.'

'One?'

'I says, what about the wife and four kiddies? And he says, yer what? I've never seen none. Bachelor he is, has lady friends, posh ones at that.'

'But….no, that can't be…that's very strange…. I need to think about that…think…' But her mind was blank.

Sophia sat down heavily in the chair.

'Alice, that's a bit of a shock in many ways, but do you know, I simply can't think about it just now. I'm exhausted. I'm going to sleep – yes, sleep. That will give me the strength to deal with everything. You go home - that's it. Don't worry, Alice. The sergeant is here, and Michel and Reverend Knightly.'

'Alright, Miss, if you say so, but I don't like it, I don't.'

'Yes, thank you.'

Alice left.

Sophia lay back in the chair and a black shroud descended on her, settled into place. Doom approaching. All was silence. The city noise outside receded along with the household bangs and creaks, Nat's steady breathing and the sighing of the old bed. Her eyes were wide open, yet she saw nothing; a colossal notion whirled about her mind, one she couldn't begin to define; it circled her consciousness, nudging for admittance, a hungry, leering devil.

'Listen,' it whispered. 'Listen…'

She had no idea how long she floated on this wave of blackness, but she suddenly heard footsteps on the stairs and then heard them approach at a leisurely pace along the landing.

*The carpet is thin, worn out. Footsteps sound so loud…*she thought, irrelevantly.

A soft knock on the door and the handle turned, the visitor sure of a welcome…the doctor; doctors are always welcome…

'Ah, Miss Kelley, I was hoping to catch you here. This *is* good,' he said, softly as he came in and shut the door quietly behind. He looked at the bed.

'Asleep I hope, resting finally. The sergeant is a strong man; difficult to find the right preparations for him,' he said pleasantly. 'Weather still blisteringly warm, but a change is coming I believe, clouds are gathering in the west. My cab driver is an expert on the likely changes in weather.'

All the while he uttered the commonplaces, he stood relaxed, facing the seated Sophia. One hand was in his pocket, in the other his leather Gladstone, his doctor's bag. The clasp on the top was polished steel and winked gently in the beam of sunshine from the window opposite. He wore a signet ring on the little finger of that hand, and captured by the light, it joined the other to create a syncopated rhythm.

He wore that ring – the mesmerist.

Sophia remained in her chair, the blackness prowling around her.

'You are weary, Miss Kelley. You need to rest,' he murmured, his voice low. 'Relax and rest a while.'

Nat turned over, grunting and muttering in his sleep, pushing his head down in the pillows. There was no rustling of the covers; he had only a sheet over him in such weather; there was no noise from bed springs; the old bed had a rope lattice to support its feather mattress. Dr Smith glanced at him again, turned back reassured.

'Rest, Sophia,' he whispered.

He stood very still, swung his bag very evenly to enable the light show; he watched it play on her face.

'I am here now. You knew I would come, didn't you? Sophia? You may nod your head when I ask you a question.' His voice had become so low, something between a whisper and a thought that it was as though she heard it only in her mind.

She nodded once, slowly, remained in her chair, her eyes open, blank; her breathing steady.

'I have wanted to speak to you alone for some time, my dear, about a very personal matter, but hold! Before I do...' he murmured as he moved quickly to the door and turned the key in the lock. 'There, all secure.' He looked at the sleeping man on the bed. 'Deeply asleep; good.' He looked at her steadily for a while then smiled, satisfied, and put his bag on the floor.

Sophia felt no fear, only sadness, overwhelming sadness. Her eyes sought Nat, held onto him, as if that would wake him to save her. She felt a tear run down her cheek but could not find the strength to brush it away; her arms were weary, her legs had no power, had never had power; she imagined she would find herself immobilised if she tried to move, so to save the horror of finding out if this were true, she did not try.

The doctor glanced down at his bag, paused, then approached her; he leaned down, supporting himself by his hands on each arm of the chair. His face was very close to Sophia's. He reached out a hand and gently lifted a curl and hooked it behind her ear.

The smell. His hands, the smell. His cologne...

'Confused, my dear?' he enquired gently, 'You may begin to see how things stand in just a little while, but first I need - no, I'd *like* to explain why I have finally chosen you.'

He straightened up and turning, lifted an upright wooden chair from its place and positioned it directly in front of Sophia, but before he sat down, he pushed her knees roughly apart with his hands, then slowly lifted the skirt of her dress up over her knees. She wore light muslin drawers that were short, so her bare knees were exposed. He stood in between her legs and pulled the chair up behind himself, then sat so that his knees pressed her thighs apart. He rested his hands on her thighs, just above the knee. His face was so close to hers; his eyes were intent, boring into hers. She noticed for the first time that he did not wear his spectacles. Perhaps he did not need them and wore them only to appear benign, kindly.

Another tear moved down her cheek; she tried to move and found herself unable. It was a reality.

'You are very privileged, my dear because you are the culmination of all my endeavours,' he told her, his voice confiding, intimate. 'You are to be my crowning glory, in this city at least. And If I'm perfectly honest, I couldn't have asked for a more propitious chain of events, events serendipitous in their appearance. The good sergeant, so strong, so diligent, so manly – becomes injured by an act of God! There, am I not sanctioned?'

Nat snorted, moved himself noisily in the bed, saliva dribbled from his half open mouth.

Dr Smith, whose back faced the bed, glanced over his shoulder, then resumed his disclosure.

'I am a creative man, you understand, astoundingly creative; I invent a fictitious assault in St Ann's Place, which I know my friend, my intimate friend Inspector Bateman, will act upon.'

Inspector Bateman...!

'I had a handy pair of men awaiting the sergeant at the appointed spot, their lead coshes ready. You see, I intended that he should be attacked and killed, thereby removing him from any interference in my plans and rendering you in need of solace.' He shook his head sorrowfully. 'You understand, don't you, Sophia?' His face was so close that she felt every breath, each word a sigh of longing.

She nodded mechanically, tears running freely, silently.

'But Fate delivered him to me for a better purpose. I thought to test your devotion, have him mortally ill, slipping away before your eyes. Concussion is handy, I grant, but his was slight following the head injury, so I was forced to resort to my old favourites of a little morphine and arsenic to keep him prostrate. And it has been enormously entertaining, this continuing weakness and lethargy, powerlessness. Wonderful concept – *powerless...*'

He stretched out a hand and roughly wiped the tears on her cheek with the edge of his thumb, looked in disgust at the moisture he'd collected.

'Distasteful, especially for a modern woman, a professional woman. I have a penchant for the type – but you already know that. All my other women, all four, have been modern women, intent on their careers, racing unchaperoned everywhere, speaking to men on equal terms, mistresses of their own fates – but no! I know you dispute that, agree with me – I was the master of their fate. You see, a man is always stronger; it is the law of nature. These professional women – oh, you are one of the deluded band; you women are wrong to think you can be equal.'

He stretched out a hand and ran the fingers through the hair on the side of her head, back and forth, a parody of a caress, his fingers raking her scalp.

'And I showed all the other modern young women to you, left you the little messages – you did get them, I know. Did you appreciate the cunning way they were worded? Hmmm? Answer me!'

He tightened the fingers in her hair, pulling it, then suddenly withdrew it and instead, snatched her chin, lifted it up. 'Answer,' he whispered. 'Speak what you know.'

His breath was hot and unpleasant, his spittle showered her face, making her shudder. The acrid scent of his warm body billowed up in her face. She spoke, her voice a dull mumbled monotone.

405

'I read the messages. I know what they said.'

'Good, well done. I wanted to have you prepare all my other women; I advised the bereaved, so that you could deal with their dead and with each one, begin to understand that it would soon be your turn. People are always ready to trust the doctor. But what am I about? You cannot prepare your own body, can you? Dealing with the dead; is it unseemly work for a woman? No, a menial task, for which women are fitted. Yet, the world of business – is this unseemly - presuming to direct men? I think so. You with your funereal garb, your nets and black lace gloves, taking command like an absurd doll. Yet, you have been quite undone by my creations, my offerings, haven't you? You see, you were not strong enough; you failed, but your time of trial is over. Perhaps your worthy father will see the error of his choice in you and indeed, see his little girl for the last time, as a corpse. He is a very sensitive man – he will feel it deeply.'

He dropped her chin, began to massage her thighs, a hand on each. Back and forth, back and forth.

'I took their lives so easily, so very cleanly. No visible marks, no damage to their hair; beautiful, beautiful golden hair just as your own is. Their lovely garments were arranged with decorum - don't you think so? - laid out as you would do later, for their burials. But, my dear Sophia, their faces! The final expressions! I believe they were shocked, felt as though I had let them down in some way, whereas I did them a great service, helped them leave the world at the very pinnacle of their charms and beauty. But a thousand pities for them to leave with such hideous expressions on their faces. Ugliness is anathema to me, Sophia. I believe you remodelled their expressions? You made them look very presentable I hear? Hmmm?'

She nodded, as instructed.

'They didn't deserve it, the ungrateful bitches. A kind death,'

406

he said. 'But you'll soon know. First, I have your own posy to award you and then my own reward is you, your own self, your own body – before I give you your release from the world, naturally. Now not everyone would do that; there are several men I know who wait until after life has ceased...peculiar, in my opinion. But you see, Fate has been my friend once more. The good sergeant is in the room with us, you and me. And as a bonus for myself I will take you in his presence. If he should wake, then all the better, he will be powerless to intervene; he is very close to his own end.'

It was then that Nat began to snore gently, as though he was very deeply asleep.

'Has he had you? Hmmm? It's of no matter. All women are whores. I have had plenty of those. But you will be my finest...' He smiled at her, leaned forward to stroke her cheek.

Nat mumbled, breathed noisily. The doctor took a swift look, decided, once more, that all was well and resumed his focus; he leaned down and opened his Gladstone bag and pulled out a posy.

'But look; this is for you, you alone.'

Sophia couldn't help but look. He held it before her eyes, steadily, turning it slowly, smiling.

She read the message immediately. The posy was formed from cypress leaves, Michaelmas daisy, nightshade and a pink carnation.

He murmured, 'Your very own. Can you read it? The last posy? You may tell me – now, so that I know you are prepared,' he said, and laid the posy on her lap while he undid his cravat, took off his jacket and hung it carefully over the back of the chair, rolled up his sleeves; his forearms were covered in very dark hair. 'Speak, Sophia.' He picked up the posy.

Her voice was quiet, but not subdued, instead it grew imperceptibly with strength.

'The pink carnation represents a woman's love; nightshade can symbolize truth, or it can accuse the recipient of sorcery and witchcraft; it can herald death; the Michaelmas daisy speaks a farewell and cypress is always for death and mourning.'

'Very good. The others, they could not read the language well – a pity. I enlightened them which gave them all a delicious thrill. Now give me the meaning of yours, my dear.' His tone was quiet and animated, overflowing with exquisite pleasure.

Sophia said, 'The message you intend with this posy is this: Farewell to woman's love which is but witchcraft and sorcery bringing death and mourning; that is the truth.' Her voice was clear.

'So talented. The others were a little disappointing, expecting too much. On their final day they expected a holiday trip, found death awaiting. It was very swift,' he said, complacently.

Sophia spoke unbidden:

'Morphine.'

His head snapped up; he was shocked. He sat straight as a bolt, alert in an instant, the posy gripped convulsively, head drawn back.

She continued, her voice in its normal tone and volume, 'Morphine. You injected them with morphine, first holding the syringe in front of their eyes before injecting them below the ear. And you stole their earrings, their right earring; you sucked them off. Then you humiliated them with the posy's message.'

She still couldn't move, and she didn't know why. She only knew that she could speak, and she would do her best to hurt him, try to stop the inevitable happening, hope to keep him mesmerised by her own revelations so that someone might come and intervene. Nevertheless, fear electrified her intent, and the encircling doom kept its patrol nearby.

Why doesn't Nat wake up? But what could he do? He's so ill. Nat! Nat!

She resumed, despite the killer's fixed and dreadful stare:

'They scratched you, reached backwards as you held them in front of you, and they scratched your neck and the backs of your hands. They had your skin under their fingernails. I can smell it even now.'

'How do you know?' His voice was cold, flat. His face twitched slightly and the veins on his temples throbbed visibly.

'I held their dead hands, cleaned their nails.'

He leaned forward and pushed the posy into the top of her dress. Now she smelt death, heard it breathing. Her neckline was a v-shape, and the awful thing sat there securely. Sophia tried to block its presence from her mind because much as she was desperate to, she could not reach up and rip it out, dash it to the floor, crush it with her foot.

'I asked how you knew the other things,' he demanded testily. 'You see, I do not deny my enjoyments.' He lifted his chin, stroked his goatee, his moustaches.

He is disturbed. Good, but he seeks to gain ground with every little nuance. I can rattle him more – help may come. Oh, Nat, wake, wake!

She made her voice ape that of the medium at the séance, made it as prophetic and eerie as she could, made her eyes appear far seeing and staring.

'I know because I saw. I have the power of clairvoyance. The spirits of the dead reached out to me across the gulf. I saw, I saw.'

He reached out a hand and lifted her hair to expose her ears.

'Garnet and gold. This one will be my own keepsake soon.' He caressed her ear. 'I saw you at the Rose and Crown, you and your reckless servant slut. I will have her killed. I would not soil my hands on her myself. I was annoyed that she interrupted my pleasure. Still, it made me keen to have you all the more, and sooner. To know you were there…I cannot tell you what an ecstasy I felt.'

He stood up in front of her, flexed his hands. He took a bottle and a hypodermic syringe from inside the bag and slowly loaded the syringe with fluid from the bottle, which was labelled Morphine. He held the syringe up, full – no need for a measure. He dropped the bottle, empty, on the floor.

'Remember that you must obey. Stand up, Sophia.'

She stood with no effort but could do nothing else. She wanted to kick him, shove him away, scream, run.

You will not kill me. You will not kill me. You will not kill me.

She chanted this as a mantra, focused on his eyes with all the negative energy she could muster.

'Turn around, face the window and look your last on the blue sky. See the gathering clouds? They are your death.'

She turned and he quickly put his left arm about her chest, pinning her arms by her side, as he had done with the others.

'But pleasure bent first, I will give you only a quietening dose. I must have you,' he explained, 'I have waited so long, Sophia, so long,' he murmured, his mouth touching her neck; he lifted his mouth to her ear. She felt the brute strength of his arms like a steel cage.

She felt his breath like a fire, heard him panting. She could see the syringe held up in front of her; his grip tightened – then suddenly convulsed. Her head was shoved powerfully forward. She saw his arm that held the syringe swing down in front of her bent head, felt his grip on her loose for a second and she suddenly knew what she could do – she moved of her own accord. She took the advantage and hit back with her elbow, aiming to punch him in the stomach, but her elbow only skimmed his side. She surged forward, fell with hands stretched out, onto the easy chair where she had been before. She heard a scuffling, grunting noise behind her and swung round like a whiplash.

Nat!

Chapter 36

'Ours is just to do or die'
Alfred Lord Tennyson

HE HAD GRABBED the doctor from behind, his forearm was round the man's throat, the other strained to keep his grip on the hand holding the lethal syringe. They swayed to and fro; the doctor, the killer, was stronger than he had appeared. They staggered forward a few paces, collided with the chest which tipped the pile of bedding onto the floor as it heaved over. In turn it fell against an upright chair, ramming it into a cupboard. There was a splintering noise like the crack of thunder. No, it was thunder! Black clouds had gathered with the usual haste of a summer storm and their thunder crashed into the room.

All Sophia's senses had returned. The noise of the city added to that in the room. Rain lashed down; lightning splintered the air. The room was filled with gloomy yellow light, then searing shards of ice white electricity illuminated everything in stark monochrome.

Smith bent forward, trying to throw Nat over his shoulder, but Nat kept his hold firm. She noticed his face for the first time since she had seen him asleep across the room, long minutes earlier; saw his features set in such an expression of ferocity that she hardly knew him. He sweated, grunted with the effort, the cords of his neck stood out, the muscles of his forearms bulged. In bed he'd worn only his long drawers and as he swung the killer around, she saw the muscles of his back were bunched tight with the strain. He was strong but was he strong enough? Could he avoid the lethal syringe?

She cast around for something to hit the killer with, saw only a little stool and snatching it up she swung it at him, catching the arm with the syringe, then felt a second's desperate triumph as it flew from his grip right across the room to land in front of the fallen chest. Her movement bunched up the front of her bodice and she felt the awful posy stabbing her skin. She snatched it frantically from the place and hurled it away across the room with a scream of revulsion, then found herself crying freely and glaring her defiance at the man who'd put it there.

He roared in fury then; Nat matched his noise and they writhed together, grunting, spitting, heaving, Nat still with his arm round the man's throat. Sophia lurched awkwardly out of the way. The killer pushed forcefully back against Nat and he was almost over balanced, until the bed post stopped him when he smashed into it. He gasped, winced, and Smith took the advantage managing to escape the throat lock and face him. Smith took a couple of deliberate steps back and Sophia saw him swing his head round frantically, looking for the syringe, she thought. It was on the opposite side of the room and she didn't dare pass him to reach it.

Nat shook his head, swiped his hand down his face, then his expression brightened with intent and it was the work of a second for him to catch up the water jug from the washstand and throw it over arm at Smith. He turned aside but it fetched him a resounding thump on the back before crashing to the floor.

'You!' the doctor snarled. 'Why are you not dying, Roberts? I gave you drugs enough.'

Nat laughed; but his eyes were flint hard. 'But I didn't take them!' he said, and suddenly rushed at the other man, head down, arms out ready to grab him, thundering incoherently at the top of his voice.

'Why doesn't someone come!' Sophia cried, looking at the door, but they had locked grips once more and reeled back to bang into it, Nat with his hands on the other's throat.

They had only fought a minute or two, but it seemed longer by its drama and the desperate worth of the outcome.

She heard pounding footsteps on the stairs and landing.

'What's going on? Hi there! Open up!' a voice shouted. 'Open up!'

The door was hammered by fists, the handle rattled. The noise was colossal.

'Open up!' yelled David.

There were two voices shouting; someone tried to break the door with their shoulder, again and again, but the locks held. Sophia ran over, ducked under the grappling arms, straining legs and managed to turn the lock. She stumbled back and crawled out of the way as the two men bound in deadly combat, fell to the floor.

David Knightly and Michel burst into the room, disbelief and terror on their faces, but nothing daunted, they both instantly understood what was happening. They leapt forward to help Nat who was now under Smith's body. Michel snatched his hair to pull him away but in return took a heavy blow from Smith's fist directly on the end of his injured arm. He fell back with an agonising cry. David cast a look around the room and seeing something he could use, he darted over to the fireplace and grabbed the long, smooth iron poker. He danced around the struggling men trying for a target, but seeing it was impossible without hurting Nat, he then grabbed the back of

Smith's shirt collar and, with all his strength, yanked him away from Nat. He in turn rolled over choking, groaning and Sophia was with him in a heartbeat, helped him rise. He staggered as she pulled him away from the killer, clasping his back and clearly in pain. He pushed Sophia behind him as David faced Smith.

But his opponent was agile as a gazelle, swiftly rolled over and up on his haunches, hands out to balance himself. His eyes flicked to the fireplace and the second poker, one with a hook on the end and he was soon in possession and up on his feet, hefting the weapon in his hand.

He sneered, his face alight with a mixture of exultation and rage. 'You have picked the wrong weapon. I am a swordsman, an exemplary one, champion of my club!' He laughed aloud, a maniacal shriek.

'We'll see,' David replied. His tone was quiet and conversational, and all the more menacing for that contrast with the very palpable danger.

A sneer was all the answer he had, and Smith began a slow circling, his weapon held up, his other arm out for balance.

David Knightly mirrored him.

'Don't kill him, David,' Nat snarled. 'Be careful, the hangman wants him, Manchester wants him. No, better still, give me that poker and I'll beat his brains in – save you the trouble.'

He tried to move forward but suddenly fell backwards and crashed heavily into the door jamb. Both Michel and Sophia were with him in a second to drag him up onto his feet.

'Stay, mon ami; wait. David can do this thing; believe me; I know this.'

Smith laughed and lunged for David, who leapt back nimbly then rebounded forward to catch his opponent off guard. The tip of his weapon grazed his target's chest.

'Expert? I think not,' Smith sneered. 'The rapier is my

weapon; you won't last long.'

'Man, you wield a fire poker, not a rapier,' David pointed out calmly and suddenly changed the angle of his own weapon. He swung it overarm and hacked down on the other poker, continued with the momentum of the movement and whirled it upwards in an arc to deliver a thrashing horizontal blow to Smith's side that made him gasp in pain.

But Smith recovered and stepped backwards, but less adroitly. He smiled grimly, his eyes dark spots of evil under lowering brows.

'How will fighting sit with your Christian beliefs, Sir Priest, Sir Prating Priest? Will you go down on your knees in contrition? No, you'll be dead. No beatitudes can save you. You can't hold me, any of you. A cripple, a sick man and a woman, a defeated woman, a humiliated woman. Oh, but Roberts, a very desirable woman. I will have her yet, see if I don't. I will make her come to me, once I am out of here.'

Smith yelled a series of oaths that were lost in the next peal of thunder. He made three rapid strides towards his opponent, then brought his weapon forcefully upwards to crash the underside of David's. It was a ringing blow and David almost let go. Sophia saw him tighten his grip, his face was flushed with the effort he made, but somehow, he found the strength to swing the heavy weapon downwards again in a wide arc and swipe it against the back of Smith's thigh. The killer dropped to his knees.

Sophia saw him make a supreme effort, stagger up, laughing again.

'No!' she cried in disbelief as David stepped back, rubbed his 'sword' arm.

It was then that Nat, lurching forwards yelled, 'Michel – move over there, throw that chair at his legs. I'll deal with him on this side. David, make your move when we do!'

He pushed Sophia behind him so that her back was against the door. They could all hear shouts from the landing and down in the yard. The thunder had not stopped, but the lightning lessened, and the room was gloomier for it. Shadows reared up the walls like an army, they lurked guerrilla like in the corners. The windowpane was obscured by rain.

Smith laughed and laughed, lunged and hit David a hard blow on the shoulder that made him drop his weapon.

'Mine, the victory!' he bellowed.

David gripped his shoulder, screwed up his eyes in pain. Smith was on him in a breath and seized him in a powerful neck hold. He backed away to the window and as he moved, he threw a swift glance behind. The bottom half of the sash was open. Sophia could see what he planned; no clairvoyance was needed, he was going to push David away and heave the sash up, take his chance dropping to the yard below. He would escape.

'Nat, the window!'

Nat reached for the stool, clearly intending to use it as a missile. David's face was contorted in agony as he struggled to breathe. Nat threw a look of despair at Michel; the end of his crippled arm dripped blood and he could only hoist up the chair with difficulty.

'Away!' Smith growled. 'Away or I will break his neck with a little twist. So easily done. Away.'

David's legs were dragged out before him as he was heaved backwards to the window. Smith reached out his arm behind, feeling for the sash.

'Away. I will not hesitate to kill him and I...'

Nat didn't wait until the killer had finished speaking – he charged. He held his head forward, his arms spread out to grab and his shoulders braced, a rugby attack. He roared incoherently as he surged across the three yards to his goal and

417

threw himself forward to tackle David's legs. His weight and the surprise loosened Smith's hold and David fell to the side, gagging and struggling for air, with Nat sprawled next to him still gripping his legs.

The momentum sent Smith staggering back alone, unbalanced; his arms flailing wildly as he desperately searched for a hold of any kind. His mouth opened wide in a desperate roar as he found no help and fell heavily back against the window. It disintegrated with an almighty crack, the splintering glass and wood screaming as loudly as the man who fell through to the yard below.

A peal of thunder heralded his fall. The rain blew in in great gusts, soaking them all as they staggered to the window to see whatever awful vision was displayed below.

There, spreadeagled on the cobbles of the vicarage yard in a spreading pool of blood, was the killer.

Sophia screamed.

'He's alive! Look!' she cried.

Michel supported David; Nat held Sophia as they watched.

They saw Smith's face. His mouth was open; rain blurred his features; he was laughing, but the noise of the rain deadened the sound of his fiendish cries.

A second had not passed when a small figure ran from the direction of the kitchen up to the fallen killer. It was Alice. She looked frantically up at the window, her expression shocked and grim. She looked at Smith, then back up to the window; Sophia bent forward to make sure Alice saw she was alive. The girl turned her face to the killer once more and they saw that he spoke to her, telling her something that pleased him, but made her lift her hands to her face in horror.

Then Smith, in his death throes, grabbed hold of Alice's skirts; she shouted something at him; they couldn't hear what. She snatched her skirts away and as his hand fell back onto the cobbles, he looked up at her, a maniacal grin on his face. She screamed and screamed, caught her skirts up in her arms, out of the way then she lifted her foot and stamped as hard as she could on the hand, again and again. She wore her clogs, and his hand was soon shattered; blood ran freely from it to mingle with the pools spread by the deluge. Just then there was a short lull in the rain, the wind chased it away, and it was then they heard her shout.

'And that's for my mistress and all the others, you bastard!' and she kept her foot on his hand, leaning her weight on it as the light went out of his eyes and he died with a grimace of pain contorting his face.

Chapter 37

'All shall be well'
Julian of Norwich

THE WIND CHANGED, and the rain came down in relentless ropes of water. Still the two separate tableaux remained frozen, that at the bedroom window and the one in the back yard. All eyes looked on the dead man and rejoiced in their different ways.

David Knightly was the first to move and break the spell. He clasped his hands together.

'Lord God Almighty, reclaim this man's soul from the devil, in the name of our Lord Jesus Christ, Amen.' He crossed himself, then said to the others, 'Now we must cleanse our own souls from contact with this evil. It has been a trying time.' He looked at Sophia who had turned to hide her face in Nat's chest. 'Especially for you, Sophia.'

He made the sign of the cross over her and spoke the words of the benediction.

'And now may the Lord bless you and keep you. May the Lord make his face to shine upon you. And may God give you his peace...'

He spoke the words softly, Nat turned Sophia around. She bowed her head and when David had finished, she simply said:

'Thank you. Amen.'

Nat and Michel crossed themselves.

Sophia felt a strange peace descend on the room.

The rain continued, and after a little while they all became suddenly aware of other people; banging noises, pounding footsteps, shouts in the yard and on the landing, but they did not yet move. Sophia saw two blurred figures run out into the rain in the yard; it was Mrs Jenkins and the housekeeper, Mrs Biggs. They threw up their hands in horror when they saw the dead man lying there in the downpour, then Mrs Jenkins wrapped a shawl around Alice's shoulder and between them they guided her back into shelter.

The bedroom door flew open. It was John Brown, the manservant, his face white with shock.

'Oh, Reverend, what's to do? That crashing...'

Nat answered him.

'The murderer has been caught, Brown. He's lying out there in the rain, where he belongs.'

'Sergeant, sir, I saw it out of the back window. It's Dr Smith. My God! Is that right?'

'Yes, Brown, it is. We all need tea. See to it will you,' Nat said.

David nodded at the bemused man, and glancing at Nat, he added to his instruction, 'I think we need the police. Nat?'

'Yes, of course. Brown, go yourself to the telegraph office round the back here, and send a wire to Inspector Caminada at Newton St Police Station. The message: *Utmost urgency. Come now. Bring men. Roberts.* Now I think on, they've a telephone at the post office. Use it to call and speak to the Inspector in case the telegram is delayed in any way. Same message delivered in two different ways. We can't risk him missing it. And don't breathe a word out of this house. Am I clear?'

When he'd gone, Michel spoke.

'David, mon ami, my arm, a dressing. The stitches have burst.

I feel it. I cannot do it myself. I need it clean and our friends here, they need time together.'

'Of course, on both counts,' David said.

Sophia said, 'I'll come and look at it in a little while, Michel, if the Reverend is squeamish.'

'Not I!' he answered.

How quick, when something so terrible happens, how quickly we move into practical matters, as though we can't even think about the obvious.

'Wait,' Nat said quickly, as if something jogged his mind. It confirmed Sophia's thoughts.

'David, indulge me here. It turns out you are a swordsman yourself– a fine one. The scar on your cheek – how did you come by that? Did an opponent get the draw on you?' He threw a glance at Sophia.

David's smile was wan but smile he did, as though pulling himself back from a great distance. He cleared his throat and Sophia saw him throw a grateful smile at Nat. The next smile was genuine to suit the memory he'd been asked for, something unimportant to break the tension left by terror.

'In a way you're right, but the tale will not colour me well.' He rubbed his face hard with both hands, a spiritual washing. 'The incident occurred at home and I but a callow youth of fifteen, full of my own importance and skill in the family's pet talent – swordsmanship. In truth, my imagination was more developed than my swordsmanship. The pastry chef my mother insisted on keeping, was French and a swordsman of some skill himself. He and my father practised for hours. So, you may anticipate my tale…We were engaged in a mock duel with long knives in the kitchens. I was not winning, and the final indignity was when I slipped and fell on my own weapon. Monsieur Emanuel laughed and mopped me up. He was not punished, naturally, but I was.'

They all managed a smile and Nat nudged David's arm. 'You were good enough just now, man.'

He appealed to Sophia. 'What did I say? I knew it would be something like that, didn't I love?'

But she pulled a wry face instead of agreeing. She could see he hoped to start pulling her back to normality. She wasn't quite ready. Her mind held questions.

David and Michel left the room. The rain began to ease. The vicarage back yard was enclosed by a high wall, but there were windows in buildings across the alley that would command a view if anyone should look. Nat and Sophia remained at the bedroom window for a time, she scanned the other buildings, he gazed at her, enclosed her more tenderly in his arms.

Below in the yard, an umbrella came in view, moving from the back kitchens. It tipped slightly and they saw it was Reverend Williams supported by David; they walked slowly to the body. They watched Reverend Williams clasp his hands and bow his head in prayer; she imagined he would petition God for repose of the man's soul; she couldn't frame a single thought about the killer. Her mind was numb.

She felt Nat shiver. The rain had soaked him, so she pulled a sheet from the pile on the floor and reached up to wrap it around his shoulders.

'Get back in bed. You're not that well yet. I can see, and this has taxed your strength.'

He obeyed and she sat next to him.

'I am well, love, not quite fit yet, but I will be. My back is a bit sore but unstiffening now. You want to know what happened. But first, let me fetch that shawl from over there and I'll wrap you in it now. You're trembling. That'll be the shock. The horror.'

He fetched the shawl said quietly:

'Sit, love. Let's be still for a little while.'

So they sat together, she leaning back on him, he with his arm about her shoulders. And there came into their hearts the beginnings of a peace and tranquillity to banish all the dark things that had surrounded them.

The rain continued and for a while all they heard was the sound of water. When eventually it lessened, Sophia noticed that the sky was washed grey after the soaking, but as she watched, a little blue seeped in at the edges. It was probably early afternoon now.

Their reverie was rudely broken by a clamour of voices and heavy footsteps down in the yard.

'People will come up here soon. That's Inspector Caminada's voice,' Nat said.

She looked at him. 'Nat, tell me everything. I thought you were too ill to move, but you weren't – thank God though.'

'I can tell you now, and you'll have to forgive the deception; I had to do it to stop him. It was Michel who realised that I was being given too much morphine for the injury. He told Smith he would give me the medication one night and next morning too as Smith was in a hurry, he agreed. He felt secure in his own arrogance. Without alerting me just then, Michel gave me an inert syrup and saw how much more alert I was and more importantly, without significant pain. My concussion was very mild. I was fine. He then told me what he had done and suggested he try another experiment with the liquid meant for me. He suspected I was also being given arsenic, due to the symptoms I showed, even after a few days. It's colourless and tasteless – so only the effect shows it's there. I was vomiting, had muscle cramps, reddened skin and my heart was erratic, I hallucinated a little too. Sometimes I was over-hot in this room and that raised my temperature. Michel took it himself in the cool of the morning and found it normal. The drugs were a high dose he said. He had seen this poisoning before. Without telling anyone he put the drugged syrup under a dresser for the kitchen mice. There were three dead next day. Smith could, of course, have poisoned my food, but that would have been logistically harder."

'Why would he – the killer (I can't call him anything else now…) want to poison you?' She was shocked.

'That was the first thing Michel and I puzzled over, he first, of course. Just now, it was all I could do not to leap up and kill him as soon as I realised he was the murderer, when he began gloating. Up until then, I thought, Michel and I both did, that he was poisoning me for jealousy – wanting you for himself, or simply hating a policeman. We had no notion of his being the killer at all. As it turns out, he obviously knew I was involved and that I was determined to discover the killer; he knew about your finds and deductions. He wanted to hurt you through me, make you perhaps turn to him for comfort or possibly just hurt you before he killed you like the others. I think he hated women, as he said, successful women, love. And he was attracted by them – you. I think you were his target all along and the others were killed to build up your fear and anticipation.'

'The posies – the messages became more and more sinister…' She felt her throat tighten.

'Damn him to hell where he belongs!'

She stared at him, knowing she couldn't hide the hurt in her eyes. 'You didn't tell me and father, and we thought it was alright for me to be alone with him. We trusted him.'

He took her in his arms.

'I thought it was jealousy, as I said, up until he started to explain himself here, *today, only here today!* His voice was too low, all that whispering. I couldn't hear until he stood, and I heard all! Then, yes, I wanted to stop him killing you – what else would I do? If I had told you about the poisoning and that Michel and I suspected him of hopeless jealousy, you, being so open in everything, would surely have betrayed that knowledge. It would've shown on your face, in your manner. You're not devious as he was. Michel and I decided that when he told me of the drugging. But I alone of we two conspirators knew about your gift, love, remember that. Only I knew that you may have told the killer all, but inadvertently, by telepathy – that may have betrayed you. And I think he also had some strange power of his own because of the way he hypnotised people. When he was murmuring close to you earlier, his voice began to lull even me. I could almost have fallen asleep, until I realised the danger and felt a jolt of pain that shocked my whole body into a terrible wakefulness.'

She said, 'Yes, I can see I may have done as you suggest – had I known about the drugging. A trap was in place for him then?'

He shook his head. 'No. No, it wasn't. We were watching him and intended to get the help of Inspector Caminada and his officers today, get him followed, having given him our evidence about the poisoning. When you came this morning with him – the trap unfolded itself before time, unravelled like a ball of twine rolling downhill, and became something quite different – as we found out. My heart almost burst when he held up the syringe. And then I had to be so careful in what I did to prevent him plunging it into you. It was like a loaded gun, cocked and ready.'

'But you let him humiliate me. He touched me, Nat, he had his hands on my legs.' She sobbed now.

'Your legs? My God – had I seen I'd have beaten him to death then! I saw nothing, my head was low on the pillow. It was only when he stood I saw he had the syringe!'

His expression was black with the horror of their talk. It struck a chill to her heart.

She stroked his face.

'Nat, you killed him in the end – and saved David.'

He hung his head, and she could see he was fighting his emotions.

When he finally raised it, he said, 'And Michel saved me – and you too by doing that. I have been trying to exercise for days and I'm getting better, but I'm still a little dizzy. But by assuming I was drugged and dying from poisoning, Smith was, as Shakespeare says, the *engineer hoist with his own petard.'*

'Now we know he was the killer he must have feared you, Nat. Or it may be he was too arrogant, too sure of his success. But when he found an accident had struck you down, he turned it to his advantage.'

'I'm glad he feared me. He had reason to. But he's gone finally and now we can rebuild and leave this horror behind.'

They kissed and he said, 'Remember the day on that bench by the cathedral, when you told me about your gift?'

'Yes.'

'You said you would marry me as soon as we got a licence, there in the cathedral if possible.'

'Yes.'

'Then marry me, this week, if I can get a licence that quickly, the first opportunity. Then we will be joined as we should be, love.'

'Yes.'

'I'll ask Arnold as soon as I see him and I'd like to ask Reverend Williams if we can have the wedding here at St Ann's, and that David should marry us, and that Michel should be the groomsman. Our lives are joined to theirs in so many ways.'

'Yes, to everything, anything.'

'You are noticeably agreeable about all this, but that's alright because I can see what your heart feels; your eyes are glowing with something of their usual brilliance, Sophia love, darling, dearest.'

She simply lay her head on his breast and sighed with the beginnings of peace.

But the time was not their own and rapid, sharp footsteps on the landing told them they would be invaded. A knock on the door came next.

'Miss Sophia! Are you there?'

'Alice, come in.'

When she entered the room, Sophia recognised the emotion written on the girl's face. It was relief tinged with the horror and an intense need to feel young and happy once more, to put recent events behind her. But she also saw that Alice's eyes were desperately searching her face to see how she fared, and she hastened to reassure her.

'Alice, I'm fine now. I am. The sergeant's fine too. He saved us all you know – his was the action that made *him* fall through the window. He and Michel and Reverend Knightly; they all fought him.'

Alice flicked a glance to each of them, struggled to keep her composure. Her lip trembled and her face flushed, but with a massive effort she managed. She spoke haltingly.

'Inspector Caminada wants to know can 'e come up yet?'

'Yes, he can, thank you, Alice,' Nat said quietly. 'And for myself, thank you from the bottom of my heart.'

She blushed, looked away, unused to this from him.

'Miss Sophia…'

'Yes, Alice?'

'I'm just glad you're alright. I don't know what I'd 'ave done otherwise, I don't. And thank you, Sergeant Roberts, thank you,' she said quickly and fled, shutting the door sharply behind her.

Nat said, 'Mmmm. I suppose you want to keep her on as your maid when we're married?'

'Of course. What would I do without Alice to be my watchdog?'

He grinned.

Noise outside had been growing all the while they'd been talking. The city had resumed its normal roaring energy, now the storm had lessened. But in the yard below, the noises were those Nat recognised from all the other scenes of disasters or crimes that he had been involved with; men called to each other, exclamations of shock, instructions barked; there were the mutterings of struggle, grunts of effort, scraping of boxes, sharp cracks from the photographer's lights. Sophia was later told by Mrs Jenkins that as the afternoon went on, the yard resounded with the clearance of the wreckage: glass, splintered wood, blood. Galvanised buckets rang like discordant bells as water was swilled over the human leavings and then came the endless scrubbing of yard brushes over the blood stains.

But before that, there was another knock at the door, and it was Inspector Caminada, as announced by Alice. He strode forward, full of concern.

'Miss Kelley, Roberts, how are you both?'

Nat answered for them, 'We are well now, sir.'

'Good. You can tell me all the details later Roberts, and a report, of course. Miss Kelley, I should say I'm very sorry to hear you'd been attacked. At the very least it must be such a shock and a betrayal to find that a person you knew professionally was such a man.' He shook his head in disbelief. 'Can I say that the men who were assigned on surveillance for you would have thought all was well because you arrived with a person known to them and to yourself. It beggars belief.'

He looked hard at both of them, appearing to be in two minds whether to tell them something else, which in the end he did.

'I got your wire and the telephone message, Roberts, and that was prompt of you. But here is news though – another shock that my men guarding you didn't know of. Only late this morning, we had a tip off at the station that Smith was the man because of an altercation at a brothel; excuse me Miss Kelley, a male brothel down near the docks. Constables were called and men arrested – interestingly enough, your own Inspector Bateman was one of them.'

'No!' Nat gasped. 'Inspector Bateman?'

Sophia recalled the brief and awful clairvoyance she'd had when she shook his hand.

'Bateman immediately sought to gain favour and betrayed this Smith as one of the members also and saying that Smith was blackmailing him to sell drugs. The buyers, the drug dealers themselves, called at Newton St to pick them up - the back door, at midnight! Dr Johnson's involved up to his neck. Bateman said, and here's the vital thing, that Smith had a collection of women's hats on shelves in his rooms in Chorlton and he wore a single earring, a woman's earring, when he came to the brothel.'

Nat and Sophia were astounded and saddened in equal measures.

'So,' the Inspector said, 'We have been to his rooms and have found all the evidence we need and when I heard what had happened here, I was just on my way to find and arrest him. I intended to send a wire to you here to that effect and caution you to keep Miss Kelley by your side, Roberts. Miss Kelley, we found the posies, and the diary belonging to Isabella Waterstone.'

He dropped his eyes and saw the one she'd flung away, on the floor near the syringe.

'I'll take these things, Roberts.'

Sophia remembered her handbag and finding it in the corner, retrieved the little tin containing the posy and earring she'd found that morning. Only that morning!

'Inspector, I found these things on the body of the last poor woman.'

'Ah – a dreadful task for you, Miss Kelley. Thank you. Although the man's dead, we will collect all evidence and prove the case. The families and the public will want to know all.'

'I agree sir, it's a duty to the dead, indeed. But Sir, can I ask that you keep my fiancée's name out of this? Can her involvement be anonymous?'

'Yes, assuredly, Roberts. Miss Kelley, fear not. I can do that and I know the judge who reviews the findings will agree. We must protect the innocent. I'll make sure of it in fact. Mind you, the news reporters are the very villains for ferreting things out, and there's a fine collection, a pack of them outside at this moment. However, I'll get an embargo on all reporting about you in this case.'

Sophia went downstairs with the Inspector while Nat dressed. Her father had arrived, and he and Reverend Williams were desperate to see her. She was weak with shock and glad to be taken into the parlour and put by the fire in a deep armchair. Everyone had tea. All at the vicarage were stunned. As evening approached, Nat returned home with Sophia; her father wanted him to have a room there for that night. He might be a policeman, but this had been a very personal culmination to a case.

Later that evening, much later, when all the staff at the yard had expressed themselves shocked and relieved in equal measures, Nat said to Arnold:

'Two things: I'd like to take Sophia for a walk now, to clear our minds, see the fine evening at the end of this long day. The other thing is that I'd like to marry her as soon as possible.'

'Nat, my boy, you must do both, directly,' her father said, 'If Sophia agrees. Lovie?'

'I do, father, of course I do. Thank you.'

The moon was clear and bright, stars filled the sky. It was half past ten. Rain had washed the air and the temperature had settled to a very pleasant level. They strolled in comfort along the busy streets, up Market St, across Piccadilly and on to Ancoats and the great area of cotton mills that gave the city its nickname of Cottonopolis, known around the world. The news reporters had disappeared from outside the vicarage and the undertaker's yard, so they were unmolested.

Lights shone from windows everywhere in the city that never sleeps. Even the great mills had lights on in the watchman's huts. As they reached the canal and took to the towpath, the way became darker. Past the streetlights, past the mills and public houses, the loading bays and warehouses, it was dark and a different, silvered light shone everywhere. Helped by a gentle breeze, it rippled like quicksilver on the surface of the water.

'Nat, look at the moon. The sky's clear for once,' Sophia said. 'We don't see the moon often in the city.'

They looked up and there it was, glorious and radiant in the deep velvet of the sky.

'It's a rare sight, but then so are you. I don't think I've seen you by moonlight for a long time,' Nat told her. 'I think we should walk more, especially after we're married.'

'At night?'

'I like the dark,' he said. 'Ah, but there's the bridge! Under those particular arches there are things a lady should not see. We'll take the way over the top and pick up the canal again near the basin. I know some of the boatsmen who moor there. We could get hot porter or tea. I can smell sausages too.'

'All I want is to walk alone with you.'

And they did; past the barges and their braziers, the coal heaps and the tenements, until they found the wisps of countryside once more and here the moon on the water danced alongside them.

They walked slowly, comfortably and after a while, Nat said:

'This is the beginning of our life together, our real life. It'll be blessed by moonlight and the sun will shine on us always – well, it may be grey sometimes.... but whatever happens, as long as I live, I will love you and care for you, Sophia.'

'I know that,' she said and leaned her head on his arm as they walked on under the stars.

Chapter 38

'Once in a golden hour'
Alfred Lord Tennyson

CELIA GARDINER'S FUNERAL was held three days later. It was as poignant and as sad as the others had been, yet Sophia felt it was a final drawing of the curtain over her own experiences too, and it gave her some relief from the guilt she'd associated with the deaths. It was gone now; she hadn't killed the young women, it was him. He'd used his position of trust as a doctor to lull them into a false sense of security and prestige. But it was her that he had really wanted; she had been his goal and the other deaths were a means of tormenting her. He had used those poor unsuspecting women to do this, each one of them young and vibrant with a life they enjoyed, ambitious, full of hopes and plans with loves and friendships now gone forever.

She was told he had been buried within the prison yard at Strangeways in an unmarked grave along with the executed criminals whose remains lay interred there. There was no ceremony of any kind and nothing to mark his place.

A few days passed, the licence was sought and obtained, and wedding preparations began. Nat and Sophia were married the following week.

The wedding was celebrated at St Ann's by David Knightly, as they wanted. She wore a cream summer dress of the finest muslin and a new straw bonnet that had been trimmed with daisies by Alice – daisies for innocence and hope, Alice said. Sophia carried a small bouquet of pink roses which stand for happiness and the little flowers were bound round with a bracelet of ivy, whose glossy leaves speak fidelity and marriage.

Unbeknown to Sophia, her father had bought a chaise, and the lads had decked it in green branches. Captain was put to, his leg healed, and they had plaited white ribbons in his mane and tail. When she and her father had stepped out of the house to walk to church, the lads, at his instruction, had brought out the bridal carriage. She was delighted. The ceremony was quiet and wonderful. The choir sang – another surprise for Sophia, and everyone they knew was outside to greet them when they emerged.

Nat drove them off in the carriage, back to the yard, because the business was closed for the day, and there they found waiting a wedding breakfast laid out on long tables in the yard, white cloths and all. Everyone followed from the church and all were entertained well into the night with music and dancing, speeches and laughter. A wedding to remember.

Autumn came quickly to the city and the few trees suddenly decked themselves in all the vibrant seasonal hues. It was cooler, pleasant to be out, if one didn't mind the noise and bustle. Sophia never did. But now she and Nat were on their wedding trip, staying at a farmhouse in the lea of Winter Hill, on the West Pennine Moors near Bolton. They had been there before and that was when they had walked to Anglezarke Reservoir to swim. This was to be a brief holiday of one week.

They sat with their backs against Nat's favourite stone wall with the beautiful scenery of the moors tumbling down before them. She lay back against him and listened to the sounds of the moor and felt that she was nearer to heaven than anywhere else she had ever been. The sun hung lower in the sky over the moors, but its warmth was luxurious, decadent, beautiful.

High overhead a skylark sang as they ate their dinner. Below in the valleys they could see the mill chimneys as busy as they were at home and the rows of terraced houses were all topped with ribbons of smoke pouring upwards and away. The difference was that the wind blew the smoke on a strong westerly and left the air above them clear and blue.

Nat heaved his knapsack down onto a level piece of ground, saying:

'I'll take you to the top of the hill later and show you where the Irwell starts. It's between this moorland, the West Pennines, and the Pennines proper. Starts off mountain-clean up here and look how it ends up in the middle of the city! And there are spots up here where you can see all of Bolton and even Wigan. You could wave at Alice's hometown!' He snorted with laughter at his own wit.

Sophia ignored this completely and instead, being reminded of her maid told him:

'Alice's young man is proving a master horseman, Father says. He's going to be kept on permanently – used to be a groom at Haigh Hall, for Lord Crawford – that's the Earl of Balcarres, no less!'

'Oh?' he grunted, unimpressed, and pulling the cork from his beer bottle he put it to his mouth and took a long pull.

'Fancy her getting that letter out of the blue. She'd refused him a few times in the past and then when she was taken on at that colliery owner's house as lady's maid, she had that trouble with the son and felt herself unworthy, she says.'

'She's still fierce,' Nat remarked, through the pie, which he had just bitten into. 'Y'know, I needed that.' He gazed at the pie appreciatively.

'They're to be married when they've saved enough and that could be a couple of years. Mrs William Martin. Just think.'

'Do I have to?' he asked.

She continued to mull over all the news.

'Michel is to join the staff at the Infirmary and help with the treatment of diseases from distant lands; the ship canal will bring more people of all sorts here.'

They talked about the night they had found him destitute under the Victorian Bridge and about how well he looked now, then they lapsed into companionable silence for a time while they ate. Sophia threw crumbs for the small birds that watched them from perches on the wall and a stunted hawthorn.

'Is he to carry on living at the vicarage?' he asked, resuming the thread of talk, and biting the last bits of flesh from his apple.

'Yes, he and David have become firm friends. When Reverend Williams retires, David's to be given the living, he says. And David says the Reverend's home is there at the vicarage, not ever to think of leaving.'

'What does *David* say about you and I living with your father?'

'He probably says you'll be very annoying wherever you live.'

'Hmmph. Pass me another apple, while you're nearest, will you?'

She stood, found an apple, and ran down the slope a little way; then she turned and threw it at him before picking up her skirts and sprinting off downhill back to the farmhouse where they were staying.

He caught the apple easily, crammed all their things into his knapsack, and raced after her as fast as he could. He arrived at the door, red faced and breathless, but Sophia was by then washing her hands in the kitchen and chatting to the farmer's wife.

'Ah, Nat. You managed to get here at last,' she said, grinning.

'As you see,' he said, and grabbed her hand then pulled her into the hall, shutting the door behind him.

'Yes, I am here at last,' he said, as he enclosed her in his arms and kissed her, 'exactly where I want to be - with you.'

*****

Acknowledgements

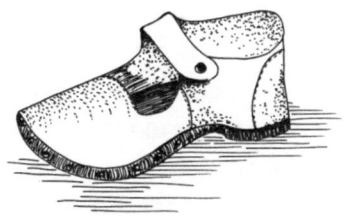

Authors have so many people to thank during the making of a book. I publish independently but that doesn't mean I can do it alone - though any mistakes really are all mine.

I was born in Manchester and lived in different parts of the city as I grew up. Later I worked in the city centre for a few years and explored in lunch hours. Four generations ago all my family worked in the cotton industry or with the many horses in the city . It feels like a legacy and listening to their tales as a child gave me ideas for many of the incidents in this book. My thanks to them for passing on the history.

I always think that Manchester's dynamism was ignited in the Victorian era and continues as ever. Industry, commerce and the arts flourish. The grand Victorian buildings are still used and stand testament to the creativity of the period. I've visited most of them.

Whilst writing this book in Lockdown 2020 I read nothing but my favourite Victorian authors. The Brontes, Mrs Gaskell, Wilkie Collins, Dickens, Sir Arthur Conan Doyle and many others gave me an insight into the way Victorians thought and spoke. It was great fun.

I also needed the essential discussions of plot and character with my daughter, Laura. Not to be left out are my writing group of fellow authors who provide very grounded criticism throughout the writing year whether we meet face-to-face or at present, on zoom; so thanks to Lizzie Gates, Jackie Farrell, Cath Cole, Carol Fenlon and Dennis Conlon.

My editor, Liz Harris never fails to find the things I've mislaid in the text and sorts out renegade semi-colons.

My three beta readers, Sue Wooff, Liz Harris and Gill Brown provide that avid reader's eye and are honest and kind enough to spot the bumps in the race-track of the story.

Every book needs the best cover and Lucy McSpirit always delivers a design I'm immensely proud of, so thanks to her too.

Researching an historical novel is intense and I use every avenue available, but there's nothing as good as talking to an expert; so thanks to Dr Andy Sutton for chats about weird illnesses and the poisons available to those creative Victorians.

Finally, my husband, Frank, keeps everything together, sorts out my computing, makes tea, reads the book and I can't ever thank *him* enough - ever.

Appendix 1
The language of the flowers

Chapter 1

ADELINE WORTHINGTON'S POSY
Honeysuckle represents affectionate devotion. A *purple carnation* represents coquetry and d*eep blue periwinkle* is a symbol of death. In Medieval times it was woven into garlands for condemned criminals. The meaning is *devotion can be distorted by coquetry*. It could also mean; *this coquetry has led to your death.*

Chapter 2 *Arum lily* - Beauty, delicacy, modesty, transition and growth

Chapter 3 *Daffodil* - Chivalry, faith, honesty, forgiveness, rebirth

Chapter 5 *Tulip* - True love, innocence, forgiveness, friendship

Chapter 6 *Snowdrop* - Beauty of spirit, hopefulness, new beginnings, consolation

Chapter 8 *Petunia* - Anger, disdain, resentment, contradictions, your presence soothes me

Chapter 10

SALLY HEPPLESTONE'S POSY
Daisy represents innocence, the *nettle* is for pain and the *for-*

get-me-not represents hope and optimism, apart from its more widely known message of remembrance. Together they say *remember the pain of this innocent.* But it could also say: *hope must bring pain for the innocent.*

Chapter 18
ISABELLA WATERSTONE'S POSY

Monkshood signifies the approach of a
dangerous foe. All parts of *oleander* are
poisonous, and its message is 'beware.' *French
marigold* represents 'jealousy'. The message is
*beware of jealousy, a dangerous foe
approaches.*

Chapter 34
CELIA GARDINER'S POSY

Buttercups represent childishness. The
orange lily speaks of hatred, pride and
disdain. The *light blue columbine signifies*
folly. The message is *I have my pride, I reject
your childishness, I disdain this relationship
as folly.*

Chapter 35
SOPHIA KELLEY'S POSY

The *pink carnation* signifies a woman's love; Nightshade can  symbolize truth, herald death, or it can accuse the recipient of sorcery and witchcraft; the Michaelmas daisy speaks a farewell and cypress is always for death and mourning. The message is *Farewell to woman's love which is but witchcraft and sorcery bringing death and mourning; that is the truth.*

Cover image : *SOPHIA'S SIGNATURE FLOWERS*

Forget-me-not : remembrance, hope, faithfulness, humility
Pink tulip : a declaration of love
Oak leaves : noble presence, bravery, strength
Dahlia : dignity, elegance
Yew: honour, leadership, strength, Illusion, mystery

Appendix 2
Chapter heading quotes

Chapter 1   *'Poor child, poor child'*
Christina Rossetti: *After death* - poem 1862

Chapter 2   *'No man is an island'*
John Donne: *Devotions upon emergent occasions: Meditation XVII* 1624

Chapter 3   *'How do I love thee?'*
Elizabeth Barrett Browning: *Sonnets from the Portuguese: How do I love thee?* - sonnet 1850

Chapter 4   *'Hope may vanish, but can die not'*
Percy Bysshe Shelley: *Prometheus unbound* - drama 1820

Chapter 5   *'Darkling in the eternal space'*
Lord Byron: *Darkness* - poem 1816

Chapter 6   *'I fear you more than any spectre'*
Charles Dickens: *A Christmas Carol* - novel 1843

Chapter 7   *'What a piece of work is a man'*
Shakespeare: *Hamlet* - play 1599-1601

Chapter 8   *'Truth is always strange'*
Lord Byron: *Don Juan* – poem 1823

Chapter 9   *'Thoughts are tyrants'*
Emily Bronte: *Wuthering Heights* - novel 1846

Chapter 10   *'I hold it true, whate'er befall'*
Lord Tennyson: *In memoriam* - poem 1850

Chapter 11   *'The wonder of a mother's love'*
Christina Rossetti: *A mother's love* - poem c 1862

Chapter 12   *'Lost in darkness and distance'*
Mary Shelley: *Frankenstein* - novel 1817

Chapter 13   *'Early one morning, just as the sun was rising'*
English folk song c 1700